Xavier Wallace

SHAW VENGEANCE

JEFFREY + WALLACE

ISBN: 9781764141208

ISBN (eBook): 9781764141215

JEFFREY + WALLACE PUBLISHING

www.jwpublishing.com.au

XAVIER WALLACE

www.xavierwallace.com

Xavier Wallace

Xavier Wallace was born and raised in regional New South Wales, Australia. He attended public primary and high schools, before studying business at the University of Newcastle. He worked in Canberra for the Australian Government in both the public service and politics for over a decade. He has a Master of Politics and Public Policy from Deakin University. Xavier's interests include politics, government, national security, media and communications, philosophy, ancient history and mythology. He is an advocate for equality and human rights, including LGBTI+ rights. Live music, thriller novels and action movies occupy his time outside writing and work. He loves spending time with his family and friends, and his groodle, Atlas.

Xavier Wallace is the author of the Max Shaw spy thriller series.

Dedication

For my parents, sister, brother-in-law and nieces.

Acknowledgements

I want to thank my parents for their constant love, support and belief in me. You instilled in me, from a very early age, a passion and motivation to chase my dreams and achieve whatever goals lay before me – and I am forever grateful and could not have done it without you.

To my sister and brother-in-law, thanks for always being on the other end of the phone for a chat or for a beer by the fire or to share the latest song. Your friendship and love mean the world to me. I may also be the proudest uncle to ever live and I look forward to spending more time with my beautiful nieces.

To the completely random and gorgeous, Gracey, your friendship has always been my guiding light. You knew me before I did and I cannot thank you enough for being there to pick me up, point me in the right direction and share this amazing life.

Finally, I want to thank my friend Tanya for painstakingly proofing and providing thoughts on my original manuscript. I also want to thank you for your support and friendship, at often trying times, over the months writing the novel.

I love you all. Thank you for being in my life.

The Max Shaw Spy Thriller Series

SHAW VENGEANCE

By Xavier Wallace

First Novel of the Max Shaw Spy Thriller Series.

Prelude

The Pilot walked into the room.

He was a short man but solid from a lifetime of physical training. There was an air about him. He commanded attention and respect, and he wore an expression that said he was used to receiving both. He was over sixty years old but even with his short-trimmed grey hair he looked younger.

Over the years, he had been in this office many times. The size and opulence still struck him every time he entered. Warm, rich polished floorboards stretched the length of the office and it was covered with a unique mix of antique and modern furniture. Clearly, a great deal of money had been spent fitting it out.

There was a long hardwood conference table with matching chairs for twelve people to his left. It was offset with one end pointing towards the door where he was standing. An extravagant vase of fresh flowers stood squared in the centre of the table. He had smelt the bouquet as soon as he opened the door.

To his right was a familiar lounge area which sat proudly on a plush rug. He figured it was at least twice the size of his lounge room at home. Two big studded leather chesterfield lounges sat either side of the coffee table and two generous one seaters faced each other at the table ends. He knew the coffee table was the same wood as the conference table. In fact, it was cut from the same tree. A smaller bunch of flowers sat on the coffee table with a selection of books from the nearby bookcase. Australian military and political history, biographies and business texts lined the shelves. There was also a selection of rare antique leather-bound books from Homer and Plato to Sun Tsu and Machiavelli.

At the end of the room, two steps ran the width of the office and led up to a perfectly centred large matching hardwood desk and high-back studded-leather office chair. A brand new computer system with two monitors sat facing the window and all the usual office accessories, phone, stationary, desk lamp and some family photos adorned the desk. It was neat and tidy, and well-organised.

A man in an expensive and perfectly tailored navy suit was sitting behind the desk. He looked up when the Pilot entered. He was a handsome man in his early fifties with greying hair, tanned skin and piercing blue eyes. He had an average build and stood at around five feet six inches. The Pilot knew people saw him as a sophisticated and charming man, and as an exceptional businessman. He was down-to-earth and relatable which was no mean feat considering he was chief executive of a major multinational company turning over in excess of thirty billion dollars every year and no doubt personally worth millions. A modest plain silver band on his left hand sat as a permanent reminder of happier times in his past when he had married.

A second man was sitting on one of the chesterfields to the right. He was pre-occupied with his smart phone, scrolling madly, impatiently with his right thumb like a teenager checking their social media feeds. He was a similar age as the man behind the office desk and wore a clean, crisp black pinstriped suit. He was slightly taller at five feet nine inches and his hair was completely grey, almost white. He was divorced too and also still wore his wedding ring to keep up appearances.

"The plans are in place," the Pilot said walking into the room. "Now he has been cleared, Mr Chang will be in the country within the week and the Arab is readying his believers. We are only days away gentlemen. How about a drink to celebrate?"

"Why don't you take a seat and I'll get the scotch," the CEO behind the desk said.

The Pilot joined the other man in the lounge area as the businessman retrieved a crystal decanter and three glasses. He sat and lounged back uncharacteristically on the chesterfield, relaxed and content knowing his plans were coming together. *Not long now*, he thought to himself.

"We have been thinking about the plan," the businessman said pouring three neat shots and passing them out to his guests.

"Right," the Pilot said taking a sip of his scotch. "I am happy to report we're ready to go. Everything is on track. Our progress is ahead of schedule."

"We're out," the second man said. "It's too risky. We cannot afford to be caught. We should walk away now. Why risk everything we already have?"

"You can't be serious!" the Pilot said sitting upright. "I have been planning this for years. It's too late. The wheels are in motion."

"It's not too late. We haven't pulled any triggers yet. We can stop this. God, it was a crazy plan to start with. We should never have gotten involved."

"Is that how you feel too?" the Pilot asked the businessman.

"Yes," he replied. "I can't believe you talked me into this in the first place. I won't have any part in it. You should stop. You will be throwing away your career, your life. It is not worth it. Let alone the damage you will cause and the innocent people who will get caught up in all this. Regardless of what you think or how much you have planned, you simply can't guarantee people won't be injured or worse. People could be killed. I cannot support you anymore."

"This is unbelievable! It is unacceptable!" the Pilot said getting to his feet. "I have planned every detail. If everything goes to plan, no one will be killed. You have been involved since the start. You can't just walk away now!"

"We can and we are," the CEO said. "If you choose to continue, you will not have our support. You will be on your own."

The second man looked down at the floor as the Pilot turned to face him.

"There are no answers to see down there you weak piece of shit. He's right about you, you know? You are a spineless, gutless wonder. You are pathetic. You'd be nothing without his intervention. I am pushing forward and I am warning you, do not get in my way or it will not end well for either of you."

The Pilot drained his glass, and glared back and forth between his two former co-conspirators.

"Fucking cowards!" he said throwing his glass and smashing it against the wall causing the second man to flinch as the shards fell to the floor. "People may get hurt now after all."

The Pilot turned and walked out of the office, slamming the door behind him before heading down the hall. At the elevator, he took out his mobile phone and dialled a pre-stored number.

"It's the Pilot," he said. "They have pulled out. Time for Plan B. Make it happen."

He didn't wait for a reply. He ended the call and left the building.

Chapter One

He laid staring up at the roof. The red numbers on the bedside clock lit up the room. It was five thirty, but he didn't need the clock, he already knew. It was the same time he'd woken every day for years. Normally, he'd now be out of bed and changing into his workout gear, but not today.

His eyes were wide open and he wasn't blinking. Slightly hungover from the night before, he just stared. The new white plasterboard roof stared back. He laid there thinking, reflecting on the events that had led him to the bed.

A pure white sheet hung loosely over his toned naked body. The room was a mess of clothes leading a trail to the bed. Two empty wine glasses sat near the bedroom door stained from the red wine they had been drinking.

He tried to remember the night that was. Piece by piece his memory was returning through the red wine haze. A series of images began to take shape in his mind.

A tall handsome blond walking into the bar, pausing ever so briefly and smiling when they locked eyes. He remembered feeling a surge of adrenaline. Excitement, maybe lust, with a familiar hint of guilt from an emotional scar which still had not healed. He remembered the blond disappearing in a crowd of friends as the big glass door of the bar closed behind the group. Disappointed he looked down to the elegant wine glass that sat almost empty on the bar in front of him. A tinge of sadness washed over him, as it had so many times in the past, as he sat there alone.

Back in the bedroom, he continued his penetrating stare at the roof as if it displayed the projected images of the previous night's events.

Wine had flowed from a dark bottle into his empty glass which sat on the solid marble bar. He remembered looking up. His eyes scanned beyond the glass, beyond the wine, to the firm, confident, steady hand holding the wine bottle. A tanned arm with clearly defined bicep led his gaze up to the smiling face of the blond he had seen in the doorway.

"The barman told me you were drinking the Margaret River shiraz," the blond said finishing the pour before filling another glass. Good choice. Can I join you?"

What did I say? He tried to remember. *Something smart, something witty, something suave?*

"Umm, yea, oh, yeah sure," he had stammered in reply.

Oh real smooth, he thought to himself.

"Do you come here often?" the blond asked before hastily answering the question with another. "Oh God, did I just ask that? Talk about dodgy pick-up lines."

They both laughed.

"That's cute," he said with a cheeky grin showing his confidence returning. "No, this is my first time here. I was walking past and thought it looked nice. I'm glad I did now,"

"Me too," the blond said returning the cheeky smile. "So, you're not from around here?"

"No, I'm travelling for work. Just in town for a couple of nights. How about you?"

"Yeah, I'm a local, I actually grew up a few blocks from here," the blond said raising the glass in a small toast to the city before smelling the wine and taking a sip.

He took a sip too. The wine was smooth and full bodied. *Probably some wanky description on the bottle about chocolate, berries and woody textures* he thought and smiled to himself. He had never understood wine culture, although his line of work meant he was often in circles with people who pranced around singing the virtues of this wine or that. *Wankers* he thought to himself. *If it tastes good drink it. If not, don't.*

He was a country boy with a middle-class upbringing from regional Australia which meant he did not stand on ceremony. He was down to earth and humble. He had always struggled to relate to the high society types. It wasn't that the city and glamorous lifestyles didn't appeal to him. He just liked them in small doses. It just wasn't who he was. He was raised by decent hardworking parents who taught him the value of a dollar and instilled in him the notion that nothing came easily and nothing was for free. You had to work to get what you want. Toil and reward. He often thought that most of the wine culture wankers hadn't likely worked a hard day in their lives. That and why waste hard-earned cash on expensive wine. Plenty of good, cheaper ones out there.

"So, what do you do for work? What brings you to Sydney?" the blond asked.

"I'm a political adviser, I work for a Federal Minister," he said.

"Oh right, you work for those guys hey?" the blond asked with that same cheeky grin returning.

"Yeah, please don't hold that against me," he laughed in reply. "I can't help it if they don't always listen to my good advice."

The blond laughed and smiled broadly showing a perfect set of white teeth.

"Don't worry I won't hold it against you," the blond said. "Not sure I could work for them though."

These were answers he had given a million times and they rolled off his tongue so naturally. The truth was it was only part of what he did for work. It wasn't a lie. He did actually work for a Minister, but it wasn't his real job.

He laid there remembering the unfolding conversation and flowing wine. The blond was charming and intelligent with a great sense of humour. They laughed and talked into the night, getting closer to each other with every passing minute and sip of wine.

He felt his adrenaline pump again as he thought about the moment the blond took hold of his hand and snuggled in close to him on the lounge in the bar. He stroked the blond's arm gently as their conversation began to slow, a consequence of wine or maybe time as it was getting late.

"How about I walk you home?" he said to the blond.

Without letting go of his hand, the blond led him out of the bar and into the street.

The blond's arm hugged him around the waist as they walked and a head full of blond locks rested on his shoulder. His arm was around the blond's shoulders and he was tenderly rubbing the soft fabric shirt with his thumb.

As they walked, he noticed the familiar stares, suddenly self-conscious. He was used to trying to blend in and he hated drawing attention to himself. An occupational hazard in both his lines of work. The blond seemed oblivious to the world around them, completely captivated by their conversation and the warmth of his embrace.

The traffic was surprisingly light for such a populated area which is why a car that drove past with music blaring from the sound system drew his attention. *God, it must be deafening in the car,* he thought. He looked at the passengers as they drove past and held their gaze for slightly too long. They started to shout through the window.

"What are you fucking looking at?" and a stream of obscenities, flew from the mouth of one of the passengers.

"Just keep driving you fuckwits!" the blond yelled.

After a few cursory looks between the passengers and a quick heated exchange, the car skid to a stop. Squeals and smoke started pumping from the tyres as the car wheeled around. It jumped the gutter right in front of the couple.

He felt the blond's grip tighten on his hand and he stepped in front defensively pulling the blond in behind him as four passengers and the driver shot out of the car with surprising speed. Yelling. He remembered them yelling awful, nasty, hateful things.

The blond's hand was shaking and trying to pull him backwards down the street to flee but he held his ground, staring at the five men standing before them.

"Fellas, we don't want any trouble," he said. "We're on our way home. Sorry for any offence. How about we just leave it and all walk away?"

The blond didn't notice how calm and controlled he sounded. He was confident and unfazed in the face of their growing anger.

"How about we beat the fuck out of you and your fucking big mouth mate there?" one of the passengers asked.

"Listen, I said we're sorry," he said. "We're leaving. I strongly suggest you get in your car and do the same."

He squeezed the blond's hand and gave a reassuring smile as he turned to face his companion.

"Let's get going," he said leading the nervous blond down the road.

"Okay," the blond said rapidly, clearly shaken. "I'm really sorry about that. Let's walk fast. My place is this way. Do you think they will go? They're so angry. God, people are so irrational, so full of hate, and for what, we haven't done anything wrong?"

The hairs on the back of his neck raised feeling the presence of someone approaching. It was one of the passengers from the car who was reaching for the blond's shoulder.

"We're not done with youse yet," the passenger screamed.

It wasn't the last time the passenger would scream, but it was the last time he would speak for the night. Less than a second had past since his outburst, when he screamed in pure agony. His elbow was snapped with lightning speed, folding his arm unnaturally in the opposite direction, with a stomach-churning crunch.

The blond realised they were no longer holding hands. Instead, the same warm, caring hand he had been holding was now hurtling for the nose of the passenger with the broken elbow. As it hit, the sound of flesh hitting flesh and bone breaking rang out. An intense sound even over the traffic and sound of waves crashing at the nearby beach.

The passenger's screams stopped abruptly as he fell unconscious to the ground.

"Are you okay?" He asked as he turned back to face the blond.

The blond nodded, slightly shocked at what had just happened.

"Stay over near the fence, I'll protect you," he said.

The blond nodded again and backed away toward the fence of a nearby house. When he knew his new friend was out of reach, he turned back to the passenger's stunned friends who were awkwardly discussing how to approach this new situation. They had just seen their comrade taken down in fractions of a second and they were trying to figure out whether to flee or seek retribution.

"I said I didn't want any trouble, but your mate here was too stupid to listen," he said. "You should learn from his mistake. Please just let us leave and do not follow."

"Fa, fuck you, you're going to pay for that," the driver stammered trying to find his courage and show some leadership to his little cabal. "Come on boys lets end this arsehole."

The driver and his remaining weary passengers approached forming a circle around him.

Four against one, not ideal, he thought. *But I have faced worse.*

"I've asked you to leave us alone and walk away, but it seems you're too stupid, too blinded by pride and hate," he said with an even tone. "I'm warning you, I am highly trained. Do not do this, it will not end well."

"Yeah for you," one of the passengers who had been sitting in the backseat spat, before running at him, head down, trying to tackle him.

He moved fluidly, darting sideways at the last moment, dodging the passenger's incoming shoulder. As he moved, he spun and reached up grabbing his attacker's swinging arm and with a sharp turn dragged it down over his chest. He drove his own shoulder up into the ribs of the passenger while pulling down on his arm. Momentum carried the would-be tackler through the air until he flipped and landed hard on the small of his back with a thud on the concrete footpath. He rammed his knee into the passenger's shoulder causing a deep pop as he felt the arm go limp. He looked down at the confused and dazed passenger who was trying to figure out what had just happened. His arm was hanging loosely by his side. Dislocated. Pain starting to hit. With violent, but controlled force, he slammed his elbow down on the top of the passenger's head.

Lights out.

Three on one. Better, but you aren't out of this yet, he thought as the passenger slumped over on his injured arm on the concrete.

"I'm warning you again, just walk away guys," he cautioned. "It's not worth it."

"I ain't going to be beaten by you!" the driver yelled. "We're going to kill you both."

He looked over to the blond who was shaking standing next to the fence, staring in shock.

"It'll be alright, these guys will either be leaving soon or taking a long nap," he said smiling confidently at the blond.

Clearly angered and full of hate, the driver sprung forward throwing a savage right hook. It was a good punch, one he did not fully block. The driver's fist partly hit his forearm which was moving to block but it still managed to hit his face, just under his eye. The speed had been reduced by his block but it would still leave a bruise.

He staggered back and the blond ran towards him.

"Just leave us alone," the blond said. "Get out of here."

The blond placed a hand on the middle of his back. Caring, loving, concerned.

"Are you okay?" the blond asked.

He was bent over holding his face dramatically playing up his injuries. He gave the blond a wink.

"Be ready to move back when they come at me again," he said.

As if a call to action, the driver and one of the passengers came running at the couple. The blond stood and quickly shuffled back. As soon as the blond's hand left his back, he jumped forward, launching himself at the driver and oncoming passenger. He sprung up off his left foot and in mid-air he drew back his right hand and clenched his fist. With ferocious speed, he punched the driver with a hard right before landing, pivoting and throwing a left hook at the passenger. The power started in his left heal and moved up his leg and torso, through his shoulder. Every muscle and every fibre of his body was thrown in behind his now clenched left fist. The force lifted the passenger off his feet, his head snapping back, as fist hit chin. The move was so fast, the passenger hit the ground only seconds after the driver.

While the passenger was clearly knocked out, the driver surprisingly was struggling to get to his feet. In a daze of semi-consciousness, stumbling each time he made to stand. The remaining passenger threw his hands into the air in the universal sign for surrender.

"Okay" the passenger said. "I'm sorry, please don't hurt me."

He nodded at the passenger.

"You lads need to change your world view," he said. "Time to grow up."

He walked over to the blond as the surrendering passenger gingerly moved to help the driver, while cautiously keeping one eye on the passenger.

He took the blond in his arms and they hugged there in the street. Even after what had just happened, the blond felt safe in his arms. Protected.

"My house isn't far from here," the blond said leading him down the street. "Come home and keep me safe."

They approached a row of terrace houses in a quiet street and stopped in front of the third. A little rusted iron gate opened into a small courtyard. It was overgrown with lush green vines and the pavers were covered in moss. A white table with two mismatched coloured steel chairs sat outside under the lounge room window. A warm light from a table lamp shone through the window. The blond fumbled for the keys.

"Come in and let me clean you up, and we'll have a drink," the blond said. "I think I need one after all that."

"Sounds good," he said smiling.

He locked the door behind them then walked into the lounge room and over to the window. He looked back out into the street making sure they were not followed, mostly out of habit, he knew the men from the car would not be coming anytime soon.

Satisfied, he looked down to the little table with the lamp by the window. It had various black and white, and coloured photos of the blond with friends and family. Each was in a different sized and coloured frame. He lent over for a closer look. Happiness stared back from each photo.

He thought about his own house. He had a similar collection of photos from the past, when his house was a home. It sat as a painful reminder of better times.

The blond came into the room and threw a bag of frozen peas and a wet cloth onto the coffee table before pouring two glasses of shiraz.

"That's my crazy family and friends," the blond said. "Love them to bits."

He turned around and looked at the blond, a sadness in his eyes.

"Keep them close," he said. "That's what life is all about, right? I don't get much time with my friends and family these days."

"Sorry to hear that," the blond said. "Why don't you come over and take a seat?"

As he sat down on the lounge, the blond knelt on the floor in front of him. Gently, the blond took his hands one-by-one and used the cold wet cloth to wash away the battle scars on his knuckles.

"How did you learn to fight like that?" the blond asked reaching for the peas.

"I grew up in a rough neighbourhood," he lied. "I'm sorry you had to see that."

"It was my fault," the blond admitted. "I shouldn't have yelled back, but I just get so angry and upset at bigots and bogans throwing insults. I don't understand why they are so full of hate."

The blond wrapped the frozen peas in the cloth and tenderly placing the cold pack on his face.

"The world is full of awful people," he said. "What's important though is knowing that there are some truly beautiful people out there too. People like you, who make it all worthwhile. You're safe now."

He let the cold pack sooth his face which was red from the driver's punch.

The blond smiled sheepishly before moving in closer, dropping the cold pack onto the couch and wrapping one arm around his back and the other behind his head. Running fingers through his hair, the blond pulled him in and they kissed passionately, holding the moment for as long as they could, both enjoying the kiss that they had been waiting for since they had first seen each other from across the bar.

Staring at the roof, he allowed himself a smile, remembering that moment. He looked down and saw the blond, still naked, wrapped in his arms, head on his chest, breathing softly, fast asleep. He watched the blond, sleeping peacefully in his arms. He missed having someone to come home to but it was the reality of the dual life he was leading. Never having enough time to make someone happy, but far more importantly not wanting to put them in harm's way. Not after what had happened.

He looked back to the roof, returning his thoughts to the night before.

After the kiss and more wine, the blond had led him to the bedroom. They sat their glasses down on the floor and stood face to face smiling knowingly at each other. Each studying, making mental notes of the other's physical appearance.

He was six feet three inches with broad shoulders and a clearly toned body from hours of work in the gym. He had short dark brown hair messed up with product, deep brown eyes and a short-trimmed dark beard over a strong chin. He was wearing a navy suit jacket with the sleeves rolled up over a tight white t-shirt with new caramel chinos and brown R.M. Williams boots. A large Tag watch on his left wrist, two rings, one on each hand, and a pair of Oakleys hanging from the front collar of his t-shirt completed the look. His name was Max Shaw. In another world, his codename and call sign was Prince.

"God, you are gorgeous," Max said after a long moment observing every detail of the blond.

The blond was tanned from hours spent at the beach and jogging in the nearby park. He wore a tight black shirt suggestively clinging to his chiselled abs and pecks which had been crafted by surfing the break after work and every weekend. The blond had a perfect V-shaped torso, broad shoulders leading down to a trim waist. He was wearing light blue skinny leg jeans, and well-loved red and blue Converse All Stars. He wore a long necklace with a ring, cross and a clear glass crystal on a thin silver chain. Shoulder length surfer blond hair hung messily framing his face. A day's worth of sandy coloured beard gave him a rugged look and accentuated his cheek bones. But it was his sky-blue eyes that drew people in. They were full of emotion and affection. More than lust, they had a connection. His name was Sam Walker.

At five feet eleven inches, Sam stepped closer, reached up and drew Max in for a kiss. Max held Sam around the waist with his left arm pulling the couple closer together. Max's right hand tenderly pushed his blond locks aside and softly sat on the left side of Sam's face. It was a long, passionate kiss.

There it was again. The adrenaline. Excitement washed over his body recalling the moment when Sam reached into his jacket, running his hands up over his shoulders and down his arms, pushing the jacket from his shoulders onto the ground. He lifted Max's white shirt up over his head and threw it to the floor beside the now crumpled jacket. Sam noticed a scar on Max's left arm near his shoulder and touched it softly as he stared at it, as if trying to reveal its secrets.

"Told you I grew up in a rough neighbourhood," Max lied again.

Sam looked up into Max's eyes then lent in and kissed the scar softly before kissing up his neck to his lips.

Starting towards the bed, Max dragged Sam's shirt off between intense kisses. His necklace tinged as it fell against his chest. They both kicked off their shoes in different directions. He remembered the blond tripping slightly as he walked backwards for the bed and the pair laughing before embracing once more. When they got to the bed, Max lifted Sam into his powerful arms. Sam wrapped his legs around Max's waist and arms around his shoulders. Max had one hand supporting Sam's weight while the other was cupped behind his head. His fingers spread into his blond locks. Gently, he lowered Sam to the mattress, never taking his hand from behind his head. So gentle and so soft for someone so big and strong. Max was on top of Sam and they kissed. Their bodies moving together. Max kissed down Sam's neck. Down his smooth, defined chest. He continued down and undid his skinny jeans, kissing his abs. The tight jeans clung to Sam's legs, taking some effort to remove. When they came loose, Max threw them playfully over his shoulder with a wry smile on his face. Max took in the view before him. Sam was laying there in purple jocks covered with small white stars. He was breathing quickly and his excitement was certainly not hard to miss.

Max's thoughts were interrupted by a kiss on the neck. He looked down to see Sam smiling up from his embrace.

"Hi," Sam said shyly.

"Good morning sleepy head," Max said.

"What, sleepy head?" Sam asked playfully. "What time do you normally wake up after a big night out and night of passionate sex?"

"I wake at five-thirty every morning, big night or not. Old habits are hard to break. And, I was just playing. Did you sleep okay?"

"Never better. How about you?"

"Great. You're a good cuddler. And, you didn't kick me or snore once."

"Well, that's good to know," Sam said sarcastically before poking out his tongue and giggling.

Max laughed and then playfully began tickling Sam.

"Oh, cheeky in the morning, are you? Well, I'm not sure what I'm going to do with you. You might have to be punished."

Sam rolled and squirmed laughing from the tickles.

The playfulness ended when the couple hugged, still smiling and laughing, staring into each other's eyes for a moment before kissing softly, romantically. They made love for the second time as the sun began to shine through the curtains.

The sun crept further across the floor as they laid naked in each other's arms, sweating, trying to catch their breaths.

"We should have a shower I guess," Sam said grabbing Max's hand leading him to the bathroom.

"So, how long did you say you were in town?" Sam asked as they returned to the bedroom to get dressed after showering together.

"Just a few nights," Max said.

"Well, umm, would you like to have dinner tonight?" Sam asked.

"Yeah, I would love to," Max said. "Although, I might be a bit late following some meetings in the city."

"That's no worries. How about you come over after and I'll cook you dinner?"

"Sure. If that's okay? That would be great."

"Yeah, of course, it's okay. Not to come on too strong, but I really enjoyed spending time with you. You're not like other guys. There is something about you. You're intriguing. I want to get to know you more."

"Oh really? I don't think I am. I'm just a normal guy."

"I wouldn't say that," Sam said. "You're gorgeous, athletic, smart, funny, sweet and heroic. And you defended and protected me last night. I would love to hear more about your home town and how you learnt to fight like you did. And, how you got that scar on your arm and the one on your right leg."

"Oh, you saw that too? Well, it's not a very interesting story. As for the fight last night, well, I just got lucky."

"Are you sure you're still talking about the fight?" Sam laughed.

They both shared a smile, laughed and hugged again.

"I better go or I will miss my first meeting, and that will mean a very awkward conversation with the Minister, but I will see you tonight."

"I can't wait."

After sharing their mobile numbers, they kissed in the doorway, neither wanting to break away from their embrace, until a shrill ringtone cut the air.

It was Max's phone. He reached into his pocket and retrieved it. The screen lit up, *Unknown Caller, Sydney Area*.

"Sorry Sam, I better answer this, but I'll see you in a few hours," Max said and they kissed, before he opened the little rusty gate and began his walk back towards his hotel.

He smiled and waved to Sam. Sam waved back then closed the door as Max went around the corner.

What an amazing night, an incredible guy, maybe I should move to Sydney, Max thought to himself. *God, it was one night. Are you really that lonely? Yeah, I am.*

Chapter Two

Lost in his thoughts Max completely missed the white sedan parked down the road from Sam's place. It was the same car which was now following him down the road.

As the car approached, the gruff old man driving pressed a button on his arm rest lowering the passenger window.

"I taught you better than that," the driver said to Max through the window.

"Which one of the many mistakes I have made in the last twenty-four hours would you be referring to?" Max replied without needing to look at the source of the familiar voice.

"Fucking all of them," the driver spat. "You've left a trail all over the city. From the dead guy laying in the street in Western Sydney to the four arseholes you put in hospital last night. Hardly your best day."

"Flash had slightly more to do with the dead guy in Western Sydney then I did. Anyway, it's not all bad. We got the files."

Max stopped and walked over to the car which was now parked on the side of the road.

Leaning through the window, he took off the ring on his right hand and passed it to the driver.

"It's all on there, copied from the Arab guy's tablet," Max said. "And, it was no walk in the park to get it."

"If you want a walk in the park, go work for the local council. Until then get over it. Oh and answer your bloody phone when I ring, off galivanting around the city with some halfwit surfer."

Max pulled a sarcastic grin as the driver placed the ring inside a hidden socket built into the volume knob of the car stereo. *Downloading* and a progress bar appeared on the car's entertainment system touch screen with a percentage slowly ticking up towards one hundred.

"When will we have the files decoded?" Max asked pointing to the screen.

"I will get the data to Blake. He's at HQ. Hopefully we'll have more for you by the time you finish your meetings this morning with the Minister. Speaking of, you better get going so you can shower and change. You stink of wine and halfwit surfer."

"I already had a shower," Max said opening the car door.

"Well, you need another one," the driver said looking Max up and down as he sat in the passenger seat. "And, what do you think you are doing getting in my car?"

"Oh, come on, it's a few blocks from here, can't you just drop me there?" Max complained.

"Nope. Get out. You're walking. Maybe you can take the time to remember some of your training, like don't get into street fights in the middle of the fucking city."

"They started it."

"I don't care. Get out."

"You're punishing me?"

"Hardly. You of all people should remember and know when I am."

"Seriously, they brought it on themselves. We were minding our own business and they started it. The guys last night had it coming. Plus, I did warn them."

"Well, that might be the case but you're still walking. Get out."

Download Complete 100% flashed across the screen with a full progress bar underlining the message.

Grumbling under his breath, Max got out of the car.

"I will text you details in a couple of hours. Until then stop fucking complaining and get to work," the driver said before throwing Max his ring through the open window and accelerating away from the kerb.

"Great, thanks Hulk," Max said quietly to himself as he put his ring back on and started for his hotel.

Patrick "Hulk" Scott was a retired Major General who had spent most of his long career in the Special Air Service Regiment in the Australian Army. There were a couple of stories about how he got his nickname, but regardless Max figured it was a perfect fit. Firstly, he was allegedly impossible to kill, according to his army mates. He was also right, Max did know from first-hand experience Hulk's ability to punish. During his training, Max had seen Hulk's vicious temper and had been on the receiving end of his brutal fighting style. On more than one occasion, Max had been bested in training as Hulk taught him how to fight any enemy, in various combat styles. He was stronger than anyone Max had ever met. And finally, he was a monster. Even now well into his sixties, he was six foot six and towered over Max, and he was carrying a lot more bulk core muscle. He had legs like an Olympic cyclist. Hulk had left the army over decade ago and had a new job now, Director-General, Australian Intelligence Services or AIS. In other words, Australia's top spy and intelligence chief.

Created after September 11, AIS brought together the best operatives from all intelligence, police and military agencies in the country under one banner. The organisation's role was to gather intelligence, frustrate attempts by foreign and domestic actors to gain intelligence from Australia and her allies, and eliminate any threats by any means necessary. AIS serves as both the country's last line of defence and the pointy end of the spear, and a critical part of military intelligence. Its budget was off the books and AIS operatives operate from various places around Australia and the world. Each agent has different skills, qualifications and covers. While many agents remained tied to their home agencies, a growing number, like Max, were recruited directly to AIS. Some of Max's AIS colleagues were full time agents based within AIS. Others, including Max, were planted in organisations with legitimate roles, indistinguishable from other employees, which provided them with cover to travel, collect intel and conduct covert missions often in plain sight.

Hulk had recruited Max while he was at university following several months of close surveillance. Max was the top of his class majoring in international relations and politics, with minors in both psychology and business. His mastery of psychology and understanding of personalities and human traits brought him to Hulk's attention as did his sporting ability. He was a gifted athlete.

Max had an interest in global and domestic politics, so Hulk arranged a low-level staffer job for Max in the office of an up-and-coming Member of Parliament. To this day, Max was not sure if the MP had willingly agreed to the placement initially out of some patriotic duty or whether Hulk had something to hold against the MP to force his hand. Either way, it was a role hiding in plain sight that gave him access to influential people at home and abroad, masses of information and unlimited travel all of which served Hulk and the AIS. He worked as a normal member of staff in the MP's office unless he was needed by AIS. As his skills grew, he was asked to combine the roles gathering intelligence for AIS through meetings he attended as a staffer. At other times, like on this trip to Sydney, he had to do assignments for AIS either side of his staffer obligations.

Max arrived at the hotel and headed straight for the elevator. Throwing his clothes on the still neatly made bed, he walked naked to the shower where he scrubbed away the lingering smell of sweat and wine.

Teeth cleaned, under-arm deodorant applied, cologne sprayed liberally, clay holding his hair in place, he moved for the cupboard and reached for his recently dry-cleaned dark navy-blue suit still in its plastic protector.

He stood and stared for a moment at his reflection in the full-length mirror. His suit was tailored perfectly to his athletic frame while providing enough room for comfort and manoeuvrability, and to hide his gun if he needed it. His brown R.M. Williams boots, rings, watch, Oakleys, white business shirt and blue tie with pink spots completed his outfit. He looked a bit tired but not too bad considering he only had a couple of hours sleep. He leaned in for a closer look at the bruise on his cheek from the driver's punch last night. He applied some concealer to cover the bruise. It was not completely gone and slightly puffy, but it was better.

Satisfied, he went to his locked suitcase and removed his dark brown leather shoulder bag which was filled with paperwork for the MP, a tablet computer, and a notebook and pens.

Time to go.

Chapter Three

Downstairs a car was waiting to collect Max and the MP who was now a Minister in the Federal Government. It was fair to say Max was not a huge fan of the Minister. He thought he was a bit out of his depth and frankly too conservative, but he respected his dual roles of Minister and Member of Parliament.

Hulk definitely did not like him at all, that was evident every time he was mentioned. Max had overheard them arguing late one evening in the Minister's office.

"I have had him in my office for several years now, he is a good staffer when he is here, but he spends most of his time working for you now, not me," the Minister had said. "Surely, I have done my time. Maybe it is time for him to move to another office?"

"Listen to me you empty suit," Hulk spat, cold as ice. "If he wasn't working for you, you would still be on the backbench trying to figure out who's dick you needed to suck to try to get promoted. I got you this role so Max can take on more work for AIS. You didn't think you got it on merit, did you? Ha. If you do not want to be a Minister anymore, that's fine. I will get Max a role in another office. Or, you can shut the fuck up and keep your job. Up to you but think quick because I am going to need to tell the Prime Minister if you are leaving."

Shocked the Minister made to argue but thought better of it and stayed silent.

"Good. You are growing into the role anyway Minister. The PM will be happy he gets to avoid another reshuffle."

Back in the hotel lobby, Max walked towards an older gentleman wearing a poorly fitting jet-black suit with the Commonwealth Crest on the breast pocket.

"Good morning, I'm Max, I work for the Minister," he said to the driver.

"Good morning, sir, please let me get that for you," the driver said gesturing for the bag.

"No that's fine, thank you, I've got it," Max said. "The Minister shouldn't be too long."

"Sorry, sorry, I'm coming," the Minister said. "Sorry I'm late, I was stuck on the phone. Good morning, Max. Hello, Driver."

Minister for Defence James Johnston was around five foot nine with a head of grey, almost white hair. He was wearing his favourite black pinstriped suit, and an ugly purple and green tie. He was as smooth and polished as you would expect of a politician, but he had an air of arrogance which people definitely did not like. Max had sat in many meetings with him and watched people shifting uncomfortably and staring at the Minister unimpressed as he dismissed their issues or showed his lack of understanding. Max remembered one senior defence official taking him aside and complaining that the Minister did not know anything about defence, intelligence or national security. *Not a good assessment for the Defence Minister* Max had thought.

"Morning Minister, how are you?" Max said.

"Good morning, sir, please let me take your bag for you," the driver said.

"Ah, thank you," Johnston said handing over the bag. "I am well thanks, Max. How are you? Get some sleep? Gee, I was tired after Sarah and I got in last night. It was a big day yesterday."

"Yes thanks, rested and ready to rock and roll," Max lied. "Here is your schedule. Should we hit the road?"

"Lead on," Johnston said briefly looking from Max to the day's agenda he had just handed him. "Whoa, just a second, what's wrong with your eye?"

"It's nothing, just a little disagreement with a door."

"Yeah right, Max. What did you do?"

"Nothing you need to worry about Minister. Everything is fine."

"Jesus. Are you wearing make-up?"

"Just a little. I didn't want to scare any of the people we are meeting with. You seem more upset about that than the eye itself."

"Hmm, well let's hope our stakeholders aren't as observant as me," the Minister said turning to follow the driver.

"Indeed," Max said under his breath.

In the car the Minister, driver and Max made small talk for the duration of the normally short trip from Bondi to the Commonwealth Building in the city. Today it would take longer thanks to the bumper-to-bumper traffic expected for most of the trip. Impatient drivers beeped their horns and cars moved in and out of lanes as they tried to find some non-existent fast lane. Max sat in the rear of the car reading news articles to the Minister from his phone.

"The Telegraph has an article providing updates on casualties from the Middle-East," Max said. "One Australian injured, twenty civilians killed in a drone strike."

"Why does the fucking Telegraph know more about these incidents then I do?" Johnston asked.

"I'm sure there is a briefing on your email Minister," Max said.

"There better be. Billions of dollars pumped into defence intelligence and I find out from the fucking Telegraph. What else do I need to know?"

"Polls are steady. The Government is barely ahead of the Opposition, but the Prime Minister is still more popular than Santa. The Opposition Leader not so much."

"Good. The public is finally paying attention. The PM is doing a marvellous job and we are ahead. We cannot let that other mob in, that would be a disaster."

"Hmm," Max mumbled in half-hearted agreement.

"That wasn't very convincing, Max. You cannot possibly think they would be better in Government."

"Some of their policies are pretty good. Why do you think the party polling is stuck around the centre considering the popularity ratings of the leaders? It is because of each party's policies. Some of ours are holding us back and some of theirs are pushing them forward. The people aren't mugs. They know what's really going on."

"Our policies are in every way superior, Max."

The driver scoffed.

"You do not agree either, driver?" the Minister asked.

"I think the kid's right," the driver said. "Some of yours are good, but gee some aren't. Same with the other mob. I think the only thing stopping them taking over is the PM. He's a rock star."

"Well you're right about the Prime Minister, but the rest is rubbish," the Minister argued. "Our platform is fair and balanced. The people love it."

"Just my opinion, sir," the driver said.

"Told you so," Max said.

Johnston pulled an unimpressed look.

"The papers are all mostly focused on the Israeli PM's visit. He arrives in a few hours here in Sydney, then he is off to Canberra and Melbourne later in the week."

"Yeah, I am looking forward to meeting him again. He was so nice when I met him in Tel Aviv."

"Yes, I remember. I was there."

"Oh that's right."

"There is another story here you might be interested in. Middle-Eastern businessman found dead after falling from a building in Parramatta overnight. The man was found with severe injuries some of which the police say were sustained before his fall. Although I'm sure the fall didn't help. Police are looking into suspected links to organised crime and possibly to terrorism."

"Does he have a name?" the Minister said.

"Police are yet to confirm although he was found on the pavement outside the Crown Constructions building," Max said. "I will get a brief for you."

Johnston didn't reply, he just stared out the window watching the passing traffic.

Chapter Four

When they arrived, they headed up to their suite on the twenty-first floor of the Commonwealth Building. Floor to ceiling windows gave way to a spectacular view of Sydney Harbour. Sunlight was glistening on the water and reflecting on the glass of the neighbouring skyscrapers. The Manly Ferry was pushing off from Circular Quay and thousands of people walked with urgency towards their workplaces. Local cafes were pumping, trains were running frequently in and out of the nearby station, and the cars in the street were still bumper to bumper.

Max's colleague Sarah was already in the office. She sat typing at her computer in the open plan office. Sarah was a highly-educated, professional staffer with a Master of Law from Sydney University. She had majored in international relations as part of her undergraduate degree and was in the process of completing a PhD. Her thesis was on the Australia and United States defence alliance, known as the ANZUS Treaty, including the inner workings of defence contracting in both countries. Sarah was good looking but did not know it. She had perfect tanned skin and a great body from spending at least an hour a day at the gym but she hid it under ill-fitting, masculine, cheap suits. Perhaps it was her way of blending in, in the blokey and masculine world of politics.

"God, can you believe this?" she said pointing to the television mounted on the wall. "What is wrong with people in this city?"

"Four men were brutally assaulted last night not far from a popular bar and restaurant strip in Bondi. One man suffered what doctors described as a devastating elbow break, severe concussion and broken nose. Three others were admitted to hospital with concussions with one of the men needing treatment for a dislocated shoulder and another needing surgery to pin a fractured jaw. Another man was lucky to

escape without injury, he is said to be helping police with their investigation," the reporter said.

"Always two sides to every story Sare, maybe they started it," Max said looking to Johnston who was giving him a questioning look.

"Good morning, Sarah," Johnston said frowning at Max who shrugged and made a face as if to say, *I don't know anything about it.* "Awful story, hopefully the police will find the people responsible,"

"Far out, Max, did you even listen to the reporter? They were seriously injured, plus there was that story earlier about some guy being thrown out of a window at some company called Crown Constructions in Western Sydney – it is just crazy. God, I hate Sydney, I can't wait to get back to Canberra. Anyway, good morning, Minister. Sorry, how are you?"

"Good thank you," Johnston said interrupted by Max's phone which tinged three times in quick succession. Three text messages.

Max looked at the phone.

Hey Max, thanks for last night. I had an amazing time. God you are sexy and charming, and so much fun.

OMG!

I can't wait to see you tonight xx Sam xx

Max smiled as he read the messages and his heart skipped a light beat, a feeling he had not felt for a long time. *It was one night. Clam down. You are not getting married. Although Sam would look good in a suit.* Max was suddenly hit by a wave of guilt at the thought. *How long had it been since Lachlan? We couldn't get married then, now I'm thinking about marrying a one-night stand. Snap out of it Max,* he thought to himself.

Hey Sam, miss me already hey? :-P Jokes! I know how you feel! Can't wait to see you tonight. I will text you later to let you know what time I'll be there. Hope your day is good. Max xx

"What are you smiling about? Got some hot bird texting you or something?" Johnston said.

"Ha, something like that," Max replied.

"I didn't know you were seeing anyone," Sarah said sarcastically. "Who is she?"

Max gave her a curt frown then smiled at her mischievous comment. Sarah knew he was gay. They had gotten drunk one night after work a few years ago and things got out of hand. She kissed him.

"I'm really sorry, but you are not my type," he had said at the time.

He knew it had hurt her feelings and, while he was definitely not one to share much about himself, he told her.

"Don't worry it's not you. You are gorgeous. Any man would be lucky to know you, let alone kiss you. I'm just not into kissing girls."

The Minister on the other hand had no idea. Max thought about telling him but their frequent heated debates on same-sex marriage and religion had exposed Johnston's homophobic and highly religious worldview. It upset Max to think that people were so easily brainwashed by religion and by culture. The Catholic Church had successfully convinced the world that homosexuality was abnormal behaviour, an impulse and feelings that could be overcome by following God's teachings or in extreme cases same-sex attraction therapies, like electro-shock.

"They, of course, completely leave out the fact that homosexual relationships have existed throughout human history, long before Christianity, the Bible and the Son arrived," Max had said during one of their arguments.

The Minister was not happy about it, but it was worse during the same-sex marriage debate as Max's guilt and heartache for his former fiancée drove into him like a knife on almost an hourly basis.

Max blamed religion for many of the world's woes. A big part of his work with AIS was stopping radicals who had been brainwashed using religion to do terrible things.

"Don't you both have work to do?" Max asked.

"Yeah, yeah, righto, Sarah where are these briefs I need to read and sign?" Johnston asked. "Let's start with the overnight security update and then we better have a look at the Crown Constructions one."

Max's phone tinged again.

"Oh God, Max, tell her you're at work and the Minister is getting cranky your phone keeps ringing," Johnston yelled out his office door.

"It's from my landlord, something about the roof," Max said.

Johnston huffed then looked down at the tablet computer on the desk in front of him.

"Gee, your landlord calls a lot, Max, it might be time to move out," Sarah said not knowing that landlord was code for AIS.

Johnston knew and clearly was not thrilled.

Max pressed his thumb to the scanner on his phone and then looked directly into the camera. The phone recognised his thumb print. The retinal scan from the camera was also recognised and his phone flashed to life. Max opened the secure messaging app. *Decrypting* scrolled across the screen.

Prince, new orders from Hulk. You are to sit in on Suit's first meeting with the CEO. Learn what you can about the organisation's expansion plans including potential new buyers and markets for their product. Any information you can gain on security of their product in transit and in country would also be beneficial. Potential link to recent chatter and intel. Following the meeting, your usual car will be waiting. Transmit meeting debrief with codename Piano Man and rendezvous at the location set on the Nav system. Hermes.

Max double tapped the finger scanner on his phone and the message erased. He took the tablet computer from his bag and walked into the Minister's office.

"Everything alright with the roof?" Sarah asked.

"Yeah, he wants to do some work for a few hours this afternoon which I said was fine," Max said looking to the annoyed Minister who understood that meant Max would be working for AIS for a few hours this afternoon.

"Have you got everything you need for the NorthStar CEO meeting, Minister?" Max asked. "I thought I might sit in on the meeting with you."

"Yeah, I know Bill Jones well. We went to university together. It's funny you know, I go on to become Defence Minister and he becomes CEO of a major Defence contractor. Not too bad for two blokes who used to sit around drinking and jamming all day instead of going to class."

"You guys were in a band?" Sarah asked.

"Oh no, no, I wasn't that good. I just played for fun. Bill though, he could play. Fantastic talent."

"Guitar?" Sarah asked.

"No, piano. Well, it was a cheap electric keyboard, but boy could he play."

Max thought to himself, *well that explains the 'Piano Man' debrief code.* It always amazed Max how much Blake knew and could find out about people.

The phone rang.

"Minister James Johnston's office, Sarah speaking," Sarah said. "Yes, please send him up."

"Minister, that was security, your guest is on his way up," Sarah said.

"Thank you, Sarah. Can you please go down to the café and get a coffee for Bill and me? And, grab one for yourself and Max too."

"No worries, can do. Long black, Max?"

"Yes please, with an extra shot thanks. Thanks, Minister."

Sarah left the office and when Johnston heard the door close he turned to Max with an inquisitive look in his eyes.

"Those guys they were talking about on the news, they were not too far from our hotel," he said.

"No, only a few blocks away in this bloody dangerous city, did you want me to increase your security detail?" Max asked mockingly.

"You know what I am asking, you smartarse," Johnston said a slight anger in his tone. "You turn up this morning with a black eye and four guys get hospitalised a short walk away. Was it you?"

"Well Minister, if it was, there would have been a good reason for it and they would have been warned, and they may have brought it on themselves."

"Oh, for God's sake, Max. You cannot just go around beating people up in the street. What if someone saw you or filmed you doing it?"

"There is nothing to worry about. Relax and focus on something that matters. Mr Jones will be here in a second anyway."

"Max, please. If you were caught do you know what would happen? I would be hounded by the media and you would be out of a job, swiftly followed by me, no doubt."

"I won't get caught. There were no cameras. Relax. Plus, they brought it on themselves."

"Max!"

The doorbell rang, interrupting their conversation. A small window appeared in the corner of the television showing footage of a man standing on the other side of the office door.

"That's Bill. I will go let him in," Johnston said. "We will talk about this later."

The Minister walked over and pulled the door open.

"Bill, come in," Johnston said. "How are you?"

"Hi James," Jones said shaking Johnston's hand. "I am well thanks. It's great to see you."

"And you, Bill."

He led Jones into his office. Jones was the same age as the Minister, early fifties and greying hair. He had an average build. Max figured he was about five feet five or six inches. He was wearing an impressive dark navy suit which Max figured would probably cost more than he made in months. He was handsome and oozed the sophistication and power of a major company CEO.

"Bill, this is my Intelligence Adviser, Max Shaw. Max, this is Bill Jones, CEO of NorthStar Defence Industries."

"Mr Jones, it is a pleasure to meet you," Max said.

"And you, Mr Shaw. Intelligence Adviser hey? Hardest job in the office trying to make him intelligent," Jones said tipping his head in Johnston's direction.

"Oh ouch," Johnston said laughing. "Let's take a seat, Sarah will be back soon with coffees. So, Bill what can we do for you?"

"Well, thank you both for taking the time to meet with me," Jones said. "I thought it would be a good opportunity to discuss the progress of our new drone fleet. I am pleased to tell you, we are weeks ahead of schedule and should be able to deliver the first drones within the week."

"This week?" Johnston asked with excitement.

"Probably early next week, but yes very soon indeed."

"Ahead of schedule? That is almost unheard of in defence contracting terms."

"Yes, we are very proud."

"That is fantastic Bill. The Prime Minister will be pleased."

Sarah arrived with the coffees.

"Thanks Sarah," Johnston said. "Hope you are still a flat white man?"

"Sure am, thank you," Jones said as Sarah sat the takeaway cup in front of him.

Max also said thanks to Sarah as she headed for the door.

"Air Force are happy with the drones?" Max asked.

"Yes, they have put them through their paces and they want them in the Middle-East as soon as possible," Jones said.

"So, have you set a delivery schedule?" Max asked.

"We were thinking of an official handover ceremony next week, pending the Prime Minister's schedule and, of course, your availability, James."

"I will be there. I will cancel anything else that's in the diary."

"Great."

"And, that's when Air Force will take control of the fleet?" Max asked.

"Yes, officially. Though they have unofficially been testing them for months and we will be embedded in their teams until they are up and running."

"This is seriously great news, Bill."

"Thanks, James."

"Mr Jones, can I ask about security arrangements? Where are the drones now?" Max asked.

"They are all based at Richmond Air Force Base here in Sydney. A couple are on trials with the Air Force, but the rest are at Richmond. I have my guys, all ex-forces, guarding the compound around the clock. Plus, the base is obviously guarded twenty-four, seven."

"How about in transit and in-country?"

"Security?"

"Yeah."

"We transport them using NorthStar's transport fleet and assemble in-country. Normally, in the Defence Force's compound on the ground."

"Normally?"

"In the past, with some of our old drones, we have assembled and launched them from Navy vessels at sea and that will be able to happen again as soon as the Navy's new carriers come online. But, for now we assemble on site. It takes an hour at most to have them ready for launch."

"How about the control modules? Where are they?"

"At the moment, the control systems are at Richmond too. Except the two on trials, obviously, their control systems are aboard Navy support ships anchored offshore near one of our ally's bases."

"Fair enough. They are that mobile?"

"Yes. The remotes are compact. They are housed in fully self-contained, reinforced steel briefcases. Ideally, you plug them into a bigger operating system, but you can launch and control the drones using just the contents of the briefcase, if necessary. It has a screen and joystick, and keyboard that all folds out. It has built in battery packs, but it chews up the juice, so it is best to plug them in to a power source. Handy for a quick or mobile launch, or field navigation."

"Not quite the nuclear football but still packs a punch. I presume these are under strict security?"

"Of course. Restricted to the highest level of security. They are locked in separate secure units buried deep in vaults under the Richmond compound. Multiple levels of security."

"All sounds very impressive, Mr Jones. I look forward to checking them out when we visit next week."

"More than welcome, Mr Shaw. It would be a pleasure to show you around."

"Thank you. I will take you up on that. Any news on how the trials are going?"

"My guys reported in last night. So far Air Force are extremely happy with the drones both for ease-of-use and responsiveness. There will always be some glitches but so far, so good."

"Well, that is good to hear. So, if you don't mind me asking, what's next for NorthStar?"

"Not at all. Assuming the trials are successful and the drones are handed over next week, we would be looking to monitor their performance on deployment then with the Government's permission we would be looking to demonstrate the capability to our allies to see if they are interested in purchasing new drones."

"Oh, that is fantastic, Bill," Johnston said. "Exports. Good for jobs. Good for the economy."

"Yes and good for our allies to have the best kit," Jones said.

"Of course," Johnston said.

"Mr Shaw, I was wondering, if you don't have any more questions, can I have five minutes with James to catch up on old times?"

"Of course, I'm sure I will have many more questions, but that can wait until next week," Max said standing to leave. "Thank you for the update. Please excuse me."

Max took his seat near Sarah but continued to watch Jones through the window. He noticed he looked agitated and fidgety. His previous calm demeanour had changed.

"How was the meeting?" Sarah asked.

"Very interesting," Max said. "Sounds like they have some impressive kit. We will need to clear one day in the Minister's schedule next week for a handover ceremony."

"Already? I thought they were months away."

"They've brought them forward. Air Force is happy."

"Oh great. Gee, I would like to chat to him sometime about my thesis."

"I'm sure the Minister could arrange that."

"I hope so. It would really help. I have been looking through their contracts for months. It would be good to ask him some follow up questions."

Max was watching Jones and the Minister. Johnston looked to be trying to calm Jones down. Max was intrigued. He wished he had left his phone in the room to pick up the conversation through his passive listening app. It was probably a personal issue but still something made Max uncomfortable.

After several minutes of animated conversation, the door opened, and Johnston and Jones walked out.

"It will be fine, Bill," Johnston said. "Trust me. Good to see you. Let's grab a drink soon."

"That would be good, James, I'm sure you're right, thank you," Jones said as they shook hands. "Good to meet you, Mr Shaw. I look forward to showing you our fleet next week. I have left a couple of briefs on the desk in there on the drones which might be of interest to you."

"Great, thank you, I look forward to looking through them and it is nice to meet you too," Max said. "Mr Jones, this is my colleague, Sarah Greene. She is currently doing her PhD on defence contracting. She would love to chat to you sometime about it, if you were available?"

"Pleasure, Miss Greene. Absolutely. James has my number. Let's find a time to chat."

"We will, thank you, Mr Jones, I look forward to it," Sarah said.

"Me too, James, Mr Shaw, Ms Greene," Jones said looking to each person as he said their names. "Good to see you. Thanks again."

"Thanks, Bill," Johnston said.

Jones left the room giving a small wave as he closed the door.

"Thanks, Max," Sarah said.

"No worries. He was there. I figured why not ask."

Max stood and followed the Minister back into his office.

"Everything okay?" Max asked. "Mr Jones looked unsettled when I left the room."

Johnston didn't answer, he just looked down at his phone. Fidgeting, almost nervously. He swiped wildly with his right thumb.

"Minister? Everything alright?"

"Umm, Max. Sorry, umm. Yeah, everything is fine. Just a few nerves before the big handover next week."

"That's odd, he seemed fine when I was in here. Everything is ahead of schedule and security is good. Not sure what he is nervous about. I'm going to have to call this in."

"No, no it's fine, Max. No need to involve AIS. The security is fine. He is just under some pressure that's all."

"If you say so," Max said. "But I think I will let Hulk decide that."

"No Max. Honestly, it is fine."
Max shrugged and left the room.

Chapter Five

Jones stepped out of the elevator and walked across the expansive lobby. The open space was bright from the sun pouring in through the three-storey floor to ceiling windows onto the white marble tiles. There was a café in the far corner and dozens of people were lined up waiting for their morning coffees. Two escalators framed the security desk leading up to the third-floor mezzanine. Two security guards sat behind the desk in their crisp white shirts and there were four matching guards manning the doors outside both entrances to the lobby.

Jones looked through the glass window to his waiting driver who was standing alert by the car. He smiled as he saw his boss approaching and opened the rear door on the powerful Mercedes town car. As the door opened, Jones saw the driver's head turn quickly to look down the path which ran in front of the Commonwealth Building. Jones could not see what his driver was staring at but the look on his face said it all. He watched in horror as his driver and most loyal staff member was mown down by a barrage of bullets. His fine suit was ripped and covered in blood instantly.

Jones stood frozen inside the lobby as a motorbike sped towards the glass doors of the Commonwealth Building. The rider levelled an automatic pistol and fired at the sentries outside who were both scrambling for their side arms after watching the driver get cut down, but they were not fast enough. A violent volley of bullets cut them down where they stood and shattered the glass doors behind them, as they fell to the concrete.

Through the screams of the masses in the lobby, Jones heard the glass behind him shatter as the two guards on the opposite door were shot and their door splintered sending tiny pieces of glass scattering across the floor.

A second bike smashed through the broken glass. The rider let loose his weapon, opening fire on the café and its patrons.

Glass, china, tables and chairs were hit in quick succession, and bottles exploded in the fridge. Dozens of people fell to the floor, some were screaming and crying in fear or pain. Others lay motionless, the life gone from their eyes. Everyone else was running in any and every direction.

Jones just stood frozen in the centre of the lobby, watching in terror.

The second bike squealed to a stop in front of the security desk for the first time revealing a gun wielding passenger on the back of the bike who jumped off and loosened off two shots. The first hit a security guard behind the desk. He had been on his feet but was forcefully thrown back as the bullet hit him between the eyes. The second security guard was on the phone calling for backup. He was moving for cover under the desk as the second bullet ripped into his throat sending a spray of blood across the government crest adorning the wall behind the security desk. He disappeared from sight, behind the desk.

The shooter turned back to the rider and nodded. The rider revved the bike and it squealed as it swung around one hundred and eight degrees on the spot. It raced across the lobby, its tyres piercing the air as they slid on the marble tiles before accelerating hard as it climbed the escalator to the mezzanine.

Jones turned back as he heard the first bike smash through the shattered glass door which led out to where his driver was lying dead in the street. It kicked up broken glass as it flew across the foyer, tyres screeching as they left black rubber marks on the white marble tiles. The rider skid to a stop in front of the café, and he and his passenger leapt from the bike and ran towards the elevator bay. Guns pressed to their shoulders, they both shot fleeing office workers in the back as they ran. The screams and gun shots were deafening as they echoed off the marble, concrete and glass of the lobby.

The two leather clad men lent down and took security passes off two of their dead victims. Jones noticed they wore backpacks over their heavy riding gear. They continued to fire shots randomly at screaming office workers. The elevator doors opened and three unsuspecting women who were in the lift were cut down by a spray of bullets. Without stopping, the rider and passenger boarded the lift, waved their security passes on the sensor and pressed the floor buttons they were looking for.

The passenger who had shot the guards manning the desk in the centre of the lobby walked to the side of the security desk and reached over to unlock the door. He walked through the small entrance and stood over the dying security guard. His previously white uniform was covered in blood which was pumping through his fingers hopelessly clutching his neck. The guard was gasping for breath. A look of sheer panic in his eyes. The passenger fired two shots into the security guard's heart, putting him out of his misery.

After a moment, looking down at his handiwork, the passenger looked up and across the lobby to Jones who had turned to face the security desk when he heard the shots. The passenger lifted his reflective helmet visor to get a better look. He walked out from behind the desk and hopped playfully between the tiles as he spoke with Jones.

As he reached Jones, his smile faded to a frown and he raised his gun and shot him between the eyes.

As he stood, again looking down at his handiwork, the rider and passenger re-emerged from the elevator, and after a brief exchange ran out into the street firing into the air to cause chaos outside the Commonwealth Building. As people ran, they climbed into the driver and front passenger seats of Jones's town car and started the engine.

The passenger in the lobby looked down at his watch as the rider who had gone to the mezzanine climbed onto the down escalator. Still wearing her helmet, her leather jacket and skinny leg pants which clung tightly to her toned body. They spoke briefly before turning and heading together across the lobby.

They walked out through the broken door as glass crunched under their feet with each step. People in the street were running and others screamed as they saw the second pair of helmeted figures emerge from the building, guns in hand. They looked around, watching the horror spreading before them then loosened off some wide and high shots to create more panic and confusion as they jumped into the rear seat of Jones's waiting car.

The car fled the scene as the passenger in the rear retrieved his mobile phone and dialled the first saved number.

Within seconds, two simultaneous explosions rang out. The electricity went out throughout the government office tower and widows on the first, second and third floor exploded out into the street. The building shook and swayed, and the foyer was destroyed in an instant. Chairs, tables and benches splintered as they were flung into the air with violent force. Bodies of slain office workers and of those who had come to aid the injured, after the car had sped off, were propelled into the walls and through the glass out into the street.

The mezzanine erupted in flames. The utilities room was torn to pieces. Sparking wires whipped back and forth as flames took hold. The conference room doors were snatched from hinges, creating lethal projectiles, mowing down men and women as they ran.

There was shear panic in the streets surrounding the building. Men and women in business suits fled as fast as they could run, while tourists and Sydneysiders alike tripped and pushed at each other as they ran in fear for their own lives. Tradies from a nearby worksite watched on helplessly from their scaffold, having downed tools when the gun shots rang out.

The second saved number was dialled from the backseat of Jones's fleeing vehicle. The twentieth floor of the Commonwealth Building was torn apart. Windows exploded and the building shook forcefully again. Office furniture, computers, paperwork and several unsuspecting victims were thrown from the building, falling to the street below. Water pipes burst and fire sprinklers started spewing water down the side of the tower.

As smoke billowed out from the bottom of the tower, and water and smoke poured from the twentieth-floor windows, the final explosion rang out when the passenger hit send on the third stored number. From the street below, it would have seemed to those watching that the twenty-first floor had suffered the same fate as glass, furniture and more than one innocent victim rained down into the street.

However, one section remained intact.

Chapter Six

As Max stood flicking through the briefs Jones had left, he thought about what Jones had said and what he was going to report to AIS. He thought about how insistent the Minister was on not telling Hulk. He probably just did not want to have to speak with Hulk. They really did dislike each other. But, there was something niggling in the back of his mind which he could not put his finger on. His face twisted in thought as he threw the brief down onto his desk and swung back on his chair in the main section of the Minister's suite.

The television news anchors were labouring on about the arrival of the Israeli Prime Minister who was to address the Parliament in a few days and visit the Australian War Memorial while he was in Canberra. He would also visit Sydney for a show at the Opera House and to climb the Harbour Bridge. The anchors made awkward small talk discussing his visit to Taronga Zoo to pat a koala and feed kangaroos. An Australian Rules football game in Melbourne was also on the official itinerary among the various meetings he was to hold on his short trip to the country.

"It is very exciting we will get to meet with the Prime Minister on his visit and I cannot wait to hear his speech to Parliament," Sarah said. "The steps he has taken towards peace in the Middle-East are nothing short of inspiring. He is an amazing leader."

"Working for the Defence Minister, we'll be out of a job if he succeeds," Max said.

"God Max is everything a joke to you?"

Just then the building shook and the lights flickered before going out. The computers and television went black. Emergency sirens started blaring.

"Jesus, what was that?" Johnston yelled.

"What the hell?" Sarah asked.

The sirens were interrupted by a commanding voice over the loud speaker. *Evacuate. Evacuate. Evacuate,* it commanded.

"Geez, that's a lot of steps we've got to walk down, but we better go," Johnston said.

"No," Max said already on his feet. "Into the safe room, now!"

"Safe room?" Sarah asked confused. "What safe room?"

The Minister shot Max a worried look.

"Go, now!" Max said pushing the Minister and grabbing Sarah by the hand dragging her out of her chair towards the Minister's office.

Johnston ran ahead. Max flung Sarah through the door and she stumbled, catching herself awkwardly on the meeting table. Max closed the door. Spinning on his heal, he ran for the Minister's desk and leapt over it using his left hand on the top to support his weight. When he landed, he dropped to his knees and smashed the thin wooden panel on the left frame of the desk with his clenched fist. Inside the panel was a red button which he hit with the same force.

Another siren sounded followed by an announcement. *Stand clear,* it commanded.

There was a clicking sound and then a faint electric motor kicked in, followed by a growing rumble. Solid metal shutters dropped with incredible speed over the outer window one-by-one each released a metal thud as they interlocked. Each shutter was a steel panel that ran the length of the window at about twenty centimetres wide and two inches thick. They each clicked into place as they fell, quickly blocking the view, creating a wall over the outside window. A solid steel wall was sliding into place between the Minister's personal office and the main suite where Sarah and Max had been sitting moments ago. As it closed, a loud explosion rang out. It sounded and felt like a truck had slammed into the metal floor of the Minister's office. The floor shook and the three stumbled.

There were a series of clicks as the shutters outside the window and wall between the offices locked into place. There was a hiss of escaping air as the room sealed itself and the noise stopped. An eerie quiet fell over the room. Max knew the shutters and solid wall had locked into the roof, floor and other solid steel walls which were built around the Minister's office creating a self-contained reinforced steel safe room.

Moments later another bomb detonated barely six feet from the entrance to the Minister's suite completely gutting the main office and most of the twenty-first floor of the Commonwealth Building.

The sound was deafening inside the Minister's safe room as the blast wave and furniture pounded into the steel wall. Max's ears were ringing and he could see Sarah was screaming, overcome by fear. Johnston had his hands over his ears, grimacing with pain. A shocked look in his eyes.

As the ringing began to subside, Max got back to his feet and reached over the table to pick up the desk phone. No dial tone.

"Shit," he said.

"Here," Johnston said trying to hand Max his mobile phone.

"It's no good, James," Max said using the Minister's first name, shaking his head. "The walls are too thick for a normal mobile phone signal to get through."

Max walked over to the bookcase and pulled out the draw on the right, removing it from its slot and tossing it to the side. Its contents spilled out onto the floor as it bounced and broke on impact. He reached into the now open space that had held the draw. After a few seconds of fidgeting about, Max produced a black carbon fibre case. It was about a foot long by half a foot wide and about three to four inches thick. He placed it on the table in front of Sarah. She just stared at Max. Her eyes darting from his face to the black case on the meeting table.

Max entered two different four-digit combinations into the tumble locks on each side of the case. The lid clicked open and

Sarah gasped as she saw a new Glock with three magazines. Max ignored the gun and pulled a small black fabric pouch from the case. He removed the contents and threw the pouch on the floor. In his hands was a small satellite phone with a large cylindrical folding antenna.

"Max, what?" Sarah asked confused. "How did you know that was there? How did you know to come to the room? What happened? Why do we have a gun?"

"It is okay, Sarah, come over here," Johnston said.

Sarah walked over and the Minister put his arms around her.

"You will be ok. Max knows what he is doing."

Max pressed the power button and the screen of the phone came to life. Max dialled one, holding the button in until a series of beeps sounded from the phone's tinny sounding speaker as it dialled a pre-set number.

"Access code?" a male voice asked after only one ring.

"India, Delta, Juliet, one, eight, seven," Max said.

"Report Prince," the male voice said.

"Transmit to Hulk," Max barked. "SITREP. Agent safe and fully operational. Commonwealth Building safe room twenty-one activated. Phone lines and power supply compromised. Suit and Tie accounted for. No harm to either. Four explosions. Two on lower levels. Two danger close. Exit strategy Alpha only option given likely damage. Fast and hard. Suit and Tie to be delivered for extract. Cannot rule out Suit as target given proximity. Rendezvous at previous set location for debrief and tasking.

"Understood and Godspeed Prince," the male voice said before cutting off the connection.

Max placed the sat phone in his inside jacket pocket and turned to face the Minister and Sarah.

"What's the plan Max?" Johnston asked. "Are they coming to help us?"

"I've reported in. I'm going to get you both to the airport where a jet will be waiting to take you to Canberra. On arrival, you will be given a federal police security detail who will move you to a safe location."

"Security detail?" Johnston questioned.

"Yes, James. Four bombs have just exploded. Two of which were very close to this office."

Max left the comment hanging as a look of realisation washed across Johnston's face.

"I'm Suit?"

"Yes."

"And, Sarah's Tie?"

"Yes."

"You think they were coming after me?"

"I can't rule it out. There will be time to figure that out later. For now, my sole focus is to get you both to safety."

"Shouldn't we wait for backup?"

"No, we will wait until we know the building is surrounded by police and emergency services then we will disappear into the crowd as fast as we can. I can handle anyone who comes at us in the building."

"How did you know to come in here?"

"The first two explosions were big enough to shake the building and I know there is nothing in this building that could cause two big explosions like that. There's no gas storage or large equipment in the building. All maintenance and services are buried under tonnes of steel and concrete next door for security reasons. Had to be bombs brought into the building."

"What is going on Max?" Sarah asked, "Who were you talking to? How do you know all of that?"

"I was speaking to AIS."

"The Australian Intelligence Service?" Sarah said.

"Yes. I work for AIS. My role with the Minister is my cover."

"Well that probably explains why you always disappear."

"Ha, yeah sorry about that."

"How do we get to the airport, Max?" Johnston asked.

"Those explosions were sure to have caused extensive damage," Max said walking back over to the meeting table. "The lifts are out. We're going with Option A, straight down the fire stairs and out the front door. We'll hopefully disappear in the confusion. I have a car nearby which we can get to and I'm going to shoot anyone that tries to stop us.

Max loaded the Glock and tucked it in the back of his pants, before placing the remaining two magazines in his left pants pocket.

They waited for around fifteen minutes which Max figured was plenty of time for police and emergency services to starting to arrive and long enough to be sure the terrorists weren't going to set off another bomb or at least that was the hope.

"Let's go," Max said, "Hit the button, James."

"Shouldn't we wait a little longer, what if there is another bomb?" Johnston asked.

"They would have blown it by now," Max said again hopeful. "Press the button."

The Minister knelt down and pressed the red button. A moment later the clicks and mechanical sounds started as the metal walls began to retract back into the roof and walls.

"Get behind me and only move when I tell you to," Max said drawing his Glock.

The outer office was devastated. Broken glass and debris, paper and smashed furniture drenched by the sprinkler system and busted water pipes littered what was left of the office space. Spot fires were slowly being overcome by the water as it rained from the roof. Wind whipped around the floor through the smashed windows.

They made their way to the fire stairs. Max moved like an athlete, fast, smooth and agile. The Minister and Sarah followed gingerly and clearly frightened from the scene before them.

"Wait," Max commanded, halting the pair in their tracks.

Max checked the stairs gun up at the ready.

"The steps are damaged. I'll go ahead to clear the path. Be careful."

The pair nodded, slowly following Max into the stairwell.

Max set off down the stairs, kicking loose objects from their path. With each turn, he led with his gun. Checking. Clearing. Some of the stairs creaked and groaned under his weight, clearly damaged by the explosions. Max yelled back warnings to Johnston and Sarah.

As he rounded the bend in the stairs on level ten, he heard footsteps and pointed his gun at the exit door. Crouching down he waited. The door flung open and a panicked man in a suit ran through the door. His panic turned to terror as he saw Max pointing the gun at his head.

"It's okay," Max said lowering the gun. "It is just a precaution."

The guy nodded sheepishly and took off down the stairs.

"Wait," Max yelled, but the guy was jumping down sections of steps in single bounds and he was gone.

Max, the Minister and Sarah picked up their pace.

On level four, they fell in behind a bunched-up group of people. The crowd was pushing, shoving, fighting, trying to get through the exit on the level below.

Max put the gun back in his pants, under his jacket.

As the line made its way through the damaged door frame onto the mezzanine level the extent of the destruction became clear. On the floor below, the café was gone. Three floors of windows were shattered. The security desk had been reduced to splinters. Bodies and limbs were strewn across the floor. People screamed and gasped as they saw the scene. Police, ambulance and fire service vehicles' lights were flashing in the street. People were running from the building. The police had cordoned off the area and barricades were being put in place to hold back onlookers and the media. When they reached the escalators, Max noticed the extensive damage in the far corner where the building's utilities room had been and extensive fire damage burned into the carpet outside the conference room.

"This way," Max said pointing to the far side of the lobby as they reached the bottom of the now motionless escalator.

They hustled across the broken marble and through the smashed window. Dodging fleeing office workers, they headed towards the far barricade. People stared as they pushed through the crowd.

"Okay, the car is a couple of blocks down, we need to move fast," Max said breaking into a run.

The Minister and Sarah started to run after him.

Two blocks from the destroyed office building, Max stopped at an unmarked door built into the side of another office tower. Max punched a six-digit code into the combination lock on the door then turned the handle and opened the door. Johnston and Sarah followed Max through the door, the sirens slowly fading as they took the stairs down to the basement carpark.

Max walked over to a black Chevrolet V8 sports sedan. He placed his right hand on the driver's door and pressed the button on the handle. The car unlocked. Max took the driver's seat, the Minister was in the passenger's seat and Sarah climbed into the backseat. Max took off the ring on his right hand and slid it into the recess behind the volume knob on the entertainment system. Max pushed the ignition button and the car roared to life.

Authenticating flashed across the screen followed by *Welcome Prince, message received.*

Max pushed the *read message* button on the screen.

Prince, proceed as indicated. Extraction confirmed. Rendezvous at pre-set location. Hermes.

Max threw the car into gear and accelerated through the garage, and up into the street.

Chapter Seven

In Jones's repurposed getaway car, the two riders and two passengers, who had attacked the Commonwealth Building, sat watching the live news feed on the car's built in entertainment system.

They had taken off their helmets, each member of the crew staring excitedly at the little screen as the news anchor's voice boomed over the Bose sound system.

The driver was an Asian man, around thirty-eight years of age. He was fit and muscular, but not bulky, more athletic. He was short at only five feet five inches, but his mass was pure muscle. His name was Chang, an international assassin and gun for hire. The Pilot had recruited the Chinese-American for his world-class driving, combat and weapons skills. He was said to have been involved in a number of international assassinations using everything from targeted explosives to long-range sniper rifles. Hand-to-hand combat was not his style, but he was not without skill.

The front passenger was born in New Zealand and had served in both the New Zealand and Australian Defence Forces. He had a tattoo on the right side of his face that started just above his eyebrow and ran down his neck. It looked like a dragon crawling down towards his chest. At six feet three inches and well over one hundred kilos, the Pilot had hired him as dumb muscle. Good with a pistol or assault rifle, and big enough to best most men in hand-to-hand combat. In a previous life he had been a Corporal, but he was dishonourably discharged for assaulting his commanding officer after a night of heavy drinking. His name was Heath.

The anchor man was talking over live rolling footage of the Commonwealth Building playing out on the screen between Heath and Chang. It showed smoke billowing from the ground and mezzanine floors, and from the twenty and twenty-first floors. Occasionally, the image would cut to vision of drenched office workers fleeing through the gaps where the lobby windows once stood. Terror on their faces. A yellow and black breaking news banner scrolled over the footage. *Sydney Terror Attack?* It read.

"It is just a, a horrifying scene," the anchor said. *"People running for their lives into the street. It is a scene of panic. A scene of chaos. The occupants fleeing the building through the smashed windows. They, they look to be wet. Maybe from the fire splinters. There is terror obvious on their faces. Many are crying. It is, it's hard to watch. This is, of course, the Commonwealth Government Building in Sydney. Police are telling us it is too early to know for sure whether this is an act of terror, but office workers and passers-by are telling us they saw a number of individuals with machine guns shooting workers inside before the gunmen got into a waiting car. We still do not know how many gunmen were involved. But, we do know they got in a getaway car and, moments later, a series of explosions rocked the building. It is hard to see this as anything but a terrorist attack in downtown Sydney. We have no idea of casualties. We have seen men and women with serious injuries being loaded into ambulances and there are reports of bodies lying in the street. I remind viewers these are live shots from the Central Business District in Sydney and well, here are some more people leaving the building. That, that looks like the Defence Minister, James Johnston. Fortunately, he looks uninjured. He is dripping wet, again we think this is from the fire splinters. He looks to be pushing through the crowd with a young man and woman, both also saturated on either side of him. Maybe staff. Interestingly, he seems to be just leaving the scene..."*

"Fuck!" Xander said.

"How is that even possible, Xander?" Sophia said.

They were sitting in the rear of Jones's car. Sophia, the crew member who had ridden the bike up the escalator, was of Italian decent but had spent most of her life living between the United States and Australia. She was stunning. Her dark brown hair was tied behind her head exposing her perfect skin and pretty face. She had piercing brown eyes and was lean, fit and athletic. Sophia had been in the US military for many years before joining the Central Intelligence Agency.

Xander, the man responsible for killing Jones and dialling the numbers setting off the bombs in the Commonwealth Building, was slightly taller than the average man, and clearly fit and athletic. He had a purple scar across his left cheek which interrupted his otherwise good looks. He rubbed the scar as anger and annoyance flashed in his eyes as he watched his target, Minister James Johnston, fleeing through the crowd on the little screen.

"The structural plans we had showed the weak points," Chang said. "He should be dead!"

"They must have changed something or maybe the plans were wrong. Either way, he is still alive and we failed.

"We still sent a signal," Sophia said. "The other teams will activate. We should regroup and work out a plan to locate the Minister and take him out to finish the job."

"Yes, the cells will activate, but I still need to assassinate the Minister," Xander said. "The Pilot was very specific about that. Let's think about it. He was pushing through the crowd. He is getting out of there. Where would he be going?"

"Police station?" Heath said.

"No, he would have gone to the police on the scene if that was his plan," Xander said.

The footage of the Minister fleeing played again on the little screen.

"He has help," Sophia said. "Look at the guy in front, he is leading him away."

"Hmm, I think you are right."

"If that's the case, they could be looking for a fast extract and they will be heading for the airport," Sophia said. "That's a standard procedure these days. Get them airborne until the authorities can figure out what is going on."

"Chang, get us to the warehouse so we can pick up some equipment and then get us to the airport VIP entrance and step on it, they have a head start. Let's take him out before he leaves the city."

Chang hit the accelerator and the powerful V12 under the Mercedes' bonnet roared, as the car took off towards the airport.

Chapter Eight

After fighting through heavy traffic, Max pulled the Chevy onto the VIP access road at the Kingsford Smith Airport. As the car approached a set of bollards, Max pressed a button on the back of the steering wheel. The bollards retracted into the ground before raising again rapidly after the car sped over them. A security hut with a red and white striped boom gate blocked their path but Max did not bother slowing down. Moments before the Chevy hit, the boom lifted allowing them through. Max knew AIS had alerted airport security of their pending arrival and would have made arrangements to let them through without stopping.

Johnston raised his eyebrows impressed at the quick response. He had been through this entrance many times, but never like that.

Max turned the car onto a taxiway and hit the accelerator. The V8 roared as the gears changed. It had great pick up thanks to the work of AIS's in-house mechanics who kept it finely tuned. A hundred metres down the taxiway, Max took a hard right and pulled the car into a large private hanger through the doors which were slowly rolling open. As they moved from the sunny taxiway to the shadowy hanger, the lights on the Chevy automatically lit up the space. Before them stood a brand new, sleek Gulfstream G650ER. It glistened in the headlights. Max wheeled the car around and stopped to the right of the plane. He retrieved his ring from the console and placed it on his right hand.

"Is that your car key?" Johnston asked.

"Among other things," Max said. "Come on, let's get you both out of here."

"Agent Shaw, my name is Tim Carrol," Carrol said presenting his badge, before shaking Max's hand. "I am Special Agent in Charge, VIP Division with the Australian Federal Police."

Max nodded and shook hands with Carrol. He was almost a mirror image of Max in build, but about five years older. Grey flecks were visible in his dark hair. He was fit and handsome. In his black suit he looked distinguished, more like a young professional ready for a formal dinner, not security detail. Max knew it was supposed to make them blend in, but with a comms unit hanging from his ear, the bulge in his jacket on his right hip where his pistol was holstered and his shear size, Max knew all too well blending in would be difficult.

"Minister, Tim Carrol nice to meet you, sir," Carrol said shaking the Minister's hand.

"And you, Agent Carrol," Johnston said. "This is my Adviser, Sarah Greene."

"Hello," Sarah said.

"Hello Miss Greene, quite the morning you have had," Carrol said with a disarming and reassuring smile. "How about we get you to Canberra and away from all this?"

"Thank you," Sarah said.

"Minister, Miss Greene, this way if you will. My colleague Agent Stevenson is on the plane waiting to make you comfortable, head on up. We will debrief on route to Canberra. Please tell Jill I will be just a moment," Carrol said.

"Thank you, Agent Carrol," Johnston said turning to Max. "And thank you, Max, you saved our lives,"

"No problem, James," Max said. "Just doing my job. Be safe. Look after Sarah."

"Will do," Johnston said shaking Max's hand before heading for the plane.

"Thank you, Max," Sarah said half-smiling before giving Max a hug. "We have a lot to talk about when you get to Canberra."

"You just get yourself back to Canberra and be safe," Max said as Sarah walked over to climb the steps up into the plane.

"Jesus, what a mess," Carrol said when Sarah was out of earshot.

"Tell me about it," Max said. "How many dead?"

"We're at forty but that number is climbing quickly."

"Shit," Max said angrily.

"Anything else I should know?" Carrol asked.

"Yeah, they hit the utilities room. One of the bombs must have been very close to it. I don't think that is a coincidence. What are the odds they would take out the former security hub in the building? They must have thought it was still there."

"If they were trying to take out the security room they might have been trying to slow our response?"

"I'd say so, they must have been trying to cover their tracks by wiping out the security camera footage. Will you look into it? AFP get the live stream from those cameras right?"

"Yes, but it is not recorded by AFP, it is solely for fast response. It is recorded locally then dispatched to AFP in twelve-hour blocks. I'll report in from the air and get my team on it. Thanks Max."

"Great. Thanks Tim. You better get going. Let me know how you go."

"Will do. Look after yourself mate."

"Cheers. You too."

Carrol started up the Gulfstream's stairs as alarms in the hanger sounded. In the gaps between the sirens, Max heard gun fire outside the hanger. Cleary Carrol had heard it too because he had stopped on the steps and swung around in search of the sound.

"Get out of here!" Max yelled up to him.

Carrol looked down at Max and nodded without arguing. He knew they had different missions that needed to be achieved. His was to get the Minister to safety. With that, he jumped the remaining step and hit a button on the side panel inside the cabin door and dashed for the cockpit. The steps began folding up as he yelled instructions at the plane's captain. Within seconds, the engines whirled, as the door locked tight and the plane started towards the hanger door which was now almost completely open.

Max was already running for his car. He hit the button to open the boot and it sprang open. Inside he lifted a flap cut out of the carpet lining in the righthand panel revealing an electronic keypad. He typed in an eight-digit code and hit the hash key. The floor of the boot lifted on light hydraulic arms. Guns, knives, silencers, scopes and an array of other items including rope, tape and cable ties were neatly arranged in the moulded foam inlay, space normally reserved for a spare tyre. Max reached for the MP5 tactical assault weapon, a favourite of special ops teams the world over. He liked the gun. It was light and more mobile than most assault weapons. While it did not have as large a range as assault rifles, it was easier to wield, especially in close quarters. A good multipurpose weapon that still packed a punch. Other than his pistol, it was Max's go to weapon and the one with which he had the most training. Hours and hours of practice on various ranges and missions.

He attached his short scope and put a magazine in the chamber. He put a spare magazine in his right pocket, not to confuse it with the pistol mags in his left pocket. He also grabbed his hunting knife and clipped it to his belt.

He closed the boot and headed towards the hanger door, the extended stock on his MP5 was pressed firmly against his shoulder.

The Gulfstream was most of the way through as Max reached the door. His gaze followed the taxiway up to the security gate he had driven through only minutes ago. There was a marked security car with orange lights flashing. Its driver and passenger doors were still open, but the car's occupants laid still on the bitumen only metres either side of the car.

Through the short scope, Max could make out a big guy dressed in what looked like full leather motorbike gear, frantically pressing buttons in the security hut. The glass of the hut was covered in blood, obviously from the fallen security guard who had let Max's Chevy through the boom gate. Max looked past the guard hut and down the access road. A brand new Mercedes town car was driving over the now retracted bollards. *He must have found the right button*, Max thought.

The car pulled up just past the raised boom gate and the big guy ran for the passenger side door. He had not even shut the door when the big Merc accelerated down the taxiway rushing towards the hanger.

Max heard sirens and looked back in the opposite direction towards the airport to see two federal police cars rushing towards the VIP entrance.

The Gulfstream had turned onto the taxiway and was picking up speed heading for the runway. Its engines whirled as they revved, pushing the plane to a fast taxi.

Max spun on his heal and ran back to his car. He kicked up the engine and slammed down the accelerator. He popped the clutch and the Chevy's wheels squealed as it skid around wildly on the polished concrete to face the hanger door. The tyres got purchase and the powerful Chevy lurched forward. As he fled through the doors out into the sun, the Mercedes went by in a flash. Max yanked hard on the wheel, turning the Chevy onto the taxiway and gave chase.

The two AFP vehicles shot past in the opposite direction. Max watched in his rear-view mirror as they slammed on their brakes and slid around one hundred and eight degrees to pursue.

The big guy from the guardhouse popped his head and upper body up through the Mercedes' sunroof. He was holding an assault rifle, taking aim at the Gulfstream. Max hit the power window button on his door, retracting the window into the doorframe. He lent forward and grabbed his pistol from the back of his pants. There was a soft sound and a green light appeared on the handle of the pistol above his hand. He took the steering wheel in his left hand then lent out the window taking aim at the biker and speeding Merc.

He loosened off two rounds one hit the back window, the other went wide. The biker spun to see where the shots had come from. He then knelt, yelling in through the sunroof and wildly pointing in Max's direction. Moments later two guns came out of the rear windows and pointed back towards Max. The big guy went back to lining up the Gulfstream taking a shot for the tyres and thankfully missing. The two guns from the back seat started firing at Max. He moved the Chevy left and right. Grass and dirt on the side of the taxiway kicked up from the bullets and his wheels as he swerved wildly to throw off their aim. Two lucky shots hit his bonnet.

Max hit the gas, gaining on the Mercedes and ramming into its boot. The big guy fell forward firing several bullets into the bonnet of the Merc. It lurched forward and swerved as Max's car bounced back from the impact and fishtailed. Max hit the gas again as he regained control and chased the Merc. He put the gun back out through his window and fired for the luxury sedan's tyres. Two of the shots hit the damaged boot and one went wide. The fourth hit punching a neat hole in the rear driver's side wheel. The Merc slowed and whipped around wildly on the taxiway as the driver tried to recover from the sudden change in handling.

Max sped up looking for an opportunity to force the car off the road. He slammed hard into the back of the Merc for a second time as the big guy was again lining up for a shot from the sunroof. As Max hit the town car, the big guy again lost his balance and he fired several shots into the bonnet of his own car. Smoke and steam began to pour out and it started to slow. Max rammed it again and it skid off the taxiway onto the grass. Max let it roll several metres from his own car before pulling on the handbrake sliding the Chevy to a stop sideways, so the passenger's side was facing the disabled Merc. He jumped out and took cover behind the front wheel.

Max put the pistol back in his pants and grabbed his MP5. He extended the shoulder support, flicked off the safety and checked for the green light. Green. Good to go. Kneeling behind the car he popped up and rested the gun on the bonnet for stability.

The two passengers from the rear of the car were scrambling out looking for cover. The big guy from the sunroof was scanning between Max and the two AFP cars now arriving behind him.

"Federal Agent, put the fucking gun down!" Max yelled.

The big guy fired a burst at one of the AFP cars. A line of bullet holes ran across the windshield. Blood spray hit the windows. Out of control, it sped off the road down the steep little slope onto the grass where it dug in and stopped abruptly. Max looked for signs of life but found none.

The big guy looked at Max and started to bring his gun around to fire. Max fired twice, hitting him in the head and the chest. The big guy crumpled as his knees buckled and he fell back through the sunroof into the car.

The driver started firing out his window as he tried to pull himself over the centre console and over his fallen comrade towards the passenger door to safety. He was desperately trying to get to cover. Max dropped behind the tyre. Bullets tore through the air over his head. He heard the AFP officers from the second car returning fire at the Merc and its scrambling occupants.

Max got back into the crouch position readying to strike. As he popped up, the two rear passengers and driver sprung up from behind the Merc unleashing a torrent of bullets at the AFP officers and at Max.

As Max and the police officers dived for cover, the Merc's driver ran for the boot while his comrades provided covering fire and he pulled out a large black military spec case.

Max was pinned down. He could see the Gulfstream turning onto the runway in the distance. The Rolls Royce engines revved hard to full capacity. Max heard the familiar shrill sound as the plane sped down the runway. Then came another familiar but misplaced sound. It was a long, loud hiss from behind the Merc and Max watched in horror as a smoke trail raced towards the Gulfstream.

The driver had fired a rocket at the plane.

The Gulfstream took off at a steep angle. Climbing fast.

The rocket gave chase.

Suddenly flares exploded from beneath the plane like fireworks lighting up the sky even in the harsh daylight. Streaks of smoke trailed the fiery flares. The Gulfstream banked hard and dived moments before the rocket hit the flares. The shockwave hit the plane, and it dropped and shook.

After what felt like the longest few moments, Max saw the Gulfstream recover as the flames and flares, what was left of the rocket, fell towards the runway. The engines whirled hard as it climbed steeply, before it straightened its course and flew off into the distance towards Canberra.

Max had been holding his breath. He breathed deeply. In and out. Relieved. *That was too close,* Max thought.

As the passengers from the rear of the Merc reloaded, Max started firing, resting again on the bonnet. He saw the two AFP guys firing and moving forward, heading for the Merc.

Get back to cover, he thought, not wanting to yell and give them away. But it did not matter. They were gunned down halfway between the cars. *Damn it,* Max thought as their bodies hit the grass.

Max returned to cover as bullets hit the side of the Chevy. The three from the Merc were making a move towards the AFP car. They had Max pinned down.

Think Max, think, he said to himself.

He laid flat on the ground and army crawled under the Chevy. Dirt flicked up as bullets ricocheted into the ground in front of him. The first two offenders had made it to the car, but the driver was still in the open. Max fired a single shot hitting him in the leg as he ran. He fell to the ground, momentum bouncing him forward twice and he groaned in pain as he came to a stop. He tried to pull himself along the ground towards the car, but Max fired three rounds into the dirt next to his head, stopping him in his tracks.

There were more sirens in the distance.

The passengers, a man and a woman, were in the police car. It reversed hard up the steep slope ripping up the grass. With a squeal of tyres, it did a one eighty before shooting down the road, heading for the exit, the VIP entrance gate, away from Max and away from the AFP cars making their way to the scene. Away from their fallen comrades.

Max crawled out from under the car. He flicked the magazine release letting it drop to the ground. He reached into his right pocket and replaced the MP5's magazine. He kept the gun trained on the driver as he opened the boot of the Chevy, and retrieved the tape and cable ties. The driver moved his arm, reaching for his gun. Two bullets hit the dirt inches from his face.

"Don't you fucking move," Max said.

Max walked over and kicked the gun away from the driver. He then dropped his knee into the driver's back, winding him. The driver was gasping for breath. Max held the gun to the back of the driver's head, pressing the barrel of the MP5 to the base of his skull.

"Give me one reason and I will blow your brains out without a second thought," Max said.

Max grabbed the driver's arms and folded them awkwardly up behind his back. With his arms pinned, his leg wounded and shortness of breath, the driver was completely immobilised. Max threaded several cable ties together creating a solid pair of plastic handcuffs. He placed them on the driver's wrists and fastened them. He made a second pair and cuffed the driver's feet.

"Well, let's have a look at that wound," Max said flipping the driver over and smiling as he dug his thumb into the bullet hole.

The driver screamed in pain.

"Fuck you," Chang spat.

Max took his hunting knife out and cut away the leg of the driver's leather riding pants. The bullet had gone right through the driver's thigh. Max grabbed his roll of tape and tightly wrapped the wound.

Chang squirmed in agony

"Get me to the hospital," Chang said.

"Ha! You're kidding, right?" Max said.

"No. I need help. I want medical treatment and a lawyer."

Max grabbed a handful of Chang's hair, pulling his head back at an awkward position. He lent down close to Chang's ear.

"Listen to me you piece of shit. No lawyer. No doctor. You are coming with me and you are going to tell me all about your mates who just left you here to die. And, you are going to give me names and details of everyone involved in today's events."

"I don't know anything."

"Good try. I am going to put you in the boot of my car now and take you for a little drive. I suggest on the way you think about names and details."

With that, Max taped Chang's mouth closed, hung his MP5 over his right shoulder, placed the cable ties in his back pocket and picked up the roll of duct tape. He walked over to the car and placed the MP5, ties and tape back in their moulded foam places. He then replaced the floor and with a click it locked into place.

He strolled back over to Chang, crouched down and lifted him onto his right shoulder. Max walked to the car with Chang hanging over his shoulder, fidgeting and moaning in pain. He threw him into the boot. The force stunning Chang and winding him. His head hit hard, putting him in a slight haze. He was breathing heavily through his nose, trying to get his breath back. Max lent in, pinching his nose closed. Chang's eyes went wide with fear.

"I am not fucking around with you," Max said his face only inches from Chang's. "You just tried to kill a Minister of the Crown. And, worse still, you tried to kill me. Make no mistake, if I think you are lying to me or not giving me what I need, I will make you suffer. Names and details. Start making a list."

He let go and Chang's nostrils flared trying to take in as much air as possible. Max slammed the boot shut just as the other AFP vehicles arrived.

"Hands over your head!" one officer said.

Max raised his arms.

"Stand down lads, my name is Max Shaw and I am a Federal Agent. I am going to reach for my security pass," Max said as he slowly lowered his hand to retrieve the pass.

The officer lowered his gun and signalled for the others to do the same when he saw Max's Commonwealth security pass.

"Special Agent Carrol reported in," the officer said. "He said you were on the ground and in pursuit. They all got away?"

"Yes. Well, except for the guy in the car. They took out your guys and stole one of your vehicles. I'm sorry about your officers."

"Thank you. I will put out an all units on the car."

"Shouldn't be hard to find. It's riddled with bullet holes. Male and female wearing motorbike leathers."

"Anything else you can tell us?"

"Not at this stage. Anyone hurt down there?"

"No luckily. Mass panic in the airport. All flights grounded. The airport is being evacuated."

"Right. Well, I better take off before the traffic gets too crazy."

"Yes, sir, good luck," the officer said.

"Thank you," Max said.

Max got into his car. He pressed the ignition button and the engine came to life. Max pressed the sat nav button on the side of the screen. He pressed *pre-set*.

For pre-set locations please insert your security key.

He took off his ring and placed it into the receiver. *Authenticating, Welcome Prince. One suggested pre-set location found. Would you like to set as your destination?* Max hit the *yes* button and a map with a highlighted route appeared on the screen.

Max opened his phone and the secure messaging app. *Hulk, coming in. I'm bringing you a friend. Prep the room. Prince.*

The Chevy took off down the taxiway. Max did not slow down for the speed bumps. He smiled to himself hearing the thud as Chang bounced into the boot lid then back onto the floor. Twice.

Max hit the freeway heading for the rendezvous with Hulk, when his thoughts were interrupted as his phone began to ring.

"Hello," Max answered.

"Oh, thank god, you are alright," Sam said.

"Hi Sam, yeah I'm fine."

"I just saw the news. It's so terrible what happened. Were you in the building?"

"Yeah, I was there. But I'm fine. Thanks for checking in on me. You are very sweet."

"I'm glad you are okay. I was so worried. What happened? The TV is saying it was terrorists. Are you still staying in town?"

"Well, I don't know what happened. I have to speak to some people, so I could be held up for a while. I'm still in town. I'm not sure if I will be able to catch up for dinner yet but I hope so. I would really love to see you, especially after all this, it would be good to see a friendly face."

"Likewise, but there's no pressure. Just let me know. You can come over anytime. I would love to give you a hug and make sure you are really alright."

"I'd like that. I'll give you a call when I know what's happening."

"Okay. Be safe. I'm so glad you are okay. Can't wait to see you."

"I will. Same here. See you later. Thanks again for checking on me."

Max ended the call. He smiled thinking about Sam and last night. It felt good having someone worry about him. It felt nice knowing he meant something to someone. It had been so long since he had let himself get close to anyone. How could he after last time?

No, Max. It's nothing. Just a casual friend on a work trip. You are going to be lonely. Get over it. You have a job to do. You can't risk history repeating.

While it was a sad thought, he was glad to have met Sam and was looking forward to seeing him again, even if it was not going anywhere.

Chapter Nine

After several kilometres, Max turned off the motorway and headed for an industrial park at Moorebank.

He pulled into the driveway of a large storage facility, stopping beside the security terminal. The sat nav beeped and Max looked at the little screen. A six-digit code appeared. Max entered the access code in the security panel and hit the hash key. The big metal gate started rolling to the side.

He drove past the first two long storage sheds and made his way towards the rear of the facility. He followed the route on the sat nav turning right and heading down the concrete road. When he reached the centre of the building he stopped the car. The voice over said *destination reached*. He looked through the windshield at the security camera next to the door.

The big steel roller door silently began raising.

Max turned the car left and went through the door into the storage shed. Once inside, he drove to the far end where he could see Hulk standing, waiting for him to arrive. There were offices and other rooms lining the walls, but the centre was a large open space with a concrete floor. The roof was about three stories high made of sheet iron and large metal beams. Max knew there was a secure communications room buried beneath the structure but had never been down there.

"Good to see you are still in one piece kid," Hulk said as Max pulled himself out the door of the Chevy. "You look like shit though."

"Thanks," Max said rolling his eyes at Hulk. "I have a present for you in the boot. Their driver."

"Get him out of there, we're set up in three," Hulk said pointing to a conference room over his shoulder. "I'll see you in there."

"You're not going to help me carry him?"

"Fuck no. What's the good of all that training and those muscles if you're not going to use them. Hurry up, get to it."

Max opened the boot and looked in at the fearful driver.

"I hope you are ready to talk," Max said as he lent in and lifted him up over his shoulder.

Max walked into the conference room. Every square inch was covered in plastic. In the centre sat a steel chair. Max dropped Chang onto the chair and Hulk threw him a roll of duct tape. Max cut the cable ties holding Chang's legs and Chang kicked with his good leg as he thrashed about now his legs were free. Max fell backwards.

"Oh, for fuck sake, get him under control!" Hulk spat.

Max scrambled back to his knees, pulled out his hunting knife and with devastating force drove it down through Chang's leather boot and right through his left foot. The colour drained from his face as he tried to scream through his taped mouth.

Max stood and grabbed Chang around the neck. The pressure from Max's big hand closed his throat, again cutting off his air supply.

"I must not have made myself clear before, "Max said. "Try that shit again and I will fucking kill you. Slowly. Painfully. Now, sit still or I will put my knife through your other foot. Do you understand me?"

Chang nodded and Max released his vice-like grip from around Chang's neck leaving behind a wash of red, white and purple blotches on his skin. Deep breaths were dragged in through his nose. Nostrils flaring. Anger and pain showing in his eyes.

Max knelt in front of Chang and duct taped each of his legs to the nearest leg on the steel chair. He then walked behind him and cut the cuffs from his wrists. His arms hung at his sides immobile from the awkward position they had been in since the airport. Max took each arm one at a time and taped them to the arms of the steel chair.

Max and Hulk walked out of the room into a nearby kitchen leaving Chang taped to the chair with Max's knife still lodged in his foot. Max grabbed a bottle of water from the fridge and took two big gulps.

"How do you want to play it?" he asked Hulk.

"Well, it looks like you've got bad cop sorted this time. Glad to see you're learning something after all. So, why don't I go in as the good cop and see if I can't get him to talk?"

"Fine by me. I'll watch through the one-way."

"Let's go."

Hulk headed for the prisoner's room and Max went into the conference room next door.

Chapter Ten

The Pilot sat collecting his thoughts. He had just heard the news. The little Prince had somehow managed to get the Minister and his adviser out of the Commonwealth Building and to the airport.

Unbelievable. Why hadn't he known of changes to the safe room plans?

He opened the messenger app on his phone and saw his previous message.

They changed the plans, I didn't know the rooms had moved.

No reply.

He was frustrated, but not just because of the failure at the Commonwealth Building. This AIS Agent Max "Prince" Shaw had also managed to get that weak Minister and the adviser on a plane before Xander's team could get there.

Obviously, the AIS Agent had slowed his team down enough for the jet to take off and for the rocket to be useless against the plane's countermeasures. If only AIS had sent one of the older planes. He had it on good authority that only the new ones had flares.

He clenched his jaw. He hated Max. He had discovered that it was Max who had gotten in the way several times, disrupting the planning and initial stages of his grand plans. Although by all accounts, Max and his handlers had been unable to link those events yet. A bit better than dumb luck but not by much.

And, now this agent had gotten in the way again. He had apparently brought Chang in for questioning. So much for a master assassin. He was caught by a child. Caught by a rookie, still wet behind the ears. Chang had been captured. He had failed. He would die. Hopefully before he sold them out.

He tapped away at the phone.

They brought in Chang, he is being interrogated as we speak.

Warning sent, he threw his phone down on the desk and went back to his work hoping that the setbacks his plans had this morning would be the day's only failures.

He did not tolerate failure especially when the risk he was taking was so high.

Chapter Eleven

The conference room next to the prisoner's hold had a large one-way glass panel allowing Max to see into the room where Chang was taped to the chair. There was a row of computer systems and televisions showing live feeds from the room. One of the monitors showed a thermal image of Chang. He was glowing red showing the heat of his anger. On the far wall, a row of televisions were each showing rolling footage of the Commonwealth Building and emergency services teams going about their work assisting people on site. The scrolling banner said more than sixty people were confirmed dead with many still unaccounted for. Vision also showed the airport in lock down. The anchor was reporting eyewitness accounts of a VIP plane under attack and firing flares during take-off at Sydney Airport. Police were yet to comment. The airport was unable to confirm when flights would resume but there was speculation it would be days, not hours.

Sitting at the bank of computers was Greg "Shadow" Lloyd. Lloyd had been an Air Commodore in the Royal Australian Air Force before taking on the role as Hulk's number two at AIS. Deputy Head of Operations was his official title. He had spent much of his time in the military in Air Force intelligence and got his nickname from his fighter days. An instructor was so impressed at the stealth shown by Lloyd's low-level flight and strike capability that he said it was like being killed by your own shadow. And, it just stuck. Lloyd and Hulk had worked side by side in their previous roles. It was a natural fit for them to continue working together. They were mates and trusted each other which was the most important thing in their line of work. Max had worked with him many times but was not expecting him to be sitting in the room. They were far from friends and neither tried hard to hide their dislike.

"Ah, Prince," Lloyd said. "How is the Master of the Dark Arts these days? Pity you can't wield that knife to get things done on the hill, right?"

"Shadow, good to see you," Max lied. "I'm good thanks, all things considered. It might make some negotiations in Parliament a bit easier, but I think I would have some trouble getting it through security."

"Really?" Lloyd asked through a wry smile. "I would not have thought that would be an issue for you."

"Well, yeah okay. I could probably find a way, but generally speaking the only knives allowed in the parliament are figurative ones, and sadly, they wield them all too frequently."

"Ain't democracy grand?"

"That's why we're here isn't it, Queen and Country, and all that?"

"Indeed," Lloyd said. "There is no higher duty."

"That's true. Where's Flash?"

"He is en route. Stuck in traffic between the airport and the city, apparently it is chaos. He will be with you from here in. We are all pairing up until we get these fuckers."

"Fair enough."

"You two sure did a job last night. Was it you or Flash that decided to send the businessman out the window?"

"Well, it certainly wasn't part of the plan, Shadow. There was a lot of them. He just fell."

"Yeah right," Lloyd said unimpressed.

Jacob "Flash" Gordon had been recruited by AIS at the same time as Max. They trained together at AIS's various training bases around the country, including the Wool Shed in regional New South Wales, and they had worked together hundreds of times, and were very close. In fact, they were best mates. They had each other's backs and trusted each other, at work and in life.

Max took the seat next to Lloyd and watched as Hulk walked over to Chang and ripped the tape from his mouth. He winced. A red inch wide strip visible across his face where the tape had been.

"I don't know anything," Chang said. "Where am I? Who are you guys? You cannot be cops, cops cannot do this here, can they?"

"That is certainly a lot of questions, but you seem to have gotten our roles reversed," Hulk said. "I will be asking, not answering, questions. Now, how about you tell me your name?"

"I have rights. You cannot do this!"

"Suddenly, concerned about your rights, hey? Well, what about the rights of the people you and your comrades killed today? They had the right to live their lives peacefully until you arseholes decided to take that away from them. Listen, I tell you what, how about you give me your name or if not, I will go and get the guy who brought you here and you can talk about your rights with him?"

Fear flashed in his eyes, then defeat.

"Fine, just do not bring that fucking psycho back in here!"

"So, what is your name?"

"John Smith."

"Hmm, are you adopted Mr Smith?"

"Yep."

"I don't believe you. I am not sure you are taking this as seriously as you should be. I'm going to get the other guy."

Hulk started for the door.

"No, wait, okay, it's Vincent. My name is Vincent."

"Do you have a last name Vincent?" Hulk asked stopping in the doorway, but without turning back to face the driver.

"Chow," he said under his breath.

"Sorry, I couldn't hear you?"

"Chow, my name is Vincent Chow."

"So Chow, not Smith?"

"Yes."

"That was your first and last chance, Mr Chow. Lie or joke again and I will go and get my colleague, and you can answer his questions. Do I make myself clear?"

"Yes."

"Who do you work for?"

"Anyone willing to pay the right price."

"And, who paid the right price today?"

"They will kill me."

"At this point in time, you shouldn't be worried about that. My friend is not far away. What do you think he will do to you if you do not cooperate? So, I will ask again, who are you working for?"

"I do not know any names."

"I am starting to lose my patience."

"I am telling the truth."

"Well, how did you come to be in their employ?"

"We were connected through an intermediary. I got a call. I quoted a price. They accepted."

"Who is the intermediary?"

"Come on man."

Hulk heard static on his earpiece.

"Vincent Chow entered the country on Friday through Kingsford Smith International," Lloyd said. *"Passport looks clean on first pass. No evidence of ever visiting Australia before now. Searching international databases."*

"Have you ever been to Australia before?" Hulk asked.

"No."

"My colleague said you were driving the vehicle at the airport. Interesting your employer would let you drive in an unfamiliar city."

He said nothing.

"You see, I have been overseas for work many times. The difference is I would not drive a getaway car unless I had been there before and spent some time getting to know the city. Too risky. Unless there was an emergency, but you had three other potential drivers to choose from, so why choose you?"

Chang said nothing.

Static.

"One result for Vincent Chow," Lloyd said to Hulk. *"MI6 flagged as possible suspect in assassination of then Lord Speaker, Lord Francis Wellington, Presiding Officer of the House of Lords 1998-2002. Not enough evidence to hold him."*

"How about the UK, ever been to London?" Hulk asked.

Chang's head sank.

"I think you made a mistake, Mr Chow. You rushed to take on this job, didn't you? And you forgot you used this fake passport on a similar job, didn't you?"

Chang stared at the floor.

"You are very quiet, Mr Chow. I never do this but is there any chance you want to take up a very generous offer, would you like a third chance to give me your real name? Look around you. You are beaten. You tried to kill a Minister and got caught. But not only that, you were stupid enough to use a flagged passport and our friends in the UK will be very interested in you, so you are done on that count too. Our facial recognition systems are working away as we speak. We'll figure it out eventually. Plus, your friends left you to die, what could you possibly owe them? It's over. Last chance, what is your name?"

"Chang. My name is Vincent Chang."

Hulk turned and walked for the door.

"Wait, where are you going?"

"I said I never give third chances and well, I'm not going to break that rule today. You get the other guy."

"No, please!" Chang yelled, but Hulk didn't stop.

Hulk walked into the room next door to find Lloyd and Max searching databases for Vincent Chang.

"Here we are, Vincent Chang," Lloyd said. "Gun for hire. Mostly personal protection. We have a note on his file, CIA thinks he may be involved in several assassinations, but they do not have enough to go on. He is a professional."

"Go see what you can find out Max," Hulk said.

"Rules?" Max asked.

"We need him alive and capable of speaking, other than that, whatever it takes."

Max stood and offered his chair to Hulk, then he walked towards the prisoner's room. He stood in the doorway, waiting for Chang to look up. When he did, Max saw the fear. Saw the terror in his eyes.

"Were you involved in the hit on the Commonwealth Building this morning?" Max asked.

"Fuck you," Chang said.

"Oh, look. Silly me. I forgot my knife."

Chang's panicked eyes darted down to the knife and back to Max. He knew what was coming.

Max walked over, grabbed the handle of the knife and twisted it in Chang's foot, making eye contact with Chang as he did it. At least one bone broke and flesh ripped, before he torn it out. Chang bounced and thrashed in the chair, but it did not move, it was bolted into the concrete floor.

"Argh, you fucking psycho!" Chang screamed.

Max walked over to a table in the corner of the room and retrieved a small sachet from a med-kit. He shook and flicked it several times to get the contents to the bottom as he walked back to Chang.

"The knife may have hurt but I can tell you from experience, that this shit hurts more."

Max tore the top off the packet with his teeth and spat it at Chang, then he poured half the sachet of white powder into the open cut in Chang's boot. Blood red, pink and white frothy bubbles started spilling out of the hole in the boot, running over onto the floor. Chang wailed and thrashed, groaning through clenched teeth in pain.

"It is great stuff. Used a lot on the battlefield. It seals the wound by cauterising it and will stop you from bleeding out. Actually, that reminds me, how is your leg?"

"Do not touch it!"

"Now, come on. I don't want you to die before I tell you, you can."

Max sliced the tape that was wrapped around Chang's thigh, intentionally cutting into the wound as he did. Chang was writhing in the chair. Max slammed his forehead down hard against Chang's nose breaking it. Chang's head flew back and he sat staring at the roof. Dazed. That's when Max grabbed one end of the tape and ripped it halfway around Chang's leg. He threw his head forward. Blood poured from Chang's nose and his teeth were gritted, covered in blood that had run into his mouth.

"I am going to fucking kill you," Chang said spraying blood across Max's face as he spoke.

Max did not say anything, instead he ripped the tape the rest of the way off Chang's leg, reopening the bullet wound on both sides.

Chang looked faint as blood that had pooled in the tape dripped to the floor, but Max did not pause. He poured the remaining white powder from the sachet into the leg wound. Pink bubbles gurgled out of the hole. The sound of thousands of tiny bubbles popping made quite a strange sound Max thought to himself as Chang's head fell forward.

Unconscious. Max checked Chang's pulse. *He'll live.*

He snapped an ammonia stick he had retrieved from the med bag under Chang's nose waking him up.

"Well Vincent, you have been a bad boy. Killing the Lord Speaker in the UK. You also tried to kill the Minister for Defence today. We know you are an assassin. We know you are a gun for hire. Why don't you save yourself pain and just tell me who hired you?"

"I do not know his name! I just know he calls himself the Pilot."

"The Pilot?"

"Yes, oh fuck, he is going to kill me," Chang said under his breath.

"What was that?"

"You do not understand. He is even more of a psycho than you. He will kill me for even mentioning that name."

"How do you contact this Pilot?"

"I don't, he contacts me."

"Searching for 'The Pilot', Prince," Lloyd said over his earpiece.

"What if you have to change your plans?" Max asked.

"He will know."

"So, he would know you failed him this morning?

"Yes."

"So, he will call?"

"Yes."

"Where is your phone?"

"Right pants pocket."

Max walked over and took Chang's phone out of his pocket. Security lock.

"What's the passcode?"

"Deadshot."

"Ha! You wish mate. I saw you shoot at the airport. Hopeless. More like Deadshit."

Max said walked from the room studying the phone.

He strolled into the monitoring room next door.

"Hey Flash," Max said tossing the phone to his AIS partner and best friend. "Welcome to the party."

"Hey Max, how you holding up?" Flash asked.

"He's fine," Hulk said. "Now, if you two don't mind, we still have some terrorists to hunt down. Get your arse back in there, and you, go see Hermes, see what you two can get off that phone and if it rings I suggest you run the trace software."

Max and Flash left the room without saying another word.

Flash set off for the bunker with Chang's phone and Max went back into the prisoner's room.

Chapter Twelve

Max strolled casually over to Chang.

"Rightio, where were we?" Max asked. "Oh right, your Pilot. Who does he work for?"

"I do not know," Chang said. "Himself."

"Well, what do you know?"

"Nothing."

"That is bullshit. Were you at the Commonwealth Building? What was the plan? Is James Johnston your target? Who were the people you were with, remember them, the ones who left you to die? Give me their names."

Silence.

"Was the Minister for Defence the target of the attack on the Commonwealth Building?" Max asked.

Silence.

Max walked around and cut a hole in the plastic sheet on the floor behind Chang and opened a panel in the floor beneath the chair. Chang squirmed trying to see what was happening. Max clipped two jumper leads to outlets in the floor, then he clipped one lead to the steel chair. He circled around to face Chang and showed him the metal clip on the lead. Chang sat upright. Horror in his eyes. Drying blood caking under his broken nose.

"Who were they?" Max asked.

Chang refused to answer so Max touched the lead to the arm of the steel chair. Chang convulsed as electricity pulsed through the chair, through his sweat soaked clothes and onto his skin. His muscles tightened and jaw clenched.

Max took the lead off.

"Was the Defence Minister the only target?"

Again, Chang said nothing.

Max put the end of the lead onto the open wound in Chang's leg. Again, electricity coursed through his body and he went rigid. As Max took the lead away, Chang breathed deeply and flopped in his chair.

"You can stop this anytime you want," Max said leaning in an inch from Chang's face. "They left you for dead. They did this to you."

Then he sat the lead on Chang's neck. His head flung back and his body went stiff as he shook, struggling against the tape.

Max left the lead on his neck for twice as long as the last time, staring the whole time into Chang's eyes. He took the lead off and a burn mark was visible on Chang's exposed neck. His muscles relaxed and he slumped over in the chair, dribbling on himself.

"Everyone breaks, Vincent. Just tell me and the pain stops. You don't owe them this pain."

"You're right," Chang said softly, choking out the words, tears rolling down his cheeks. "I will tell you. Please, please just stop."

"Make it quick or I will clamp this to your broken nose and leave you to die."

"No, please!" he screamed.

"Were you involved with the bombing at the Commonwealth Building?"

"Yes."

"Was the Minister for Defence the target?"

"Yes."

"Was the attack and assassination the end game or is there more to come?"

"I do not know."

"Who is the Pilot?"

"I do not know."

"Who were you with at the airport?"

"Their names are Heath, Xander and Sophia."

"Which one is still at the airport?"

"Heath."

"So where can I find Xander and Sophia?"

"We planned the mission at a safe house in Parramatta. I do not know the address."

"They will be there?"

"That is where we were heading until you and your boss stumbled out of the building on Sky News."

"My boss?" Max shot a look through the glass to Hulk. "How do you know he is my boss? How do you know who I am?"

"The Pilot knows who you are. He does not like you. You have wrecked his plans more than once. He was hoping you would die in the attack too. Now, can you get me a doctor?"

"Nope. Got to make sure you weren't lying."

"I was not lying. Please."

"You'll be fine," Max said as he walked out of the room.

Lloyd walked out of the monitoring room.

"Good job," Lloyd said. "Not quite textbook stuff and a bit too brutal for me, but like your mentor Hulk, you get results and I cannot argue with that. Come with me."

Chapter Thirteen

Max and Lloyd walked across the large concrete space towards a room marked *storage*.

A crew of workers were busily running around Max's car. Panels and windows were being replaced. Supplies were being restocked and it was being cleaned. Soon it would be as good as new.

"No expense spared," Lloyd said looking from the car to Max.

"I've not seen them do it so fast before," Max said.

"Well, that's because you normally just piss off, leaving the car in a wreck or abandoned somewhere."

"Nature of the work," Max shrugged as they walked into the storage room.

"You are a real smartarse you know that?"

Max just smiled.

There was an elevator in the storage room. Lloyd hit the call button. When it arrived, they walked in and Lloyd waved his right hand in front of a sensor. The door closed and the elevator sunk into the ground. When it came to a stop several floors beneath the storage room, the doors opened and the two agents walked out into a wide industrial concrete room with a set of large thick steel doors recessed into the far wall which looked like a bank vault. Lloyd swiped his right hand over a key pad then typed in an eight-digit code. There was a prolonged soft screech as metal bars retracted inside the doors. A hiss of air escaped as the doors began to open. The space beyond was huge. Not quite as big as the storage shed above but close. There were glass walled offices and conference rooms. Sunken lounge areas. A solid concrete bar ran in front of a long row of fridges lining the righthand wall and in the distance Max could see an operations centre.

"What the hell is this?" Max said. "I knew the place existed, but this was definitely not what I expected."

"This is a safe house and a war room in one. It was set up by AIS as a backup operations centre and a place for VIPs should we need to get them off the radar. It would also be a place for certain individuals should the worst occur. It is fully stocked and has its own air supply. There are bathrooms, bedrooms, an operations command centre and a weapons vault. Everything we need. It is bigger and better than the White House bunker."

"This place is nicer than my house and about a thousand times bigger, it must have cost a fortune," Max said as they walked through the glass doors and set off towards the operations centre at the far end of the complex.

"It did, but since nine-eleven and seven-seven and Bali and Paris and Germany. Well, you get the point. The politicians give us free reign. Plus, the intel committee thinks they will be safe in here if the world ends."

Max held the door open and Lloyd walked through into the operations centre. Three rows of computers and desks ran the length of the room with keyboards for more than twenty analysts and chairs for at least double that. There were six analysts in the room spread out randomly at the desks. It was like a small version of NASA's Houston Operations Centre Max remembered seeing in so many news clips and movies.

On the far wall three massive screens hung from the ceiling. The left had nine equal sized boxes showing the news feeds from Australia's free-to-air and satellite news services, as well as CNN and BBC. They all had rolling footage of the two terrorist attacks in the city and back-to-back interviews with security experts. Video rolled showing the Commonwealth Building, access to the building had been cordoned off and water was still pouring out of the windows but the smoke had stopped. One of the scrolling banners said traffic was backed up on the freeways and motorways out of the city, and the airport was still closed.

The right screen showed CCTV footage from inside the Commonwealth Building. It was a live feed flicking between multiple cameras. Max watched as it changed to one of the lobby cameras. It was a devastating scene, but the most chilling footage panned over a row of white sheets concealing bodies. The row ran the full length of the far wall of the lobby and halfway back. Glass, marble, tiles, tables, chairs, everything from the lobby was smashed. Debris was lying everywhere and vision from more than one security camera was obstructed or the camera lens was cracked, while footage from others was non-existent, the explosions having taken out a few cameras.

Max scanned across to the centre screen which showed a satellite image from high above the Sydney CBD. The Commonwealth Building was at the centre of the image. Several blocks around the building had been blocked off and emergency vehicle lights were flashing. Masses of people had come to see what all the fuss was about.

A male voice came over the speakers.

"Sydney, confirming Suit and Tie have landed in Canberra. They circled for an hour until the route and safe house were secured. Special Agent Carrol is still with them and continues as lead agent. Package en route to location Foxtrot."

"Acknowledged Canberra," Blake "Hermes" Smyth said. "Thanks for the update. Please confirm when they are locked down."

"Acknowledged, Sydney. Will do."

Flash was standing behind Blake looking over his shoulder and pointing at his computer monitor. Blake was an officer in the Royal Australian Navy. His dress uniform was a clean and crisply starched white shirt, black pants and jacket with epaulettes indicating he had reached the rank of Lieutenant Commander. He had an impressive number of medals for someone his age. His sandy blond hair was cut short and neat. Handsome was an understatement. He was shorter than Max, but just as fit. In fact, since they met at the Wool Shed years ago they'd become close friends. They trained together most mornings and had dinner together when they were in the same cities. Blake's official role was supposed to be aide-de-camp to Hulk which meant he would be everything from secretary and personal assistant to adviser. But Hulk trusted Blake, which put him on a very small list, and hated the idea of someone fussing over him, so instead Hulk made him his Chief of Staff. Though not officially in the chain of command, the role meant Blake was effectively third in charge of AIS.

Blake had a reputation as Hulk's go-to man and when he came knocking, you answered. He got his nickname from a former Brigadier after delivering a particularly stinging message from Hulk. The Brigadier had said "I don't envy your role son having to deliver this message from God." Word spread from there.

Max and Blake often trained together at the gym and went on early morning jogs. Even with similar fitness levels and builds, and only a year separating them, Max was always pushed to his limits by Blake. Max thought the nickname was perfect, not only was he young and fit, Max too had received many messages from Hulk via Blake – Hermes, the quick and cunning emissary, messenger of the Gods and second youngest God of Olympus.

"Hi, Blake," Max said.

"Oh hi, Max," Blake said. "Good to see you're in one piece."

"It will take more than a few bombs to get me."

"You're not bulletproof, Max, you need to be careful out there."

"I always am."

"Sorry we missed our training session this morning," Blake said coyly.

"Yeah, sorry about that."

"Oh, are you two right?" Lloyd asked annoyed. "Time to flirt later."

He was interrupted before he could continue berating them. One of the nine television feeds expanded, filling the left screen. It was Sky News.

"The Israeli Prime Minister has been moved to a secure location in Canberra," the anchor said. *"After arriving earlier today, the Prime Ministers of Israel and Australia met to*

discuss the ongoing security situation in the country following the two attacks on the Commonwealth Building and at the airport. The Prime Minister agreed to stay in the country as a sign of strength and friendship in the face of terror."

"Oh, as if we weren't busy enough, now he is staying too," Flash said.

"Anything useful from the phone?" Lloyd asked.

"We're running tracking pings on each of the stored and dialled numbers," Blake explained. "A few are bouncing around the world running through multiple satellites. They will be hard to trace but we will get there. One seems promising. It is static in the Western Sydney area."

"Parramatta?" Lloyd asked.

"Could be."

"Focus on that one. Chang told us his partners in crime from the airport were heading to Parramatta."

"Okay, just give me a minute," Blake said frantically typing commands into the computer. "Did he give you anything else?"

"He confirmed it was the same team that hit the Commonwealth Building," Max said. They were after the Minister for Defence. Can you get word to Agent Carrol?"

"Yes, of course."

"Thanks."

The computer pinged and Blake typed in a string of commands. The centre screen on the wall changed from the Commonwealth Building to a satellite image of Western Sydney. It zoomed in on a pulsing green dot which was hovering over a house in a suburban street in Paramatta.

"Found them," Blake said pointing to the screen.

"Prince, Flash – go now," Lloyd said.

"I will upload it to your car's nav system," Blake said.

"Great. Thanks," Max said. "Oh and our friend Mr Chang upstairs. He says the guy we are looking for is called The Pilot. Chang says he doesn't like me and that I wrecked some of his plans. Can you run a search on some of my past missions and look for any correlation?”

“That could be a long list, with all the people you’ve pissed off, especially in the last few years, but I will get straight on it,” Blake said.

“Yeah true but it’s a start. Thanks Blake,” Max said as he and Flash headed for the elevator.

Max waved his ring in front of the sensor and pushed the button to take them back up to the storage shed. The elevator started moving.

At the top, the doors opened and the two agents ran out into the storage shed and towards the car.

Hulk was waiting.

“Here,” he said passing over two communications units. “We will put a drone above the house. I will be watching and running the operation from the bunker. At this point, it’s just the two of you. I will try to re-route an AFP Spec Ops team, but they may not get there by the time you do.”

“Rules of engagement?” Flash asked.

“Detain if possible, shoot if necessary. I will send forensics as soon as a team comes online to sweep the house for evidence.”

“Ack. Let’s go Flash,” Max said.

“Good luck and Godspeed,” Hulk said.

The two agents pushed the comm units into their ears and did a quick test. Working. Flash jumped into the passenger seat and Max slid behind the wheel. The car had been completely overhauled. It looked like new. Flash took off his ring and inserted it into the car’s receiver. After the usual authentication process had confirmed the agent’s security identification, Flash hit the sat nav button and a map appeared with a highlighted route. Blake had already loaded it up.

Max drove out of the shed, off the compound and headed for a series of backstreets as shown on the map. Avoiding the motorways. They past rough neighbourhoods. Broken down and jacked up cars sat on front lawns. Graffiti was everywhere, tags covered houses, abandoned shopfronts and street signs. They drove down the main street of a suburb. Locals were drinking in the street and staring as they drove by in their brand-new Chevy. One heavily tattooed man shouted at them and gave the middle finger. *Charming,* Max thought to himself.

The afternoon sun was streaming through the windshield as they drove deep into a tidy residential area. It was cleaner and much nicer than the suburbs they had just been through.

Max pulled the car up a few blocks from the target location and killed the engine.

Chapter Fourteen

Xander and Sophia laid naked in each other's arms.

After fleeing the airport, they had ditched the AFP car and their motorbike jackets. At a local shopping strip, they had stolen two new shirts of a rack outside a small fashion retailer and put them on a block down the road.

A combination of bus, train and taxi had gotten them close to the safe house. The remaining blocks they had walked, once the taxi was out of sight.

In the safehouse, they had discussed calling the Pilot but thought it was better to come up with a plan of attack first. He did not tolerate failure and they had failed twice. They knew they had to clean up their mistakes and they needed to tell the Pilot how they planned to do it.

Xander had paced back and forth on the orange and black shagpile carpet. The little safehouse had been built in the late 1960s and the interior looked like it had not been updated since. What were once white walls were stained and faded with a yellow tinge from decades of cigarette smoke. Big old faded green corduroy covered sofas and solid dark brown hardwood tables with rounded edges filled the room in front of an old oil heater. A matching credenza with glass doors ran the length of the lounge room proudly displaying a lifetime collection of ceramic ornaments and crystal. Xander had purchased the fully furnished house from a deceased estate, months before today's operation. He rubbed the scar on his cheek as he paced. A nervous tick.

Sophia walked across the room and grabbed his wrist halting his frantic pacing. They locked eyes as she placed her hand on the side of his face, her thumb rubbing his scar gently. They both had a nervous energy after all they had been through and were shaking slightly from their rapid heartbeats. He grabbed her firmly and drew her in, and they kissed roughly, overcome by their adrenaline and animal instincts. He pushed her back against the hallway wall as they stumbled towards the nearest bed. A framed painting of a mountain range fell to the floor. Its glass shattering into the carpet. They bumped into the walls and crushed the broken painting and glass under their feet as they headed for the master bedroom.

Sophia ripped Xander's stolen shirt open, sending the buttons flying. He did the same to hers exposing her black lacy bra. They stumbled through the bedroom door and it swung hard into the wall with a loud thud before they left a trail of clothes across the room. As they approached the bed, Xander picked Sophia up in his arms and threw her down onto the bed. She bounced on the springs as she landed before taking off her underwear and throwing them at Xander. He dropped his briefs and with a smile leapt onto the bed.

They had passionate, wild, rough sex, letting out their nerves and adrenaline.

As they laid naked, breathing hard both their phones beeped in unison.

"I guess we better face the music," Sophia said.

"Yeah, we can't hide from him forever," Xander said as he got to his feet and retrieved his phone.

Sophia watched his face change as he read the message.

Chang gave up the safe house, if you are still there GET OUT NOW!

"Fuck Chang gave us up, we've got to go now!" Xander said.

"What?" Sophia asked. "Fuck. That arsehole! AIS better kill him or I will."

The pair scrambled for their clothes and got dressed while stumbling back down the hallway. Sophia ran for the back door.

"No, this way," Xander said pulling her arm towards the front door.

"What about the…" Sophia said.

"We don't have time. Leave it."

They sprang through the front door, and looked left and right down the street.

A few blocks down a new black Chevy was parked on the side of the road.

Xander wrapped an arm around Sophia and led her in the opposite direction and around the corner.

Chapter Fifteen

Max jumped out and ran around to open the boot, as Flash retrieved his ring.

"Silenced MP5s and pistols?" Flash said as he joined Max at the rear of the vehicle.

"Yep, here you go," Max said handing the weapons to Flash. "Watch where you're aiming."

"If my memory serves me correct, it's you who's nearly shot me twice."

"I was just seeing if you were on your toes."

"Stop fucking about you two and get going," Hulk said over the earpieces.

Max closed the boot.

"You take the front door, I'll take the back door," he said.

"Typical," Flash joked.

"Oh ha-ha," Max said as he started running for the house with Flash in tow.

As they approached the house, Max stayed low to keep under the windows as he made for the backyard. Flash took a position crouched by the front door.

It was a little suburban home. The yard was slightly overgrown, but nothing an afternoon or two's work couldn't fix. A large gum tree shaded the house and yard. It was painted a mild grey with white eves and window frames. It was a bit rundown after a few years of neglect.

Max reached the backdoor.

"Three…Two…One…Breach," Max said over the comms unit as he swung around and kicked the door open at the same time as Flash kicked in the front door.

"Laundry clear," Max said.

"Foyer clear," Flash said.

"Kitchen clear."

"Lounge clear."

"Dining clear."

"Master bed clear."

"Sitting room clear."

"Second bedroom clear."

"Bathroom clear."

"You better come up here Max, second room on the left," Flash said.

Max ran down the hallway, gun up, finger on the trigger. Broken glass crunched under his feet as he trampled a painting which had fallen from the wall.

As he went through the door he knew why Flash wanted him to see the room. It was lined with surveillance photos.

Picture after picture pinned to the wall was of the Commonwealth Building. Multiple angles. Multiple targets. Max stood and stared at the pictures. Friends, colleagues, Ministers, Government officials, hundreds of people were photographed coming and going from the building. He saw his boss and Sarah in several photos. And, his own photo hung on the wall too. There was also a structural blueprint of the building in the centre, framed by the pictures.

"This is too much, Max," Flash said.

"Yeah, tell me about it," Max said as he tapped his photo.

"No, I mean too much evidence. They knew we would find this."

"It could be a distraction," Hulk interjected. *"There could be more to find. Guns up boys. Parameter check."*

On cue the two agents raised their weapons and in unison headed down the corridor. They walked through the front door and broke. Max went left and Flash went right. They circled the house and met by the back door. Nothing.

"Check the garage," Hulk said.

Max looked up into the sky searching for the drone but to no avail.

"On it," he said.

Guns up, they made their way across the yard. Just like the front yard, the backyard was overgrown with long, thick grass. An old concrete path led from the backdoor of the house down to a rusted hills hoist clothes line which was leaning hard to the right. The wooden shed was painted to match the house. Paint was peeling from the surface and was chipped and water damaged. The door was locked. Max stepped back and fired one bullet. There was a short thump as it left the silencer and hit the lock. Flash kicked the door open and went in scanning left. Max followed scanning right. Clear.

"It's clear, Hulk," Max said.

Max opened a row of cupboards down the right side of the garage. Nothing out of the ordinary. Left over grey and white paint tins from the exterior of the house, and useless brushes stiff with old paint. A collection of tools, drill, sander, all relatively new looking seemingly at odds with the other contents in the cupboards given the state of the house. Maybe the new owners were going to fix it up.

A lawnmower and yard working tools were gathering dust at the far end of the shed.

Oddly, there was a scattering of new chrome tools in the centre of the concrete floor set in a large circle. Clearly someone had been working on something recently. Max knelt down and inspected a small empty bottle of motorbike oil. Then he saw something familiar, but without doubt, completely out of place in a suburban garage. He picked up a small stiff plastic packet from the floor. It was dark green with camouflage print and one of a handful of similar packets from the floor.

"Flash," Max said showing him the packet. "C4?"

"Looks like it," Flash said walking over to get a closer look.

He took it from Max and examined it closely.

"Yep," Flash said looking to Max.

"You keep looking around. Hulk, you there?"

"Yes Prince. Report."

"We've got motorbike oil and new tools spread around the shed, and about twelve or more empty C4 packets. Army issue. Green cam print."

"Looks like we have the right place then. Eye-witnesses accounts from the Commonwealth Building have recalled motorbikes breaching the foyer."

"There are partial serial numbers on the packets, Hulk. Is Hermes on the line?"

"I'm here, Prince," Blake said.

"Standby, I'll take pictures of the serials and send them through. See if you can track down where these could have come from."

"Ack. Will do."

Max retrieved his mobile and began photographing the C4 packets' serial numbers.

"Max, I've got something here," Flash said as he opened a cupboard under the workbench at the rear of the garage.

Inside was a solid metal safe. It had a combination lock like an old bank vault. It was bolted into the cupboard which Max noticed was bolted into the concrete floor.

"Hulk, we've got a combination safe," Max said.

"I can crack it, but I'm going to need some tools," Flash said. "I'm going to the car. Be back soon."

"Alright, I'll head back into the house and see if we missed anything," Max said.

Max did another sweep of the garage before heading out into the yard and towards the house.

Max's phone rang. It was Sam.

"Hey Sam," Max said.

"Hi Max, how are you feeling?"

"Yeah I'm fine thanks. How are you?"

"Good thanks. I have been thinking about you all day."

"I've been thinking about you too. I did have a building blow up and a few other minor things happen around me, but other than that I've been thinking about you."

"Oh babe, I wish I was there to give you a hug. I can't even imagine the day you have had."

"It's still going sadly."

"Oh gosh, sorry I should let you go. I just wanted to let you know I'm making pasta and I have stocked up on Margaret River's finest. Come around whenever you are free."

"Thanks Sam. Sounds amazing. I'm probably still a few hours away. I'll text to see if you're still awake before coming around."

"Okay. Can't wait to see you."

"You too. See you later."

Max ended the call and smiled to himself thinking about Sam. So cute. So innocent. So sweet. A stark contrast to the horrors of his day.

"Anytime you want to get back to work, Prince, that would be great," Lloyd said over the earpiece.

"You heard all that? Sorry Shadow."

"While I hardly like your life choices, I understand the need for companionship and love. We do not always have time for family and friends in jobs like these so enjoy it while you can. Just not now. Get back to work."

"Yes, sir."

Flash arrived and headed back into the garage to start breaking into the safe.

Inside the house, Max had a closer look at the painting on the ground. Maybe it had been knocked in a hurry to get out of the house. He looked in the master bedroom. The bed was not made. Sheets and pillows were strewn across the room. He saw several shirt buttons amongst the glass on the floor.

No, not in a hurry to leave, quite the opposite, Max thought to himself.

Max walked back to the room covered in photos. He stared at his picture. He was angry that they had gotten so close to taking him out. It was a reality he faced in his line of work, but he liked to think over the years he had gotten better at detecting someone following him. The surveillance crew was clearly a professional outfit. It was a long time since he had worried about how upset people would be if someone took him out. Since Lachlan, he had not thought about it at all. Instead, he had thrown himself into danger repeatedly without a care for his own safety, instead only caring for the safety of his team and the people they were all charged with protecting. He felt lonely again at the thought. He wanted someone to go home to. Shaking off the feeling, he looked to the blueprint of the Commonwealth Building. He noticed the logo in the bottom right corner. It was a construction company logo.

"Hulk are you still online?" Max asked the empty room.

"Yeah I'm here. Find something?" Hulk asked over the earpiece.

"Crown Constructions. Ring a bell?"

"From last night?" Blake said.

"One and the same," Max said.

"What have you got, Prince?" Hulk asked.

"Let me show you," Max said taking his phone back out of his pocket and hitting videocall.

In the AIS bunker, the centre screen which had been showing drone footage of the house in Parramatta cut to the live feed coming in from the camera on Max's phone. He held it firmly in front of the wall of photos before scanning over the blueprint.

"Jesus, that's the classified blueprint of the Commonwealth Building. Not many places you can get one of those," Hulk said.

"Who would have access?" Max asked.

"An electronic copy is stored at ASIO and with the Feds. And, the construction company have a copy for advice on maintenance and upgrades."

"Time to start making a list of who may have had access. Wait, check this out."

Max walked closer to the blueprint.

In the bunker, Hulk sat upright and leaned forward.

"It's the original," Hulk said.

"Yeah, there are no safe room structures on this plan," Max said moving the camera down to the mezzanine, "and, this is still the security room on this plan."

"Prince, I've run the search," Blake said. *"Crown Constructions was asked to tender for the Commonwealth Building upgrades however when AIS suspected the businessman had connections to some suspect individuals, so we vetoed their application and changed the designs for security reasons."*

"Well, it's a fucking pity, you two idiots threw the Arab through a window last night," Lloyd said.

"That's not exactly what happened," Max said.

"From what we can tell so far, a bomb went off next to the old security room," Blake said. *"The other two went off one floor down and across the hallway from your office. So, using these plans, it is clear, that they were targeting your office and didn't know the safe room was fitted to the Minister's suite."*

"Have you seen the footage yet?" Max asked.

"It is being uploaded to our servers now."

"Right, we'll be back soon. I wouldn't mind seeing it for myself."

"Go check on Flash," Hulk ordered. *"Bring whatever he finds back here. Forensics are ten minutes out, they will photograph and document everything then bring it to the bunker for analysis."*

"Got it," Max said. "Hermes, you will need to put some more guys on the Crown files we recovered last night which I gave to Hulk this morning."

"I will check on the progress of the decryption and give you an update when you get back," Blake said.

"Thanks mate," Max said.

Out in the garage Max found Flash with a set of headphones in his ears leading to the safe. Max watched Flash as he slowly twisted the combination lock and moved a set of picks inside a separate lock.

Max pulled his phone out, six o'clock, still time to see Sam. Suddenly, he remembered he was still wearing his suit from earlier in the day. He must look a wreck. He looked down at his crumpled suit.

"Don't worry it's not the suit he's interested in," Flash said setting down the picks and removing his headphones, seeing Max in the reflection of the cabinet.

"Hmm, hope you're right," Max said. "How did you go?"

"Let's take a look," Flash said turning the handle, opening the safe.

Inside was a tablet computer. Flash picked it up and opened the case. Password protected. He showed the lock screen to Max.

"Hulk, we're en route," Flash said. "We've got a tablet computer from the safe. Have your best IT analyst ready."

"Give it to Hermes, he'll get it done," Hulk said.

Max and Flash headed back down the driveway as the forensic team arrived.

"All yours boys," Flash said to the first agent out of the car.

Chapter Sixteen

Max and Flash made their way back to the car and drove to the storage compound. They parked next to a line of other vehicles then took the elevator down into the bunker. Once they were through the bunker's doors they saw a hive of activity.

"Looks like the troops have been rallied," Flash said.

"That it does," Max said watching for a moment as analysts and aides moved around the bunker. Some were shuffling paperwork between offices while others were stocking the fridges and topping up supplies.

"Guess they figure we are in for a few long nights," Flash said.

"Guess so."

Max and Flash walked into the operations centre. Every computer had at least one person busily typing away. The left screen still showed rolling news footage. The right was showing vision from the Commonwealth Building. Police and forensic teams were inside reviewing the evidence under big flood lights. The centre screen showed the inside of the house in Parramatta. One of the forensics guys was filming the scene. His voice was coming in over the speakers, calling in what the team was seeing.

"Hulk wants us, he's in the Director's suite," Blake said.

"Thanks, Blake," Flash said.

"Follow me."

Hulk was talking to an analyst and looked up when the agents walked into the room. Lloyd was sitting at the conference table tapping his pen on the glass top and staring at the wall.

"Are you ready to go?" Hulk asked.

"Yes," Blake said.

Flash gave the tablet to Blake who hustled over to join the analyst as Max walked in.

"This system is completely isolated from the AIS network to protect us in case of viruses and to ensure no one can hack in," Blake said.

He plugged in the tablet and began typing fast keystrokes on his own computer. Blake and the analyst began hushed conversation.

"What is it?" Lloyd asked.

"It's military spec software, like the Crown files we are still trying to decrypt," Blake said. "We are going to have to do this the very hard and very slow way."

"Fuck," Hulk said.

"Sorry sir, one mistake and the system will erase," Blake said.

"How long?" Hulk asked.

"Hours."

"Well, get to it."

"Yes, sir."

Hulk, Lloyd, Flash and Max left Blake and the analyst to work in peace.

"How the hell did they get this level of security software and all that C4?" Lloyd asked.

"Has to be an inside job," Flash said. "These sorts of supplies are under tight security. Maybe some grunt trying to earn a bit on the side. Wouldn't be the first time. Remember Corporal what's his name?"

"Johnston?" Max asked. "No, Jackson. Corporal Jackson. He was pinching Berettas and ammunition from Holsworthy Barracks and erasing the inventory logs. We thought he was selling to one of our watchlist targets, but he was only pushing to local dealers and crackheads."

"Yeah that's him, Jack-off Jackson, the boys called him," Flash said. "Wonder where he is now? Might be worth dropping in and having a chat."

"Good thinking," Lloyd said. "We will track him down and you two can go see what he knows. He has been in gaol for several years now though, not sure how useful he will be?"

"He might be helpful in figuring out what we are looking for and nailing down exactly how this could be done," Max said.

"You look like shit Max," Hulk said. "Why don't you boys go get some rest while we track Mr Jackson down and wait for Blake to decrypt those files?"

"There is a room for you down the hall, past the kitchen," Lloyd said. "I had your things brought over from the hotel and settled the account."

"Thank you, good idea," Max said and started for the room. "Call me as soon as you have anything,"

Max showered letting the hot water soak into his skin, washing away the day's dirt and grime. He threw his old suit and shirt into a dry-cleaning bag in the corner and changed into a new suit and put on a new pair of R.M. Williams boots. He picked up his rings and mobile from the charging pad next to his bed. He stared at himself in the mirror. He still looked a bit tired but, all things considered, he felt fine. He checked the bruise on his eye and put some more concealer on to hide it. He felt his heart race a beat hoping to escape the bunker for a few hours to see Sam.

He headed back down the hall to the conference room. Flash and Hulk were sitting there.

"What's up, where's Shadow?" Max asked.

"He's gone upstairs to have a chat to your friend, Mr Chang, and show him some footage," Flash said.

"From the Commonwealth Building?"

"Yep. It hasn't long finished downloading from AFP. Want to see it?"

"Yes."

Flash typed away on the laptop in front of him and a television screen turned on at end of the room.

Max watched as windows shattered and bullets struck down his colleagues. The gunfire was loudly pouring through the speakers in the conference room. He saw friends from other Ministerial offices gunned down. Two motorbikes entered and stopped. One by the security desk dropped someone off before speeding up the escalator to the mezzanine. Two men from the other bike shot several of Max's colleagues before taking security passes and heading upstairs in the lift. The security guards were shot with the terrorist standing looking down at them behind the security desk. He looked like he was enjoying the sight. Then he looked up and across the lobby to Mr Jones who was standing frozen on the white tiles.

"Ahh, Mr Jones, how was your meeting? Productive I hope."

"You, what have you done?" Jones asked.

The passenger walked out from behind the desk and with a spring in his step, hopped playfully between the tiles, as he spoke.

"I did, what you, refused to do," he said as Max watched him hopping tile to tile on the screen. *"I took action. This is act one. The Pilot has taken command and we are putting his plan into action. You remember the plan, right?"*

"Killing some security guards in a Government building is not going to help you. That was never part of the plan," Jones said.

"No, sorry. I meant Plan B. Did you ever discuss Plan B? It involves killing you and your Minister mate to send a signal. Each of our cells will activate in the country, triggering an escalating series of terrorist events. And, while the police and ASIO, and AIS are busy trying to control the growing panic and work out how to stop the attacks, we will finish what we started together."

Max watched as Jones looked over to the elevator bay and saw the two men in their leather riding gear exiting the lift and walking back towards him at a fast pace. Max noticed they were no longer wearing their backpacks.

"It is a pity you couldn't get on board with Plan A, Bill. You could have become obscenely rich and powerful, but instead you betrayed us. So, Plan B it is."

His smile instantly faded to a frown as he raised his gun and shot Jones between the eyes. Jones's lifeless body fell to the floor with a hard thud as his skull slammed into the marble tiles.

"Oh well," the passenger said.

Max's blood ran cold at the sight of Mr Jones, a man he had been speaking to only hours ago, being assassinated. He watched as Xander stood for a moment taking in his handiwork, before kneeling down and opening Jones's briefcase. He flicked through the contents then clicked the case closed and stood carrying it in his left hand.

The two men from the elevator arrived at his side.

"Go get the car," he barked.

"Yes, sir," the men said in unison still wearing their reflective helmets.

Chang and Heath I presume, Max thought.

The passenger looked at his watch as the rider from the second bike walked onto the down escalator. Still wearing her helmet, her leather jacket and skinny leg pants which clung tightly to her toned body.

"It won't bring it down, but it is going to do a great deal of damage," Sophia said.

"It doesn't have to, as long as it gets that fucker upstairs," Xander said. *"Let's go."*

Max watched as the remaining two, who he knew were Xander and Sophia, walked out through the broken glass into the street.

"Mr Jones was assassinated," Max said mostly to himself. "Can we get a better shot of his face, the guy with his visor up, Xander, Chang said his name was?"

"The tech guys are working on it," Flash said.

Max just nodded and watched as people from the street nervously entered on the screen when the four from the bikes had left the Commonwealth Building. They bent over injured office workers to check for signs of life. One man took off his jacket to put under a young man's head.

"They came in to help?" Max asked himself. "Oh God."

Then the bombs exploded. The sound was dramatic in the conference room making the three men jump. Max shook his head as a wave of sadness hit him, followed by anger. The lobby was ripped apart. People who had come to help, including the man who had taken off his jacket, were thrown violently around or out of the lobby. The flickering footage that followed showed the devastation. Max remembered the lobby from earlier in the day. Horrific.

"So many innocent people," Max said. "Terror is right."

"We are cross checking our watch lists with threats made against the Minister and Mr Jones," Hulk said. "They seemed to know each other. He mentions Plan A and Plan B. Maybe they were blackmailing him or maybe he was in on it. We'll need to look into it."

"So what now?" Flash asked.

"We wait," Hulk said. "It is unlikely we will know anything for a few hours. Our teams are working on the connections and the files. Until then we have nothing to go on. You should go and get something to eat and some rest. I need you two fresh and ready. Oh and if you do head out, please keep your phones on. I will call when I know more."

"Okay, thanks Hulk, "Max said. "Yeah, let me know as soon as you have anything. I am going to kill everyone involved in this for what they've done."

Max and Flash left the room.

"Are you going to see him?" Flash asked as the pair walked down the hallway.

"Yeah, but let me know if anything happens and I will come straight back," Max said.

"I haven't seen you like this for a long time, Max. He must be a special guy."

"Don't tell me you're jealous, Flash, you know I love ya, right?" Max asked playfully.

"Oh that's sweet, but I think I will pass, besides what would Jane say?" Flash replied with a laugh.

"Oh, my broken heart," Max said clutching his chest dramatically. "She's one lucky gal."

"Get out of here," Flash said walking off towards his room.

"Call if you need me," Max said heading for the elevator.

Chapter Seventeen

Max parked outside Sam's place.

He pushed open the little rusty gate, walked over to the front door and knocked. There were lamps on inside and the house looked warm and welcoming in stark contrast to the cool air and shadowy street.

He heard footsteps and the door opened. Sam was standing there smiling warmly. He flung open the screen door and jumped into Max's arms. He hugged him tightly and kissed his neck, then they kissed passionately.

"I was so worried when I saw the news," Sam said. "I didn't know what to think. I'm so glad you are okay."

"You're beautiful, thanks Sam," Max said. "It's been a sad day, but I am glad to see you. I need a hug."

Sam hugged him tightly. Max felt warm. He felt secure. He felt safe. In Sam's arms, the day washed away and for that moment his mind was at peace.

"Come on, let's go inside," Sam said.

Max watched as Sam led him into the terrace. He was wearing a pair of tight black sweatpants and colourful spotty socks. A grey jumper, about two sizes too big, hung loosely from his shoulders. His blond hair was tied back in a high ponytail.

The pair had dinner and a glass of wine. Sitting on the lounge Sam reached over and held Max's hand as Max told him some of what had happened during the day. Leaving out the airport, the bunker, the prisoner, the house in Parramatta and, of course, the fact that he was a spy.

"I'm so sorry to hear about your friends and colleagues, it is so tragic," Sam said.

"Yeah, it's awful," Max agreed.

They sat in silence for a short while until Sam snuggled in close and hugged Max.

"I know it's really soon and I never do this, but I have to tell you, I really feel something for you," Sam said.

"I know how you feel," Max said. "I feel the same."

They locked eyes and Max reached over and placed his hand on Sam's cheek. Sam rested his head in Max's palm and lovingly smiled. Max drew him in and kissed him with the intensity of long lost lovers. Sam pushed Max's jacket off his shoulders and threw it on the armrest of the couch then he undid his tie. Max grabbed the bottom of Sam's jumper and t-shirt, and lifted them both up over his head exposing his chiselled chest and abs. Max watched as Sam unbuttoned his shirt. Sam pushed Max down, laying him on the couch. He kissed up Max's chest and neck, and then he kissed his lips as he lowered himself down onto Max's strong muscular body. His pants clung to his toned arse and legs. He kissed back down Max's body, unbuckled his belt, undid his button and zip, then slid his pants off onto the floor, taking his socks off as he went. Max laid there in his pink and blue striped briefs.

"God, you are so sexy," Sam said admiring Max's athletic body.

"Look who's talking," Max said cheekily. "Now, get back over here."

Sam playfully leapt onto Max and they made love there in the lounge room.

They laid in each other's arms sweating and panting. Holding each other tightly.

"Let's go shower and head to bed," Sam said standing to lead Max to the bathroom.

They showered. Hugging and kissing under the hot water, and they made love again in the shower.

Sam led Max to the bedroom and they climbed into bed. They snuggled, hugging each other tightly and fell asleep without letting go.

A few hours later, Max woke to banging on the door and his phone ringing.

"Hello?" he said groggily answering the phone.

"Wake up lover, time to go to work," Flash said.

"Is that you banging on the door?"

"Yep."

"Well, I'm awake stop banging."

The knocking stopped.

"What is it?" Sam said barely awake.

"I have to go babe sorry," Max said.

"Why? What time is it?"

"I have to go to work, because of what happened yesterday. It's still really early. I'm sorry, Sam."

"Okay, well, when will I see you again?"

"It may not be for a couple of days. I may have to go back to Canberra soon, but I promise I will come and see you when I can."

"You better. I miss you already."

"So cute. You too babe."

Max lent in and kissed Sam, before he snuck quietly down to the lounge room to get dressed. Flash was looking in the window and laughed seeing Max totally naked sneaking around.

As Max put on his boots, he looked up and saw Sam standing in the doorway. The light was catching his toned naked body, accentuating every muscle. Max was hit with a wave of sadness knowing he had to leave.

"I'm sorry, Sammy, I really want to stay," he said walking over and hugging him. "I don't know where this goes, but I know I want to see you again. We will work something out."

"I want to see you again too, Max. I meant what I said last night, I really like you. Be careful today. Can I call you later?"

"Of course. Any time."

They kissed passionately before being interrupted by a tap on the glass.

Flash.

"Who is that?"

"That's my colleague Jacob. We call him Flash."

"He's cute."

"Hey, I'm standing right here."

"Not as cute as you, don't worry."

They kissed again.

"I've got to go babe. I will talk to you soon."

"Okay bye, Max."

"Thanks for last night and for dinner."

"Anytime."

They kissed before Max walked out into the street.

Sam watched as they walked to the car. Max and Sam waved to each other.

"Wow, I think he's fallen for you," Flash said.

"Yeah, I know how he feels," Max said.

"Oh gee, that's fast. You gay guys move quickly."

"Such a cliché."

"Well, I'm happy for you either way. It's good to see you smile."

Max looked at Flash. He smiled and nodded understanding what he was saying without needing anymore discussion. Flash was Max's best friend and he had always been there for him, since the day they met at the Wool Shed.

A few years ago, at the most challenging time in Max's life when he lost his fiancé, Lachlan, it was Flash and Blake who were there to pick him up and help him pull himself together. They both provided emotional support and friendship. And it was Flash who was beside him on every mission and Blake who helped them plan every mission. The three of them were inseparable.

Max had been heartbroken and completely devastated. He felt like his life was over and not worth living. Lachlan was murdered and Max had always blamed himself. At the time, Flash was not sure his friend would make it, but he did, and he smiled to himself, pleased to see his friend happy again. He hoped this might see a return to some kind of normal for his heartbroken and changed friend.

Chapter Eighteen

Flash pulled the car up to the gate at the Silverwater Correctional Facility and, after a brief exchange, the gate rolled open for the two agents. They parked near the administration building and made their way over to meet the warden and the captain of the night guard who were standing at the top of the stairs waiting.

It was an old brick building, one of a dozen originals built on the site and it stood in stark contrast to the modern state-of-the-art perimeter security and new super-max facilities which had been completed shortly after nine-eleven to house the worst of the worst from across Australia. Silverwater is home to rapists, murderers, terrorists and a number of highly trained thieves like the man they were there to visit.

Warden Bradley Hill was several years older than Max. He was a tall man, over six feet tall, and his thin build was crafted over a lifetime of marathon running. He was standing on the steps in an ill-fitting, cheap jet-black suit with a greying white business shirt and light blue tie. He had short sandy hair and olive skin from time in the sun training on the circuit which ringed a nearby lake, and wore a chunky big Casio sports wristwatch.

"Agent Gordon, Agent Shaw?" Hill asked looking from Flash to Max as they climbed the stairs.

"Yes, hello Warden Hill," Flash said as he and Max took turns at shaking Hill's hand. "I'm Agent Jacob Gordon. This is my colleague, Agent Max Shaw. We appreciate you taking the time to meet us."

"I'm not sure I had any choice in the matter Agent, but it is no hassle at all. This is Captain Davidson. He is the head of the guards on night duty."

"Nice to meet you, Captain Davidson," Flash said.

"And, you too," Davidson said before both agents shook the guard's hand.

He was a short nuggetty man but solid, like a bodybuilder. Given the size of his arms, Max guessed he was taking some serious steroids. His biceps were straining against his short-sleeves like he could rip the shirt with one good flex. It was not just the sleeves, he was bulging out of his tight guard's uniform as if it was bought years before he started training and he had not bothered to update it. Max wondered if the light blue, short-sleeved business shirt and brown slacks were up to the challenge of holding him in. He looked ridiculous, especially next to the warden in his suit.

"I believe former Corporal Jackson is one of your guests?" Max asked.

"Yes, he has been with us for about three years now," Hill said. "He is in the workshop waiting for you, as requested."

"Good. Did you tell him who was coming to see him?"

"No, your office said not to."

"Good. Let's go say hello."

Davidson and Hill led them into the prison. The new buildings were painted a stark grey blue. There was concrete and steel everywhere. Cold. Unforgiving. Depressing.

They crossed the prison yard which was mostly dust and dirt. The grass was worn low from overuse. A concrete workout area and basketball court sat alongside the concrete path they were on. Everything was ringed with razor wire fencing on top of long shear sheets of steal, which was close to impossible, but definitely extremely dangerous to climb.

"We will be fine from here gentlemen," Max said as they approached the workshop. "Thanks for your time."

"Umm, no. I will be staying to supervise and then escort you back out," Davidson said.

"Supervise?" Max asked. "Let's get one thing clear, I don't need supervision and trust me you might not want to see what happens next."

"You can't," Davidson said before getting interrupted by the Warden.

"Davidson, stay outside and escort the agents out when they have finished," Hill said. "Gents, I will leave you to it."

"Thanks, Hill," Flash said.

Hill turned and quickly walked back across the yard smart enough to not want to stick around. Nothing like plausible deniability.

Davidson unlocked the door then held it open for Flash and Max. Max stared him down as he walked past. The door closed behind them and they walked across the open workshop where Jackson was handcuffed to a workbench.

"Oh, fuck me," Jackson said as he looked across to Max and Flash.

"Jack-off. It has been a while, how's it going?"

"My name is Tom," Jackson said.

"Yeah, but the boys on base called you Jack-off, right? I thought you would like the name. I mean, it is quite appropriate for an arms-dealing, oath-breaking, wanker."

"You seem nastier, then last time we met," Jackson said. "Speaking of, how is your dead boyfriend?"

Max sprung off his left foot into the air and unleashed a powerful right jab to Jackson's face as he landed. Jackson stumbled and fell, his handcuffed wrists holding his weight.

"Pretty good punch for a fag," Jackson said spitting blood onto the concrete floor. "Pretty weak though punching a guy that's tied up. Why don't you uncuff me and try it again?"

"Happily, you piece of shit."

"We didn't come here for this Max," Flash said.

Max stepped back and let Flash talk to Jackson.

"Military grade C4 and IT equipment has turned up in the hands of known terrorists," Flash said. "How well connected are you with your old buddies?"

"Thanks to you two, I have been locked up for years. How would I know how they got their hands on it?"

"Interesting response. That is not what I asked. I asked how connected are you to your old buddies? Ever hear from them?"

"It's not really the place for a few beers with old pals from either side of the law, now is it? My old army mates think I'm the bad guy and there is no way any of the others would come near a prison or be seen with me."

"Aww, do you need a hug?" Max said busying himself with some of the tools on the bench to calm down.

"Fuck you!" Jackson said.

"So, we're here, talk to us," Flash said. "We just want to know how they could get the equipment and weapons, and who might be involved?"

"I'm not telling you who's involved. I mean, not that I would know."

"Not telling us who is involved?" Max said. "You're a bit defensive. What aren't you telling us? Are you involved in this?"

"No. How could I be? You locked me in here. I haven't seen anyone or talked to anyone since I got here."

"Yeah, you see the thing is Jack-off, I just don't believe you," Max said. "Flash, why don't you go ask Captain Steroid for Mr Jackson's call and visitor logs. Let's see who he's been talking to?"

"No worries," Flash said as he headed out to speak to the captain of the guards who was still standing sentry at the door.

"You see Jack-off, we just came to ask a couple of quick questions like 'how could they do it?' and you've gotten all defensive and you look nervous. You also said you wouldn't tell us who was involved. Now, I'm a naturally inquisitive guy and your reaction to our little visit has made me really interested in what you know."

"Nothing. I'm just nervous because you're here and I've heard you have gone off the rails since, well, since, you know. People say you've lost it, since. Since, your boyfriend got whacked."

"He was my fiancé and yes, I'd say there's some truth to that, so why don't you tell me who you have been talking to or you can find out for yourself just how far off the rails I will go to get information?”

“Shit.”

“Good to see you’re still an idiot. I think you’re nervous because you are involved somehow, so former Corporal, why don’t you just tell me, and I can be on my way and you’ll remain pain free.”

“No. Please. I don’t know anything.”

“So, how do you know about Lachlan and how do you know I have apparently gone off the rails? Who have you been talking to?”

“No one. I swear. I don’t know anything about you.”

“Well, let’s find out hey?” Max said walking back over to the tool bench.

Max reached across the workbench and plugged in a power cord. He flicked the switch on. Jackson saw Max pick up a plastic Tupperware container and pour out the nails it had been holding. The nails fell like metal rain onto the steel tool bench. Then Max turned back to face Jackson. In his hands, he held the plastic container and a soldering iron.

“Now, while we are waiting for this to heat up, why don’t you tell me how someone could steal equipment from a military base?” Max asked as he slowly walked towards Jackson.

“Okay, okay. I’m sure it’s not as easy as it was when I did it,” Jackson said stiffening and shifting nervously as he watched the soldering iron heating up. “The army would no doubt have changed handling protocols, but the idea would be the same. Find a way to disappear inventory logs.”

“What about getting equipment off base in the first place?”

“The IT equipment would be easy enough. A lot of people carry mobile devices, so they probably just walked them right out the front gate.”

“These aren’t your everyday items. They had military spec encryption software and encrypted tablets.”

"Well those are a bit harder to come by. The commanding officer and executive officer on a base would have them, plus maybe a handful of senior NCOs and junior officers."

"So, they would know they are missing?"

"Yeah, but they would still be able to walk them out the door. The whole idea is that they look just like a normal tablet."

"Right, well, what about the C4?"

"The easiest way would be to leave a box behind after an exercise and go pick it up later or give the buyer the location, so they can go get it."

"It couldn't be that easy, they would check inventory before and after exercises."

"Oh, they do, but it's easy enough to say they used more then they thought. A few shoulder shrugs later and they load up and move out."

"That's pretty sloppy."

"Yeah, but it's possible. That's how I used to…"

"Used to what? Steal military equipment and sell it to drug dealers?"

"I'm not saying anymore. They will kill me for even telling you this much?"

"Who will?"

"No. I'm not saying anymore. I shouldn't have said this much. He will kill me."

"Who will?"

Jackson was silent.

Max stood staring at Jackson then held the container up and sat the soldering iron on its side. The plastic melted and smoked as the soldering iron effortlessly burned a large hole in the container. The plastic blackening as it turned in on itself. Smoke rose between the two, slightly obstructing their eye contact.

"Who have you been talking to?" Max said throwing the smoking melted container on the floor.

"God, you can't do this. I'm handcuffed inside a prison. This cannot be legal."

"I work for AIS. My job is to get information at any cost to save people's lives. If that means badly hurting a criminal arsehole in the process, it won't matter and trust me, no one will care about you. So, I ask again, who have you been talking to?"

Silence.

"Fine," Max said as he sat the soldering iron on soft skin inside Jackson's right elbow.

The smell of burning flesh filled the air as smoke poured off Jackson's burning skin overpowering the lingering burnt plastic smell. After a few seconds, Max removed the iron and Jackson trashed about trying to free himself.

"They're right, you are a fucking psycho!" Jackson said.

"Did they also tell you I will not stop until I get what I want? Save yourself some pain and just tell me. Trust me, there are more tender spots than your arm to put this."

Max waved the iron in front of Jackson's face.

"Alright, alright, alright. Jesus. Just put that down. Please."

"Start talking."

"I never stopped running my side business. I still sell equipment. Some of it's new and some I stored before I got busted."

"So, are you telling me you sold the C4 and the tablets?"

Jackson winced and lowered his head. Max stepped forward and grabbed Jackson by the throat. He hovered the soldering iron an inch above Jackson's right eye.

"Yes! Jesus, don't. Please!" Jackson said. "I sold the two tablets to an Arab businessman from Western Sydney."

"We know about him. What about the C4?"

"Some guy. He was Chinese or Korean or something. Chang was his name."

"We have Mr Chang in custody. He used the C4 to blow up half the Commonwealth Building in the CBD. A building I happened to have been in at the time. He also tried to shoot down the Minister for Defence's jet not long after that with a rocket launcher. Don't suppose you know where that came from?"

Jackson's eyes fell. A look of defeat.

"That's right you piece of shit. You sold weapons to terrorists. You are responsible for the deaths of everyone in the Commonwealth Building, many of them friends of mine."

Flash walked back into the workshop with a bundle of transcripts from Jackson's calls and visit logs. He saw Max with Jackson pressed against the workbench, soldering iron in hand.

"How are things going in here?" Flash asked.

"We are just having a little chat about how Jackson here is selling weapons to terrorists."

"There are a number of calls which were scrambled Max. No transcripts just timings. That's high-end tech to block the prison's listening devices. Who were you talking to?"

Jackson said nothing.

Max casually leaned forward and sat the soldering iron on his face. Jackson screamed and started thrashing about again, but Max was too strong. He held him tightly as smoke poured from a burn trail running down Jackson's left cheek.

"The Pilot!" Jackson yelled. "His name is the Pilot!"

"Who is he?" Max asked lifting the iron.

"I don't know, but he is well connected and has a limitless bucket of cash. I charged him a fortune for everything he bought."

"What else did you sell him?" Flash asked.

"Guns. Lots of guns," Jackson said.

"You are coming with us back to AIS. Should I bring the iron or will you cooperate?"

"I'll talk. I'm a dead man anyway."

In the prison yard, Davidson was waiting with a worried look on his face that turned to anger and slight panic when he saw his prisoner being led out of the workshop with a huge burn mark on his left cheek.

"What the hell have you done?" Davidson asked.

"He had a little workshop accident," Max said. "Should have been wearing his safety goggles."

"You can't do that. He was handcuffed for Christ's sake! And, where do you think you are taking him?"

"AIS."

"He can't leave," Davidson said as Max looked at Flash. "You don't have that sort of authority."

Flash retrieved his phone from his pocket and called Hulk.

"By the time we get to the gate we will have it," Max said. "I suggest you get your keys ready."

Chapter Nineteen

After Max and Flash had dropped Jackson off at the AIS bunker and locked him in the holding cell next to Chang, they got back in their car and drove off.

"So, what did Shadow say when I was dealing with Jackson?" Max asked.

"He gave us new orders," Flash explained. "We're going back to Canberra. The Prime Minister has held a press conference and he is recalling Parliament. He wants to make a statement on the attack. The Israeli Prime Minister will also address the Parliament. Show of strength. We won't be beaten. That sort of thing."

"Oh well that is just fucking great. What a waste of time. Wouldn't I be better off here trying to figure out who Jackson and Chang were working with and where the two others went?"

"Yeah mate, but Shadow thinks that you can provide closer security for the Minister if you're in Canberra and you might also be able to do some digging on Mr Jones and his connections to the Minister."

"Connections to the Minister?"

"The footage is pretty clear, Max. They assassinated Jones and tried to take out the Minister too. There must be something connecting them. And, it sounded like Jones may have been involved or known something."

"They went to uni together. They were best mates. It wasn't just work."

"Interesting. We should definitely try to get some time with the Minister to ask him some questions."

"Come to think about it, he was acting weird when I left the room."

"Who was?"

"Jones."

"How do you mean?"

"He was fidgeting and looked agitated. Completely different to when I was in the office. It slipped my mind, given the explosions and escape."

"We will definitely need to ask the Minister about that."

"Yeah we will. Did you get my stuff from the bunker?"

"Bag's in the boot. The jet is waiting for us."

"Us?"

"Yep. I'm coming with you."

"Good. I'm glad you'll be there to have my back. What's your cover?"

"Always. Cover is, I'm there to provide the Minister with legal advice on a defence contract."

"Right. So, what about the tablet we picked up in Parramatta, did Shadow say whether they have found anything?"

"They have broken through several layers of security, but the files are heavily encrypted."

"Will they look into who stole the tablets for Jackson, might give us a lead?"

"He is pulling a special team together to look into it."

"So, we're basically nowhere?"

"Yep."

"Fuck."

They drove down the freeway and took the same exit Max had taken the day before to the airport VIP entrance. Police vehicles were barricading the entry gate. The cars reversed and the bollards lowered on sighting their vehicle. Red and blue lights flashed on the police cars, as orange lights flickered on top of the airport security vehicles. Max could see police had cordoned off the site of the shootout. Police tape was running between cars in a wide square around the wrecked Merc which was still parked there on the grass. Forensics teams were tidying up after pulling an all-night shift to document the scene. Brown paper and plastic evidence bags were being loaded into a blue police van. A tow truck was on the grass in front of the

Mercedes with its back tilted down readying to load it up and take it away.

In the distance, a second forensics team was combing the grassed areas either side of the runway. They walked in a straight line. There must have been twenty or more of them looking for any remaining fragments of the rocket or debris before they could reopen the runway.

Max and Flash drove into the AIS hanger. The same white Gulfstream had returned to collect them. They walked up the stairs and said good morning to the pilots and flight attendant. Hulk was waiting on board. He was sitting in one of the rear business class seats reading the local tabloid.

"Good morning Hulk," Flash said.

"What's so fucking good about it?" Hulk said not looking up from the paper.

"Don't worry about him Flash, he is not a morning person," Max said.

"I see that," Flash said.

Hulk lowered his paper and raised an eyebrow unimpressed at Max. He picked up the phone in his armrest.

"Let's go fellas," he said to the pilots.

The engines started and the door folded itself into place. Max and Flash took seats facing each other across the aisle from Hulk.

"Where are we at?" Max asked as Hulk stuffed the paper into a side pocket.

"Forensics are still on the scene at the Commonwealth Building," Hulk said. "Blake and the analysts are still working on cleaning up the image of the guy who shot Jones and they are getting close to cracking the tablet's encryption. We need to debrief on your meeting with Mr Jones."

"He spoke about the company's new drone fleet and the delivery schedule. They have moved it forward, hoping to organise a handover next week. The PM and Defence Minister are doing the big media circus handover ceremony at

Richmond Air Force Base where the fleet is based on NorthStar's compound."

"Any issues with it?" Flash asked.

"Jones left me with a written briefing. It said trial runs at Woomera have shown it to be highly effective in strike capability. Sea trials have proven its stealth capability is next generation, and its range and performance tests have exceeded even the company's expectations. Plus, about thirty to forty percent on publicly released figures."

"Any threats?"

"Nothing out of the ordinary. Usual suspects, lefties, greenies and do-gooders protesting. Middle-Eastern and some Eastern-European opposition to the purchase. Some footage of the drone is being used in radical propaganda."

"Do you think the Jones hit was related to the launch?" Flash asked.

"Certainly possible," Hulk said. "Some terrorist nut-job takes out the CEO of a defence contractor about to launch a drone fleet which will devastate their fight in the Middle-East. A warning maybe."

"Becomes a pretty strong warning if they successfully take out the Minister who signed the contract too," Max said.

"True," Hulk agreed looking out the window to reflect on that thought.

"The biggest feature, but also the highest security risk of the fleet, is how mobile their operation systems are. They each have a suitcase which can control the drone from anywhere in the world. They've got built in screens and joysticks, the works."

"And, where do they keep those cases?" Flash asked.

"Jones said they were buried under the compound at Richmond. He seemed quite sure that the security was high."

"Then he got shot in the face," Hulk said. "I think we should keep an eye on Richmond."

The plane had taxied to the runway. It had been given special clearance for take-off. The engines whirled and the captain released the brakes sending the jet speeding down the runway. After only a short distance, it lifted off the ground at what felt like ninety degrees. Straight up. The force pushed the passengers back into their soft leather seats. It punched through the clouds and levelled out, then banked heading for Canberra.

Max text Sam.

Hey Sam, sorry I had to shoot through early this morning. I had a great night and miss you already. So, I'm on my way back to Canberra because Parliament has been recalled. I'll be there for a few days I think, but I'd really like to come back to Sydney to see you after that. I really like you and want to spend more time with you. I know it's complicated but I'm sure we can figure something out. Miss your face xx

"Hulk, any progress on the files we recovered from Crown a couple of nights ago?" Flash asked. "Max said Jackson told him he sold the businessman the IT equipment."

Max thought back to the previous morning and the files he had transferred to Hulk near Sam's house.

The night before he and Flash had run an operation in Western Sydney. Intelligence had confirmed a Middle-Eastern businessman was sending money offshore to fund radicalised groups in their fight against the West. It was also suspected that the man was part of a wider terror cell operating in Sydney. He was CEO of a large company called Crown Constructions. Hulk authorised the operation. Max and Flash were to enter Crown, gather any further intelligence they could find and take the businessman into custody.

Max and Flash had met several blocks away from the Crown building in a dark alley. They were dressed head-to-toe in black ops gear. Both had silenced pistols on each thigh and a hunting knife. Max had a small tablet computer in a nylon case Velcroed to his lower back. Small green lights on silenced MP5s lit up in unison as Max and Flash gripped the handles.

The two agents made their way through the dark backstreets to the alley behind the businessman's building. Dust and paper skipped along the alley from the light wind. Dumpsters were overflowing from nearby businesses. Crown's building was around thirty storeys from the ground to the top floor.

Max extended the stock and raised his gun sighting the security camera on the corner of the building watching the alley. With a soft thump, a bullet spat from the end of the MP5's silencer and smashed into the camera disabling it. Flash shot the camera above the building's service door. *Crown Constructions Loading Dock*, the sign on the door read.

The pair ran to the door. Max swiped an access card through the door's security panel as Flash provided cover. The tablet on his back beeped as it finished decoding the door's access code. He swiped the card again and the door opened with a soft mechanical buzz.

There was minimal lighting on throughout the building and the service garage was barely lit by two small lights on each wall. It was a big space, filled with crates and boxes. Like the dumpsters outside, the bins in the building were overflowing with paper, cupboard and plastic sheeting. Max and Flash silently moved through the garage using the stacks for cover. To reach the far end they crawled on all fours, making their way under the window of the security room. Silently Max stood and very slowly opened the door of the security room. He snuck up behind the security guard and with violent force slammed the stock of the MP5 into the back of his head, knocking him out. Flash threw Max a wad of cable ties which he used to secure the guard to his chair.

"Check this out, Prince," Flash said.

Max looked at the guard's computer screen. He had been scrolling through a jihadi website showing images of beheadings of western prisoners of war. Preaching death to infidels. The footage was horrific. Men in orange jumpsuits were dragged one at a time into the shot and forced to their knees in front of a black flag. A blunt machete the weapon of choice. Max angered watching the screen.

"Hmm, well looks like we are in the right place," Max said.

Flash took out his phone, snapped a picture and sent it to the operations centre with the message: *Hermes, Send backup and a cleaning crew – proceeding to target. Flash.*

The door opened behind them revealing a second security guard.

"I cannot get the external cameras rebooted," the guard said in Arabic.

He looked up and saw Max and Flash levelling their guns at him then to his companion fastened to his chair. He was a big guy, at least two inches taller than Max. He wore a security uniform with the company logo on the right breast of his shirt. He had a dark black beard and tanned skin.

"Hands up and get on your knees," Max said.

The guard raised his hands slowly. His eyes were burning with anger. In a split second, he leapt forward lunging at Max. Max threw the butt of the gun towards his oncoming head. It connected just as the guard's hand came down on the alarm button and he fell to the ground as the alarm sounded. Red lights started flashing and the alarms whooped.

"Oh, fuck me," Max said raising the gun and pointing it at the door.

Flash hit the alarm button again silencing it. He then cable tied the second guard to the first.

"Time to move," Max said heading for the door, finger on the trigger.

Flash followed. Moving together as one they swept the fire stairs floor by floor. Passing the tenth, they heard doors fling open and movement above and below as men ran into the stairwell on at least two floors.

They pushed open the door on the eleventh floor and instinctively dived to the floor as bullets hit the doorframe and wall behind them.

Max scrambled left, flipping a table.

"Federal Agents, throw down your weapons," Max yelled.

Bullets hit the table Max was using for cover.

"Fine, we'll do it your way," he said.

He sprung up from behind his makeshift cover, sighted a man in full Islamic robes with the gun and fired a quick volley of shots into the terrorist throwing him off his feet.

Flash moved quickly in behind the cover as the terrorist fell and two more similarly dressed guys appeared at the far end of the room.

"We can't stay here," Flash said readying to shoot anything that came through. "They will be through the door behind us in seconds."

"Got it," Max said removing a flashbang grenade from his ops vest and throwing it over the table in one smooth motion.

"Move now," Max yelled just before the flashbang exploded piercing the air with sound and blinding white light.

As they ran for the left-hand row of offices they each shot in the direction of the terrorists who were hunched over clutching their eyes and ears. The bullets hit their mark reddening their white robes with blood as they fell to the floor.

Max and Flash clambered through the door and tucked in behind the office wall as the fire door flung open. Bullets were sprayed everywhere, shooting at nothing and everything. Glass shattered and plasterboard puffed as holes were ripped open from the impacting bullets. Four guys came into the room searching for targets.

Staying low, Max quietly laid on the floor and army crawled to the door. He stuck his head around the frame for a sneak peek.

"Four by the door, I'll take the two on the left," Max said. "On three. One, two, three."

On three Max slid himself halfway through the door as Flash stood up behind the office window. The agents loosened four shots each. Two for each terrorist. The four men fell.

"Let's move," Max said.

In unison they moved, covering each other back to the door and up the fire stairs. Again, they swept each level in the stair well.

Level thirty. Top floor. The agents loaded new magazines into the guns.

"Ready?" Max asked.

"Let's do it," Flash said.

Max swiped the card in the security panel reader. The tablet beeped and Max swiped the card again unlocking the door.

A man was sitting behind the desk at the far end of the opulent office space and two Arab men were sitting on lounges halfway between the agents and the businessman. The businessman was wearing a new charcoal suit and white shirt. He had a trimmed and neat beard, and a bald head. He was an average build and podgy around the mid-section. He had a gold necklace and six gold rings on his fingers.

"Welcome gentlemen," the businessman said. "You could have just made an appointment."

"Shut the fuck up, you're coming with us," Max said.

"Please. There is no need for the language."

"You must be kidding. You just sent a bunch of arseholes to kill us and you're worried about some swearing?"

"We were defending ourselves against intruders. We are legitimate businesspeople and you have no right to be here."

"Legitimate my arse mate," Max said. "I announced us as Federal Agents and they started shooting. You are a terrorist and you are coming with us. You are under arrest."

"Under arrest," the businessman scoffed. "I do not think so."

On cue the men on the lounges sprung from their seats and ran at Max and Flash. The two agents shot the men as they ran. Max nailed his guy between the eyes and he fell at Max's feet. Flash's shot had only grazed the guy's neck. Non-fatal.

The businessman was on his feet running towards the exit door. Max gave chase. He shot twice, the bullets hitting the doorframe as the businessman ran through.

Flash was tackled by one of the Arab men from the lounge. He dropped his gun and the two men wrestled on the floor.

Max left Flash to deal with the guard. He needed to get the businessman.

Max flew through the door into the private stairwell that led to the roof, following the fleeing businessman. He ran up the stairs and out onto the roof. The businessman was scrambling for the door of his helicopter. Max shot the helicopter smashing the pilot's side of the windshield with a volley of bullets. The businessman fell to the ground and started crab walking backwards away from the helicopter.

"Please, what do you want? Money? I will pay whatever you want. Do you want the helicopter? It is yours."

"Why the fuck would I want that? It's got a smashed windscreen."

"I will buy you a new one."

"No thanks," Max said as he shot the businessman through the left kneecap.

The terrorist screamed in pain and yelled a long string of expletives in Arabic. Max recognised a few words. Infidel. Death. Hell.

Max hung the MP5 on his back and drew his hunting knife and the tablet. He held the knife to the businessman's throat and said, "Put your hand on the computer screen."

"Fuck you!"

"Please. There is no need for the language," Max said mockingly repeating his earlier phrase.

Max drove the knife into the Arab's right bicep and twisted it disabling his arm. His left hand shot across to protect the wound when Max removed the knife. As his left hand wrapped the wounded arm, Max stabbed the businessman through the left hand. The knife past through his hand and went back into the bicep wound, pinning his hand to his disabled arm. He screamed in pain and started cursing again.

Max ignored him as he placed the guy's right palm on the tablet screen. He hit the home button three times and the screen flickered. The terrorist leader was still cursing and spitting, rocking back and forth in pain. Max kept ignoring him as he put the tablet back on his back then began searching his pockets. He retrieved keys, a wallet and a mobile phone. He placed the items in his vest pockets.

"Alrighty then let's head back downstairs and see if my partner has killed your last minion yet," Max said standing the businessman up.

"You will pay for what you have done. My Arab brothers and sisters will no longer sit by as the West destroys our faith and our countries, and spreads its filth. Your nations are plagued by your lack of faith in the one true God, Allah. Christianity, atheism, rampant promiscuity, your so-called democracy led by hypocritical and selfish men, false pretence warmongering, killing innocent Arab women and children for oil, and your willingness to accept the scourge of the repugnant unholy sin that is homosexuality. The West will pay for its insolence and interference."

Max spun around and lent in towards the fundamentalist. Their faces were only a few inches apart. He grabbed the knife and twisted it ripping muscles and tendons. Forcing the man to scream in pain.

"Listen to me you terrorist piece of shit," Max said. "You will never win. Freedom. Equality. Love. Democracy. These are the things that will overcome your radicalised, nonsense view of the world."

The severely injured man went to speak, but was interrupted.

"Oh and by the way," Max said. "I'm gay."

With that he lent around and kissed the businessmen on the cheek before laughing in his ear. The man started swearing and backed away from Max. Max grabbed him and led him down the stairs back into the office.

On the left of the room was the man from the lounge. Flash was on the right a few metres away standing with his hands in the air looking into the barrel of his own gun. The man from the lounge laughed when he saw Max and his boss re-enter the room.

"Let him go or I will shoot your friend here," the guard said.

"That won't be happening," Max said.

"You do not care about your friend's life?"

"I do. Very much."

"Well, let the boss go or I will fucking kill him."

"Gee whiz again with the language, your boss does not like that."

"Right. That is it, say goodbye."

Max laughed.

"I will but not to Flash, I'll say goodbye to you."

The guard pulled the trigger, but the weapon didn't fire. Confused, he looked down at the gun and tried again. Nothing. He frantically looked at Flash then to Max.

"Goodbye," Max said.

The man from the couch looked at Max confused before he turned to see Flash draw his pistol. The guard pulled the MP5's trigger repeatedly but nothing happened. Flash shot the man twice. Head and chest. Dead. Then walked over and reclaimed his gun.

"That looks painful," Flash said to the businessman seeing his arms pinned with Max's knife as he joined them at the far end of the room.

"If he moves shoot him," Max said walking to the Arab man's desk.

Flash pointed the MP5 at the terrorist, as he made to follow Max.

"Stay away from my desk," he said.

"Stop, I won't warn you again," Flash said.

"I am not worried, your gun is empty," the businessman said mockingly.

Flash squeezed the trigger and the bullet hit the window behind the desk missing him by millimetres. The terrorist froze.

"How?"

"Magic, now stay still or I will kill you," Flash said knowing all AIS weapons were synced to Agents' security rings.

Max removed his tablet and connected it to the businessman's. It flickered to life, revealing the lock screen. *Enter password or touch the scanner,* appeared on the screen.

"Get over here," Max demanded.

Just then the door at the end of the room opened and four guys stormed into the room, guns drawn. The windows behind the desk cracked and groaned as they were hit with bullets. Max and Flash dropped to the ground, moving quickly for cover.

The gun fire stopped.

Flash looked up to see the businessman coughing up blood. He had been hit in the chest. He fell back on the cracked glass. Flash lunged for him as the window shattered and he began to fall.

Flash grabbed for him catching Max's knife handle which was still lodged through his left hand and in his right bicep. It sliced right out of the man's hand and came free.

The terrorist fell thirty stories to his death, screaming the whole way down.

Max jumped up and fired in the direction of the door, scattering the four guys. It gave Flash enough time to turn and run back to join Max behind the desk.

"Here's your knife," Flash said smiling.

"Ha. Thanks," Max said putting it back in its holster.

Max knelt behind the desk and peered over the top. Bullets kicked up on the desk. He slid back in beside Flash reaching up with his left hand feeling for the tablets. Bullets hit the desk as he grabbed one of the mini computers and dragged it off the edge into his lap. It was his, so he opened it and tapped away starting an app designed by the AIS tech guys. The app opened on the screen and he typed a combination of words into the space. *Download contents AND backup. Execute.* A progress bar and a familiar, *Authenticating,* filled the display.

Max left the tablet hanging from the cable before springing up and shooting in the direction of the bullets that had hit the desk moments before.

Flash moved left. He saw the top of one guy's head appear trying to look around the chair he was hiding behind. Flash hit it with a bullet and watched as the head hit the floor and did not move.

"One down," Flash said.

As he went to return to cover he saw another guy stand and start firing. Bullets whizzed past Flash. He swung his MP5 around and shot the guy in the heart.

"Two down," Flash said.

"What are we keeping score?" Max asked.

"I was thinking more like, I've done my bit. Your turn."

"Oh, that's how it is hey?" Max said as he knelt and rested his gun on the table for support. He shot the lights and panels out above where the last two guys were crouched behind the far lounge.

The panels and pieces of neon light fell towards the guys below. They moved to flee the falling debris only to be hit by a bullet each to the head.

"Three and four down," Max said sarcastically.

"Wow, that was pretty impressive."

"Still surprised I can out shoot you after all these years?"

"Nah, surprised your fragile office worker hands can still handle the gun," Flash said jokingly.

"Like you can talk lawyer boy."

"Let's get out of here."

"Good idea," Max said checking his tablet.

It had copied the files from the businessman's computer and had begun to start the backup process. *Uploading backup to personal identification and security key* scrolled across the screen to indicate the information was being transferred to Max's ring.

Sitting in the Gulfstream, Max remembered he and Flash had exited the building as the backup teams and clean-up crew arrived. They shook hands and went their separate ways. Max had changed in the back of his car before returning to his hotel. He showered, changed and then went to the bar where he would soon meet Sam.

Sam, he smiled thinking of his new friend.

Hulk lifted the phone in his armrest.

"Put me through to Shadow in the bunker," Hulk said.

"Hello?" Lloyd said thirty seconds later.

"Was there anything in the files Prince and Flash retrieved last night?" Hulk asked.

"I took a few people off that to work with the forensics teams and the tablet tech guys, so we haven't gotten through it all yet," Lloyd said.

"We're thinking this could be an assassination and attempted assassination related to the drone purchase. If so, then our splattered friend they peeled off the pavement in Western Sydney the night before last is likely to have known something about it, especially now Jackson has linked the tablet sales. Look into it, will you?"

"Sure thing Hulk," Lloyd said.

The flight attendant brought them coffee and breakfast. Max's phone beeped with a message from Sam.

Hey handsome, I'm sorry you had to leave early to go back to Canberra. Sad face. I miss you too. I really like you too. Let me know when you are coming back to Sydney. I agree. Complicated. But, I think we definitely have a connection that I've never had before so I want to see where we can take it. Come back soon. Xx

There was an AIS Landcruiser waiting for them in a private hanger at Canberra Airport. It was black with heavily tinted windows and it was completely bulletproof. Sitting behind the wheel was another member of Max's team, Alpha. Alpha was several years older than Max. They had worked together many times and Max knew how well she could drive. In fact, he could not think of anyone better behind the wheel, especially when you needed to get out quick.

"Good to see you, Kate," Max said to the driver.

"Hi Max," Kate said.

Kate "Alpha" Matthews had been a Lieutenant in the Australian Army. She was the first female Commando in the Special Forces and came to Hulk's attention on a mission he was commanding in the Middle-East before joining AIS. Hulk had been impressed by Kate's skills and her intelligence, and recruited her several years before Max had started with AIS. She was actually part of the team, along with Blake, who had trained Max and Flash at the Wool Shed. She was about Max's height and build with dark brown hair which she had all but shaved off. She was a masculine figure, tough as nails and she could match any opponent in strength and skill. Max knew she had a softer side under her rough demeanour but not many got to see it. She was in a business suit which Max knew she would hate wearing. One of her Commando crew gave her the nickname Alpha after she bested three of their teammates sparing to become the Alpha in the group.

"Hey, Alpha," Flash said climbing into the back seat.

"Hey, Flash," Kate said. "You boys have been fucking busy. Still in one piece?"

"Yeah mate thanks, but I'm glad to see you. Looking sharp in that suit. Are you with us for the day?"

Kate gave him an unimpressed look.

"She's with you until further notice," Hulk said climbing into the front seat.

"Hi Hulk, welcome back to Canberra. Straight to the Parliament?"

"Yes, please."

The big V8 roared off the mark and headed for Capital Hill.

Chapter Twenty

When they arrived, they parked under the Ministerial Wing of Parliament House and headed for the elevator.

"I'm going to see the Prime Minister, then I'm going to head back to AIS to get a progress report," Hulk said. "You three head to Max's office and maintain your covers. I will be in touch when I know more."

When the doors opened, Hulk walked one way and the others headed down the opposite corridor.

"Okay, so Flash you are a corporate lawyer in town to provide legal advice to the Minister," Max said.

"Right," Flash said.

"And, Kate, you're extra security given what happened yesterday?"

"Yes mate."

"Alright, let's do it."

They approached the office, following the blue carpet of the Ministerial Wing. The office had a large polished hardwood set of doors in an ornate matching oversized doorframe. It had polished brass doorhandles and doorstops, and a large brass light fitting which ran the length of the set of doors hung from the recess above. A small glass plaque gave the suite number and read *Minister for Defence James Johnston.*

"Rightio, here we go," Max said as they walked into the foyer.

It was a relatively small space. Two stiff, uncomfortable, green almost grey, lounges sat on either side on the foyer. There was a small coffee table with an assortment of magazines and books between them. A large polished reception desk sat in front of a Picasso-like painting of random shapes and colours. Max hated that painting. He didn't like abstract art. There was just something about it. He liked art that looked like whatever it was the artist was trying to recreate, not some impressionist's mind-melting view of the world.

Black and white, and some coloured photos of military service personnel and hardware dressed the remaining walls throughout the office. Max particularly liked the photo chosen for his office of an F/A18 Super Hornet breaking the sound barrier. A perfect light blue sky was interrupted by a white vortex which circled the rear of the plane as if it had just smashed right through a cloud. Max had always wanted to be a fighter pilot but given his frame, he was too tall to fit in the cockpit. He had his pilot's licence and he had flown the AIS Gulfstreams a couple of times, although they basically fly themselves these days. He enjoyed it either way, but it still was not a fighter jet.

Max introduced Flash and Kate to the office. Max's colleagues were all visibly nervous and upset from the events of the previous day. The death toll was over seventy, most of whom worked for Ministers and various lobby groups. Max's colleagues all had connections to someone hurt or killed at the Commonwealth Building and their pain was clear and real. Max did his best to comfort those he spoke to about the incident. His own anger building inside with every story of heartache. He was going to find the people who did this and make them suffer.

Sarah hugged Max.

"Hi Max," Sarah said. "Thank you again."

"Hey Sarah," Max said. "You don't have to thank me. I was just doing my job."

"Without you, I wouldn't be standing here. The Minister and I were going to run out of the office. You stopped us and protected us. I…the bomb…so close to our office…we'd have been killed."

"We were lucky, Sarah," Max said giving her another hug. "I'm just glad you're safe. Let me know if you need anything. Is the Minister here?"

"Yeah, he is in his office. I'm sure he'd like to see you."

"Thanks, Sarah. Hey, look after Kate and Flash, will you?"

"Of course, friends of yours?"

"The best. I'll go see the boss."

Max knocked on the Minister's door.

"Come in," Johnston said.

Max walked in and closed the door behind him. It was a decent sized office. The far wall behind Johnston's desk was all windows looking into the Prime Minister's courtyard. Sunlight streamed in through the slatted wooden blinds. A bookcase ran the length of the left-hand wall, filled with official gifts from world leaders and books on various subjects from politics to military strategy. Three computer monitors and two phones as well as a stack of paperwork sat on the Minister's hardwood desk. An open briefcase was sitting on the conference table next to a vase of flowers, a tablet computer and a teleconference phone. Another ugly painting hung next to the conference table. Max hated it too. The Minister's choice again.

"Hi, Max," Johnston said standing and walking around from behind his desk to shake Max's hand. "Thank you for yesterday, Max."

"It's really no problem at all. As I said to Sarah, I was just doing my job."

"You don't need to be modest Max. I can't thank you enough."

"It's my job Minister."

"Well still. Thank you. So, have we gotten any closer to finding out what happened?"

"No, but we have a few leads to follow up. I'm with you until further notice and so are my colleagues Flash and Kate."

"Three of you?"

"Yes, Minister."

"And, Agent Carrol and his team?"

"Yes, he will be escorting you everywhere until the threat has cleared. Is he here?"

"Yeah he drove me here. He's in the conference room with another Fed. I've got five highly trained agents in close proximity and you mentioned the threat. What aren't you telling me?"

"We are just being extra cautious. Although, I was wondering if you might be able to help me with something?"

"What's that?"

"Well, given a few of the details we have pieced together already from the bombing, we're looking for connections between you and Mr Jones, and the attackers. Is there anything else, other than the obvious links you have in your current roles? Any other links you think might be worth exploring?"

"No, Max," Johnston said after a brief pause. "Not that I can think of. We've been friends for a long time. Why?"

"We think that the two of you might have been the targets. The working theory is radicals who are upset about the new drone fleet wanted to take you out."

The Minister shifted uncomfortably, reflecting on the thought.

"Maybe, Max. I'm sorry I just can't think of anything else it could be. Poor Bill. God, I'm just devastated about losing him."

"Yes, I'm very sorry about your friend. Let me know if anything else comes to mind."

"I will. I will. The Prime Minister's speech is in thirty minutes and then the Israeli PM is going to speak too. The PM's asked me to make some remarks after the Opposition Leader's reply from a Defence perspective and given I was in the building. I better have another practice. I'll see you after. Thanks again."

"Okay, probably best to leave out the safe room details. Something like 'I got lucky. I was in a stronger part of the building.' You know what I mean. Good luck."

"Yes. Good point. I won't mention the safe room. Thanks again, Max."

"Anytime Minister."

Max went to the conference room and after knocking on the door he walked in.

"Agent Shaw, I hear you had quite the day yesterday," Carrol said.

"You could say that, and please, call me Max. How are you?"

"I'm fine. Not the first time someone has tried to shoot me out of the sky, but certainly one of the closest to actually achieving it. Thank God for the new jet hey?"

"Yeah, it's an impressive plane. Flew up on it this morning."

"Max, this is Agent Jill Stevenson, my deputy," Carrol said.

"Agent Shaw, nice to meet you," Stevenson said.

Stevenson was a tall and broad-shouldered woman. She was wearing a dark blue suit with light blue shirt, all of which was about two sizes too big. She was not wearing makeup and her hair was cut short achieving a masculine look with the bulky attire, no doubt all designed to fit in with the boy's club.

"And, nice to meet you too Agent Stevenson," Max said. "I take it you have both seen the footage from the Commonwealth Building?"

"Yes," Carrol said. "We're working with AIS to get an ID on the man who shot Mr Jones."

"Good. Hulk's in with the PM now then he's going back to AIS to get a progress report. I'll let you know if I hear anything."

"Likewise. Thank you, Max," Carrol said.

"The speech will be on shortly. The video conference screen over there streams the Parliament if you want to watch."

"Great, we will indeed," Carrol said as Stevenson walked over and turned on the television.

Max left the room and headed for his office. He turned on the television and tuned into the feed from the House of Representatives. Members of Parliament had started to gather, quietly speaking with each other and milling around. It was an impressive Chamber. Max had read that the green colour had been altered from the green of the Westminster Lower House. It was lighter, with a blue tinge, symbolically coloured to look like gum leaves from native Australian trees. Sunlight poured down from a large glass pyramid built into the roof above the centre table which held the dispatch boxes where the Prime Minister and Opposition Leader sat across from one another. Max watched the MP's enter until he was interrupted by his ringing phone.

"Hello," Max said.

"Prince, it's Hermes," Blake said. *"I'm calling to let you know we have unlocked the tablet and the files are moments away from being decrypted."*

"That's good news. The Prime Ministers are about to address the Parliament. How far off are we on the decryption?"

"Maybe sixty seconds."

"Great. Loop in Hulk and Shadow. I'll go get Flash and Alpha."

"Ack," Blake acknowledged.

Max ran across the office.

"Flash, Kate, come with me," Max said not stopping to discuss. "The tablet and files are close to decryption. I'm on with the Bunker."

Flash and Kate followed Max back to his office and closed the door. Both Flash and Kate paused to take in the Super Hornet photo on the wall before taking a seat opposite Max. Max laid the phone down on his desk and the speaker crackled.

"We're here Hermes," Max said.

"Acknowledged, Prince, Hulk and Shadow are on the line and the line is secure," Blake said. *"Prince, I'm remotely accessing your computer and Hulk, I've accessed your vehicle's entertainment system, you will all be able to see what Shadow and I are seeing."*

Max turned the screen so Flash and Kate could both see it.

"Confirmed, Hermes, we can see it," Flash said.

"Receiving clearly," Hulk said. *"I'm two minutes out from AIS Canberra."*

The television mounted on the wall of Max's office showed the Prime Minister and Ministers arriving in the Chamber. The Sergeant-At-Arms proceeded the Speaker of the House with the gold mace. The symbol of the Queen. It was placed on the rack and the Speaker climbed up to his seat at the front of the Chamber. They conducted the normal opening of Parliament rituals, including the acknowledgement of country and prayers.

"Sergeant, please ask the Senate to join us for an address from the Prime Ministers of Australia and Israel," the Speaker of the House said from the television.

"They have done the prayers and acknowledgement of country in the Parliament," Max said. "The Speaker has just invited Senators to the Chamber. It'll take them a couple of minutes to arrive then they'll invite the Israeli PM in."

"Alrighty, here are the first few documents," Blake said as everyone's screens slowly loaded the documents.

"This is a biography of Mr William "Bill" Jones, Chief Executive Officer, NorthStar, a defence industry contractor based in Sydney, New South Wales. Sadly, we do know Mr Jones."

"That confirms he was a target," Flash said.

"The second document is a schematic. It looks like wires and a mobile phone."

"And, C4," Hulk interrupted. *"This is a backpack bomb design. No doubt the bombs they used at the Commonwealth Building. Next."*

"Okay, umm here we go, document three," Blake said as the screens simultaneously closed the previous file and began opening the third. *"It looks like a blueprint."*

Level by level the building blueprint loaded on the screen from the top down.

"It's the Commonwealth Building," Flash said. "Same one Max and I found on the wall at the house in Parramatta."

On the television, the Israeli Prime Minister had just entered the Chamber and was shaking hands of Ministers as he approached the front of the House where a chair was waiting for him next to the Speaker's. When he took his seat, the Australian Prime Minister got to his feet and began his address to the Parliament.

"The blueprint had the Crown Constructions logo on it Hulk. Looks like it's all connected."

"I just arrived back at AIS, I'll get a progress report from the team going through the files you downloaded from Crown after this call," Hulk said. *"Next file Hermes."*

The window was replaced with a new one.

"It's a video file," Blake said.

"Play it," Hulk said.

The video started. A series of speeches from former Prime Minister's from both major parties played. One by one they were arguing the virtues of Australia's commitment to various wars and Australian values. World War One, World War Two, Korea, Vietnam, the Gulf, Iraq, Afghanistan, Syria.

"We will increase defence spending and investment, and we will strike down those who would silence democracy. We will kill those who seek to terrorise our nation and our allies, and those who would destroy our freedom. We will end the radicalisation of vulnerable young adults and we will halt the spread of fundamentalism. We will prevail. We will succeed. We will not rest until we have peace.

Those were the words of the current Prime Minister. The same Prime Minister who was on his feet in the Chamber giving a very similar speech to the Parliament.

The video cut to the Defence Minister signing a contract with Mr Jones for the purchase of the new drone fleet. A heavily accented voiceover said: *"you will not prevail. You will not succeed. What happened at the Commonwealth Building was just the beginning. No one is safe. We will spread fear throughout your nation of morally bankrupt sinners. We will punish you for your past wrongs. We will continue to cripple your Government and continue to spread terror until you pull all of your troops out of the Middle-East. Death to the unbelievers. Praise be to God. Allah Akbar."*

"Well, that was fucking ominous," Kate said.

"Just the beginning? What could be next?" Flash asked.

"He said 'cripple your Government,' do you think he was referring to the Minister?" Max asked.

"No, he said 'continue to cripple your Government,'" Hulk corrected. *"This was made before they knew James Johnston got out. Something bigger is coming. Are there any other documents on the tablet?"*

"Just one," Blake said. *"Here."*

The video player closed and the final file opened. It was another blueprint. It was loading painfully slowly. Line after line of solid blue until right in the centre of the blueprint a spire of some sort was taking shape. Then Max saw it. It wasn't a spire. It was a flag pole. The distinctive thirty-two tonne stainless steel flagpole which rose above Parliament House.

"Fuck me," Max said. "It's Parliament."

An horrific sound came from the television on the wall as two hundred and twenty-six Members of Parliament and Senators, and the Israeli Prime Minister screamed as they were covered in glass from above.

Chapter Twenty-One

Two vans arrived on Capital Hill.

Each van escorted by two motorbikes.

One van and its accompanying bikes sped up to the front of the building, while the others accelerated towards the Ministerial Wing at the rear of the building.

At the front, one of the bikes broke from the group, mounted the kerb and sped across the forecourt towards the front door of Parliament House. It past the water fountain which was carved out of the centre of the forecourt and raced across the crushed red rock. The rider and passenger opened fire on the heavily armed federal police guards, killing them instantly. They rode to the front door and jumped off the bike and began shooting wildly into the crowd of tourists, public servants, lobbyists and businesspeople who had been lining up to visit the Parliament. The crowd began running for their lives. One by one they were gunned down as they ran. Men and women in business suits fell. Tourists in jeans and t-shirts with cameras and backpacks scrambled and fell as they were hit with bullets. A large group of school children who had been standing in line waiting to go inside and their teachers were mercilessly cut down where they stood. The two men shot the heavy glass doors and jumped through the empty doorframes into the marble foyer. The spectacular foyer was filled with terror as screams echoed off the ten-thousand-year-old marble from Greece and Belgium. Security guards were shot down behind their sign in desks. Attendants and visitors, most of whom had been gathered around a television showing the Prime Minister's speech, were hit by sweeping gunfire. It smashed into ornate wood panels and chipped the marble. Once the screams had stopped the two men stopped firing and headed for the elevator.

As innocent people fell in the forecourt, the front van had reversed up to the security bollards which blocked access to the building's roof. The back doors flew open. Four men dressed in black paramilitary uniforms jumped out dragging two metal beams out over the bollards. Each beam was made of a flat section about three feet long which sat on top of the bollards and a seven or eight feet long slopping section which unfolded to create a ramp from the bollard down to the grass. The two men on each side dragged a second set of metal planks out the door of the van. The short, sharp zip of electric drills, filled the air as they bolted plank and beams creating makeshift ramps over the bollards.

The second motorbike darted between the bollards. Its rider and passenger fired wildly at security guards and police who were making their way down the sloped hill, taking them down.

The four men jumped back in the van. It drove forward letting the beams fall into place leading up to the bollards. The van made a U-turn, accelerated and hit the ramp. It scrapped as it went over the beam mid-section between the metal planks, but the driver had enough speed. It bounced over the bollards and onto the grass. The driver gunned the van flying past its escort bike, climbing the grass hill leading to the top of Parliament House. The van smashed hard into the new metal fence buckling it with surprising ease and tore up the grass creating a path for the bike.

At the Ministerial entrance at the rear of the building, one of the bikes broke away and climbed the stairs towards the new guardhouse. The passenger shot one of the Feds who had been on sentry duty near the guardhouse. A second police officer jumped clear and scrambled behind a potted plant for cover. She sprang up from behind the concrete pot and sprayed the bike, and its rider and passenger with bullets. The bike toppled and fell halfway back down the stairs, pinning the passenger.

The police officer turned to see a matt black van. Its passengers were dressed in black military kit and they were heavily armed. They looked like they were assembling some sort of ramp from beams and planks over the bollards. She reached for her radio to call it in, but she didn't get the chance. The bike passenger shot her twice in the chest from his position pinned under the bike and his fallen comrade. Blood dripped from her mouth and poured from the holes in her chest. She fell to the ground as the second bike used the new ramp to jump the bollards. It was closely followed by the black van, both now heading up the grass slope. She watched as the van ran down two of her fellow officers who had run into its path firing their pistols. Another shot hit her in the shoulder and she turned her attention back to the passenger on the steps. She fired two shots killing him before her world went black.

The two vans met at the top of Parliament House under the iconic flagpole. They were both damaged from smashing through the fences that ringed the House. Each van held four people, and the two bikes each had a rider and passenger. The crew were all wearing the same black paramilitary gear, plus machine guns, pistols, knives, tactical vests and balaclavas.

A crew member from each van opened their respective side doors. Inside the vans, identical industrial steel frames were mounted to the floors. Their A-frame design stood around one metre high, joined at the apex by a solid steel pole which ran the length of the vans' cargo space. The pole held six climbing ropes which were attached to individual winches. All twelve men connected their lines to the shackles on their vests.

The men ran to different locations above the House of Representatives trailing their rope lines. When they were in position, the lead crew member raised his hand above his head. His index finger raised then his middle finger. As he raised his ring finger, each man threw a small plastic explosive at the glass panel of the pyramid in front of them. The explosives hit the glass and shattered it instantly.

As the shards rained down inside the Parliament, to the screams of the MPs and Senators, each of the men from the roof leapt through the now open window frames. Ropes spooled out before slowly stopping each man inches above the floor.

The men cut their ropes.

Five landed on the table in the centre of the Parliament. It sat between the dispatch boxes, and the Prime Minister and

Opposition Leader, and in front of the Israeli Prime Minister and Speaker of the House. The seven others landed in various places around the outer perimeter of the Chamber forming a ring around the Parliamentarians. The seven ran to their nearest door and locked it. Those with glass panels in their doors, pulled out cans of spray paint from their vests and began spraying the windows so no one could see into the Chamber. The others took aim at the closest group of MPs, freezing them in position.

One of the five men on the table ran towards the Prime Minister who was still close to the dispatch box but bleeding from multiple superficial wounds from the splintered glass. He was looking down at his arms and the blood, when the man from the table kicked him in the sternum sending him flailing backwards onto the front bench into the arms of his Ministers.

The Prime Minister was gasping for breath as the man who kicked him jumped from the table onto the small table in front of the Speaker of the House. He loosened a volley of bullets into the Speaker's face, spraying the chair, the Israeli Prime Minister and himself with blood. MPs and Senators began screaming and crying. They were all on their feet, but they were completely surrounded and had nowhere to run. The man on the Speaker's desk, kicked the Speaker's body to the right and it dropped to the floor then he spun around and fell backwards into the now vacated chair.

"Silence!" he yelled into the microphone but the MPs kept screaming.

He fired his gun at the roof.

"Order!" he yelled mockingly.

The MPs slowly quietened, though there was more than one late whimper, to hear what the man had to say over the sobs of many of their colleagues.

"Prime Ministers, elected representatives," the terrorist said, removing his balaclava and looking around the Chamber and at the Israeli Prime Minister on his right with disgust, before finding a camera and looking down the lens. "People of Australia. My name is Dalir. I have taken your Parliament and your Government hostage. We bombed the Commonwealth Building in Sydney. We have gunned down hundreds of your fellow citizens here in Canberra and in Sydney. We killed your Parliament's Speaker. And, we will kill every Minister, Senator and Member of Parliament one-by-one until your Prime Minister agrees to withdraw Australian troops from the Middle-East and agrees to contact his American and British allies forcing them to do the same."

"We, of course, also have the infidel leader of Israel in our possession," Dalir said looking back to the Israeli PM with pure hatred. "A man whose very existence insults me. You are a parasite on the Middle-East and we will not rest until you and your people are dead and erased from the earth."

"You are insane! We will not surrender to the likes of you!" the Attorney General said.

"That is a shame Mister Attorney General, maybe you just have not grasped how serious we are," Dalir said nodding to one of his men from the table.

The man leapt from table and punched the Attorney in the face before grabbing him by the neck and dragging him to the table. Two of his comrades grappled the Attorney and dragged him up onto the long hardwood desk and forced him onto his knees. Dalir nodded again and one of his men raised his gun and shot the Attorney-General in the back of the head. He fell limply and rolled off the table at the row of Ministers' feet.

"Two down," Dalir said. "I am going to cut you down one-by-one until it's just my team and I left in here with you, Prime Ministers. What is it going to be? Why don't you both take a moment to call your allies? And, by the way, for the police and intelligence services listening, each of my men is willing to die for our cause. So, do not try to enter this Chamber or we will open fire. How many of your representatives do you think we can kill before you take us down?"

Chapter Twenty-Two

When the glass fell into the Parliament and the men abseiled in, Max ran to main door leading into the Minister's suite. He bolted the door as the building's alarms sounded.

"Lockdown, lockdown, lockdown," came over the emergency intercom, followed by a whooping alarm.

"Half of you in there and lock the doors," Max shouted to his colleagues and pointed to the Minister's office.

"The rest of you in there and bolt the door," he said pointing to the conference room.

"Carrol, Stevenson, with me," Max said.

The three agents ran back to Max's office while the other staff ran to their secure rooms.

Flash and Kate were already checking their pistols.

"Behind the Hornet, Flash," Max said pointing to the photo of the Air Force fast jet on his wall.

Flash lifted the photo off the wall revealing a wall safe. He waved his ring in front of the access panel and typed in his ID number. The safe opened revealing a weapons cache and various other items including passports and money. Flash pulled out three MP5s and three flick-knives. It was an emergency supply Hulk had fitted years ago, but neither he nor Max genuinely ever expected they would ever be used.

"What about us, have you got spare MP5s?" Stevenson asked.

"Sorry, no can do," Flash said. They are security coded and won't fire unless you are AIS personnel."

"That's what the rings are for?" Stevenson asked mostly to herself.

Flash raised his eyebrows as if to confirm without speaking.

"Clever," she said. "Well, our Glocks will have to do."

"Hulk, any thoughts?" Max asked the phone still connected sitting on his desk.

"He says they will open fire if anyone tries to go in there but we sure as shit can't give this arsehole any real time to inflict damage," Hulk said. *"He'll kill them all eventually. We need to go in, but we can't risk taking them out one-by-one, we need to take them all out in one hit."*

"Right, but how?" Max asked. "He's got them surrounded."

"Divide and conquer," Hulk said. *"Agent Carrol, do you have your radio? Can you reach the other feds in the building?"*

"Yes, General," Carrol said.

"Good. Protocol says they should have opened the weapons vault and should be getting into their ops gear as we speak. Tell them you and Agent Stevenson will meet them. You will need to take command. Once you are geared up, break into four teams. One team for each of the main entrances to the Chamber. You'll be responsible for taking out the perimeter team."

"Okay, General. Not an easy task by any means. There's a huge risk to the representatives."

"I agree, Agent Carrol. But, they'll all be dead if we don't get in there. The risk of inaction is much higher."

"Agreed, we're on it," Carrol said. "We've got this."

"And, us?" Flash asked.

"Flash, Prince and Alpha, get yourselves to the roof. You've got the arseholes on the table and arsehole number one, Dalir. Shoot to kill, but if there is a window to keep one or two breathing for a few minutes do it."

"Got it," Max said.

"Good luck and Godspeed," Hulk said ending the call.

"This is Special Agent Carrol. From this point forward, I am assuming command. Hold at the vault, I'm on route," Carrol said into his radio.

"Understood Agent Carrol. Awaiting your arrival," an officer replied.

"Stevenson, give your radio to Max," Carrol said.

Stevenson unclipped the radio and passed it to Max.

"Thanks," Max said. "The vault is in the basement. Under the Prime Minister's office. Turn right when you leave the suite. Take the second corridor to the left and you'll see the elevator. Follow the signs to the AFP Ops Centre. When you are en route to your positions around the Chamber let me know."

"Roger that, see you on the other side," Carrol said. "Let's go, Stevenson."

"Flash, Alpha put these on," Max said throwing the two agents balaclavas and putting on his own. "There are cameras everywhere. Right, let's move."

Flash was on Max's left and Kate on his right. The three agents had the balaclavas on but were all still dressed in their business suits as they cleared the hallways. Flash and Kate had their MP5s raised, scanning the corridors as they moved. Max had his MP5 slung over his shoulder and had his silenced pistol drawn with both hands providing support. The three agents moved as one in a crouched walk.

Staff had heeded the warnings and were bunkered down in their offices meaning the hallways were all clear. There was an eerie stillness in the corridors. Thousands of staff huddled behind close doors in silence was an unnerving break from the usual hustle and bustle of the building. The footage from the Chamber was still rolling on some televisions throughout the building. Dalir was taunting the Prime Ministers in the Chamber. Sky and ABC News were broadcasting on other televisions. The anchors were describing what had just happened over looped footage which had been edited to pause before the assassinations of the Speaker and the Attorney. The channels clearly did not want to show that distressing footage. The anchors also spoke about the devastating scene outside Parliament where hundreds lay dead in the forecourt, including groups of school children who had been on excursion to the nation's capital.

Max raised a closed fist, stopping the group in front of one of the televisions.

After watching for a moment, Max gave the signal to move forward. At the end of the hallway, they took the stairs up to the roof. Max swiped his access card in the security panel and pushed the door open an inch. A stream of daylight poured through the gap. As Max's eyes adjusted, he saw the two terrorists who had shot up the forecourt and marble foyer on the roof near the vans. They were heavily armed and dressed in full tactical kits over leather riding gear. One of the men was facing the rear of the building over the Ministerial Wing. He was staring down Adelaide Avenue towards The Lodge – the Prime Minister's official residence. He was standing to Max's left. The second guy was to Max's right looking out over the front of the Parliament back towards the city and the Parliamentary Triangle.

It was a strange sight, seeing vehicles parked on the roof. Max could see the rope lines still leading from the vans to the now smashed glass pyramid. There were bodies strewn about the lawns that covered the Parliament's roof. Men, women and children who had started their days visiting the iconic building, Australia's symbol of democracy, only to be cut down where they stood. Max tried not to think about the fear and panic they must felt before the end. Anger choked in his throat.

He turned to Flash and Kate, and used hand signals to indicate the plan of attack. Flash left. Max right. Kate centre. He held a finger to his lips. Flash and Kate holstered their MP5s and drew silenced pistols. Max didn't want the sound to carry across into Chamber below. He could not risk Dalir hearing the shots and firing wildly into the assembled MPs.

Max held up his hand. Three. Two. On one he flung open the door and tracked right heading for the terrorist watching the front of the building. He fired three bullets into the terrorist's back, the third hitting him at the base of the skull. Dead.

Flash was through the door fractions of a second after Max and went left. He fired four shots, two into the head and two into the back of the rear facing terrorist. Kate came through third and took a knee, sweeping left and right covering Max and Flash, and checking for any remaining terrorists.

All clear.

Sirens sounded in the distance. Max looked down the hill following the left side of the Parliamentary Triangle, a major feature in Walter Burley's design of Canberra, over Commonwealth Avenue bridge towards the city. He saw a line of police cars racing to get to Parliament. Ambulances and fire brigade vehicles were also fighting their way through the traffic. Two helicopters were hovering overhead. Max looked up and saw *ABC News* and *Sky News* written on the side of the aircrafts. No doubt they had just recorded and televised the takedown of the two terrorists. He could not risk them filming what was to come next. He did not want Dalir to be tipped off.

"Carrol, you there?" Max asked holding Stevenson's radio up to his mouth.

"Yes Max, go ahead," Carrol said.

"Your boys able to clear the skies? Don't think we want to advertise our moves."

"On it."

Chapter Twenty-Three

Inside Dalir was still in the Speaker's chair, staring down the Australian Prime Minister.

"I understand how your Parliament works Mister Prime Minister," Dalir said. "As much as I hate this country, I have spent a lifetime here studying it. Working out the best way to destroy it. Your Parliament and so-called democracy is a farce. One party is in for a while, then the other takes over for a while and so the cycle goes. But, both parties are complicit in the actions and inactions of your country's foreign affairs policy and defence strategy. While you fight and beat your chests over petty domestic policies, you say nothing when it comes to international policy. You all just agree with each other. Puppets of the Americans and your old masters the British. So Prime Minister, why don't I spare you some pain for a moment? Given there is no opposition to war. Given there is no voice for the dead women and children your wars have inflicted in my homeland. I will hold the Opposition Leader to the same account as I do you. So, Mister Opposition Leader which of your Shadow Ministers do you like the most?"

"The Attorney General was right," the Opposition Leader said with a slight tremble in his voice. "We will never backdown to the likes of you."

"That is not what I wanted to hear," Dalir said. "You, Deputy Opposition Leader. On your feet."

The Deputy Opposition Leader did not stand. Instead, she clung to the Shadow Ministers either side of her. Dalir nodded and two of his men jumped down from the table and grabbed her. She fought and screamed. Her colleagues did not try hard to hold her, not wanting to be the next victim and in fear for their own lives. She was desperately clinging to her colleagues, trying to grab anything to hold off the attack and crying in fear. The Opposition Leader jumped up and punched one of Dalir's men in the face causing him to stumble, releasing his hold on the deputy. Seeing an opportunity, the Opposition Leader grabbed his deputy and dragged her behind him for protection.

"Take me instead," he said.

"How exciting. What a surprise. It seems you do have a spine after all. Valiant effort, but worthless."

Dalir raised his gun and fired.

The bullet hit the Deputy Opposition Leader in the back of the skull. The Opposition front bench was covered in her blood. She stood perfectly still for several seconds before swaying and falling onto the green carpet. People screamed throughout the Chamber, while others wept silently in fear and shock. The Opposition Leader stood staring at his fallen colleague and tears fell down his cheeks. He removed his jacket then knelt-down and covered his deputy with his suit coat. He lingered a moment, taking time to compose himself, upset at the loss of his friend and colleague.

"I suggest you have a word with the Prime Minister," Dalir said to the Opposition Leader. "He can make this stop. He alone can save the rest of your friends."

The Opposition Leader got to his feet. Nervously, he cleared his throat.

"I stand with the Prime Minister," he said softly.

"I beg your pardon?" Dalir asked.

"I said, I stand with the Prime Minister," he said louder with more confidence. "We will not back down to terrorists."

There was a resolve in his eyes. A decision. A peace. Accepting of his fate. Dalir fired a shot into the table in front of the Opposition Leader making him jump and more than one of his colleagues scream.

"Sit down," Dalir said and he did.

Chapter Twenty-Four

The Pilot sat watching his television. Sky News was helpfully broadcasting live vision from the top of the Parliament and from inside the Chamber. He was watching in delight as Dalir was raining down terror on the Parliament. It was all part of his plan. Create mass panic and fear.

Even the most protected building in the country was vulnerable. The most guarded people in Australia were not safe.

People would panic, he was sure of it. They would call for the Government to act. Well, they would call for what's left of the Government, after Dalir was finished with them, to act.

He picked up his phone and dialled.

"Hello," Xander said.

"It's me," the Pilot said.

"Sir."

"Are you watching this?"

"Yes, he's certainly causing havoc. I didn't think he would get as far as he did. Maybe he's not as dumb as I thought."

"Yes, I'm impressed he got in there. Regardless of how far he gets, the damage is done. Anyway, how are the plans coming for the next stage?"

"We are on track, sir. Sophia is already in the city and supervising delivery of the items."

"And, what about you?"

"I'm staying in Sydney to plan the fourth wave."

"Good, good. It's all coming together. Good work with Jones. Pity you missed Johnston, twice."

"Yes, boss. Thank you and apologies. We put the devices in the required places. We had no idea about the safe rooms. They were not on the plans."

"No, it turns out Crown lost the contract. AIS apparently vetoed their involvement. I didn't know. But since they have found the safehouse and the tablet, and the little Prince has retrieved files from Crown, it is only a matter of time until they are on to us."

"Yes, sir. I'll make sure we are ready to get you out of the country if it comes to that."

"Good. But hopefully I won't need it. I am going to see if we can't make a play for those files. Still, be ready for my signal in case the plan fails. They will have them closely guarded."

"We will be ready."

"Thank you, Xander. I will not forget your loyalty and your efforts on this."

"Thank you, sir."

"Get back to it and keep me updated," the Pilot said ending the call.

He turned back to the television just as three people in suits and balaclavas burst through a side door on the roof of Parliament.

The first moved with silent athletic speed and control. The Pilot watched as the terrorist on the roof towards the front of the building fell to the ground. The second terrorist suffered a similar fate to his comrade at the other end of the building as the second and third agents burst through the door onto the roof.

Efficient. Practiced. Skilled. Well-trained. Hard to see those three agents as anyone other than AIS agents.

The little Prince rides in again to save the day. I can't wait to kill him, the Pilot thought.

He thought about warning Dalir but thought better of it. He was expendable and he had done his job. No doubt he could take out a few more MPs before he was taken down.

The Pilot watched the little screen and saw the first man that had come through the door look up at the helicopters before using his radio. A few moments later, the footage being broadcast from the Sky News helicopter changed as it cleared the area.

Clever boy.

Chapter Twenty-Five

Up on the roof, Max watched as a police helicopter arrived scattering the two news crews. The choppers cleared the skies above Parliament and moved into a hover several kilometres away from the House.

Over the whip of the helicopter blades, Max heard a familiar sound. Approaching fast, three F/A18 Super Hornets which had been scrambled from Sydney swept in low over the building before moving into a patrol formation circling the skies above Canberra. It was a chilling sound but one which projected power and military might. They were not only patrolling to protect, they were sending a signal to the Australian people from their military, 'we're here to protect you'. And, to the terrorists watching, 'we will find you and hunt you down'. Max watched them circle for a moment listening to the shrill engines tearing up the sky and drowning out the sirens below.

"Max, we're moving and we'll be in position in a few minutes," Carrol said.

"Ack." Max replied. "Thanks, Carrol. We're ready when you are."

Max clipped the radio back on his belt.

"Okay, Flash you're going to take my left," Max said. "You've got the two on that side of the table. Remember, danger close to the Executive. If there is a risk, move to disable. Alpha, you're on the right. You've got two arseholes to take out. Same goes, shoot to disable if you can't risk a kill shot to protect the MPs. I've got arsehole number one. Roger?"

"Got it," Flash said.

"Ack," Kate said.

"Flash, as soon as you have dropped your two, secure the Prime Minister," Max said. "Alpha, you secure the Opposition Leader. I'll secure the Israeli Prime Minister."

"Got it," Flash said.

"Ack," Kate said.

"The time has come, Prime Minister," Dalir said in the Parliament below. "We have seen the Opposition Leader at least has some balls. He is not a clever man but at least he is tough enough to punch one of my guys and try to help his late deputy. He failed but he tried. Let us see how tough you are. Get the Deputy Prime Minister on his feet."

The two guys left on the table jumped down and grabbed the Deputy Prime Minister. The Prime Minister made to move but his Deputy held up his hand, stopping him.

"No," the Deputy Prime Minister said. "Stay strong. Never give in to these fuckers. Tell my wife and kids I love them."

"I will," the Prime Minister said.

The Deputy Prime Minister smiled to his boss and friend. Accepting the inevitable, he stood tall and looked Dalir in the eyes.

"Go fuck yourself, Dalir, and fuck your cause," the Deputy Prime Minister said before spitting at Dalir. "You'll never win."

Dalir's face went red, angered by the comment and the insult. He bounded out of the chair and down onto the floor. He ran at the Deputy Prime Minister and got within inches of his face then threw a violent headbutt into the Deputy's nose. It broke and blood burst through split skin on the bridge of his nose and from his nostrils.

"That all you got? I had worse when I played rugby," the Deputy Prime Minister said and laughed before he spat again at Dalir.

This time the spit and blood sprayed across Dalir's face and the Deputy roared laughing again. Dalir was infuriated. His eyes were staring like a man possessed.

"You will pay for your insolence you filthy infidel," Dalir said.

"Do your worst. We have the best police and security agencies in the world. They will hunt you down. You're already dead."

Just then Dalir saw movement to his left. A twitch of the ropes that they had used to abseil in on. His eyes followed the ropes up to the roof just as three people in suits and balaclavas leapt through the opening where the glass pyramid above the Chamber had once stood. They were using the ropes to fast repel into the Chamber. Without thinking, Dalir spun and wrapped his arm around the Prime Minister's neck using him as a human shield.

There were four simultaneous explosions and doors on each wall flew open, and the Chamber was filled with gunfire.

Dalir turned keeping the Prime Minister between himself and the men who had come through the roof. He raised his gun and shot the police officers who had entered behind the Speaker's chair and started dragging the Prime Minister out through the door by the neck.

Flash was on the left rope, on the Government's side of the Chamber. He fired two shots while he was in mid-air, halfway down the rope. He had taken out his two targets before he even hit the table. He let go of his rope and dropped to the table immediately assuming a crouched firing position on one knee. Aiming left, he fired multiple shots over the heads of the cowering MPs assisting the feds take down three terrorists around the perimeter. He watched as police officers were hit as the terrorists returned fire.

Kate slid down the rope with her left hand. She was on Max's right, on the Opposition's side of the Parliament. Clenching her MP5 tightly in her right hand, she shot two terrorists who were standing looking to the nearest door, distracted by the explosions. Two bullets each. Mirroring Flash, she hit the table and went into a crouch position. She fired a volley of bullets killing the two terrorists on the right-hand side of the Chamber just as they fired several shots into the crowded MPs.

In unison, Flash and Kate spun on their knees to face the rear of the Chamber. They both fired at the same time the Feds at the rear of the Chamber fired. The two remaining terrorists were shredded by an onslaught of bullets from all directions.

Flash and Alpha swept the room.

"All clear," Flash said.

He looked around surveying the room looking for Max and the Australian Prime Minister.

"Prime Minister, my name is Flash," Flash said to the Israeli Prime Minister. "I'm a Federal Agent. You are safe now."

"Thank you, Agent," the Israeli said.

"Are you hurt, Sir?"

"No, I am fine. I need to speak to my security chief."

"Yes, sir. I will make that happen. So you are aware, the Chamber is surrounded by Australian Federal Police and Parliament Security guards. And, there are three Royal Australian Air Force Super Hornets and a Federal Police helicopter patrolling the skies. You are safe. I am very sorry you had to witness these events."

"Thank you, Agent."

"Alpha, let's move," Flash yelled to Kate who had been speaking to the Opposition Leader.

The two agents headed for the rear door behind the Speaker's chair which was the only place Max could have gone.

As Flash and Kate had taken out their targets, Max had followed Dalir and the Prime Minister. He couldn't get a clear shot. Right at that moment, he was aiming his MP5 at the Prime Minister, who was still being used by Dalir as a human shield.

"Stop, Dalir," Max said. "It's over. You've lost."

"Stay back or I will kill him."

"Don't worry, sir. You will be fine. Dalir is going to surrender any minute now."

"Shoot him," the Prime Minister said.

"Shut up," Dalir said grabbing the Prime Minister's neck even harder.

Dalir pushed open a set of doors leading into the Speaker's courtyard.

"Sorry, PM," Max said.

"Why?" the Prime Minister asked.

Max fired a round into the Prime Minister's leg. He fell to the ground dragging Dalir down. It was the opportunity Max was looking for. He shot Dalir in the shoulder shattering the ball. His arm fell to his side and his gun fell from his hand and scattered across the floor, since his arm could no longer bare the weight and his grip failed. While Dalir stood in shock trying to grasp what had happened, Max was running at full sprint. He dived over the Prime Minister. His shoulder hit Dalir in the sternum and he heard a rib break on impact. The two men flew backwards into the courtyard and clear of the Prime Minister who was laying on the floor clutching his leg in pain. Max straddled Dalir, pinning him to the ground. He pressed his MP5 into Dalir's good shoulder and squeezed the trigger, shattering it. Dalir cried out in agony.

"Time to talk, Dalir," Max said. "Who else is involved in this? What is your end game? Who is The Pilot?"

Dalir laughed through the pain.

"These attacks are just the beginning," Dalir said. "We will never stop. My brothers and I have martyred ourselves in service to Allah. More will rise up and they will not stop. Not until every last one of you is dead."

"You are not a martyr, Dalir. You are still breathing. And, you are going to tell me who else is involved or I am going to make you suffer until your last breath. Then I'll revive you and make you suffer all over again."

"Pain is but a human reaction. Allah will end my suffering when he takes me in his arms in paradise."

"I wouldn't be so sure of that but either way you won't be finding out for a while. You've got some talking to do first."

Flash and Kate had arrived. They were providing first aid to the Prime Minister. Carrol ran through the door and on seeing the Prime Minister he radioed for medical assistance.

"Alpha," Max said. "Get this piece of shit to the car. We're going to AIS."

"Done Prince, with pleasure," Kate said.

Kate stood up and walked over to Max. They dragged an enraged but groggy Dalir onto his feet. Kate removed Dalir's belt and used it to tie his arms together. It was just a precaution, she was pretty sure Dalir couldn't use them, but better safe than sorry. She grabbed the belt forcefully making Dalir groan in pain.

"Come on you fucking piece of shit," Kate said leading Dalir away.

Max walked over to the Prime Minister.

"Prince?" the Prime Minister asked.

"Yes, Sir. Prince is my codename," Max said removing his balaclava.

"Oh fuck, Max. You shot me in the leg."

"Yes, very sorry, Sir. I thought it was our only chance. He was cornered. He was going to kill you."

"Well, thanks for saving me, even if I may never walk again."

"You should be fine, Prime Minister," Flash said. "It missed all the vital bits. It went right through and missed the bone. You should make a full recovery."

"Hmm, well that's good to hear, I guess. Thank you both."

"Just doing our job, PM," Max said. "Sorry again."

"What is going on in the Chamber," the Prime Minister asked as two ambulance officers arrived to tend to his injury.

"Looks like we have eleven dead terrorists," Carrol said. "I'm sorry to report we also have four dead federal police and two critically injured officers. Sir, the Speaker, Attorney-General and Deputy Leader of the Opposition are all deceased. Four MPs were also hit, one of whom is in critical condition. Everyone else is safe and accounted for, including the Israeli Prime Minister who is being moved to a safe room with his security detail."

"Thank you, Agent Carrol."

Defence Minister Johnston walked out of the Chamber.

"Max? Wow, that was you in there?" he asked.

"Yes, Minister," Max said.

"I knew we trained you boys well, but that was something else. Bloody hell. Zip. Bang. Done. Thank you. Thank you both and thank you, Agent Carrol. Please pass on my thanks to your agencies."

"Yes, Minister, thank you," Carrol said.

"Will do," Flash said. "We're glad you are safe. Sorry we didn't get in there sooner."

"What's your name, Agent?" the Prime Minister asked.

"Jacob Gordon, sir, but most people call me Flash," Flash said removing his balaclava.

"Flash Gordon," the Prime Minister smiled. "You lads crack me up with your nicknames. Well done and thank you, Flash. You saved a lot of lives here today. We owe you. The country owes you."

"Well, thank you, but as Max said, we were just doing our jobs."

"I'll be sure to tell General Scott how impressed and thankful I am," the Prime Minister said.

"Thank you, sir," Max said. "We better catch up to Alpha and our prisoner before she kills him. Minister, I'll be at AIS for the afternoon. Agent Carrol will look after you. Carrol, I will be in touch. Good job in there. Sorry about your officers, they died heroes every one of them."

"Thanks, Max," Carrol said. "Appreciate that. We couldn't have done it without you three. That was some real hero shit diving through the roof like that."

"Thanks, mate."

Max and Flash shook hands with Carrol, the Prime Minister and Minister before briskly walking back towards the Ministerial Wing. They met Kate in the basement. She was in the car with the engine idling. Dalir was tied up in the back. Max and Flash jumped aboard, and Kate drove out of the underground carpark slowly to allow the police vehicles to clear their way.

Chapter Twenty-Six

The Pilot could not believe what he was seeing and hearing.

Moments after the news feed changed as the helicopter pulled away from the roof of Parliament the live feed from the Chamber had also been cut. The police, military and intelligence agencies obviously did not want the live assassinations of Ministers and Members of Parliament broadcast, but more importantly, they could not risk the Israeli Prime Minister being assassinated on live television. Such an event would cause an international scandal of unprecedented proportions which would have ramifications the world over.

The Pilot had gone back about his work as the commentators spoke to looping rolling footage and speculated about what was happening inside. After a long while, the commentators said that the Prime Ministers and most Parliamentarians were safe. They said there were a number of injuries and fatalities, but they couldn't release any details until next of kin had been informed. The commentator said they had been given permission to show some of the footage of federal agents and police retaking the Parliament.

He watched the footage of Dalir standing in front of the Deputy Prime Minister. It looked like he had blood on his face. Then he looked up, released the Deputy and sprinted towards the back of the Chamber with the Prime Minister. The scene then cut to a series of other camera footage which variously showed three people abseiling into the Chamber and multiple explosions around the perimeter of the Chamber. It cut away without showing any bloodshed, but they kept the audio playing. Gun shots rang out over screaming and shouting. A cacophony of horror and chaos. As the footage cut back to the commentators, the Pilot got to his feet and paced back and forth. He took several deep breaths and rolled his shoulders and stretched his back. He took a long, deep breath to calm down.

Once he settled, he left his office. There was chaos. People crowded around screens watching the scenes unfold. With all the distractions and noise, no one saw him slip into the conference room.

He pulled a small tablet computer from his bag and plugged it into the laptop which was sitting unattended in the conference room. It was running a decryption programme on the files recovered from Crown Constructions. *Enter command*, appeared on the tablet. He typed *Erase all files* and he hit 'execute'. The fan in the laptop kicked in hard as the files were being deleted. *Complete*, flashed on the screen. *Enter command*, reappeared. He typed *upload virus*. The fan whirled again as the virus was downloaded from the military spec tablet onto the desktop.

When it finished uploading, he bundled the tablet and cord back into his bag and with another calming breath and roll of his shoulders to loosen up, he left the room. That would at least buy him some time.

When he was sure no one was watching, he slipped back out of the conference room unseen.

Chapter Twenty-Seven

Kate gunned the engine when they got into clear space. She headed down the hill and up Kings Avenue towards Russell, home of the Department of Defence, famous for its tall spire and eagle which rose above Sir Thomas Blamey Square. It was a gift from the Americans as a symbol of friendship and military relations. It was an impressive structure.

The big Landcruiser turned right instead of heading into the Defence Headquarters. It sped down the road and made a left into the Royal Military College, Duntroon. The security level had been elevated. Armed military personnel were manning the gates already.

Kate wound down the window and presented a security pass.

"We are here to see General Scott," Kate said. "He is expecting us."

"Says here he is expecting four of you," the junior officer said.

"Fourth one's in the back," Kate said pointing over her shoulder with her thumb.

The officer walked over and peered through the window.

"Not quite what I was expecting, but if Hulk says you're good to go that's fine by me," the officer said.

"Thanks," Kate said.

They drove through the compound until they came to a new large glass building. Kate turned the vehicle right onto the ramp leading down under the building. She waved her right hand in front of the sensor and looked into the camera mounted on the wall.

"Access code?" a voice said from the security panel.

"Papa, Juliet, Alpha, six, four, twenty, X-ray," Kate said.

"Access granted, welcome Alpha."

The bollards lowered and the large steel garage door rolled open.

"Home sweet home," Flash said as the vehicle pulled into an available space.

The AIS facility had been purposely built away from the defence and intelligence agency headquarters at Russell for security reasons. It was designed to look like a lecture theatre from the outside. Just another random building on the grounds of Duntroon. Hiding in plain sight. But, what the public didn't know was that the impressive glass structure housed the Australian Intelligence Service Headquarters.

Max opened the rear door, grabbed Dalir by the shirt and dragged him out of the car.

"Well, Dalir, you've had some time to think," Max said. "Now, we're going to find out who else is involved in all of this and what other plans you have in place. There are a couple of ways to do it. Two of your colleagues in Sydney chose the hard way, but they both ended up talking. Everyone does. Think you are in pain now? I can assure you, you have not experienced pain yet. But, I can end your pain if you like? All I need is your cooperation."

Dalir said nothing.

"The hard way it is then," Max said.

Max pushed Dalir into the elevator, and Flash and Kate followed them in. Max swiped his ring on the sensor and hit level eight, but the elevator did not go up, instead it sank into the ground. Eight floors beneath the new glass building, the doors opened to reveal a long grey concrete hallway lined by a series of rooms. Yellow paint and signs showed there was a medical room, six cells with solid steel doors as well as a bathroom and kitchenette on level eight.

Dalir was ushered into one of the cold concrete and steel cells, and handcuffed to the solid steel chair. He was in shock and the pain from his shattered shoulders was taking over. He looked moments from unconsciousness.

Max slapped him across the face.

"Wake up! You're about to tell me all your secrets."

Dalir did not respond.

"Flash, can you please grab a med-kit?" Max asked. "Alpha, do you want to go find Hulk?"

"No worries," Kate said.

"Be right back," Flash said.

Max's phone started to ring. Sam. Max stared at the phone without answering it. *Later*, he thought.

"Go freshen up and answer the call if you want Prince," Flash said walking back into the room.

"Nah, it's fine," Max said ending the call. "I'll call him after."

"It's okay, you know?"

"What is?"

"To have feelings for him. He's not Lockie. That won't happen again. I will never let that happen again and neither will you. You deserve to be happy. It's time to move on."

Max was hit with a wave of sadness. He had spent the last few days trying not to think about Lachlan. It was the same every time he met new guys. Never wanting to get too close. Never wanting to put them in harm's way. Not after what happened to Lachlan. He did not think it was fair innocent people had to suffer because they were close to him. He did not want to see them hurt. He did not want to take the risk. But, the pain he felt the most was that he did not want to fall in love again only to end up with a broken heart. He could not let what happened to Lachlan happen to anyone else. And, he could not experience the pain of loss again. It had nearly killed him. It had certainly changed him.

Max felt like a knife had stabbed him in the heart just hearing his name again.

Lachlan was perfect. They were in love. Max remembered the first time he had seen him, and every conversation and every moment they had spent together. He remembered him and would never forget him. And, he remembered the last time he held him, the last time he saw him, the last time they kissed.

He did not have a photographic memory, but he remembered every detail when it came to Lachlan.

They had met at university. Max was in his second year when Lachlan moved into the college to start the first year of his studies. Max noticed him straight away. It was hard not to. He was cute. More than just tall, dark and handsome. He had personality, charm and charisma. He was smart. He was popular and funny. He was the life of the party and from the outside looked to have it all. But to those who knew him, they knew there was more to him. More than the showman and the infectious smile. Deep down he had buried a hurt. Deep down he was fragile. Deep down he needed someone to hold him and care for him and love him.

Max and Lachlan got to know each other over the course of that year. They became close friends. Nothing more. Until that night. That one night would be engrained in Max's memory until he took his last breath.

There was a party on campus in their college's home room. Max and Lachlan had organised the party and they were revving up the crowd. They held the whole room's attention as they took it in turn to joke and sing and lead the games. They felt like princes circled by hundreds of their college friends in the centre of the room. Music was blaring. Drinks were flowing. Laugher and frivolity surrounded them. Then the lights went out and the music stopped.

Total darkness.

Laughter and playful screams rang out as people pretended to be scared of the dark. In the chaos came a calm. Max felt a warm strong hand take hold of his and pull him closer. Through the darkness, Max could feel a presence. Tall, masculine, full of energy but silent. The figure embraced him and for a moment they held each other. A moment of peace in a storm of drunken noise. A moment of tender, longing embrace in a raging alcohol fuelled tempest. He could feel the figure's breath on his neck. He felt its racing heart. He felt it tremble. He felt right. He felt safe. He felt something long overdue had taken hold.

Then the lights came on and the chaos stopped as the room was left staring at Max and Lachlan holding each other tightly in the centre of the room.

They let go of each other as the laughter grew louder, and they tried to save face by playing it up and pretending they were just joking to see what people would do. After what felt like an eternity, people laughed and joked buying their story, the music started and the party kicked-off again, and Max and Lachlan went their separate ways.

Max left the party to get more drinks from his unit. He went into the bathroom and splashed water on his face, and stared into the mirror. Confused. Questioning. Wondering.

Did I just feel that? Why is my heart racing? I'm not gay. I've had girlfriends. I've thought about it, but I would never do that. Why would anyone? The rejection. The hate. The scorn, that came with it. It wasn't right, was it? No, that's not who I am.

But, still he could not shake what he had felt. He stood looking in the mirror questioning everything he had previously thought about himself. After a long period, he left the bathroom and walked towards the kitchen.

Drinks. Party. Everything is okay. Forget it. It wasn't anything. You're just confused. You were just mucking around.

Lachlan was waiting in the kitchen.

"Hey, quiet up here compared to down there," Lachlan said.

"Sure is," Max said suddenly short of breath.

"How funny was that, in there, before?"

"Yeah man, hilarious. Think they all fell for it."

"Ha, yeah," Lachlan laughed.

"Do you want a drink?" Max said after a moment of silence.

"Definitely."

Max got two beers out of the fridge and passed one to Lachlan. They clinked the glass bottles, said cheers and took big sips.

"Hard work all that dancing, want to sit for a minute before we go back down?" Max asked.

"Good idea, I'm buggered."

They sat on the floor on opposite sides of the kitchen, leaning back on the cupboards. Their legs sat inside each other's. Sipping their beers, they sat quietly listening to the raging party going on across the college. They both sat looking at everything in the room except one another. Although there were the occasional quick looks. After quite a few longer stares, there were wry smiles forming on each of their faces. Their legs were now touching. Lachlan rubbed his foot gently on Max's leg.

Max's mind was racing. He was confused and his heart was beating out of his chest. He hoped he did not look or sound nervous or give away his feelings. He was suddenly unsure of himself. His normal confidence, replaced by an overwhelming feeling of not wanting to make a mistake. He felt sick in the stomach and his head was spinning.

This is what I want. It is who I am. I've been fighting it. I won't fight it any longer.

"Why are you sitting all the way over there?" Max asked.

"I don't know," Lachlan said.

"Well, if you're not coming over here, I'll come over to you," Max said as he slid on the floor over to sit beside Lachlan.

They were close. So close their legs were touching, hips to feet. Their arms laying against each other's, elbows to hands, shoulders and biceps touching.

"You're right," Lachlan said.

"What about?"

Lachlan grabbed Max's hand and turned and looked him in the eyes.

"You were too far away, sitting over there," Lachlan said looking to the other side of the kitchen.

They both smiled. Max remembered his cheeks hurting from smiling. Not once did either of them look away. Neither blinked. Electricity was flowing through their hands and every inch that was touching.

Then they kissed.

Max was overcome. There was a strength, masculine and passionate, behind the kiss but it was so soft and gentle. It was his first kiss with another man and he felt a surge of adrenaline. A rush. Every nerve, every muscle pulsed with that same electricity.

"Wow," Lachlan said.

"Yeah," Max said. "I can't say I was expecting tonight to turn out like this."

"Me either, but I'm glad it did."

"Me too."

They kissed again. Longer this time as their hands started to explore each other's trembling bodies. Desire. Lust.

After a while, they stood up and headed back towards the party, not wanting people to wonder where they were. They walked hand-in-hand in the shadows. As they approached the door, they let go of each other. They did not want anyone to know, unsure of their reactions. As Max went to enter the room, Lachlan grabbed his hand again and led him straight past the door. They walked down into the quad and Lachlan pulled Max in and they kissed under the trees in the open outdoor space. They held each other in the darkness as the sound of the party carried across the cool night air. Then they went to Lachlan's room. Their nerves were overcome by desire and they made love for the first time and held each other until the early hours of the morning.

Snapping back to reality, Max realised he was staring at the floor.

"Come with me," Flash said and they walked out into the hallway. "I'm sorry Max, I didn't mean to make you upset. I just want you to be happy. Give him a call. You'll figure things out."

"It's okay, Flash. I know you are looking out for me and your friendship means so much to me. I'm just worried. I don't want to risk anyone getting hurt. And, I don't think I could go through it again."

"I know mate. What happened to Lockie was fucking horrible, but you need to move on and find someone to be there for you. There is more to life. There is more than work and, as I said, we would never let anything like that happen again. I would never let anything happen like that again."

"Thanks Flash," Max said. "God, it's only been a couple of nights anyway we're not eloping."

"I know but you've got that look in your eyes. I've seen it so many times before."

"What look?"

"That look like you want to end it before it's started, but this time, I can tell you don't really want it to end."

"Oh, fucking hell Oprah, I thought I was the gay one," Max said jokingly.

"I wish I had her money for all this good advice I am imparting," Flash said sarcastically.

"Don't we all. Thanks Flash, seriously you are a great friend. I really appreciate it. Oh and Jane's a lucky girl to have such a sensitive new aged guy for a boyfriend."

"I will make sure I tell her you think so."

"Please do. Now, how about we go see if our friend in here is ready to talk and get away from all this emotion?"

"After you," Flash said motioning for the door.

Chapter Twenty-Eight

Flash followed Max into the cell to find Dalir out cold in the chair.

Max removed one of the cauterising powder sachets from the med bag Flash had brought in. He poured half in each shoulder's bullet wound. It bubbled and gurgled as it sealed the wounds.

"Can you please call the doctor?" Max asked.

"Yep," Flash said before leaving the room to call the AIS Head of Medical.

Max took out an adrenaline shot and forcefully stabbed it into Dalir's leg. Seconds later he spluttered awake.

"Wake up sunshine, it's time to talk," Max said.

"You might as well kill me, you will get nothing from me," Dalir said.

"You'd be surprised how many people say that in your position, but you'd be even more surprised at how many of them can't follow through. Everyone breaks. It is just a matter of time. And, I've got all the time in the world."

"Do you?" Dalir whispered.

"What was that?"

"Nothing."

Max walked over and placed his hands on Dalir's knees and leant in close.

"Whatever happens you're going to endure more pain than anyone has ever felt."

Flash and the doctor entered the room, and Max stood and stepped back as the doctor went about hooking Dalir up to a drip. He placed the needle into Dalir's arm then connected the long plastic tube to blood and an IV. The liquid from both bags started to flow as he taped the needle in place.

The doctor nodded to Max and left the room without a word.

"There we go," Max said. "That should keep you going for a while. At least long enough for me to get every detail I need from you."

"Fuck you, Allah protects me," Dalir said.

Max grabbed Dalir's belt which was sitting on the floor. It had been used to tie his hands but now he was handcuffed to the chair it was not needed. Max whipped the leather tip across Dalir's face, hard. He winced, then laughed.

"Is that all?" Dalir asked.

It was the response Max knew was coming. Like lightning, he whipped the buckle end of the belt around in a loop behind Dalir's neck and caught it. He inserted the leather tip through the buckle and pulled the belt tight. The buckle lodged in under Dalir's Adam's apple and the skin instantly whitened in stripes running beside the leather and metal. Max put his right foot on Dalir's chest and pushed hard with the heal of his boot on Dalir's cracked ribs from the tackle at Parliament House, then he lent back pulling the belt tighter. Dalir's windpipe closed. His eyes widened. His mouth opened and closed like a fish out of water as he tried to scoop in air. His skin was reddening either side of the belt and his general complexion started to go blue.

Max let go.

The belt loosened slightly but stayed in place. Colour returned to Dalir's face as breaths were inhaled through his still partially closed windpipe. It was strained like breathing through a thin straw. He was making a shallow, drawl, gasping screech, trying to take in the air. It would have felt like he was suffocating or drowning, but he was still getting just enough air.

"There's something you need to know, Dalir," Max said. "I hate you. I hate everything you stand for. I will stop at nothing to protect the innocent from you and defend our way of life. I have no issues with your people. I love many of your people more than you ever will, and I will defend them from the likes of fundamentalist radicals like you. Understand that I feel these things, even more passionately than you believe in what you believe. Am I really the sort of person you want to upset? Is it worth going through all of this? Just tell me, who are you working for and what is coming next?"

"You do not understand my faith," Dalir choked out. "You could never comprehend that level of devotion and from what I heard earlier, you never will. Your sins will see you burn for eternity. The Quran says that homosexuals will be draped in cloaks of fire and flogged with iron staves. When you meet Allah, it is you who will know pain."

Max laughed and smiled.

"And, I guess you'll be in paradise with your seventy-two virgins enjoying yourself?"

"Inshallah."

"Well, God-willing, I'll keep you locked in hell on earth for the rest of your days. By the time, I am finished with you, you will beg for fire and iron as it will seem like a relief."

There was a commotion in the hallway outside. Voices getting louder with the sound of hustling footsteps. Flash walked into the hallway to see what all the fuss was about. Kate and Hulk were heading towards the cell Max and his prisoner were in. Between them hung a young semi-conscious Arab man in black paramilitary gear.

"Get another chair Flash, we've got one of his mates here," Hulk said.

"How's that possible?" Flash asked.

"One of you dumb fucks needs to spend some more time training on the gun range. That's how. Maybe then you'll be able to shoot a fucking terrorist and make sure he stays down. Til then, get a fucking chair."

Flash ran to the room next door and dragged in a heavy steel chair. Max watched on as Hulk and Kate plonked the new guy down into the chair directly opposition Dalir. Max noticed Dalir's expression change. He was visibly shaken by seeing his companion in the room. Max kept his gaze on Dalir. Reading him. Studying him. Looking for something to use. As Hulk and Kate cuffed the new comer to the chair, Max watched as Dalir's eyes betrayed him. He was worried about the new guy. His eyes were darting up and down as if trying to assess his comrade's injuries.

"Friend of yours?" Max said.

Dalir looked up briefly but said nothing.

"He is. Well, how fortunate," Max smiled. "Maybe you're not worried about your own pain but maybe you will worry about your friend's pain or maybe he will just tell me everything while you watch as he suffers."

"Do not fucking touch him!" Dalir spat.

"Your emotions betray you Dalir. I am going to make him scream in pain while you watch. Give me the room fellas," Max said.

Hulk, Kate and Flash went into the observation room next door.

"I wonder what you would hate more," Max said slapping the new guy hard across the face. "Your friend here suffering more pain than he has ever felt while you watch on helplessly?"

Max's hand fell onto the new guy's shoulder. He walked around then crouched behind him and rubbed his hands on his chest, hugging him from behind. Resting his head against the terrorist's.

"Or maybe you would be even more upset if my sinner hands ran over his body and my lips kissed his neck and made him consider doing a little sinning of his own? I am sure I could find a way to take his mind off his pain. All while you watch of course."

"You fucking faggot infidel get away from my son!" Dalir yelled.

"Your son?" Max asked. "Mmm, does he have a name, other than handsome?"

Max's face was turned in towards the son's neck like he was moving to whisper something in his ear. As he spoke he got closer. His lips were so close they almost touched his skin.

"So, who are you working for and what is coming next?" Max asked.

"Get away or I swear I will fucking kill you," Dalir said.

"Wrong answer."

Max pulled out his knife.

"What are you doing? Leave him alone. Izad. No. Please," Dalir said.

"Izad hey? Well, tell me what I want to know or Izad's in for a terrible afternoon."

Dalir was squirming but did not speak. Max grabbed Izad's left hand and with a couple of hard pulls on his knife, he cut Izad's little finger off. Izad woke and screamed in pain. His eyes darted from his left hand around the room taking it in, sobbing through the pain.

"Father," Izad said. "What is going on? What happened? Help me."

"Argh! Fuck you!" Dalir screamed at Max. "Izad, I am sorry my son. Argh! I will kill you."

Dalir rocked and shook in his chair. Izad was crying in pain. Max threw the finger onto Dalir's chest.

"Nine more to go, then we'll start with the toes," Max said.

"You are a psychopath," Dalir spat.

"That might be true, but you have only got yourself to blame. I wasn't always like this. Friends of yours made me this way. I lost someone to your so-called cause and now I will do whatever it takes to tear you all apart. And, if you feel even half the pain I feel before you set off for paradise, then I will have gone part the way to avenging him. Maybe you need to feel my pain to understand my motivation? Maybe you need to suffer a loss? Maybe I will just stab little Izad here in the neck and let you watch him slowly bleed to death?"

Flash shot Kate a nervous look. He could see it in Max's eyes. The pain that drove him. Lachlan was his motivation. Vengeance, revenge and anger had forced him back to work. God help anyone that came up against him. Max was determined and ruthless. He would stop at nothing to make sure no one else felt the pain he felt. He knew Max had changed since Lachlan, but this was the first time he had heard him admit it.

"You are out of time," Max said.

He took his knife in his right hand then grabbed Izad by the hair pulling his head back getting ready to cut his throat.

"Wait, please," Izad said his throat tight and dry.

"You hear that Dalir, your boy wants me to wait? 'Please', he said. He is begging for his life Dalir. Are you going to let your boy die knowing his dad could have helped him but didn't?"

"Father, please just tell him, I don't want to die," Izad pleaded.

"Come on, Dalir," Max said placing the blade against Izad's neck and drawing some blood.

"Okay, okay, wait, wait, I will tell you what I know," Dalir said. "It is not much but I will tell you. Just leave him be."

"He stays and if I think you are lying or not telling me everything you know, I will kill him without hesitation," Max said. "What is your plan?"

"We are creating panic and striking fear into the hearts of all Australians by hitting those people thought to be the most protected and by attacking sites you think are protected. We want to show your country that no one is safe and we want your people to know in their hearts they have condoned the abuses my people have suffered and know we are seeking our retribution."

"Why? What's the end game?"

"He wants me to spread fear. He wants your people to know the Government cannot protect them. How could they when they cannot even protect themselves. But, I want to go further. I want their fear and their lack of trust to see your Government collapse. Chaos will ensue and your country and precious democracy will crumble."

"Who is 'he'?"

"He calls himself the Pilot."

"Who is he?"

"I don't know," Dalir said.

Max waved the knife in front of Izad's eyes.

"Who is he?" Max asked.

"I swear, I do not know."

"So, you just started working for some guy you don't even know?"

"He found me. He had money and equipment, and gave it all to me on one condition. Create panic and kill as many as possible in the process."

"You said you want to go further. What do you mean by that?"

"He is weak. I know he is only using me and using my cause for his own. But, I will not stop until your country is destroyed."

"I see. Well, considering how much you hate this country, you certainly know very little about it. Australians will never backdown and never succumb to your threats. We will rise up against you and we will prevail. We will not hide in fear or let you kill our freedoms and way of life. So, why don't you tell me what's next?"

"We have hit your Government but that was just the beginning," Dalir said grinning.

Max returned the knife to Izad's neck.

"Are you sure you are happy about that, sitting there smiling in my face?" Max asked before walking out from behind Izad, pointing his knife at Dalir as he walked. "If your plan succeeds, you are talking about the death of millions of people I am sworn to defend and you are sitting there smiling. I don't think you're taking me seriously, Dalir. Izad knows I am not fucking around with you. Maybe I should cut off another one of his fingers. Will you be smiling then?"

"Leave him alone you, you mad man!"

"Mad man, really? You kill innocent people and call me mad?" Max said pausing. "Well, maybe I am."

He spun on his heal and with precision, slashed his knife through the air and sliced an artery in Izad's arm. Blood sprayed and pumped from the deep cut. Izad began to cry and plead with his father, his voice cracking and softening as the life started to quickly drain from him.

"Argh! Get help! Izad! What have you done?" Dalir yelled.

"Father, please," Izad said groggily, consciousness already starting to fade.

It would not be long until he was overcome and passed out.

"I'd say he has only minutes to live Dalir! Tell me what I want to know or watch your son bleed to death!" Max yelled.

"Alright. Alright, the next target is a large public event," Dalir said.

"Where?"

"Melbourne."

"When?"

"Some time in the next forty-eight hours."

"What event?"

"I do not know. Please get help for my son. I have told you what I know."

"What is the event?"

"I do not know, I swear! The cell was just told to hit a large public event to prove that no one is safe. If you spit on God's laws, we will be His hand and strike you down. That is all I know. Now, get him help!"

"Doc," Max said to the one-way mirror.

The doctor and his medical team rushed in and started working on Izad. Max headed for the observation room.

"Fucking hell Max, that was intense," Flash said. "Is he going to make it?"

"Fuck him, he's a terrorist piece of shit, with a terrorist piece of shit father," Hulk said. "You did good kid. Let's call the bunker and see if they have anything in the files or any chatter mentioning Melbourne."

Flash moved closer to Max and put a hand on his friend's back. Max gave him a reassuring look.

"I'm fine, Jacob," Max said, his tone slightly colder than expected.

"Alright, mate," Flash said patting him on the back before pulling his hand away.

Kate tapped away on the computer and a video screen appeared. A telephone symbol popped up with a circle of dots which were fading and reappearing in sequence as it tried to connect. Lloyd came on the screen. There was commotion in the background.

"What's going on there?" Hulk asked.

"We've got a problem," Lloyd said. *"The files from Crown Constructions have been erased."*

"You have got to be kidding me," Hulk said. "How the fuck could you let that happen? It's not like their terrorist owner, they can't just fly out a fucking window!"

"I'm reviewing everyone that has been in the room and accessed the files," Lloyd said. *"I will find out how it happened."*

"Is there any chance of recovering the files?" Flash asked.

"I am not sure yet, Hermes is on it," Lloyd said. *"But we have another problem, a virus has been uploaded into our in-house security systems knocking out our cameras and alarms. I will find the person responsible but until the camera systems are back online it will be impossible. I will keep you updated."*

"You do that," Hulk snapped. "Where's Hermes?"

"I'm here, Sir," Blake said appearing on the screen next to Lloyd.

"Good. I want you two to track down whoever deleted those files then I want their head. Got it?"

"Yes, Sir. I am already on it."

"Dalir says the next target is a large crowded event in Melbourne. Forty-eight hour window from now. This is the highest priority. We need to know possible targets and we need to review security for each event. Get to it."

"We will, Hulk," Lloyd said.

Kate ended the call.

"Who could have deleted those files?" Max asked.

"Some fucking traitorous piece of shit," Kate said.

"Too early to tell, but God help them," Hulk said. "They are fucking traitors and will be treated as such. You three get to the airport and get to Melbourne as fast as possible."

Chapter Twenty-Nine

A delivery truck pulled up at the loading dock. This was the second stop it had made on its short journey from the warehouse.

An attractive woman stepped down out of the truck with a clipboard and opened the rear doors. Two guys jumped down and set about unloading their cargo onto the cold concrete of the dock. She made a note on the delivery sheet on her clipboard as items were unloaded. As the last steel container was lowered from the truck she lent in to inspect the serial number stamped into the metal. One of the men tilted it forward for her to get a better view then placed it on a moving trolley.

"Just a moment," she said before taking out an old smart phone.

She rested the mobile on top of the object and felt it pull gently from her hand as the magnet on its rear stuck to the metal. She opened an app on the phone and entered a sequence of numbers on the keypad. A timer appeared on the phone and started counting down. *Device armed,* glowed from the small phone screen. She locked the phone's screen and placed a plastic cover over it.

"Good to go," she said to the man with the trolley who smiled back at her.

A man in a polo shirt and chinos walked briskly into the loading dock.

"Oh, that's great, thank you so much for dropping these off," he said. "Can never have enough supplies for an event like this!"

"That is no problem at all, sir," the woman said. "Happy to be involved. Should be a great event."

"Oh, yes. We are very excited. Not long now until it starts. Did you need me to sign anything?"

"Yes please," she said handing over the clipboard. "Just down the bottom there."

"There we go and thank you again," he said before handing back the clipboard and turning to walk away.

"It is a pleasure. Hope it all goes well. Thank you."

As she climbed back into the truck her phone beeped with a message.

I've deleted the files which should slow them down but I'm going to need to get out of here soon, it won't take long until they're onto me.

As she was about to type a reply, two more messages arrived.

Dalir is here, they are torturing him for information.

Shit, they've got Izad too, Dalir is talking.

She deleted her draft reply and called a number stored in her phone. After three rings, it was answered.

"Xander, it's Sophia," she said. "Did you get the Pilot's messages?"

"Yes, I just saw them," Xander said.

"God, they are getting close now. We need to get out of here."

"Relax gorgeous. They are miles away. When stage three starts, you will be free and clear on the highway. And, when you get back here we will finish all of this with stage four then fly out with the Pilot until the heat dies down."

"Okay babe. I am just a bit nervous. How is stage four coming along?"

"Good. I am getting ready to head over there now. With the access card we picked up it will be quick and then we can get on the plane. How about you? Nearly ready to hit the road?"

"I have one more thing to do then I will change and find a new vehicle and head back to you."

"That's good babe. I cannot wait to see you."

"You are so sweet. I love you, Xander."

"Love you too. Be careful. See you soon."

Chapter Thirty

Kate was speeding down the Tullamarine Freeway towards Melbourne. Flash was on the phone in the passenger seat and Max was on his mobile in the backseat of the big bulletproof Landcruiser. While Max had a Chevy in every city when he needed it, the Landcruiser was Kate's preferred vehicle.

Three unmarked federal police vehicles were escorting them. Lights flashing and sirens wailing. Cars, buses, bikes and trucks all pulled to the side to allow the small convoy through.

"Hulk, has he given you anything more?" Max asked.

"No," Hulk said. *"He says each of the cells were deliberately kept in the dark about the plans of the other cells."*

"Well, there has to be someone in charge. Any details on the Pilot?"

"Not yet. I'm pushing him but I'm not sure how far I'll get."

"How's Izad?"

"He's still in surgery but it's looking like he'll pull through."

"Good. We might need him. Anything from Shadow?"

"Not much of use. He said only a few people had access to the files and Hermes is getting the virus under control, so it won't be long until we figure out who did it."

"What about Chang?"

"He didn't have access to the files. He's still tied up in the bunker."

"Yeah I know. I was thinking we could use him against Dalir, make Dalir think Chang has given us something or vice versa? Bit of a rope-a-dope."

"That could work. How about I set up a video link so they can see each other, no sound just video? We'll play both of them to see what else we can learn."

"It's worth a shot."

"I'll get it done and call you back," Hulk said ending the call.

Flash ended his call.

"The list is getting shorter," Flash said. "Three major events today. The tennis is on at Rod Laver Arena, there's a diversity and multicultural parade through the CBD this evening and there's a concert at the Melbourne Cricket Ground. Two major events tomorrow. The tennis is still on and the races are on at Flemington. The police have been alerted at all events. The State Premier doesn't want to cancel any events, nor does the Defence Minister. He said, 'then they win' which is probably true but a huge risk in the present environment."

"Defence Minister?" Max said.

"Yeah, he's taken over operational control of the country's security until we're sure we've gotten to all of the cells."

"Right, God help us," Max said.

"Could be any of these fucking events," Kate said.

"Let's think it through," Max said. "They all have a large audience. Sport is engrained into Australian culture. Bradman's batting average is part of the citizenship test for God's sake. So, striking a sporting crowd would have a big impact."

"So would taking out the MCG where that concert is on," Flash said. "The ground itself is an icon."

"That's true, but it can be rebuilt. He said he wanted to show that no one is safe and he spoke about striking down those that spat on Allah's laws. Surely, that means the crowd is the target?"

"Yeah, maybe," Flash said.

"Has to be the parade then, doesn't it?" Kate said. "A large gathering of people from all over the world celebrating diversity and multiculturalism."

"Certainly would fit their normal MO," Flash said.

"Given they fight for the supremacy and domination of their religion and culture, blah, blah, fucking, blah, you know how they go on – it would be a big target," Kate said.

Max opened his phone and dialled Carrol.

"Carrol, it's Shaw," Max said. "Can you get me the security details for the parade in Melbourne? We think it is the highest likely target."

"Yeah Max, I'll have the details emailed to you," Carrol said. *"I have spoken to the teams on the ground, let me just get my notes. Here we are. Two man uniformed teams on each corner of the route. Snipers and spotters on several roofs. Hard perimeter two blocks out in all directions using concrete barriers and council vehicles to block the roads. Two birds in the sky. It's pretty tight Max."*

"We can't rule out the other locations, but we thought this sounded like it could be a symbolic hit."

"You're probably right. You should have that email now."

Max pulled out his tablet computer and opened his emails. He found Carrol's email and double clicked the link to download the parade route map.

"Got it, thanks," Max said.

"We changed the route to avoid any pre-planted explosives and to throw out any plans they may have made," Carrol said.

"Good thinking. Any checks being done on the vehicles in the parade?"

"Yes, full sweeps of all vehicles but there are too many people involved to check every individual. We also have not been able to sweep all buildings."

"Well, it seems like the highest likelihood of an attack. So many moving parts. They used backpack bombs in Sydney, so we know they have the technology. What will it take to shut the parade down?"

"I don't think it is an option that is on the table at the moment. If we get specific intel, I can make a call. There is something else Max. The Prime Minister and Israeli Prime Minister are making an unannounced appearance at the tennis."

"Fuck. Why?"

"Another show of strength and determination. You won't scare or change us. That sort of thing. You know better than most what politicians are like mate."

"Yeah but Jesus that's just another huge target. Have they got secure evac procedures?"

"Yes, a corridor will be prepared for their motorcades and they have full security details to keep a look out for anything suspect. Security at the tennis will be tight. I have already got boots on the ground there, so your focus on the parade is probably a good thing."

"I don't like this Carrol. There are too many moving pieces and with intel on a likely attack. We need to shut it all down."

"I agree Max. I'll make some more calls, but I don't think I will get too far. I am with the Defence Minister, he is calling the shots and the Prime Minister is apparently supporting his decision."

"Okay, we're on our way into the city now, keep in touch."

"Will do, Max, and be safe mate."

"Thanks," Max said ending the call. "This is getting out of hand fast. The Prime Ministers will be at the tennis now. Any thoughts lads?"

"Shit," Flash said.

"Bloody risky," Kate said.

"They are checking bags and x-raying at the concert and the tennis today, so backpack bombs at the parade would be an option and result in heavy casualties," Flash said.

"I agree with Flash, if the crowd is their MO," Kate said.

"Flash, you and I are going up in one of the birds to watch from the air. Kate, we will put you into the parade line up at about the halfway mark, so we have eyes on the ground. We'll put these three other AFP cars in to assist."

"Roger that," Kate said.

"Guess that's all we can do for now," Flash said as Kate pushed the big car to its limits. "Let's go Alpha, double time to the police headquarters."

Max's phone rang again. Hulk.

"Check your email," Hulk said, not bothering with greetings.

Max opened the tablet and clicked the link Hulk had sent. The screen divided into four windows. One was Max's image streaming from the tablet's front-facing camera. The second window was Chang, covered in bandages sitting taped to the chair in the bunker. Dalir was on the third window, looking worse for wear. Hulk appeared in the fourth.

"They both have monitors in their rooms and they can see each other, but their mics are muted," Hulk said.

"Can they hear or see me?" Max asked.

"Just a second. They can now."

"As I am sure you have figured out by now, you're not the first person I tortured today for information," Max said his voice booming in his prisoners' rooms.

"You've been a chatty pair. Now, I want you to think long and hard about the man you see on the screen in front of you, Chang, Dalir. Tell me everything I need to know about him. His place in the organisation. His role and tasks in all of this. Do that and we can discuss options for your future, because you will have one. Tell me nothing or feed me lies, there will be consequences and any future you have won't be long or pleasant. You do not have long gentlemen, I suggest you talk to my colleague in your room as soon as possible. Cut the feed."

The screens went blank.

"Right, we're out," Hulk said. *"Good job, kid. That should make them think. Especially, Chang. He's a gun for hire. He's the most likely to want a future and he will think he can talk his way out."*

"I hope so, Hulk. We're in some shit here and we need to narrow down the targets if we have any hope of stopping an attack."

"What's your plan, kid?"

"Flash and I in the chopper. Alpha on the ground with support in the parade. The parade is our assessment of most likely target, given the crowd and the security checks at the other two events. Plus, Carrol says the PMs are rolling in heavy to the tennis so I'm not sure how much more we can add."

"I don't think we can rule out any of the events especially now the PMs are going to visit."

"Oh I agree but we are scrambling here. It's ridiculous, Hulk. Have you spoken to the Prime Minister about it?"

"Yes. About thirty minutes ago. I tried to talk him out of it, but he said he was happy following the Defence Minister's advice. I told him I did not think that was a good idea especially putting James Fucking Johnston in charge. What a joke. But, he didn't want to hear it. I also spoke to my opposite in Israeli Intel and he said he was having the same trouble with his PM. Neither are listening. They want to go to the event as a show of solidarity against terror."

"Carrol said the same thing. Fuck."

"Lots of moving pieces in all three locations. I'm doing a final check on security details now. Patch me in when you get in the chopper."

"Will do, thanks Hulk."

Chapter Thirty-One

The delivery truck was stopped at a police check point. Heavily armed police and sniffer dogs were inspecting the truck. Sophia and her delivery guys were out of the truck speaking with police.

"Sorry ma'am, this should not take too long," an officer said. "Just being extra cautious given everything that has been going on lately."

"Ma'am?" Sophia said. "How old do you think I am?"

"Sorry. Oh gosh, I…I…"

Sophia smiled.

"I am just playing with you. Bit of humour doesn't hurt given what is going on."

"Oh thank goodness. You had me worried there for a moment. You're right, a bit of humour goes a long way."

"All clear, boss," an officer said approaching from the rear of the truck.

"Great. Ma'am, you are free to proceed. You will have to park two blocks back and go on foot from there. I hope you brought your trolleys."

"Ma'am?" Sophia said with a wink. "That's no problem officer. Thank you."

"Have a good day," he said blushing.

"Thank you and you too," Sophia said climbing back into the truck.

Two blocks from their delivery point, the truck braked and pulled into a free drop-off space. It was a big open concrete carpark which normally would have been full of cars. It had been cleared for security reasons, but it was full of people making their way to the event.

Sophia watched as the large crowd moved past the truck. Men, women and children of all ages and races. Some of the children had their faces painted while others waved flags. There was laughter and joy in their eyes.

Sophia felt a brief pull of hesitation and doubt. She looked down to collect her thoughts and caught a glimpse of her own reflection in the window. She stared for a long moment before snapping out of it.

"Let's go," she said to the delivery guy in the passenger seat.

They climbed out and went to the rear of the truck. They unloaded several items, including a similar metal container to the one they had offloaded earlier, and placed it on the trolley before making their way through the crowd to the drop point.

Chapter Thirty-Two

Flash was piloting the helicopter and Max sat beside him. They were hovering above the parade route watching as people from all walks of life moved into position along the roads beneath. The crowd jostled for the best spots on the parade barricades. Flags and banners were being waved, and confetti was being thrown into the air.

Max could not hear it above the sound of the helicopter but knew there would be music blaring along the route. He watched as people danced and drank in the street waiting for the parade to start.

Flash had made two passes over the Melbourne Cricket Ground and Rod Laver Arena before taking two slow trips above the parade route. Max noted the positions of the police snipers on the buildings overlooking the parade.

"This is impossible," Flash said after finishing another lap of the parade route.

"Yeah," Max said. "It is going to be hard to spot anything."

"Alpha, come in," Flash said into his headset.

"Here, Flash, got anything?" Kate asked.

"No, we're flying blind here. Too much movement. How about you?"

"Nothing suspicious yet. I am with the other drivers. There are people everywhere putting final touches on their floats and the Feds are sweeping each vehicle with mirrors and dogs."

"Not good, but do what you can and keep your eyes open," Flash said.

"Hulk, are you there?" Max asked into his headset.

"Just a minute Prince," Blake said. *"The General is on the line with the bunker."*

"Thanks, Hermes," Max said. "Flash, head over to the parade assembly area and let's have a look at the police sweep."

Flash tilted the chopper forward, heading for the showground where the floats and vehicles were waiting to start the parade. There were mobile stages for choirs and bands, dancers and ensemble groups milling around, and various vehicles covered in colourful messages of love and inclusion. There were also a number of organisations there to advertise their businesses.

"Hulk to Prince, you there Prince?" Hulk said over the headset.

"Receiving, Hulk," Max said. "Any news?"

"Your friend in the bunker is singing. Clearly you made an impact."

"Chang? What's he saying?"

"Yeah, says the guy you killed at the airport was a grunt. He was a Corporal in the Army, dishonourably discharged for assaulting a senior officer. Suspected of weapons theft and trafficking. Heath Wilson. Born in New Zealand. He's been working for a US-based private contractor. Involved in several private security operations including a few stints in the Middle-East with the US Army."

"Do we know who his last client was?"

"We are looking at his accounts now."

"Okay. What else?"

"Chang says Heath was hired just for the Commonwealth Building operation. Doesn't think there is an ongoing relationship between him and the other two, but we are looking into it."

"Well that's a start. We need the full names of the other two from the Commonwealth Building so we can run a search. Anything else?"

"Yes. He says Dalir is more than just a cell leader. He says Dalir is the head of the radical group here in Australia."

"Their Australian leader?"

"Yes."

"So, why isn't he on any of our lists?"

"He's been deep cover all his life. Born and raised here. Bred for this role."

"And Izad?"

"Chang says Izad was not supposed to be on the operation. Says he was being groomed to take over as leader. Dalir was not planning on making it home after the Parliament siege. Izad would have been in charge once Dalir took a bullet. He must have been added to the team last minute."

"Well, that is interesting. It also shows our friend Mr Chang is more involved in this than we previously thought."

"Have we ID'd the others from Parliament yet?" Flash asked.

"Yes. A couple from the watch lists, a couple from the close surveillance lists and a couple we didn't know."

"How did the guys being monitored by our close surveillance teams get away without detection?" Flash asked.

"Their surveillance teams were taken out."

"How is that possible? AIS surveillance teams are all but invisible."

"They had a tip off," Max said. "They knew what to look for."

"Looks likely," Hulk said.

"Hulk, are you on alone?"

"Just a second," Hulk said pushing a combination of buttons to make the line private. *"I am now."*

"We have a terrorist tip off leading to the deaths of our surveillance teams. We have leaked blueprints of the Commonwealth Building and Parliament House. And, we've got the deleted files from Crown Constructions. Someone is helping them. From inside AIS."

"Fucking hell," Flash said.

"From here in you, Flash, Alpha and I should be the team until we can find out who's with us and more importantly…."

"Who's not," Hulk said finishing Max's thought. *"My thoughts too, kid. I trained you well."*

"Learnt from the best. Watch your back boss."

"Will do. Anything from your end?"

"Hundreds of vehicles. Thousands of people. We are looking for a needle in a haystack, Hulk. It is pretty much impossible. My recommendation is still to shut it down."

"The Prime Ministers aren't changing their minds. I have tried, but they're following your Minister's lead. God help us."

"Shit, I don't like this at all," Flash said. "Something is coming and we aren't ready for it

"I agree," Max said.

Beneath them the parade had started. Vehicles were slowly heading down the route. Max was watching and scanning the ground when he saw something out of the corner of his eye. He turned his head to the left and his eyes widened in horror as a shockwave hit the helicopter and an explosion could just be heard above the rotating chopper blades. In the distance, a pillar of smoke was billowing out of Rod Laver Arena.

"Jesus Flash, look," Max said pointing towards the stadium. "We were wrong. They hit the tennis. Oh fuck, no. Let's move, Flash."

"Oh God," Flash said gunning the big police helicopter in the direction of Rod Laver Arena.

"Hulk, Alpha," Max said into the headset. "It was Rod Laver. They have hit the stadium. We are en route. Where are the Prime Ministers?"

"They are both in the stadium, Prince. Get in there!"

"Oh shit," Max said.

They swept in low to survey the scene. An explosion had wiped out a large section of the stadium. Bodies were strewn across the court and what was left of the seats in one section. Thousands were running for their lives inside and outside the arena. Advertising signs had been ripped from the concrete while others hung loosely, the metal torn from the explosion. Spot fires were burning all over the stadium and smoke was pouring out and up into the sky.

"Flash, bring it down inside the stadium. I'm going to go in to find the Prime Ministers."

Flash steadily lowered the chopper into the stadium. The rotors swirled the smoke throughout the arena. Max climbed into the rear of the chopper and loaded up. When it was about a metre from the ground Max leapt through the door and dropped softly on the blue court. No sooner than his boots had hit the ground, he began running for the corporate boxes.

"Hermes, patch me in with the Prime Minister's security detail," Max yelled over the chopper's rotor wash as he ran.

"One moment," Blake said. *"AFP Team One, AFP Team One, this is AIS. We have an asset on the ground at Rod Laver making his way to you. Do you copy?"*

"Copy AIS," an agent said weakly over the radio after a few long seconds.

"Agent, this is Prince, from AIS," Max said. "What is the status of the Prime Minister?"

"I...I'm not sure. I was outside the room. Making my way in now."

"I'm sixty seconds away," Max said sprinting up the stairs.

The smoke was thick and it was burning his lungs as he ran. He had his MP5 raised. People were running down the stairs. They screamed and moved aside when they saw him running towards them.

"Federal Agent, move aside!" Max yelled as he bound up the concrete steps.

Max hurdled bodies and chairs as he made his way along the concrete walkways. He reached the door to the corporate box and kicked it open. He found the AFP agent he had spoken to moments ago digging through debris. He was throwing chairs and broken sections of table clear.

"Give me a hand with this," the agent said.

Max ran over, holstering his MP5 on his back. The two agents lifted a large leather lounge up and walked back and placed it down a few metres away.

The Prime Minister of Australia was lying beside his Israeli counterpart.

"Prime Minister, can you hear me?" Max said to the Australian Prime Minister.

"What, what happened?" the Israeli Prime Minister asked.

"Sir, are you okay?" the AFP agent asked the Israeli.

"I, I think so."

"Sir, we are going to get you out of here," the agent said before pressing his radio button. "AFP Command, this is Agent Smith. We have the Prime Ministers. Need assistance ASAP for evac."

"Roger that, Agent. Support is on the way, thirty seconds out," came the reply.

"Prime Minister, can you hear me?" Max repeated leaning in over the Australian Prime Minister.

"Is that you, Max?" he said gently opening his eyes.

"Yes, PM."

"My leg is pinned. It feels like you have shot me again."

Max scrambled, throwing clear loose debris then he found it. A large shard of glass was piercing the Prime Minister's thigh in almost the same place as Max had shot him at Parliament House.

"Okay, well, you have a minor cut there," Max said reassuringly. "You'll be fine. Help is on its way. Not a good day for that leg."

"Are you trying to be funny, Max?" the Prime Minister asked through pain laced smile. "Bad jokes and lies. Have you thought about a career in politics?"

"Well, sir, I think your jokes are always good and I'm sure all politicians are truthful at all times."

"Now, that is funny."

The Israeli PM was on his feet and the AFP agent was helping him to the door as it swung open. Ten agents from Australian and Israeli police services stormed into the room.

The Israelis grabbed their Prime Minister under the arms and rushed him out of the room towards their waiting motorcade.

"Who's got the med-kit?" Max asked.

One of the Australian police officers ran to his side.

"Here, Agent Shaw," the officer said passing Max the kit.

Max and the agent spent the next few minutes rebandaging the Prime Minister's leg, careful not to move the glass.

Once it was secured and bandaged in place, the agents stood him up. Max was under his left arm, the agent under his right, both easily taking his weight.

"Let's move," Max said. "Clear the way you lot."

Half of the agents ran ahead, guns up to clear the way. The others formed a protective ring around the Prime Minister as they headed for the motorcade.

"How many dead, Max?" the Prime Minister asked.

"Unclear, PM," Max said. "Hundreds. I'm sorry we failed you again."

"No, Max. You warned us. James said the intel wasn't there. It's not your fault. It's mine. I should have made a different call."

"This is not on you. But I promise I will find out who did it and I will make sure justice is served."

"Thank you for saying that, Max. Happy hunting."

Max and the agent helped the Prime Minister into his waiting vehicle which sat idling to make a quick exit. Agents were scrambling into motorcade support vehicles.

"Max," the Prime Minister said. "Thank you. I will shut down the other events before I get to the plane. Sorry, I didn't listen to Hulk's advice. Will you tell him?"

"I will," Max said. "Get to the plane and get better. The country needs you now more than ever."

"Thank you, Max."

Max shut the door and tapped on the roof, "get out of here!" he yelled to the first car. Tyres screeched on the polished concrete as the motorcade accelerated towards the arena's exit.

Chapter Thirty-Three

Max climbed back into the helicopter. Once he was strapped in, it lifted off the ground.

"Hulk, put me through to Dalir," Max said over his headset.

Hulk barked a few orders and pressed a series of buttons.

"You're on kid," Hulk said.

"Dalir, you son of a bitch!" Max said. "Hundreds are dead and injured. You did this. You are going to pay for it."

"Hundreds? Excellent!" Dalir said. "See the pain my brothers can inflict? Anywhere, anytime. And, your precious MCG is in ruins too, I hope? Please tell me, did it take out the singer and his infidel audience? So many disgusting sinners, worshipping at that homosexual's feet dead and injured. Inshallah."

"Hulk, evacuate the MCG!" Max yelled.

"It's happening as we speak, the Prime Minister just gave the order," Hulk said.

"What?" Dalir said confused, before laughing. "Oh, it has not gone off yet? Must have been the tennis first then? Well, no matter, you are too late anyway!"

"Izad is as good as dead and so are you, Dalir, you piece of shit!" Max yelled.

"Oh, the pain in your voice is worth it, Agent," Dalir said. "We are ready to die for our cause."

"Cut the line, Hulk," Max said hearing Dalir laughing as it disconnected.

During the call, Flash had moved the helicopter over the MCG next door to Rod Laver Arena. As they hovered over the centre of the field, the MCG lights were coming on and early evening inside the stadium became day in their light. Max watched as the concert stage lights were extinguished. Security guards were running onto the stage. Three guards grabbed the performer and dragged him away from the piano and down under the stage. Another guard was at the microphone. Max watched helplessly as the crowd began pushing and shoving one another scrambling for the exits. Max could see the terror in their faces.

Then it happened.

The bar in the Members' stand exploded violently throwing flames and debris over the crowd. A whole section of the stadium was engulfed. Hundreds of people were thrown forward from the shockwave.

The bar opposite shattered as a ball of flame shot out over the crowd and up into the air. Chunks of concrete and plastic seats were hurled through the air taking out people as they ran.

The helicopter shook as the second blast washed over the aircraft, but Flash kept it level. Even with the noise of the chopper and their headphones on, Max and Flash heard the loud explosion.

"Hulk," Max said barely able to speak. "They've hit the MCG. Two bombs. They must have taken down at least two hundred people. There is mass panic inside the stadium."

"It's a warzone, Hulk," Flash said his voice cracking.

"Jesus Christ. Every available emergency worker is en route to the sports precinct but it's not going to be enough," Hulk said. *"We need reinforcements, I'll make the call."*

"Prince, Flash, it's Hermes, Hulk has gone off comm to call in the troops," Blake said. *"What else can you tell me?"*

"It's just chaos," Flash said.

"What about the location of the bombs, can you pinpoint where they were?"

"The bars," Max said thinking aloud.

"What about Rod Laver?"

"Flash, move us back over to the arena."

The helicopter moved quickly and hovered over Rod Laver Arena. But for the bodies of the fallen spectators, it was empty. Fires were still burning and smoke was billowing out. Emergency vehicles were pulling into the carparks around the perimeter.

"Check it out," Max said. "Hermes, the damage seems to be focused on the area where the bars were. They must have used the bars to smuggle in the explosives."

"There are bars on the parade route too, Prince," Blake said.

"Alpha, come in," Max said. "They've hit the tennis and the concert. We think they were using the bars for cover to get the bombs in."

"Copy Prince," Kate said. *"The parade is still moving. The news hasn't travelled yet."*

"Roger. Get the AFP to hit their sirens and use their megaphones to start clearing the area. We will sweep in low and do the same from the air."

"Ack," Kate said.

The chopper spun and hurtled back towards the city.

"Prince, I've called it in," Hulk said through the headphones. *"The local guys should be getting a message within the next few minutes to clear the area. I've also called the Chief of Defence. He's mobilising troops as we speak."*

"Roger that, Hulk," Max said. "We're going in to try to clear the parade route."

The helicopter swung in low, only a few storeys above the parade procession. Max saw the local cops on the roof tops and on the street corners all looking at their radios. Moments later they all sprang into action. At first the crowd was slow to move but then the sirens started. Kate and her escort vehicles were approaching. In their wake, people were starting to flee.

Max pressed the speaker button, activating the chopper's megaphone.

"This is the Federal Police," Max's voice boomed from the chopper. "For your own safety, please evacuate the area. Return to your homes. This is not a drill. This is not a stunt. This is an emergency! Please clear the area as fast as possible. I repeat, evacuate, return home, this is an emergency."

"Max, look," Flash said pointing ahead to the bar strip on the parade route.

"Get me above it," Max said before climbing back over into the back of the helicopter where he checked his MP5 and pistol.

Max opened the helicopter's side door and kicked out a rope which was buckled to the airframe. Without another thought, he grabbed the rope and jumped from the chopper. His left leg wrapped around the rope to control his descent.

Max hit the ground only a few metres away from the first mobile bar. He immediately raised his MP5 and walked quickly towards the first bar. He kicked the door. A nervous staff member was gathering up the takings before fleeing.

"Get out of here," Max yelled.

The young man dropped the money and ran past Max out the door. Max checked the bar, moving the register and beer kegs. He checked the fridges and kicked open the maintenance panel. Clear.

"Two minutes out, Prince," Kate said.

"Ack," Max acknowledged.

He moved and cleared the second and third bars in the same way. Checking kegs, fridges and equipment.

Max heard the big four-wheel drive pull up a few feet behind him. Kate jumped out and immediately raised her MP5, mirroring Max.

Together, they swept the fourth mobile bar. As Kate checked the beer kegs, the door of the fifth bar swung open and machine gun fire peppered their bar. The thin wall was riddled with bullet holes.

Max scrambled for the door to get to better cover but Kate stayed put by the kegs and returned fire through the wall.

Max stood using the bar for cover. Leaning around the wall, he fired in the direction of the fifth bar.

A large family wagon pulled up next to the fifth bar. The driver fired at Max, forcing him back behind cover. The bullets tinged loudly as they hit the metal structure flicking up yellow paint and tearing holes through the promotional posters hanging on the massive metal box.

Two figures ran from the fifth bar and jumped into the rear seat of the wagon under the cover being provided from the vehicle's driver. The car sped off as one of the assailants slid the side door closed.

"Alpha," Max yelled. "Let's go!"

"Just a second, Prince," Kate shouted through the door.

Moments later, Kate leapt through the mobile bar's door and ran for her big Landcruiser. Max ran for the passenger seat.

"Flash, stay with them," Max barked into his comms unit.

"On 'em," Flash said. *"They're four blocks ahead following the parade route. It's clear. Most people have moved away from the street already."*

Kate was pushing the big V8. It roared through the gear changes, closing in on the slower wagon.

The wagon's rear window opened and the two rear passengers started firing at the pursuing Landcruiser. Bullets bounced off the toughened windows and bonnet harmlessly. Max opened the sunroof and fired his MP5 through it towards the wagon. Several bullets went through the opened window, impacting inside the wagon. It swerved widely trying to evade. It sideswiped a car to its left bouncing on impact but kept moving.

Max saw an opportunity. The passengers had fallen on each other on impact with the parked car. He stood exposing his upper body through the sunroof. He shouldered his MP5 and fired at the passengers in the wagon. Bullets hit all around the passengers and hit the rear tailgate.

The vehicles took a hard left onto the on-ramp for the motorway. Max stumbled. His right arm catching on the sunroof. He quickly recovered but not before gunfire rang out from the fleeing wagon. Bullets hit the windows and roof next to Max. He ducked back into the cabin for safety and took a moment to reload his MP5.

"Get us some support," Max said to Kate. "Block the road ahead."

"Got it," Kate said picking up the two-way. "AIS to AFP Command, come in Command. In pursuit of suspected terrorist subjects from today's bombings. Nepean Highway, just past St Kilda, heading towards the Mornington Peninsula Freeway. Requesting immediate backup and roadblock assistance. Priority one."

Max heard a reply from the police dispatcher as he was standing to return fire at the wagon.

There was traffic on the highway. The two big vehicles were weaving in and out. Max was careful not to fire if there was any danger to civilians. Unfortunately, the wagon did not have the same restraint. The rear passengers started firing at vehicles at random. Cars braked hard, squealing as their rubber tyres bit into the road. There were several collisions as cars smashed into the back of those braking. Glass, lights, bumpers and wheels were torn from vehicles on impact.

Kate drove masterfully through the pile ups and stopped vehicles. Made even more impressive considering the size of the Landcruiser.

"Get me closer," Max yelled through the sunroof.

Kate gunned the big Landcruiser bringing it within metres of the wagon.

Max fired.

A rapid onslaught of bullets ripped into the wagon's rear panel and seats. One of the rear passengers was hit in the chest. Blood sprayed from the wounds and the life drained out of his face as he fell onto the back of the seat.

"The local guys have put the roadblock in place, Prince, just a few kilometres ahead," Kate yelled up through the sunroof.

After a couple of kilometres, Max looked into the distance and saw a line of police vehicles blocking the road ahead. Red and blue lights flashed awaiting their arrival. Kate backed off letting the wagon get ahead.

The wagon braked as the driver sighted the police barricade.

Max jumped back down into his seat and put on his seatbelt.

"Ram it Alpha!" he said.

Kate pushed the accelerator to the floor.

Impact.

The heavy bulletproof Landcruiser smashed into the back left-hand side panel of the wagon as it was beginning a U-turn. It hit hard. The wagon's front right-hand wheel gripped on the roadway causing the wagon to flip. It flew through the air end-over-end, landing on its nose before falling and skidding to a stop on its roof only metres away from the police road block.

Police surrounded the vehicle guns drawn as Max and Kate's car pulled up a few metres down the highway on the city side.

Max was in full sprint towards the overturned car. Kate was close in behind him. Both had their MP5s drawn at the ready. Max shot the rear window raining glass down on one of the passengers who had been shooting at him. She was unconscious.

The driver had not been wearing a seatbelt and was thrown wildly around in the crash. He was in bad shape. Clearly, he had several broken bones and internal bleeding. They all knew he was unlikely to survive.

Max holstered the MP5 behind his back and retrieved his knife. He cut the seatbelts that the passenger was tangled in and she fell awkwardly out of the seat onto the roof. He grabbed her by the jacket and dragged her from the car through the window.

"Alpha, get the med-kit," Max said. "You two, drag the other guys out."

Kate ran back to her car to get the first-aid kit and the two police Max had given the command to ran over to the vehicle to pull the driver and the shot passenger out.

Max began to check the woman for injuries. Her breathing was shallow. He lent in closer to listen to her chest. She was struggling to breathe. He looked up. Her lips were turning blue. He felt her ribs and found what he was looking for. A broken rib and likely punctured lung.

Kate arrived with the med-kit. Max pulled out a tube, water bottle and scalpel. He made a deep incision in her chest then pushed the tube through into the cavity. The other end of the tube went into the water bottle. He then bandaged the area around the tube locking it in place and sealing it. Her breath was still shallow, but it was not as strained, as the pressure was lifted from her lungs. He had saved her for now but she needed a doctor badly.

"See if she has any belongings in the car," Max said.

Kate went over and rummaged through the wreckage.

"Sorry, Agent, this guy is dead," one of the police officers tending to the driver said. "So is the guy from the rear."

Max nodded to the policeman.

"Time to wake up," Max said to the woman as he waved smelling salts under her nose.

She woke with a start and winced in pain as her body came back online. She looked down at the tube sticking out of her chest. Adrenaline made her heart race. Max grabbed his silenced Glock and rested the barrel on her forehead.

"I work for AIS," Max said. "I have tortured two of your colleagues in two days, do not make it three for three. Be smart. You will die here on the road without medical attention. Tell me what I need to know and I will let you live. I'll get you the help you need. Do you understand?"

She nodded.

"What is your name?"

"Sophia," she said weakly.

"What's your surname?"

"Capaldi."

"Who do you work for?"

"Dalir Rashidi."

"What is Dalir's role in this?"

"He is the leader of a terrorist cell here in Australia."

"What is your objective?"

"Create chaos and fear. Spread the word of Allah and wipe the infidels from the Earth."

"So, you're a true believer Sophia?"

"Yes."

"What is the second verse of the Quran?"

Max saw her squirm and her eyes flinched.

"You see Sophia, I just don't believe you," Max said grabbing the tube in her chest and shaking it.

Sophia screamed through clenched teeth in pain.

"Stop, please," she begged. "I will tell you everything. I don't want to die."

"Well, start talking," Max said.

"My name is Sophia Capaldi, I was a Major in the US Army, before I joined the CIA," her voice trailing off.

"Why are you helping terrorists?"

"Means to an end," she said weakly, her eyes starting to close.

"Wake up, Sophia. Why are you helping them and don't tell me it's money?"

"I have done so many terrible things and seen so many terrible things, I just have to get away from it all. I want to live the rest of my live with the person I love and try to forget the pain that I have caused."

"Tell me who is involved and what's next, and ease some of your guilt."

"Prince, I've got her phone," Kate said.

Kneeling down she placed Sophia's finger on the scanner unlocking the phone.

"Stay with me, Sophia, what happened to you? How can you turn your back on everything you once believed in?" Max asked.

"We have risked our lives for this ungrateful country and mine too many times, and for what, a medal and a pat on the back? No more. We were getting out of here to live free of all of this. Dalir was just for cover."

"Who is we?"

Sophia shook her head, refusing to answer.

"Who else is involved, Sophia? The man that was with you in Sydney, Xander?"

Sophia looked at Max with shock in her eyes.

"That's right. I know who you are. You blew up the Commonwealth Building trying to assassinate a Minister of the Crown after killing the CEO of NorthStar Defence Industries Mr William 'Bill' Jones. I also know you were together at a safehouse in Parramatta yesterday. You have now been caught fleeing the scene of a terrorist attack in Melbourne. It is all over for you, Sophia. So why don't you tell me where your boyfriend Xander is before he hurts anyone else?"

Sophia just stared at Max for a few seconds before shaking her head again.

"I'm not going to tell you. He will get away from you and live for both of us."

"Well, that's a lovely thought. Selfless even. I wonder if he would be the same in your position? I guess we will find out soon enough when I catch up with him. Although, since you have not been very helpful, I am probably going to take out my frustration on him. He is going to be in for a long, painfully slow death."

"No, please. Don't hurt him."

"All you need to do is tell me where he is and I will save him some pain."

Sophia closed her eyes tight trying to decide what to do. Her mental anguish drawing more pain on her face than her physical pain.

"I won't tell you where he is. He will beat you."

"Well, pain for Xander it is then. So, now that's decided why don't you tell me who you really work for?"

"The Pilot."

"Who is he?"

"He does not like you," Sophia said coughing.

"Who doesn't? Give me a name."

"He is closer than you think," Sophia said slowly and softly before closing her eyes.

Sophia passed out and her body went limp. Max waved the smelling salts under her nose. Nothing.

"Fuck," Max said. "Get her to the hospital now! Call me when she wakes up."

Two policemen ran and picked her up. A third grabbed the water bottle and tube still hanging from her chest. They placed her in the back of a police car and it sped off towards the hospital.

"Prince, you need to see this," Kate said passing Max Sophia's phone.

"Jesus. Let's get back to the plane and regroup."

Max signalled for Flash to land the helicopter.

"Flash, get us back to the plane," Max said climbing aboard.

"Roger that," Flash said, as the helicopter lifted and banked heading north for the airport.

Max started reading from Sophia's phone.

"We need to speak to Hulk," Max said without lifting his eyes from the screen.

"Sure do," Kate said.

Chapter Thirty-Four

Xander slowed his car on approach then stopped just short of the gate between two small grey guardhouses. Two guards, one on either side, walked to his car. The guard on the right kept his eyes locked on Xander as the window started to lower into the doorframe. The guard on the left scanned the backseat before inspecting the car.

"Good evening, sir," the guard at his window said. "ID please."

"Good evening, no problem mate, here you go," Xander said handing over his new identification card.

"Thank you, I won't be a moment," the guard said walking over and scanning the card at a computer inside the guardhouse.

A green light flashed and Xander's photo appeared on the computer monitor. The guard checked the photo on the screen matched the one on the card before making his way back over to the car.

"Here you are, Sir. You're free to enter."

"Thank you. Have a good night."

"And you, Sir."

Xander drove through the gates, his headlights stretching down the long road, as the sun was setting in the distance. He kept his vehicle at the signposted speed until he found the building he was looking for, pulled into the carpark and shut off the engine. He sat in the fading light and dialled a pre-set number on his mobile phone.

"It's Xander. I'm here. Making my way in now. I will do a recon of the site and update you with details, before proceeding to pick up the package. I should have it done within a couple of hours."

"Good, thank you, Xander," the Pilot said. *"But, we have a problem. I was not going to tell you until your mission was*

complete, but I want you to know. It's Sophia. She's been killed."

"What? No. That's not possible. She was just making the last drop. She should be on the road."

"He found her. The bombs went off as planned at the tennis and the concert, but he found her planting the third. There was a car chase. He rammed her car and she died of her injuries on the way to the hospital."

Xander sat in silence.

"I am sorry Xander. I know you two had become close. Sophia knew the risks. We have to keep moving forward. You must get to the package and you have to ready the jet. We need to get out of here. I will be there soon, they are close to finding me. I have stayed too long. Do you hear me, Xander, are you still with me?"

"Yes, of course. Sorry. It is just, I…"

"I know you loved her and I am sorry, but we need to push on or we will both be joining her when he catches us."

"Yeah, you're right. I'm on the way to the package, but know this, I will kill him for this."

"Good. Use your pain Xander. Channel it into revenge. Max "Prince" Shaw is your number one target. But, first you need to secure the package, ready our escape and complete your mission. Do you hear me?"

"Understood," Xander said. "He is a dead man walking."

Xander ended the call and sat in silence. A tear fell down his cheek. After a moment, he wiped it away before returning his hands to the steering wheel gripping it so tightly his knuckles went white and began to shake. He clenched his jaw as hatred ran over his body.

"I will kill you, Prince," he said, before composing himself and getting out of his car.

He walked over to the nearest building and pulled an access card out of his pocket. He swiped it in the panel next to the door. It was a different pass to the one he used to get through security. Only a select few people could access this building.

Once he was through the door, he walked across the open space and through a door on the opposite wall. Inside was an elevator which he took down into the basement. When the elevator stopped at the bottom of the shaft the doors stayed closed until he swiped the same security ID card on the access panel. It opened revealing a small concrete room with a solid steel door and hi-tech security panel which looked better than any bank vault he had ever seen. He inserted the card halfway into a reader with a light click. As he looked down he saw the smiling face of Mr Bill Jones looking back from the card.

Xander took out Jones' tablet computer. He had found it and his access card in Jones' briefcase after he shot him in the Commonwealth Building's foyer. Xander plugged the little tablet into a socket next to the card reader. The black screen was suddenly filled with rapidly scrolling white text computer code. When it stopped the cursor sat blinking on the screen patiently waiting for a command. Xander typed away on the screen's keyboard then hit 'enter'. A green light flashed and a small alarm sounded, as four big, thick steel bolts smoothly retreated into a recess in the wall and the door opened with a hiss as air rushed into the space beyond.

He took a moment to assess each item before him lined up perfectly square in the secure room. When he found the right serial number, he connected Jones' tablet and typed an eight-digit combination into the keypad. A similar green light and alarm preceded a small click as the package was released from its hi-tech security lock.

With package in hand, Xander made his way back to the elevator as the security doors closed behind him.

Chapter Thirty-Five

Max, Flash and Kate sat in the comfortable business class leather chairs on the Gulfstream which was still parked in the AIS hanger at Melbourne's Tullamarine airport. Max and Flash were going through what they had learned from Sophia and Chang, and trying to piece together what might be coming next. Kate was typing away on a laptop but she paused when it beeped with a new message. She clicked the link, read the message then reached for the remote. Kate found the button she was looking for and the screen on the wall changed to show a video feed from AIS. On the left of the screen, Blake appeared. On the right, Hulk sat down and looked at the three agents.

"There was nothing you could have done," Hulk said seeing the broken looks on his agents' faces. *"They were way ahead of us on this one but well done stopping the bomb at the parade. You saved a lot of lives."*

"It was concealed in a beer keg," Blake said. *"Looks like you were right, Prince. Early indications show that's likely to be how they got them into the stadiums too. Well done Alpha for disarming the fourth bomb."*

Max and Flash gave Kate a smile and a nod, acknowledging their team member's heroics.

"Thanks, boss" Kate said. "It was only possible because Prince was laying down covering fire."

"Well, good work to you all," Hulk said. *"Now, enough backslapping. I want you all back in Sydney as soon as possible."*

Max looked at Kate and nodded his head. Without speaking Kate got up and walked to the cockpit. As she was walking back, the stairs folded in, the door locked and engines started.

"Hulk, we got a phone off Sophia," Max said picking up Sophia's phone. "You need to hear these messages. Message one, 'They changed the plans, I didn't know the rooms had moved'. Message two, 'They brought in Chang, he is being interrogated as we speak'. Message three, 'Chang gave up the safe house, if you are still there GET OUT NOW!'. Message four, 'I've deleted the files from the tablet which should slow them down but I'm going to need to get out of here soon, it won't take long until they're on to me'. Message five, 'Dalir is here, they are torturing him for information'. Message six, 'Shit, they've got Izad too, Dalir is talking'."

"Jesus, you were right, Prince," Hulk said. "This confirms we've got a traitor in our camp."

"Whoever it is has got to be in Sydney to delete those files," Flash said.

"Hermes, watch your back," Max said. "Someone there is working against us."

"We are running an investigation as we speak," Blake said.

A man appeared to Hulk's right and walked in to hand him a note.

"Your friend Sophia died en route to the hospital," Hulk said looking up from the note.

"She wasn't in good shape when we sent her off," Max said.

"That happens when you not only ram a family car with three tonnes of bulletproof Landcruiser, but you do some dodgy emergency field surgery on someone," Hulk said.

"Hmm, how is the Prime Minister?" Max asked changing the topic.

"He is upset he didn't follow our advice and feeling a bit sorry for himself," Hulk said. *"He's called in the Defence Minister for a 'please explain'. Otherwise, he is fine. The doctor and staff on the plane have fixed him up. No permanent damage."*

"He's going back to Canberra?" Flash asked.

"No, Sydney. Once he gets to the residence, he and the Defence Minister will be holding a press conference," Blake said.

"And, the Israeli PM?" Max asked.

"He is on the jet with the Prime Minister. Once they land, he and his team will head for their plane and fly out," Blake said.

"That is probably for the best," Flash said.

"Agree," Hulk said. *"I'm going to get to the airport. I'm coming to Sydney. Hermes, can you contact my pilot and make the arrangements?"*

"Yes, of course, General," Blake said. *"See you all when you get here."*

The screen faded to black just as the jet sped down the runway taking off as the sun was disappearing over the horizon.

Chapter Thirty-Six

He dialled the familiar number from memory.

"Hello," Xander said.

"It's the Pilot. I'm on my way to you. Is our plane ready?"

"Yes, it is. Fuelled and waiting."

"Good. Do you have the package?"

"Yes. I'm set up and ready to go."

"Good. Good. Right, when I get there two of my guys will come and make sure you are not disturbed."

"How far out are you?"

"Not far. Signal our other men to get ready. See you soon," he said ending the call.

"Sir, you might want to see this," the Pilot's driver said as he ended the call.

The Pilot pressed the button on the small television screen mounted to the back of the chair and the screen came to life in front of him, Sky News. The anchors were explaining over the car's speakers what they knew so far. Three explosions at Rod Laver and the MCG. News was coming in of a fourth that may have been stopped at the culture and diversity parade. Reports of a car chase on the Nepean. The breaking news banner in its distinctive yellow with black text proclaimed *Australia under attack.*

The rolling footage cut away to a blue room adorned with six brand new Australian flags standing proudly behind two lecterns. The Prime Minister and Minister for Defence walked up to the matching lecterns embossed with the Commonwealth Coat of Arms. The Pilot and the watching world noticed the Prime Minister was using a cane and limping heavily. The Pilot smiled at the sight.

"We take you now to the Prime Minister and Minister for Defence," the anchor said.

"It is with incredible sadness that I stand here tonight with the Defence Minister to tell you that our nation has suffered a catastrophic series of terrorist attacks," the Prime Minister said. *"Following the attacks on the Commonwealth Building in Sydney and Parliament House in Canberra, Melbourne has suffered simultaneous attacks at the tennis at Rod Laver Arena and at a concert at the iconic Melbourne Cricket Ground. The death toll is still rising. Hundreds of people have been killed or injured and the number will continue to rise. I urge all Australians to return and stay in your homes. The terror alert has been raised to the highest level and I have called in all Defence, Police and Intelligence Officers to work on preventing any further attacks. We have a number of leads and we will pursue them rigorously to get to the bottom of how these attacks were possible and most importantly to stop any further loss of life. Rest assured we will find those responsible and hold them to account for what they have done."*

"The Israeli Prime Minister is safe and is his way back to Israel. I thank him for his support and friendship during this very difficult time. I have spoken to my counterparts in the United States, United Kingdom, Canada and New Zealand all of whom have offered immediate assistance and support. I have also spoken to a number of other world leaders who have condemned these attacks. I also contacted the Heads of State and Heads of Government in the Middle-East whom I have assured we will continue to support in their fights for freedom from tyranny and terror. We will not stop until there is peace in the Middle-East and we will not be deterred in our fight for freedom, liberty and democracy."

"On my direction, the Australian Defence Force in conjunction with our Defence industry contractors have moved forward plans to bring our new Defence capability online and send it into battle. Of note, our new aircraft carrier, HMAS Barton, which was on sea trials, has been joined by an armada of ships from the Royal Australian Navy, and the New Zealand and United States' Navies, and they are headed for the Gulf. Additionally, several of our new unmanned drones have been

launched and, on my direction, have commenced bombing raids over the Middle-East on known terrorist targets with our F/A18 Super Hornet fleet which was already on patrol. My message to every person who chooses to spread tyranny and terror here and abroad is this: there is no building or cave, no crevasse or bunker where you can hide. We will find you and we will end you."

"Our thoughts and prayers are with the families of those who have suffered loss on what is sure to be one of our nation's gravest days. But, we will overcome this threat, we will heal together and we will endure, because that is who we are. We can be hurt but our spirit can't be broken."

"The Defence Minister will now outline the details of our increased commitments in the Middle-East and of our new defence capability we have deployed into the field. We will then take questions. James."

"Excellent," the Pilot said. "Just as planned."

Chapter Thirty-Seven

Kate drove the car into the storage garage above the AIS bunker.

Hulk was climbing down from the backseat of a big black Landcruiser with tinted windows at the far end of the garage. He waited for the three agents and they walked to the elevator together.

When the door to the bunker opened at the bottom of the elevator shaft, Blake was waiting.

"General," he said walking with Hulk and the three agents into the bunker. "I have recovered the files from Crown Constructions. My computer is piecing them back together very slowly. So far, we have recovered information on Dalir and his organisation, as well as the Arab businessman, that umm, fell from the window at Crown Constructions and his network in Australia. We also have information coming in on suspected terrorist cells in Adelaide, Brisbane and Perth."

"Great work Blake," Hulk said. "As soon as the information comes in we need to get our teams around the country out there arresting or killing these fuckers. Send Shadow in will you?"

"Umm, there's more, General. It looks like the terrorists planned to hit NorthStar Defence Industries. The files contain a massive amount of information on the company. Mr Jones's profile as well as files on each of the members of the board and senior management were recovered. It looks, at this point, like the terrorists are holding NorthStar at least partly responsible for the strikes in the Middle-East."

"The Prime Minister said in his press conference that he had sent NorthStar's drones to the Middle-East," Flash said.

"Only half the drones. There are four on the HMAS Barton heading for the Gulf. Two drones were on trials in Germany. They are all fully loaded and will aid our F/A18 Squadron in strikes on Syria, Iran, Iraq and Afghanistan. The final six are still at Richmond Air Force Base."

"And, you think the terrorists know this and that they are going to try to take them out before they can be deployed too?" Max asked.

"Yes, Max, or worse."

"Turn them against us?" Hulk said.

"Yes, General."

"Flash, Alpha, go get our tactical gear ready," Max said. "Full kit, fully-loaded and comms. I'll be in, in one minute."

"I'm coming with you," Hulk said.

"You've got it," Flash said as he and Kate ran for the weapons vault.

"Where is Shadow?" Hulk asked.

"He's leading the first tact team to NorthStar," Blake said. "They have already left."

"Good. Anything else?"

"Yes, sir. Mr Chang was found dead in his holding cell about twenty minutes ago. Looks like he bled out."

"How is that possible?" Max asked. "We patched him up and got the doctors in to see him."

"Blake, from this point forward you are to only communicate with Shadow, Prince, Flash, Alpha or me," Hulk said. "I want to know who deleted the files as soon as possible. There is a rat in the ranks and we need to flush him out."

"Yes, General, understood. The final files are decrypting now and I will update you as soon as we have them."

"Thank you. This stays between us," Hulk said.

"Of course, good luck," Blake said jogging back to the conference room.

"You think our mole took out Chang?" Max asked.

"It's possible. Blake will call us when he has more. Let's make a move."

Max and Hulk joined Flash and Kate in the equipment room. All four changed into their new black tactical gear. They loaded smoke and flashbang grenades, and spare magazines into their vests. They fitted and tested their comms units.

Backup pistols were holstered to their thighs as well as flexicuffs and hunting knives. Each of their vests displayed their callsigns in grey stencil. Prince. Hulk. Alpha. Flash.

"Let's move," Hulk said.

Chapter Thirty-Eight

Kate pulled her new Landcruiser up to the gate at NorthStar's compound on Richmond Air Force Base. It looked like a fortress within a fortress. Men dressed in similar tactical gear were on guard. They took aim at the vehicle as it approached.

Kate slowed the big four-wheel drive to a stop.

Surrounding the gate, Max noticed a number of dead bodies lying on the roadway and the green lawns. Each was a man in his mid-twenties or thirties, with dark skin and dark beards. They looked Middle-Eastern. There must have been fifteen or twenty in total.

On the other side of the gate, he saw several dead NorthStar guards laying face down on the concrete.

"What the fuck?" Kate said.

"Looks like they already tried their luck getting in," Flash said.

"You in the front, wind down your windows then put your hands on the windscreen!" a guard yelled.

Kate and Hulk complied.

"You in the rear. Hands out the windows!"

Max and Flash wound down their windows and put their hands out.

"Seems we missed a hell of a fight," Kate said to the guard as he approached gun at the ready. "We're from AIS. Our colleague Air Commodore Greg "Shadow" Lloyd is expecting us. This is General Scott, Agents Shaw and Gordon, and I'm Agent Matthews."

"General, gentlemen, ma'am, apologies," the guard said lowering his weapon. "Welcome to NorthStar, please come through quickly, we're unsure if they are sending reinforcements. Air Commodore Lloyd is in the mess preparing our team to defend the site. Follow this road, take the second right. It is the last building on the left."

"Thank you," Kate said. "Sorry, for your loss."

"Sorry?" the guard said.

"Your men. I am sorry you lost men."

"Oh yes, of course, thank you."

After driving through the gate and following the directions to the mess, Kate pulled the car into a park near Lloyd's. The four men walked into the mess and found Lloyd commanding a group of private soldiers. He was barking orders to the group about securing the compound.

"Lockdown the hangers and secure the perimeters of each," Lloyd said. "The engineers need to be pushing to ready the drones for launch as requested by the Prime Minister. Air Force personnel will be on the compound in a few hours to take command of the drones. They need to be ready by then."

"Yes, sir," one of the men said snapping off a salute before heading out of the mess.

"Looks like you've got everything under control," Hulk said.

"Ahh, hello Patrick," Lloyd said. "Max, Jacob, Kate, good to have you all here. You missed all the action though I'm afraid."

The agents nodded.

"Think we've seen enough for a while anyway," Flash said.

"Quite possibly," Lloyd said.

"Where are we up to?" Hulk asked.

"We are locking down the compound and the Air Force have locked down the wider base. The final six drones are all but operational. The final checks are being done now and weapons are being fitted for deployment. NorthStar has brought in their whole security unit to guard the compound."

"Where are our guys?" Max asked.

"They are out advising and supporting NorthStar's guys to lockdown and secure the facility."

"Hulk, if you don't need me, I might go see if our guys need a hand," Max said. "Flash, Alpha, stay with Hulk."

"Got it," Flash said.

"Ack," Kate said.

"Good idea, report in when you have spoken with each of our guys," Hulk said.

"That is not necessary, Max, my boys have got it covered," Lloyd said.

"All the same, an extra set of hands can't hurt," Max said.

"I agree, off you go, Max," Hulk said overruling Lloyd.

Max left the mess and started walking down the road towards a row of hangers. Up ahead Max saw guards jogging between the structures and others standing sentry on the entrances.

"How's it going?" Max asked a short nuggetty man guarding one of the hangers.

"Can I help you, Sir?" the sentry said.

"Yes, I am looking for the AIS agent who is helping out in this hanger."

"No one here from AIS. I suggest you head back to the mess."

"No, I think I will go in here and have a look."

"Sorry, that's not possible. Weapons are being loaded and I cannot let you in."

"This is going to happen one of two ways. You either move aside or I will move you aside."

The guard went for his gun.

Max sidestepped grabbing the guard's arm in his left hand. His right arm flew up and under the guard's shoulder. Twisting and lifting with both hands, Max dislocated the guard's shoulder then he slammed his forehead down on the bridge of the guard's nose knocking him out. Max caught him before he hit the ground and dragged him around the corner away from the door. He flexicuffed the guard to some pipes then took his security pass which he used to open the hanger door.

Inside the hanger, one of the drones stood gleaming in the neon light. It was a sleek, smooth, gun-metal grey, windowless plane. It had a bulbous head, running down a long cylindrical body to a V-winged tail.

It was an eerie figure.

Its most impressive feature was its wingspan. The wings easily matched those of a jumbo jet. Max knew from the briefing Mr Jones' had left him it could fly for days without needing to refuel and it was as stealthy as they come. Four clusters of Hellfire missiles could be loaded on the drone in its standard configuration with two larger bunker buster missiles either side. Other more devastating missiles could also be fitted if necessary. The drone class was known as Gungnir or Odin's spear.

Men and women in lab coats were busy at computers connected to the front of the drone in the centre of the large white sterile room. A team of men in military tact gear were busy loading missiles onto the drone from metal trolleys. The two larger missiles were already in place. Max watched the organised chaos for a few minutes then started walking across the hanger.

Halfway across the laboratory-come-hanger he saw a man hurry through a door marked as storage. There was something about the man. He could not place him, but there was something about him, something not right. He had a gut feeling, so he decided to follow.

Max crossed the hanger, walked through and clicked the door shut behind him.

Two men clad in AIS tactical gear stood in the foyer-like room before him guarding the door opposite.

"Hello, lads," Max said. "I thought it was weird when the guard at the door said there were no AIS agents in here. What are you two doing?"

"Prince, good to see you," the agent on the left said. "Harry and I are guarding the access point for the drone control units."

"Good to see you too, Scraper. Harry," Max said nodding to each before looking at the elevator doors beside him. "This is the access point for the bunker and the drone control units?"

"Yep," Scraper said.

Max knew the two agents. He had only worked with them once but knew Lloyd trusted them. Scraper was short for Skyscraper. He got his nickname for obvious reasons. He was easily six feet seven inches tall. He literally towered over most and he was supposedly made of steel. The second agent, Harry, got his name from looking like a famous royal. Max knew it was mostly the orange tint in his hair that sealed the deal.

"So you were sent here to guard the suitcases?"

"Yes," Scraper said. "The elevator takes you down to the security storage unit. High tech security systems. You need a tablet and an access card to get in, but we are here as an extra layer of protection."

"Right. Well, we certainly don't want anyone down there. Good stuff. What about the man who came in here before me?"

"What man?" Scraper said shifting slightly on his feet.

"There was a man who came through this door before me. Who is he and where did he go?"

"Sorry, I'm not sure what you're talking about. You're the only one who has come through as long as we have been here. Look, we've got everything covered here. Maybe you should head back to the mess."

"Why does everyone want me to go back to the mess?"

An alarm sounded behind Max. He backed back towards the door and stole a glance through the small window into the hanger.

"Oh fuck," Max said as he watched the hanger doors opening and the drone rolling towards them.

It knocked over ladders and scuttled trolleys. The men and women in lab coats, as well as the guards ran out of its path, shouting in obvious confusion.

Max stood looking through the little window when he felt a shiver run down his spine. The hairs on the back of his neck stood up. Instinctively, he ducked just before a bullet smashed the little glass window he had been looking through.

He spun to see a look of astonishment on Scraper's face. He had come to within inches of Max and missed. Max was impressed someone so big could get the drop on him.

Max grabbed Scraper's gun-wielding left hand, dragged him forward and brought it down hard on his knee snapping the agent's wrist. He groaned and dropped the gun before throwing a massive right hook towards Max. Max dodged the incoming blow by millimetres. Using Scraper's momentum against him, Max grabbed his arm and pulled it, spinning the big man around and into the wall.

The second agent, Harry, had his gun drawn and pointed at Max.

"Stop, Prince," Harry said. "Don't make me shoot you."

"You better or I am going to fucking kill you, you traitor!" Max said.

Scraper ran at Max, but Max was too fast. He ducked the incoming blow and looped the big man into a sleeper hold in front of him. But, Scraper was too big and strong. He broke the hold. Even with one hand, Max knew he was going to be hard to beat. Max threw a left jab into Scraper's jaw, followed by a quick right cross which hit him on the right eye. It swelled quickly.

Max kept Scraper between himself and Harry for cover.

The big agent ran at Max again. Max moved like lightning, drawing his knife as he dropped to one knee. As Scraper came level with Max unable to stop his forward momentum, Max pushed the knife up into the right side of Scraper's body finding the soft tissue beneath his ribs and severing his oblique. In one smooth motion, Max spun Scraper around using the agent as a shield. He kept hold of the knife with his right hand and wrapped his left arm around Scraper's neck. Every ounce of his strength was being used to hold the agent up and awkwardly march him forward.

"Stop Prince," Harry said.

"Put the gun down Harry and I will let you live," Max said as Scraper's blood ran down over his hand and onto the floor.

"Jesus, hang on, Scraper."

"Oh, isn't that sweet. Still looking out for each other. Guess your country is the only thing you turned your back on today but not your traitor mate here."

"I am sick of risking my life for nothing Prince. You, of all people, should appreciate that. Look what this job did to your life. How is you're fiancé, anyway?"

Max thought about Lachlan and felt sadness wash over him. Then, anger. White hot anger.

"How dare you! You don't get to say his name you traitorous fuck!" Max said ripping the knife from Scraper's side and throwing it with all his might.

The knife flew through the air end-over-end until it punctured Harry's throat. The force drove the knife through his windpipe and lodged the blade in his spine, knocking him back towards the door. Harry blinked in shock and fear, before he dropped to the floor.

Dead.

Scraper fell to the floor at Max's feet. He was clutching his wound and bleeding out on the concrete.

"That what this is about for you too, money?"

"Please Max, don't kill me."

"You tried to kill me and you have clearly played some role in everything that has happened over the past few days. Those deaths are on you. You are a traitor!"

Scraper was weakly dragging himself towards his gun which laid on the cold concrete floor not far from him. He sprung towards it using the last of his fading strength. Max was faster. He drew his silenced pistol from his right thigh holster and shot him through the temple. His body went limp. Max fired two more shots into Scraper's body just to make sure he was dead.

"Hulk, come in," Max said into his comms piece. "Flash, Alpha, are you there?"

Silence. His communications were being jammed.

Max stepped over the bodies of his former colleagues, grabbing his knife on the way past Harry and opened the door they had been guarding.

It was dark, just a faint glow coming from exit and safety lights. The storage area was full of stacks of crates and rows of shelving. Ahead the man he had seen earlier stood in the darkness next to a row of computer monitors which sat on an upturned crate.

"Agent Max "Prince" Shaw, it's good to put a face to the name, I've heard so much about you," the man said. "Now I understand why he really hates you. In fairness, he hated you before you got involved in all of this, but after you saved the Minister, tortured information out of Dalir and Chang, and stopped the fourth bomb. Well, let's just say his hate has grown. And after what you have done, I hate you too."

"Who are you?" Max asked. "Come into the light and let me see the face of a dead man.

The man moved from the shadows into the weak light. Max had seen his face before. He was the man from the lobby of the Commonwealth Building. The man who assassinated Mr Jones and who tried to kill the Minister, and who had tried to kill him twice in the Commonwealth Building and at the airport.

Max raised his pistol and fired at Xander as they both leapt for cover behind the crates.

"I heard you were a better shot than that!" Xander yelled.

"Step back out and I will show you how good I am," Max said.

"Ha! Good one."

Xander fired two shots hitting the crate Max was kneeling behind. Max pulled the pin and threw a flashbang up and over the crate. It landed only a few inches from Xander. Max covered his ears and waited. Once he saw the light flash on the wall he sprung to his feet and started running towards the crate Xander had been behind. Firing at the wooden box.

Out the corner of his eye, he saw something but it was too late. Xander charged at him and tackled him to the ground. Max dropped his gun as they wrestled. Xander had obviously heard the flashbang land and ran. He was on top of Max pressing down hard with his forearm on Max's jaw and throat.

"You couldn't just die in the Commonwealth Building, could you? You had to be a fucking hero. Well, I missed you twice but third time lucky, I won't miss you again."

"Chang's dead you know, your inside man killed him. What's to stop him doing the same to you?"

"Chang was a pawn, who cares?"

"And, what about Sophia, she a pawn too?"

"I am going to kill you for what you did to her," Xander said his tone giving away his emotions.

"She should have been wearing a seatbelt. Vehicle safety is very important."

Max felt Xander's grip soften slightly. He capitalised kicking Xander up and over his head. Both men scrambled to their feet.

"So, not just a pawn then?" Max said smiling again.

Xander ran at Max unleashing a rapid flurry of punches. Max guarded his head and deflected the punches with his forearms.

Then it was his turn.

He threw two left jabs which hit Xander's forearm. Not getting through there, he threw a savage right uppercut into Xander's abdominals right above the liver, winding him. Max jumped from his left foot into the air and threw a hard-right knocking Xander down onto one knee.

Max landed and went to throw another punch, but Xander sprung up bearhugging him and trapping his arms above his head. Xander squeezed hard making it difficult for Max to breathe. Max squirmed trying to break his grip, moving enough to swing his legs. He drove his knee into Xander's groin. Xander immediately loosened his hold enough for Max to get his hands around Xander's throat. He tightened his grip cutting off Xander's air supply. Xander let go and clawed at Max's hands, but he did not release him. Instead he kneed Xander several times in the stomach. One of Xander's hands was clutching at Max's chest then it came up holding something. Xander locked eyes with Max as they both looked at the grenade pin in Xander's hand. Max immediately let go and looked down at his vest. Xander stumbled backwards looking for cover. In a single action, Max pulled the flashbang from his vest and tossed it after Xander. It exploded with a blinding white flash and its deafening bang rattled the storage room halfway between the two men.

Max had closed his eyes but only managed to loosely cover his ears. They were ringing as he fell towards cover.

A crowbar swung through the air and hit Max in the back as he fell. Luckily his vest took most of the blow, but it still knocked him to the ground where he slid forward on his chest. He rolled over just in time to see the crowbar coming down towards his face. He rolled to the left and the bar hit the floor hard millimetres from his head. Xander flung the bar back over his head readying for another attempt. But, he was too slow, taking his time to put every available inch into his swing. Max grabbed his knife, sat upright and plunged it into Xander's stomach as he reached the top of his arch with the crowbar. The bar dropped to the floor behind Xander. His hands wrapped around Max's right hand which still had hold of the knife. Xander looked down at Max, blood starting to flow from his mouth. Max used the knife to push Xander back and take some of his weight, so he could stand.

"Why were you helping terrorists?" Max asked.

"They were just a means to an end," Xander said through bloodied teeth.

"You're not the first person to say that to me. So, why don't you tell me what the end game is and I will let you join Sophia without any more pain?"

"Dalir and his terrorist mates were supposed to inflict as much damage as possible to frighten Australians and pressure the Government to act."

"How does that help their cause?"

"It doesn't. Quite the opposite. Dalir was in it to bring pain to a western nation and try to force a withdrawal from the Middle-East, but we were just using him. We knew the Government would not back down. We used him."

"Another pawn. So, tell me, who is the King? Who's the guy pulling the strings? Who is the Pilot?"

"He has been planning this for a long time. As I said before, he hates you for interfering. And, the best thing is he has done it right under your nose."

Xander laughed through bloodied teeth and winced as he fell to his knees.

Max followed him down, still holding the knife, kneeling on one knee. Xander went to speak but just smiled as blood flowed from his mouth. Staring at Max, he fell backwards. The life gone from his eyes before his head hit the ground.

Max took Xander's security pass and searched him for a phone. He pulled out Xander's mobile and pressed his finger against the scanner. It unlocked. Max scrolled through the messages.

Max saw the messages he had seen on Sophia's phone but then read two new messages. The first said *'I'm my way to you. Four AIS guys with me. Two on side. Two who will need to be handled. I'll assume command when on the scene.'* The second message said, *'The precious little Prince is on his way to you. You know what to do.'*

Chapter Thirty-Nine

Max's phone started ringing.

"Prince, the last files downloaded," Blake said with uncharacteristic panic in his voice. *"I found a bio and headshot of Air Commodore Lloyd. His name is also on a number of the remaining files. They look like emails and encrypted messages to NorthStar, someone named Xander and to the businessman from Crown Constructions. There are also forged immigration papers and passports. There's a spreadsheet listing financial transfers between several players including Chang and Dalir. It shows both cash and stocks. Shadow has amassed a large share in NorthStar. The businessman from Crown Constructions must have been their banker. Payments also went to Harry and Scraper. They're on site with Shadow."*

"Xander's not going to be a problem, nor are Harry or Scraper," Max said. "They attacked me. I had to put them all down. Hermes, Shadow is the Pilot. He is the one behind all of this. Can you get a message through to Hulk?"

"Christ, Shadow is the Pilot. I can't get Hulk on the line. He's not on comm and not answering his phone. I can't reach Flash or Alpha either."

"They were with Shadow in the mess."

Max had walked over to the bank of computer monitors Xander had been standing in front of and his eyes widened as he registered what was on the screen.

"Oh fuck, Hermes, we've got an even big and more immediate problem," Max said.

"What is it, Prince?"

"One of the drones launched and it has two targets locked."

"What are the targets?"

"One of the markers is above Sydney. It looks like Bondi."

"Can you make out the exact location?"

"Yes, I have been there recently, it's the hotel the Minister and I stayed in the night of the Crown Constructions job."

"How far out is the drone?"

"It is out circling over the ocean getting to altitude. We've only got a few minutes."

"Okay, I am bringing up the schematics for the control unit, I will talk you through it. What is the second target?"

"That's strange. It's in Western New South Wales. What do we have out there?"

"What? Western New South Wales. Nothing."

"No, wait. It's above Western New South Wales and it is moving fast. It's a plane."

"It's the Israeli Prime Minister's jet," Blake said.

"Oh God. Have you got the manual up?"

"Loading, yes. Here it is. Alright, there should be a joystick and a keyboard?"

"Confirmed," Max said.

"Good, right. You need to enter an override code into the system. Hit Control F5. A new window should appear. Have you got it?"

"Yes hurry, Hermes, it has turned back towards the city."

"Type 'command override' and hit 'enter'."

"It says 'enter access code'."

"You need to look at the briefcase and give me the serial number. It should be engraved on the side of the case."

Max turned the case left and right. Nothing. He spun it around.

"Got it. Alpha, Kilo, Juliet, Hotel, two, zero, one, two, nine, zero," Max said.

"Searching," Blake said.

An alarm sounded from the drone's suitcase. Max looked at the screen.

"Hurry mate, it's arming one of the missiles. Sixty seconds."

"Okay, here it is. Hit Papa, Juliet, Juliet, Sierra, four, one, six, one, one and hit 'enter'."

"It says 'override sent', but nothing is happening," Max said grabbing the joystick. "Ten seconds until launch Hermes."

"It should be yours. That's the right code."

Override confirmed. Missile Launch Aborted, appeared on the screen.

"Oh, thank God," Max said. "It aborted, Hermes. Good job mate."

"That was too close."

"Let's not celebrate too early. It's doing something else, it says 'second target coordinates acquired'. It just banked hard and took off across the city."

"Shit, it's still going after the Israeli PM."

Max hit Control F5 and typed 'command override'. The box reappeared. He typed 'P-J-J-S-4-1-6-1-1' and hit enter.

"I re-entered the commands but it's not responding."

Max typed it in again.

"Nothing," Max said. "Shit, it's gone supersonic! I didn't even know they could do that."

"Yeah, that's a feature only codeword cleared operatives know about. Above Top Secret. You weren't going to read that in Jones' brief."

"Well, what are we going to do? It won't be long before it starts to gain on the PM's plane at that speed."

"Ok, here we are. Open the command window and type 'manual operation'."

Max typed it in. *Command sent* appeared on the screen.

"Done," Max said.

"Good, in a moment you will take control of the drone using the joystick."

"Ack. Just like flying the Gulfstream right?"

"Umm, sure. Let's run with that."

After a few very nervous minutes, *Manual Operation Confirmed* appeared on the screen.

"I got it, Hermes," Max said. "How do I slow it down?"

"There is a lever on the side of the joystick, pull it back towards you."

"Alright, here it goes," Max said pulling the lever. "Okay, it's slowing down. I'm trying to drop the altitude, but it's fighting me. It's still locked on target."

"Type 'target abort'."

Max typed in the command. *Command sent.*

"Sent, Hermes. Cross your fingers."

Target Abort Confirmed flashed across the screen. Max breathed deeply.

"Aborted, Hermes. You did it, well done."

"Good job, Prince!"

"Hermes, my comms unit isn't working either. I think they must be blocking it. Is there any way you can disable their block so I can reach Hulk?"

"Yeah, that should be possible. I will boost the signal and reroute the traffic over the emergency frequency. It may take a few minutes."

"In the meantime, I'm going to land a multimillion dollar drone in the middle of the desert."

"Piece of cake."

Max brought the drone down on an abandoned road in the middle of Western New South Wales. It skidded hard on the gravel, kicking up rocks before sliding off the road into the sandy red soil. The little monitor showed a cloud of red dust engulf the drone before settling on the dry and hot landscape.

"Better get the local cops out there to watch it, Hermes, and scramble the nearest military unit," Max said.

"Already on it."

Chapter Forty

"Hulk, Flash, Alpha – it's Shadow! He's behind all of this!"
Max yelled through their earpieces. *"He's the Pilot. Here's my
SITREP. Shadow has taken control of NorthStar and they
funded Dalir's attacks! He just tried to take out a hotel in Bondi
and the Israeli PM with one of the new drones. I have aborted
both with Hermes' help and we crash landed the drone in the
desert in Western New South Wales. I also took out two of our
guys, Scraper and Harry, who were working with Shadow and
I killed Xander, the guy who assassinated Mr Jones."*

Lloyd looked at Hulk and his two agents, Flash and Kate,
then to his NorthStar contractors. On cue, the contractors all
raised their guns surrounding the AIS agents.

"You son of a bitch!" Hulk said.

"Oh please," Lloyd said. "I have spent over thirty years in
the Air Force and AIS, and I have nothing to show for it. I
watch on as people like James Johnston, the so-called Defence
Minister, throw around directions like they have some small
clue about the world. They do not. It is a joke! How many lives
have they taken? Innocent men, women and children the world
over, and the disadvantaged kids they gave a uniform and a gun
and sent to war – all for political point scoring and dick
measuring. It is all just a game to them. I cannot do it anymore.
It's time for them to get involved. Time for them to bleed and
time for them to payback everything I have sacrificed."

"You've killed innocent people today you hypocrite!" Flash
yelled.

"They are a means to an end Jacob."

"You are a traitor," Hulk said. "You won't get away with
this."

"I already have," Lloyd said. "The dead terrorists we
planted at the front gate are responsible for all of this, under
Dalir's command. I cannot believe they got in and took
command of a drone. They are resourceful fellows. And, just

as I planned the Prime Minister has ordered the Gungnir drones into action. Our munitions factory is working overtime to fill missile orders. I have spent years silently acquiring NorthStar shares. I am now a major shareholder and soon to be Chairman of the board now Mr Jones is out of the way. I am going to make billions. But first, I am going to kill your precious Prince in front of you, then I will kill the three of you. Then all that is left is to handover the drones and retire due to the sadness of losing my dearest old friend Patrick 'Hulk' Scott. Put down your guns you are outnumbered. You have lost."

"I hate to burst your billion-dollar bubble, but Prince has aborted your strikes and disabled the drone, and he will come for you with an unwavering desire to kill you," Hulk said smiling. "It's you that's lost."

Chapter Forty-One

Max had been listening to Hulk and Lloyd as he made his way out of the hanger. In the process he had taken out four guards. He had his MP5 up sweeping left and right. In the dark of night and completely dressed in black, Max made his way through the shadows back towards the mess. He had put a silencer on the MP5. It took some of the sound out but reduced his range. Max hid behind a wall and connected his mobile to his comms unit. He dialled Blake.

"Prince, how can I help?" Blake said.

"Shadow has Hulk, Flash and Alpha hostage," Max said. "I need you to contact Special Agent Carrol at the Federal Police. Tell him everything. Send him the files you recovered. I will contact him now to let him know you will be making contact. I am going to get our friends back and take out Shadow."

"Understood, good luck and Godspeed," Blake said ending the call.

Max dialled Carrol.

"Max, what can I do for you?" Carrol asked.

"Carrol, I don't have long. One of our agents has gone rogue. This is all tied to NorthStar Defence Industries. Every attack. Lieutenant Commander Blake 'Hermes' Smyth is going to contact you and transfer you the evidence we have collected. I am sending it to you because I don't know who else to trust. He has Hulk, Flash and Alpha hostage at the company's Richmond RAAF Base Compound. I am on my way to get them back."

"Understood, Max. I am in Sydney with the Minister. We're at the hotel in Bondi. Let me get a team together and I will come and back you up."

"Bondi? Shit. I don't have enough time to wait. I'm going in. Thanks, Carrol. Hermes will be in touch soon."

Max ended the call.

Max was only two buildings away from the mess. He army crawled forward slowly in the darkness. Dragging himself across the grass. NorthStar guards were running along the street towards the hanger he had just left. He stopped moving as they passed. Keeping a low profile, he laid flat in the shadow of a nearby building staring through his scope, surveying the scene. The curtains had been drawn inside the mess completely blocking his view.

Only one way, he thought to himself.

He slowed his breathing and gripped the trigger. He sighted in the two sentries on the mess's front door. He felt his heart rate slow.

There were two short hisses in very quick succession as he squeezed the MP5's trigger twice. He knew he was pushing it to its limits with the silencer on, but he did not want to give away his location. The bullets found their targets, the necks of the mess guards. They fell on top of each other.

Max waited. Nothing.

He ran in a crouch towards the fallen guards. He checked for pulses. Nothing. He dragged them around the corner into the darkness before trying the mess door.

Locked.

He retrieved the security pass he had taken earlier and waived it on the scanner. It beeped three times and a red light flashed. Max cringed. Taking a knee and levelling his gun at the door. No one came so he stood and tried Xander's security pass. One beep and a green light unlocked the door.

Max entered the foyer silently, clicking the door gently back in place behind him. The doors to the main mess hall were closed. Max crawled up to the doors and rested a moment. Listening.

He pulled out his phone and plugged in a long cord which he drew from his vest. After opening an app on his phone, he thread the other end of the cord under the door. An image of the room came into focus on the phone's screen. Hulk, Flash and Kate were flexicuffed to chairs at the far end of the room.

Lloyd and four of his NorthStar men were a few metres to the left of the door huddled around a computer. Max left the camera under the door as he set about removing his last flashbang and three smoke grenades from his vest. He loaded a fresh mag into his MP5 and removed the silencer. He sat one of his pistols next to the grenades, once he reloaded it.

Max scanned the camera to the left. Shadow and his men were still occupied by the computer. He moved the cord bringing Hulk, Flash and Kate into focus. He pressed the button on the cord several times in quick succession. Flash saw the little light blinking under the door and silently got Hulk and Kates' attention. They saw it too. When Max knew they had seen his signal he got to his knees and flashed 'ready' in Morse Code with the little light. All three agents nodded gently. Max slowly and softly opened the door a few inches.

The flashbang landed on the table next to the computer. Shadow saw it and jumped out of his chair. His men were not that quick to react. The three smoke bombs which Max had pulled the pins on before throwing the flashbang left a trail of smoke as they soared through the air towards Hulk, Flash and Kate. Smoke instantly started covering the three agents. The flashbang went off with a similar result as the two from the hanger. Blinding light and ear-piercing concussion rang out. Hulk, Flash and Kate had each tipped over their chairs lowering their mass to the floor making themselves smaller targets behind the smoke in case Shadow or one of his team got a shot off in their direction.

Max rounded the door and loosened a volley of bullets from both his MP5 and his pistol in the direction of Shadow's men. Two men were hit while the other two dived for cover. As Max made it to cover behind a pillar, he saw Lloyd running through the side exit. The door behind Max opened and three guys ran in. Max squeezed the trigger emptying his MP5 into the three men, killing all three. But not before one of them got a shot off which luckily hit Max's vest which was lined with Kevlar. It protected him, but he was winded by the force of the impact.

Bullets splintered the pillar, from shots fired from behind the table. Max blind fired around the pillar in the direction of Shadow's remaining guys. He pulled the camera and smartphone back out and pressed his chest against the pillar facing the table. Aiming the camera around the pillar he found his target. Taking aim using the footage on the little screen, he shot four bullets into the chest of one of the guys behind the table. His pistol clicked. Empty. The remaining guy heard it and sprung to his feet. Grinning from ear-to-ear he levelled his gun at the pillar and pulled the trigger.

Five bullets slammed into the pillar. Max pulled his arm back behind it for protection. The firing stopped as the gun jammed.

Max capitalised and stepped out from behind the pillar dropping the phone and empty pistol, and with practiced precision drew his hunting knife and threw it at the NorthStar guard with astonishing force. Just like Harry from the hanger, the big knife lodged in the guard's neck with the force throwing his head backwards. He fell to the ground. Max picked up his MP5 and pistol and reloaded both. Then he went and got his knife before walking into the smoke filled rear section of the room. He cut the flexicuffs from the wrists and ankles of each of his colleagues, and one by one they got to their feet, coughing from the smoke.

"Thanks, kid," Hulk said trying to catch his breath.

"Are you all okay?" Max asked as they walked to Shadow's table clear of the smoke.

"Yes, thanks to you mate," Flash said, coughing out the smoke.

"I can't believe fucking Shadow did this," Kate said, spitting on the ground.

"Neither can I," Hulk said. "I have known him for over three decades. He is the last person I thought would be a traitor. But, he is. And now, he is a dead man. I need to contact Blake."

"He helped me take down the drone, Hulk. It was only seconds away from hitting its first target."

"Jesus, that close?"

"Yeah."

Hulk nodded reflecting on what he had just been told.

"We should go after Shadow," Kate said.

"He will already be off the base," Max said. "But we have bigger issues. NorthStar guards are no doubt on their way. We can find him once we're clear."

"Max is right," Hulk said. "Grab your gear. We are going to have to fight our way off the compound."

Hulk, Flash and Kate retrieved their weapons which had been stripped from them before they were tied up. Mags were checked and guns loaded. The whole process took about two minutes.

"Safety off, you lead the way kid," Hulk said to Max.

"You got it, boss," Max said.

Flash, Kate and Max all raised their weapons to their shoulders in unison. Hulk joined them on Max's right.

Max was first through the door and crouched aiming straight ahead. He was followed by Flash who took a knee and swept his MP5 left searching for targets. Hulk was through third, mirroring Flash to the right.

Max found two targets ahead and fired. A bullet hit the first target in the bicep spinning him around and he dropped behind cover. The second guy moved fast, diving behind a tree. The bullet sailed past the attacker.

Flash had seen a NorthStar guard duck behind the corner of the building. He drove two warning shots into the wall an inch from the corner.

Hulk fired three shots. Three targets fell. All three were shot in the head. Two fell in the open as they ran towards the agents. The third fell as he stuck his head out from the cover of the building.

"Move," Max said.

Max, Flash and Hulk formed a V, and began making their way to the car. Kate joined them walking backwards, scanning and guarding their rear flank. The four agents in a diamond formation headed across the carpark. At the halfway point, Kate found Flash's guard from the corner of the building and dropped him with two shots. More guards were running in across the fields next to the mess. All four agents began shooting.

"Double time," Max yelled picking up his speed.

Guards fell as others ran for cover. Those safe behind trees and barriers were firing at the agents.

"Fuck!" Kate said as she fell to the ground. "I'm hit."

Max, Flash and Hulk stopped, and crouched around her, still firing.

"You still with us, Alpha?" Flash asked. "Can you walk?"

"Nah, fuck, it hit my quad, think it broke the fucking bone," Kate said through clenched teeth.

"Well grab your gun and get ready to fire, I'm going to drag your arse to the car," Flash said. "Prince, Hulk, ready to move?"

"On your call," Max said.

Flash gave Kate his MP5 and grabbed her under the arms.

"Move," Flash yelled.

Max and Hulk laid down covering fire. They were in a crouch walking as fast as they could without leaving Flash and Kate behind. Kate moaned and winced as her legs dragged along the bitumen. Anger was rising in her eyes. Through the pain, she fired both MP5s taking down another three guards and firing in the direction of others sending them diving for cover.

"Come and get your bullets you fucking traitors, I've got enough for each of you!" Kate screamed as she fired at the guards.

As they got to the car, Max opened the rear passenger door and Flash climbed in dragging Kate up and in behind him. Max closed the door before jumping in the passenger's seat. Hulk fired another volley taking down two guards then he jumped into the driver's seat. Bullets harmlessly bounced off as the big bulletproof Landcruiser's engine kicked over.

Chapter Forty-Two

Hulk took his ring off and inserted it into the car's entertainment system.

Authenticating. Welcome Hulk.

"Call the bunker," he said pressing a button on the steering wheel and slamming the car into reverse.

When the speed was right, Hulk pulled the handbrake. The vehicle spun one hundred and eighty degrees. Hulk shoved the gearshift into first, dropped the handbrake, hit the accelerator and popped the clutch. The tyres bit and flung the big car forward.

"General?" the operator said.

"Get me Hermes!" Hulk yelled.

"General?" Blake said answering the call. *"All safe and accounted for?"*

"Yes. Prince got us out. Shadow is compromised and he got away. Cut off all access and inform the relevant channels."

"Already done, General," Blake said. *"I spoke with Prince. Access has been cut and I have informed the Prime Minister's office and Defence Minister's office as well as Defence and Federal Police commands."*

Hulk swerved to hit a guard sending him up over the bonnet and windshield, and over the roof. Hulk watched him bounce on the road in his rear vision mirror.

"Good work. We are en route to the bunker and may be coming in hot. Get two teams on the roof to assist."

"Right away."

"Get the Doctor and med bay ready too, Alpha's been hit in the leg and will need attention."

"Roger that."

"Thanks, twenty minutes out."

Hulk ended the call as the Landcruiser came under heavy fire from guards on the back gate of the compound. NorthStar men jumped clear as Hulk hit the gates at over one hundred kilometres an hour. Sparks flew as the gates were whipped back and broke from their hinges thanks to Hulk's bull bar.

As they headed down the rear access road, three NorthStar branded Jeep SUVs pulled in behind them giving chase having sped through the broken gates. Hulk slid the car onto a boundary road and headed for the motorway.

Flash had pulled a belt tight around Kate's upper thigh to stop the blood loss. He injected a small amount of antiseptic and painkiller into the wound. Kate winced and gritted her teeth. After waiting a few moments for the morphine to kick in, Flash applied a field dressing and tight bandage.

"That should keep you with us until we get to the bunker at least," Flash said smiling at Kate.

"I've had worse," Kate said. "Now, stop fucking around and go kill those arseholes."

Flash laughed.

"With pleasure," he said climbing over the back seat into the cargo space.

Max climbed over into the back seat next to Kate.

"Think we might need something bigger then these," Flash said throwing his pistol and MP5 down.

He typed his code into the security panel and opened the weapons hold. He pulled out two HK416 assault rifles. Max climbed over into the rear with Flash and took his HK and fitted a scope, front grip and under-barrel grenade launcher. Flash did the same. When they loaded their magazines, Max nodded to Flash.

"Let's do it," Max said.

Flash pressed a button lowering the rear window. Max fired a burst into the first Jeep's windshield causing it to swerve wildly. Unlike the Landcruiser, the Jeeps' windows were not bulletproof.

Shots were being fired at the Landcruiser from all three chasing Jeeps. Max and Flash took turns returning fire.

"Hulk, we're going to need back up!" Max yelled as he sighted two NorthStar assault helicopters sweeping in over the chase vehicles.

"Got it," Hulk said dialling the bunker.

Bullets ripped into the road either side of the Landcruiser as the front helicopter started firing. Flash fired at the helicopter. Realising he was hopelessly outgunned, Max turned and fired at the leading Jeep. The windscreen finally cracked. There was a low thump and pop as a grenade cleared the cylinder and was expelled from Max's under-barrel launcher. Finding its mark, the grenade smashed through the Jeep's cracked windshield. Seconds later the Jeep burst into flames from within. The windows all shattered and the roof tore open. A ball of flame shot up into the air in front of the firing helicopter. It was hit by the flames and smoke. The bullets stopped but the chopper did not, it just powered through and kept coming. The Jeep rolled on engulfed in flames, eventually crashing into a parked vehicle.

The remaining Jeeps dodged around and continued chasing as Hulk hit the on ramp for the motorway.

The lead helicopter fired a missile at the Landcruiser.

"In coming!" Max yelled.

Hulk pulled the wheel hard to the left and the missile hit the road a few metres behind the right tail lights. Max and Flash bunkered down behind the rear panel. The explosion blasted chunks out of the roadway. Dirt, concrete and steel flew up into the air. The shockwave lifted the Landcruiser up onto three wheels, but it was too heavy to flip, thanks to the bulletproof steel panels. As the rear wheel hit the ground again, Hulk gunned it. Max and Flash resumed firing at the helicopters and Jeeps. Max's phone rang and he answered using his comms unit.

"Max, it's Carrol. The Prime Minister has given me command to get you and your team to safety, and to help capture your rogue agent. What's that noise?"

"Good," Max yelled. "We need help. We are being pursued by two NorthStar gunships and a couple of Jeeps."

"Right, I have just been handed Hulk's message. Can you lead them away from public areas?"

"Yeah, we're on the motorway. They are not fucking around, whatever you're planning you better do it quick."

"Got it. Get Hulk to turn off the motorway as soon as he can to get them into open space."

"Hulk, Carrol says pull off and away from civilians when you can!"

Hulk drove the car off the road, kicking up dirt and grass. He smashed the car through a light wire fence and some soft scrub. The Jeeps followed and the helicopters pulled up and hovered on the spot as the vehicles made the turn cutting across onto a suburban street. The vehicles wound their way through the streets until finally they entered an industrial estate. Hulk swung the car left. It mounted the kerb and drove over what was left of an old rusty fence. Hulk led the Jeeps on a chase through a long-abandoned steel manufacturing site. It was huge. A large factory ran for several football fields in length down the left side of the site. Old furnaces and rusted machinery littered the right.

"All clear Carrol," Max said. "Do you have our location?"

"Yes Max, I'm tracking your phone."

Over the noise of the choppers, vehicles and gun fire came a sound like rolling thunder. It was low and rumbling but building. Within seconds the sound changed to a loud, high-pitched shrill whirling. Max could not place the source of the sound, but he knew what it was.

Moments later two smoke trails blasted through the clouds. The choppers both violently veered trying to evade but it was no use. The missiles were locked on the choppers' heat signatures. The explosions were loud and dramatic as the helicopters were ripped apart in balls of flame. The falling debris rained down on the site as the F/A18 Super Hornet screamed by overhead and off into the distance.

One of the big choppers fell into the path of one of the Jeeps. It slammed into the flaming heap, crumpling the SUV. Petrol from the Jeep ignited and another explosion rang out as the car was torn apart.

Hulk drove off the site and headed for the storage yard, which sat above the bunker, only a few kilometres from their current location.

"Thanks, Carrol, the two choppers are down," Max said. "And one of the Jeeps was taken out by the wreckage. We will handle the remaining Jeep."

"Got it. Good luck."

Max and Flash riddled the remaining Jeep with bullets.

"This is Hulk, Hermes are you on comm?" Hulk asked.

"Here, General, in position and standing by," Blake said.

"One minute out, lower the bollards."

"Done. See you in one minute."

"As soon as our Landcruiser passes through hit the button. Danger close."

"Understood, sir."

Blake heard wheels screeching and gun fire then the big Landcruiser shot through the gate. He slammed his hand down on the red button. Three small explosive charges forced the bollards out of the ground within fractions of a second to devastating effect. The front of the Jeep was ripped free of the vehicle pinning it to the bollards. The agents on the rooftops unleashed wave after wave of bullets into the Jeep. Impossible for anything inside the vehicle to survive.

Hulk's car sped through the open door of the rear storage unit. A maintenance team and medical team were both waiting as the car pulled up. The medical team dragged Kate from the car onto a stretcher.

"Look after her, Doc," Max said. "You're in good hands, Alpha."

"Will do," the doctor said.

"Looks like it," Kate said smiling as she sighted her attractive doctor as they wheeled her off towards the medical room.

Max and Flashed laughed as they followed Hulk to the lift.

Chapter Forty-Three

Blake joined the team in the elevator and passed a tablet computer to Hulk.

"General, I'm sorry but you need to see this," Blake said.

Hulk hit the play button. The footage showed Chang taped to the steel chair in the interrogation room.

"*Oh it's you,*" Chang said. "*What do you want?*"

"*You have said too much,*" Lloyd said stepping into the shot.

"*Fuck you, did you see what he did to me? I did not want that psychopath coming back in here to torture me again.*"

"*Well, Xander and Sophia only just made it out the first time you opened your mouth. Now, it looks like the little Prince is going to piece this all together thanks to you and that prick Dalir.*"

"*I cannot be blamed for Dalir and all his mistakes. You recruited him.*"

"*Hmm, he should be fucking dead. Bloody terrorist piece of shit. He had one job then all he needed to do was get shot but he fucked that up too.*"

"*Well, you do not always get what you want when you hire people, especially Middle-Eastern radicals. Who would have thought they could not be trusted.*"

"*You are not helping your situation.*"

"*Just let me out of here and we can finish what we started. I will find the others and kill them.*"

"*No. I said before that you said too much. You have proven you cannot be trusted. You are a gun for hire and you will turn for the right price.*"

"*No, please. I will do anything.*"

"*See. Whose point are you trying to prove?*" Lloyd said before sliding a needle into Chang's neck.

"What the fuck are you doing?" Chang screamed as he thrashed about in his chair.

"Goodbye Mr Chang."

"Fuck you," Chang said weakly.

Seconds later Chang stopped moving and Lloyd left the room. Hulk looked distressed. Max had never seen him like that before. Hulk was always so tough and unbreakable. He had seen footage like this many times before and had done far worse, but this was different. His fellow officer, trusted colleague and life-long friend turned traitor. It had clearly gotten to him.

"I'm sorry, Hulk," Blake said. "He was the one that deleted the files too. Did you want to see?"

"No, I have seen enough. Thank you, good work today. Where are we at in finding Shadow?"

"They ditched their vehicle and split up, and we haven't been able to get a location yet."

"They?" Max asked.

"Yes, Shadow and four guards from NorthStar. They went five separate ways, to slow us down."

"Clever," Max said.

"We are still looking. We will find them."

The group walked into the conference room. An aide was busy laying out sandwiches and getting coffee.

"Welcome back, General, agents, is there anything I can get for you?" the aide asked.

"No, thank you," Hulk said. "Right Blake, put the satellite feed up on the screen and let's try to find this son of a bitch."

Chapter Forty-Four

In the dark of the night four figures all dressed in black exited the car. They moved slowly in the shadows of night towards the door.

One of the men set about picking the lock while the others stood guard. Through the window the men saw outlines of furniture faintly lit by television and appliance standby lights, and the digital clock of a microwave, but otherwise darkness. Their target was no doubt sleeping given the hour and they worked silently to keep it that way. They also kept quiet not wanting to rouse any nosey neighbours. After a few seconds, the lock-pick set was put back in the leading man's pocket. He stood and softly opened the door.

The four men gingerly entered the room, carefully placing their feet with each step hoping the floor boards would not creak and give them away. Inside, they started searching. Room by room they swept silently looking for the target. In a room at the end of the hall, they found him.

The second guy removed a roll of tape from his backpack. He unwound several inches of the tape and tore it from the roll. He crept across the bedroom and stood silently watching for signs the target might wake. Nothing. Just a faint rhythm of peaceful sleep in the target's breathing.

A second later, he slapped the tape down over the mouth of the target and held his hand in position waiting for it to stick. The target's eyes opened in a mix of confusion and horror. He began kicking and flailing his arms, and he tried to scream but the second man's hand and the tape made that impossible. The other men restrained the target and taped his hands together. The target was trembling in fear and tears fell down his cheeks. He was wriggling and bouncing trying to break free from the men's hold. He was strong but not strong enough to loosen their grip.

They stood him up and he tried in vain to get away. The balaclavaed man who had taped his mouth shut punched the target hard in the face causing him to stumble but he remained conscious. The same guy stood him upright using his left hand to clutch the target's shirtfront then punched him again with a hard right. This time the target passed out.

One of the men retrieved a black hood and pulled it down over the target's head. With it secured, two of the men took the target's weight and started for the car led by their comrades who went ahead to make sure the path was clear.

Outside the men hastily fumbled their tall unconscious target into the boot of the getaway car, climbed into their seats and drove off into the night.

Chapter Forty-Five

Max and Flash were busy talking and pointing at maps and other documents that were spread over the far corner of the conference table. Hulk was on the phone providing updates to various agency heads and senior ministers. Analysts and agents were shuffling papers and typing on computers. They had worked for hours through the late night and into the early hours of the morning.

Blake came into the room and passed Hulk a note. He smiled at Max as he looked up and Max returned it with the same warmth. They held each other's gaze, partly through exhaustion but there had always been a lingering feeling between the two. Maybe something that might have been had circumstances been different. Blake had strong feelings for Max but had never shared it, because he knew Max was not ready. It had only been three years since Lachlan had died. They also worked so closely together he did not know how that would play out. And, they were friends and he couldn't risk losing that. They were not ready, but maybe one day.

"I will have to call you back Mister Secretary," Hulk said reading the note. "Appreciate the support your agency has provided. Thanks again."

Hulk hung up the phone and shared a worried look with Blake whose focus had returned to work.

"Clear the room," Hulk said. "Max, Flash, Blake, stay put."

The agents and analysts all stood and left without needing to be told twice.

"Is he still in the city?" Hulk asked.

"Yes, he is scheduled to tour the Commonwealth Building as a show of defiance in a couple of hours," Blake said. "Full media, the works."

"We need to have a little talk with him."

"Who?" Max asked.

"Your boss the Defence Minister, James Johnston," Blake said. "Hulk asked me to hack into Shadow's computer. I found emails between the two from months ago on a ghost drive. They discussed NorthStar shares and management. We know from your debrief, Shadow planned to takeover NorthStar. We are hypothesising that Mr Jones the former CEO found out and tried to warn the Minister, but his attempts fell on deaf ears. Looks like the Minister was going to be Shadow's number two. Seven figure salary plus bonuses and shares."

"Jesus," Max said. "And he is still here in Sydney?"

"Yes, but there's more," Blake said. "It looks like he let Mr Chang into the country. I found his signature on security waiver documents for Sydney airport. I am sorry Max."

"Nothing to be sorry about, Blake. I never really liked the guy anyway. Plus, now I get to tell him Shadow tried to have him killed using a drone."

"What?" Flash asked.

"He was at the hotel the drone was targeting in Bondi. I spoke with Carrol, he's on site. The Minister had to be the target. It makes sense now, Shadow was trying again to cover his tracks."

"Right, yeah of course, the first target," Blake said. "Before it took off after the Israeli."

"Let me make the arrest," Max said looking to Hulk.

"Let's do it together," Hulk said. "You two stay here and see if you can find Shadow. Keep us updated."

"Yes, General," Blake and Flash said together.

"But there is one thing I have to do first," Hulk said as he picked up the desk phone and pushed the broadcast button.

"This is General Scott," Hulk said. "We are at war. This is a battle where we have all suffered loss and heartache especially knowing that these acts could be perpetrated on our watch. We have all sworn to protect this nation and her allies, and now is the time for us to fight back. These terrorists and traitors have been hiding in plain sight, and it is time we flushed them out. One of our own has turned and we need to hunt him down. We will not rest until he and his fellow traitors, and conspirators are brought to justice. With Shadow gone, it also means we are without a Deputy. To ensure continuity of command, on my authority, Lieutenant Commander Smyth is being awarded a jump-step promotion. He will herein be referred to as Captain Blake Smyth, Chief of Staff, Australian Intelligence Service, and he will serve as Deputy Head of Operations. You will afford him the respect the position and rank deserves, and in my absence, he will be considered Acting Head of Operations. I thank each and every one of you for your tireless work. But, we are not done yet. Let's go get these arseholes."

Hulk put down the phone as agents and aides went busily about their work with renewed momentum. Without speaking, Hulk walked through a side door into his office. Moments later he returned and stood in front of Blake, who was standing at attention. Max and Flash stood smiling in silence. Hulk removed Blake's epaulettes and replaced the Lieutenant Commander rank slides with those of the rank of Captain.

"Congratulations Captain Smyth," Hulk said.

"Thank you, Hulk," Blake said. "I am honoured."

"The Chiefs of Defence and Navy have approved the appointment, as has the Governor-General and Prime Minister. There will be time to celebrate later but for now you have command. Let's go, Max."

"Congratulations, Blake," Max said hugging Blake and kissing him on the cheek. "Drinks on me when this shit is all over."

"Yeah congrats, mate," Flash said shaking hands with Blake.

"Good luck, Max," Blake said. "I will definitely hold you to drinks. Thanks, Flash."

Hulk and Max left the room heading for the elevator. Max dialled Carrol.

"Hello, Max," Carrol said.

"Hi Tim, thanks for your help earlier," Max said. "First time calling in an airstrike?"

"Yes, that was a first. Amazing piece of equipment the Hornet. I meant to mention the picture on the wall of your office earlier but obviously circumstances didn't permit. Anyway, what can I do for you?"

"Hulk and I are on our way to you. You are still with the Minister, right?"

"Yeah, we're at the hotel in Bondi."

"Good. Please keep this conversation between us. Do not tell James we are coming and don't let him leave."

"Everything alright?"

"No. I can't go into it over the phone. I will explain when I get there. Do you understand?"

"Yeah, I think I get where this is going. Understood we will stay put and I won't mention the call."

"Great. Thank you, Tim."

Chapter Forty-Six

The target woke.

He could not move.

His world was dark. He tried to scream but the tape was still firmly in place over his mouth. He began to shake violently trying to break free. He rubbed his head on his shoulder trying to remove the hood. He moved his mouth and jaw trying to break the tape.

Nothing.

Then it hit him. A wave of pain in his face. He remembered being hit in the face. His head ached from the black out. The steel of the chair was cold through his light bamboo pants.

There was a chill in the air. He could hear machines and beeps. A forklift maybe. He clenched and flinched as the sound rushed towards him, breathing heavily as it passed underneath him.

He began to cry in fear.

Chapter Forty-Seven

Hulk knocked on the hotel door.

Agent Stevenson, Carrol's partner, answered the door.

"Agent Stevenson," Hulk said. "I am General Scott, Head of Operations, Australian Intelligence Services, and I believe you have already met Agent Shaw. Special Agent Carrol is expecting us."

"Yes, of course, please come in, General," Stevenson said.

"Thanks, Stevenson, good to see you again," Max said.

"Max, Patrick, what are you doing here?" the Minister asked.

"We need a word," Hulk said. "Agent Carrol, Agent Stevenson, you might want to give us the room?"

"Jill, did you want to take a break for a bit?" Carrol said. "I'm fine to stay."

"Sure, can I get anyone anything?" Stevenson asked.

"No, thanks Jill," Carrol said and with that she left the suite.

"You sure you want to stay, Tim?" Max asked.

"Yeah, I'm sure."

"What is going on?" Johnston asked.

"Shut the fuck up!" Hulk said backhanding the Minister knocking him off balance.

"How dare you! I am a Minister of the Crown! I am the Minister for Defence!" he said using a nearby chair to stand back upright and moving to within inches of Hulk.

Hulk punched Johnston in the stomach winding him and dropping him to the ground.

"I remember, but it seems you're the one that forgot, you traitor!" Hulk said leaning down over Johnston.

Johnston's eyes widened in horror, in a sudden realisation.

"That's right," Hulk said looking him in the eyes. "We know."

"I do not know what you are talking about. Max please get him away from me."

Max walked over and helped Johnston to his feet.

"That's it, thank you Max. Now please get me out of here and away from him."

"I have known you for several years now James," Max said. "I helped you get into high office and spent hours listening to your mind-numbing bullshit. Queen and country. Family. National Security. You are a hypocrite, a liar and a traitor."

Max stepped back and punched Johnston square on the bridge of his nose. The room filled with that old familiar sound of flesh, cartilage and bone breaking, and the slap of skin hitting skin on impact. Johnston fell back to the floor clutching his face as blood started to pour from his broken nose.

"You will pay for this! You will both fucking pay! You have nothing on me. I am the Minister for Defence. Agent Carrol arrest these men!"

"Sorry, Minister, I'm on a break with Agent Stevenson downstairs getting coffee," Carrol said.

Max and Hulk looked at him and smiled.

Johnston's eyes revealed his shock but then he saw his phone on the floor in front of him. He had dropped it when Hulk punched him. He pulled himself forward with his free hand towards the phone. As his fingers wrapped around it, Max stomped down hard, his combat boots crushing Johnston's fingers under the phone. Max was not sure whether it was bone or the phone itself he heard crack under the pressure.

"Where is Air Commodore Greg "Shadow" Lloyd otherwise known as The Pilot?" Max asked without removing his foot.

"I don't know!" Johnston said trying to pull his hand out from under Max's boot.

"Not good enough," Max said.

He lifted his boot and Johnston recoiled clutching his broken hand to his chest. Max stepped forward and swung the same boot through the air kicking the Minister hard in the ribs.

"Please, stop," Johnston said gasping for breath.

Max kicked him again.

"I don't know where he is. He said he had to pick something up before he left."

"What did he have to pick up?"

"He didn't say."

"So, what is his plan after he picks up the mystery package?"

"Please, he will kill me."

Max drew his pistol and shot a neat hole in the wall inches from Johnston's head.

"And, you think I won't? After the shit you have put this country through over the past few days, I would welcome the chance."

"No, please. Bill and I tried to get out of all of this. In Bill's office a week ago, we told Greg we didn't want to be involved anymore. I tried to stop him. I am not a traitor. Please believe me."

"A week ago? Shadow said he had planning this for years. How long have you been involved?"

"A year."

"A year? You piece of shit. What and you got cold feet a week ago? No wonder he has already been trying to kill you."

"What?"

"Oh, you didn't know?" Max said. "His man Xander assassinated Mr Jones in the foyer of the Commonwealth Building the day they bombed the building. Shot him point-blank, right between the eyes, then he set off the bombs which were planted to take you out. Turns out they were after both of you. It was a clever plan. Blame Islamic fundamentalists for wide spread terror and the assassinations of a Minister and his warmongering defence contractor mate. But, it was all bullshit. A rouse designed to hide the greed of traitors. And, now it all makes sense because you turned your back on him. He was trying to cover his tracks and make you pay for your betrayal. He gave the plans for the building to Xander to take you out for breaking your word. Luckily enough for you, Shadow gave him the old plans which didn't show the safe rooms. Then he very nearly got you again with a rocket at the airport and with fundamentalists terrorising the Parliament and, only a few hours ago, he again nearly succeeded. I stopped a drone from levelling this building with only seconds left on the clock. You are a liability to him. A weakness. He will stop at nothing now to kill you."

Johnston said nothing, he just stared at Max in shock.

"I saved your life too many times this week, James. I have watched as hundreds died, helpless while you knew all along who was behind it. It is all because of you. Their blood is on your hands. Tell me why I shouldn't put a bullet between your eyes right now?"

"Okay, alright, he's scheduled to fly out in a few hours," Johnston said.

"Where is he going?"

Johnston did not answer.

Max dropped a knee into the Minister's thigh and pressed the silenced Glock to his head.

"Where is he fucking going?" Max said.

"South America!"

"How is he getting out, I thought flights were grounded?"

Johnston squirmed and grimaced.

"You cleared the flight?"

"Yes."

"Fuck. Where is your phone? You are going to cancel the clearance."

Max fished around and found Johnston's second phone in his jacket pocket. He scrolled through the phone and found the number.

"One wrong fucking word and I will put a bullet in your brain without a second thought. No mistakes. Do you understand me?"

Johnston nodded. Max pistol whipped him with the silencer to re-enforce the point.

"Am I fucking understood?"

"Yes! Jesus."

Max hit the speaker and call buttons.

"Kingsford Smith Airport, Managing Director's office," the assistant said after only two rings.

"It's James Johnston, I am the Defence Minister. Can you please put me through to the Director?"

"Yes, Minister. Please hold."

"James, how can I help?" a woman's voice asked.

"Sally, I am going to need to cancel that request I put in for the NorthStar VIP jet."

"Is everything alright?" Sally asked. *"You sound a bit off. We only just spoke a little while ago. Anything I need to know?"*

"I just need you to ground all flights, including the NorthStar jet. Can you do that?"

"Yes, of course. Consider it done. Anything else I can help with?"

"No, thanks Sally."

"Anytime, Minister."

Max hit the end button.

"Right, one down, one to go," Max said standing.

"What? What do you mean?"

"You're not real bright, are you?" Hulk asked.

Johnston frowned and then there was that realisation again in his eyes.

"That's it," Hulk said. "You fucking idiot."

"I am not calling him. He will fucking kill me Patrick."

Hulk pulled his pistol and shot Johnston in the knee cap, shattering it. He screamed in pain. Max saw Carrol flinch.

"You don't have to be here, Tim," Max said.

"I'm fine, just keep him quiet, would you?" Carrol said tossing Max a pillow from the couch.

Max stuffed it in Johnston's mouth and lent back in over the Minister's face.

"One of your best friends was killed so you and Shadow could steal his company out from under him. You let Chang and who knows who else into the country. You are responsible for the deaths of hundreds, if not thousands in the Commonwealth Building, Parliament House and in the terrorist attacks in Melbourne. You are a traitor. You are a terrorist. If you want to live, you will make this phone call and find out where he is. Got it?"

Tears streamed down Johnston's cheeks as he nodded that he understood. Max took the pillow out of his mouth and he breathed deeply given he only managed very shallow strained breaths through his broken nose.

"I am sorry, Max. This was never supposed to happen. When we started planning, a few civilians were supposed to be hurt. No one was supposed to be killed but Shadow was adamant people had to die. He wanted panic to force the Prime Minister to ramp up defence spending. You cannot kill me, Max, you saved me."

"Save it. I don't want to hear it. Time for you to make the call. Oh and I definitely can kill you and I will kill you if you fuck this up."

Max again scrolled through the phone and found Lloyd's number.

"That's not it," Johnston said. "He has a disposable, so you couldn't track his mobile. Hold down seven."

Max pressed and held seven on the mobile. A prestored number began dialling. After three rings, it was answered and Max pressed the speaker button.

"What is it?" Lloyd asked.

"Just checking in, everything on schedule?" Johnston asked.

"Yes, I have picked up that item. Now I am just waiting for my co-pilot to call."

"Yeah, about that. I haven't been able to get you cleared."

"What? You said you already cleared it. What is going on?"

Johnston did not answer.

"He is there isn't he, the little Prince? He is there with you? And Hulk, I suppose he is there too? I shouldn't be surprised you are supposed to be dead by now."

Johnston looked at Max who was again kneeling on him with his gun to his head.

"Who is the little Prince? No, no one here, but me."

"For a politician, you are a fucking bad liar James. Put him on the phone."

"I'm here you piece of shit," Max said.

"Do me a favour golden child. Pull the trigger. James is useless to me now. Always was pretty useless come to think about it. Just put him out of his misery, otherwise he will spend the rest of his short life looking over his shoulder. Waiting for his Shadow to snuff him out."

"We have just been having a chat about you. He says you are the brains behind all of this and didn't tell him your full plan."

"Well, he sure as shit isn't the brains, but don't listen to a word he says, he has been in this from the start. He and Bill Jones were both in on it, but they got cold feet. Cowards. That is why I brought forward my plans and had Bill killed. My team tried several times to kill your boss there, but you just kept saving him. That must piss you off, all that effort saving a traitor?"

"How are those plans working out for you? You are a fugitive on the run and we have cancelled your travel plans. You cannot hide for long."

"You have always been too clever for your own good. I presume Hulk is listening? I told you he was arrogant when you hired him. Well, now his arrogance is going to get another boyfriend killed."

Max's face flushed with anger and grief. Hulk said nothing.

"What...what have you done?" Max asked.

"I have your little surfer friend Sam here with me. He is the package I had to pick up before my flight. Do not worry I have not hurt him too badly. Yet. His pretty face will recover in time. He has been crying a lot though since he woke up. I guess when four men break into your house and take you hostage in the middle of the night, and leave you chained up in a dark, cold warehouse for hours it would be pretty scary, especially for a little fairy like your mate."

"He has nothing to do with this. Let him go."

"I will, that is, if you get my flight clearance back. Otherwise, well, it looks like he will meet a similar end to the last one. It truly was tragic how Lachlan died. So brutal what they did. He was so fragile. Did he blame you Max, when he was dying in your arms? Did you see the sadness in his eyes or was it hurt and disappointment knowing you were the reason he was about to die? It was your fault you know? Don't let history repeat itself, Max. Get me out of the country or Sam dies."

There was a long pause. No one spoke. Max was almost catatonic. His vision blurred through teary eyes, then he blinked letting a tear fall down each cheek. His focus returned as he wiped the tears away.

"You son of a bitch," Max finally choked out through a broken voice laden with pain. "Let him go. I'm the one you hate. Don't punish him because of me."

"Get my flight cleared, and you come and meet me to trade places with him. When you get here, I will let him go."

"You have a deal, but if anything happens to him the deal is off and I will kill you."

"Deal. I am at the docks at Port Botany, Foreshore Road. You remember the place, I am sure. Come alone. If I see anyone else, I will make his suffering last. I will make Lachlan's death look like a mercy killing. Got that? Do not forget. Come alone, that's very important. You know the drill."

"I'm on my way," Max said after a few seconds.

The call ended and Max stared at the wall thinking about Lachlan. Tears in his eyes.

"You're gay?" Johnston asked the disdain showing in his eyes even through all the pain he was experiencing from his damaged knee.

Max pushed the gun hard into Johnston's head. Tears streamed down his cheeks and his jaw was clenched. His face was red and full of pain.

"After all that, that's your question? What is wrong with you?" Max asked through clenched teeth.

Max's hands were shaking and his finger tightened on the trigger. Johnston's eyes closed.

"Don't do it, Max," Carrol said. "He isn't worth the bullet."

After a long moment, Max let go of the trigger and holstered his gun.

"James Johnston," Max said his voice cracking. "You are under arrest for murder, terrorism and for being a traitor to this country. You are not obliged to say or do anything unless you wish to do so, but whatever you say or do may be used in evidence. Do you understand?"

Max did not wait for him to answer. He stood as Johnston slowly opened his eyes.

"He is all yours, Carrol," Max said walking from the room.

"Are you alright, kid?" Hulk asked following him into the foyer.

"No. No I am not. Every time I think I am starting to move on, there he is dying over and over again in my thoughts, like it was only yesterday."

"I'm sorry, Max. I know how much he meant to you."

"Yeah, I know. I will be fine, once I put a bullet in Shadow's face."

"I know you will, kid. You are the toughest son of a bitch I know. You were my best student during training and you have done nothing but get stronger every day. Anyone else would have run far away from all of this after what happened, but you stayed because you know the job is bigger than you or me. We sacrifice our lives to protect others and to save them from feeling the pain you feel.”

“You’re right, I know. I’m not worried about myself. I’m worried about the people I get close to and the fact that they can get hurt. I’ve put someone else in harm’s way, Hulk. They deserve better than that. Lockie deserved better. Sam deserves better. They did not choose this life.”

“Evil exists in the world, Max. That’s why we do what we do. So, people like Sam and Lockie can live and enjoy freedom and democracy and everything that life should be.”

“I’m going to kill him, you know that, right?” Max was shaking with anger and pain.

“Yes. He is a traitor. As far as I am concerned it is an easy out for him.”

“You’ll put Flash and a team in place as backup?”

“Yes, they will be out of sight.”

“Thank you. See you on the other side.”

“Good luck and Godspeed, Max.”

Max walked silently to the lift. He crossed the foyer and the doorman opened the door for him. His Chevy was parked at the front door.

Chapter Forty-Eight

Blake was sitting in his office in his tactical gear. He was getting ready to join Flash in the field supporting Max. There was no way he was going to let Max suffer through this on his own. Not after what had happened last time. He was struggling with the thought that Lloyd was involved in all of this and that he had been so vindictive in the location he had chosen to confront Max. Blake could only imagine the horror of the thoughts Max was having and the pain he was going through. His thoughts were suddenly cut short as an alarm sounded in the bunker. Blake looked up as Flash ran into his office and locked the door behind him.

"We found two guards down near the weapon's vault," Flash said.

"What? When?" Blake asked.

"Just now. We're checking into it, but for your safety we need to lock you down."

"No, I don't think so," Blake said opening the bottom draw of his desk.

He retrieved a small black box, similar to the one Max had found in the Commonwealth Building behind the draw. He opened it and assembled his Glock.

"With all due respect Blake, you are the second-in-command now, I am supposed to lock you down."

"I am not sitting here when there are people out there gunning down my staff. You want to protect me, get my back and follow me."

Blake headed for the door.

"Right behind you, boss," Flash said smiling.

"Good. Let's move."

Blake and Flash moved in crouched formation through the open empty space. Agents and aides had fled into nearby safe rooms as part of the lockdown procedure. Side by side they swept clearing the way to the weapons vault.

When they arrived, Blake saw his two dead guards laying in a pool of their own blood. He did not stop to check them, he knew they were dead. He holstered his pistol and entered his code in the panel to retrieve MP5s from the vault then they headed for the elevator. As the doors opened in the storage facility upstairs, Blake and Flash hugged the wall in a crouch making themselves smaller targets for anyone waiting for them. The little room was clear so they moved out of the lift towards the door. Blake stole a look into the large space beyond the door. He saw two more bodies laying near the prisoners' rooms and two down near the medical centre to his right.

"Shit, Alpha," Blake said mostly to himself. "On me."

Flash followed in close formation heading for the medical centre. Inside they found a nurse crumpled over a table. He had taken a bullet in the back of the head. They moved across the room and stood either side of the door to the surgery. Blake held up three fingers. On three, he swung open the door. Blake went in first and took a knee sweeping to the right. Flash followed fractions of a second later, sweeping left. Clear.

"Where are they?" Blake asked when the door of the supply room opened.

Blake and Flash took aim at the door but immediately lowered their weapons on seeing Kate and the doctor.

"Boy are we glad to see you," Kate said.

"What happened?" Blake asked.

"We heard several shots ring out across the storage garage, so we ducked in here and locked the door. The doc's got an app on her phone so she can monitor the medical rooms remotely, so we turned it on and watched as one of our guys came in gun up. We were going to come out but then he loosened off a few shots into the door. So, we just bunkered down. He left when he figured he couldn't get in. Then we waited until we saw you guys come in."

"We only just got up here. We still need to clear the rest of the storage area. Can you walk?"

"Barely, but the drugs are helping."

"Good, here," Blake said throwing Kate his MP5. "Give us some cover. Stay here, Doc."

The doctor nodded calmly.

"Go get 'em," she said.

The doctor was a veteran of the first Gulf War, so she was used to being shot at, but this was a first inside a secure facility.

"You alright?" Flash asked.

"Yeah, the doc's been looking after me well," Kate said.

"Good to hear. Stay close to cover."

"Will do."

Blake led the two agents back out into the storage area. Several vehicles stood gleaming under the industrial lights.

Blake and Flash started towards them as gunfire rang out across the space. The agents all moved for cover. Blake and Flash ran and dived behind one of the vehicles returning fire as they moved. Kate ducked left bouncing on her wounded leg for one of the offices near the medical centre. No sooner had she made it behind the wall, bullets slammed into the doorframe. They were all pinned down.

Four rogue agents who had been working downstairs only minutes earlier were running for one of the vehicles closest to the prisoners' rooms with a prisoner in tow. Blake sprung up and fired in their direction. Flash followed his lead and using the boot of the vehicle for support loosened off several shots. Kate ducked out from behind the wall and took sight of one of her former colleagues through the short scope attached to the MP5. Three bullets spat from the barrel of the MP5 with all three hitting the leading assailant centre mass taking him off his feet. Kate sighted one of the other fleeing agents but before she got a shot off they hustled in behind a car using it for cover to return fire. Blake, Kate and Flash all ducked back behind cover.

"They've got Jackson," Blake yelled over the gunfire.

"That fucking gun running arsehole," Flash said. "Must be more useful than he looks."

"Yeah, take him if you get a shot."

The two agents bounced back up into position to fire as the vehicle their former colleagues had hidden behind started up. Kate fired her MP5 into the passenger window of the fleeing car, when it clicked dry she saw the smiling face of Jackson sitting behind the bullet proof glass. With a little wave from Jackson, the vehicle sped off towards the storage hanger door.

"Son of a bitch," Kate said to herself as she watched Flash and Blake jump into their own car to give chase.

Chapter Forty-Nine

Outside the hotel in Bondi, Max got in behind the wheel and fired up the Chevy. Its big V8 engine roared as he accelerated towards the motorway.

As he drove, he thought about Lachlan. His heart was beating out of his chest in pain, in confusion, in disbelief his past was back again to haunt him.

It was Lachlan's smile. Not the smile he showed others. Not the Lachlan 'life of the party' smile. Not the pretending to be someone else smile. It was the smile that only Max could see. They could lock eyes anywhere, from a crowded nightclub to the moment of pure intimacy when they were alone in each other's arms and he would smile. It was that smile. In that moment, Max felt his love. Felt his happiness. Felt his heart. Felt his warmth. Felt his history, his present and his future. He knew his sorrow and knew his joy. He understood what he was feeling and thinking. He knew it without words. In that moment, in his smile, they were one and would be forever.

Hulk had recruited Max at university and started his training while he was still studying. Max was a natural. He could out shoot a veteran sniper. He could drive like a rally driver with a decade's experience. He could tail even the best spies from ASIO and ASIS without a trace. And, he had a mastery over human behaviour and could use them to his advantage – the so called dark triad. But, he had a caring and loving soul which always clawed at him and kept him grounded. Hulk knew it held him back at times, but he also knew it kept him human and helped drive him to help others.

Hulk had told him AIS was established to stamp out terror and that agents would be spread throughout the country and the world, hiding in plain sight, in normal nine-to-five jobs until they were needed. Hulk found him a job with an up and coming Member of Parliament, James Johnston, who was being touted as a future leader of his political party. Hulk needed Max in

Canberra both for his cover role with the MP but also to complete his training.

Max said he was in, as long as Lockie wanted to move to Canberra. Max remembered the conversation. He and Lachlan spoke about their careers. They spoke about Canberra. They spoke about the future, about getting married, starting a family and growing old together.

Lachlan had said, "You have been given a great opportunity to work for an MP Max. I love you. I'm in. It doesn't matter where we go. All that matters is being together."

"I love you too, Lockie. You are my world and I will do anything for you. If you don't like Canberra, we will move. I promise. I just want you to be happy."

"I am happy when I'm with you, Max," Lachlan said and then they kissed.

A tear ran down Max's cheek as he remembered the moment and he clenched the steering wheel tightly manoeuvring the big Chevy through the traffic.

He thought about their first apartment in Canberra. *God what a shithole, but it was home*, Max thought.

Lachlan graduated university with a degree in medicine. Hulk made one phone call and with that Lachlan had a job offer that afternoon. Max told Lachlan it was the MP who had made the call. Lachlan worked shifts during his internship which helped Max sneak out for training with Hulk and Flash. Max hated keeping a secret from Lachlan but knew it was only for a little while. When he was a full agent Hulk said he would be able to tell him, if he was genuinely 'the one'.

They lived happily in Canberra for several years and their group of friends grew. Lachlan and Flash became close friends too. Much to Lachlan's playful protests, Flash was straight and so Lachlan made it a goal to help find Flash a girlfriend. After a month or two of searching, Flash started dating one of Lachlan's colleagues, Jane, and soon they were going on double dates every weekend.

Life was good.

Max was Flash's best man, when he and Jane married a few years later. After the wedding, Max surprised Lachlan with a trip to Maui for his birthday. He remembered telling Lachlan that since they could not get married yet, they would have a honeymoon to celebrate Flash and Janes' marriage instead. The resort was beautiful. Max could still see the cabin they had rented on a jetty out over the aqua blue ocean. It was perfect. One evening after a long day of swimming and snorkelling, Max and Lachlan sat looking out at the clear blue water drinking wine on the cabin's deck.

He remembered it in vivid detail.

"I'll just duck in and grab some more wine, and the cheese platter," Max had said.

"Okay, babe," Lachlan said. "Do you need a hand?"

"Nah, that's cool. I won't be a second."

Max had gone to the bedroom and retrieved a little box from a hidden pocket in his luggage. Then he went to the fridge and got a bottle of Champagne, two elegant glass flutes and the cheese platter. He walked back out onto the deck, juggling it all and Lachlan jumped up from his chair.

"Here, babe, let me help," Lachlan said taking the platter.

He turned around to place it on the table.

"Champagne hey?" Lachlan said setting the platter down giggling. "What's next a ring?"

Lachlan turned back around smiling at his own joke and saw Max down on one knee. The little box resting in his hands. His arms outstretched. Tears welled in Lachlan's eyes.

"Lockie, I love you more than anything in the world," Max said. "I want to spend my life with you. Oh wait, I forgot something."

Max fumbled in his pocket and produced a remote. He hit play. Savage Garden's *Truly, Madly, Deeply* started to play. Lachlan smiled cheekily.

"Let me start again," Max said. "Lockie, I have loved you since the day I met you and I have never doubted my feelings for you. From that first hug in the common room in the dark at uni to now and until the end of time, I know you are the one. I love you. Will you marry me?"

"Yes, Max, oh God, yes!" Lachlan said pulling Max to his feet. "I love you so much! You are my world. I want to spend the rest of my life with you."

Max remembered the pure joy and happiness he felt. He was overcome, lost in emotion. They hugged and kissed, and danced right there on the deck of the little cabin over the water.

"You are so corny by the way," Lachlan whispered playfully in Max's ear. "Truly, Madly, Deeply? You are adorable. The song we first danced to. So corny but so beautiful. I love you so much."

They had been engaged for several months before moving into a new house when Lachlan finished his internship. It was a large house just outside Canberra. It had more bedrooms and bathrooms then their apartment and a good-sized yard. It was going to be their family home. They wanted to get married in Australia with all of their friends and family, but the laws at the time would not allow two men to marry. Lachlan said he did not want to have to go overseas to marry the person he loved. So, they waited.

Max's anger grew through his pain and he gripped the steering wheel tighter still as he drove towards the docks to confront Lloyd. He was upset and his emotions were overwhelming. They were overpowering his reason.

His thoughts were interrupted by his phone.

"Hello," he said.

"Max, it's Flash. Hulk told me what happened. Are you okay?"

"No. I am really not. I am going to kill every fucking one of them."

"Well, that's why I'm calling. Shadow has called in reinforcements. The original four he had with him are there plus the satellite has picked up another six on site."

"I won't let it happen again, Flash. I am going in and I am going to kill him."

"There's more Max. Four more of our guys have turned. They killed guards and agents and some of our support staff as they fled the bunker. And, they busted out Jackson. Blake and I gave chase, but we let them get ahead of us when we realised they were heading to the docks. We didn't want to risk Sam's life by getting too close. Alpha took one of them down at the bunker but there's still fourteen of them at the docks now, plus Shadow. Going in there is suicide, Max."

"He wants me to come alone. I can't risk Sam's life. I won't let it happen again. I can't."

"I know. I can't believe he is dragging you back down there. So fucked, but you know he is doing it to get in your head. Don't take the bait mate. We will follow your lead, but we will only be back a block or two. If you get into trouble Blake and I will be coming in to get you."

"Just get Sam out, that is all that matters to me."

"I won't let you down Max. We won't let you down, we have your back."

"I know Jacob. You always have. You are always there for me. Thank you. I'm only a couple of blocks out. I'm going onto comm and will kit up. See you on the other side."

"I will send you the satellite pictures of the compound now. Be safe mate. Remember, we will be in on your word."

"Roger mate. Thank you."

Max was still wearing most of his tactical gear. He pulled the car over and went to the boot to refill his supplies. He put the silencers on the MP5 and his two Glocks which he put in his thigh holsters. Once the grenades were in, he holstered his knife and slid in his extra magazines.

He looked at the photos Flash had sent. Eight red dots were visible outside guarding the perimeter and eight were inside. Max tried to determine which one was Sam and which was Lloyd. Impossible to tell. Max was not going to just walk in like Lloyd wanted. Like Flash said, that was suicide. Max knew Lloyd had no intention of letting Sam live. He was going to take out the guards silently. One-by-one until he reached Lloyd.

Chapter Fifty

Lloyd entered the room where Sam was fastened to the chair.

"Well, Mr Walker," Lloyd said making Sam jump nervously. "I guess you deserve an explanation."

Sam shifted uncomfortably in his chair, his head moving from side-to-side as if trying to find the source of the voice, which was impossible given he was still wearing his hood.

Lloyd smiled as he noticed Sam shaking in fear.

"You have gotten yourself into the middle of something very serious. You see, I have spent many years planning the attacks in Sydney, Canberra and Melbourne, and between you and me in some other locations around the country too. But, a friend of yours has interfered and if I am to prevail, I need to teach him a lesson. I need to break him. I need to slow down their chase, so I can get away. I have disliked him from the moment I met him. Such a cocky, know it all, smartarse. Too clever for his own good. It pains me to say that he is the quite possibly the best agent AIS has ever produced. And he is so loved by all of them. I can't see why. Whether he knows it or not, he has disrupted my plans more than once and I am going to make him suffer."

Lloyd walked over and placed his hands on Sam's knees making him flinch, then he pulled Sam's hood off and threw it to the ground. Sam's blond hair fell down over his face covering swollen eyes from the beating he had received.

"And, I am sorry to say for you Mr Walker, I am going to use you to break him then I am going to kill him. What you may not know is that your friend was previously engaged. Their love was sickening. It is just so unnatural what you people do. Disgusting. Anyway, his fiancé was killed right here in this very building. In fact, it was in this very room only a few years ago. A terrible death and I am afraid you are going to meet the same fate. History repeating itself. I will finally break the little Prince and get retribution for his interference and slow AIS down in the process. His heartache and pain will break his spirit, giving me the chance to finally kill him and have enough time to escape and see my plan through to its conclusion. Prince is his codename, but you know him as Max Shaw. He works for the Australian Intelligence Service as a Field Agent. But the little Prince will be of no use to AIS after today and his loss will affect them all."

Sam stopped shaking hearing Max's name and raised his head looking Lloyd in the eyes. Anger and confidence. Resilience. Lloyd took his hands off Sam's knees and stood up.

"Defiant in the face of certain death Mr Walker, maybe you are stronger than you look. Stronger than the last one that's for sure," Lloyd said before punching Sam hard in the side of the head knocking him out cold again.

Chapter Fifty-One

Max laid motionless surveying the scene and checking the satellite feed. The eight guards were moving about in seemingly random patterns outside the warehouse. The dockyard was filled with shipping containers and crates waiting to be loaded onto outgoing ships.

Max waited for his window. Then it happened. Two guards on his side of the compound both slipped behind different containers.

Max leapt up and sprinted towards the fence. He pulled out his pliers and snipped the fence wires creating a long slit which he climbed through quickly but quietly. He drew one of his silenced pistols and his knife. He clenched the knife in his left hand in a stabbing grip and the pistol in his right hand which he rested on his left wrist for stability. The pistol swept for targets.

"Flash, can you hear me?" he whispered.

"Yes, Prince," Flash said over the headset.

"Have you got me on the satellite?"

"Yes, you have two guards one row closer to the warehouse. Head left and get ready to take out the first guy."

Max walked quietly to the left in close to the shipping container using the shadows created by the site's poor lighting which was failing to fight the dark of night.

"Hold there," Flash said watching the satellite image on his little screen. *"Three, two, action."*

Max fired a single round into the unsuspecting temple of one of the NorthStar guards as he came around the container. He ran forward and caught the guard before he hit the ground, and dragged him around the back of the container, resting the body in the darkness against its metal frame.

"The second guy is coming Prince," Flash said.

Max rounded the corner of the container and waited. This time he didn't need Flash, he saw the guard's shadow created by the site's flood light. As soon as the guard was close enough, Max plunged the knife into the guard's neck severing his spinal cord. He lowered him to the ground and dragged him around resting him next to the other guard.

"Clear on that side of the building, Prince," Flash said.

"Copy that, making my way to the warehouse," Max said.

Max moved silently between the shipping containers. Scanning left and right at each intersection, weary in case the satellite had missed anyone. He led the way with his pistol and knife.

"Shit, Prince, two coming towards you," Flash said. *"Nine o'clock."*

Max spun left and scrambled for the cover of a shipping container as the two guards walked around the corner of the warehouse. He waited, listening as Flash relayed their movements. Max heard their boots on the concrete path closing in, so he slipped out from behind the container. He shot the guard on the left between the eyes. The guard on the right was faster than he anticipated and was already moving for cover. He got a shot off as Max trained the gun towards him. The guard's bullet grazed Max's left arm but did no real damage, other then to his shirt which was ripped by the impact. Max shot twice. The second bullet tearing a neat hole in the guard's calf muscle. He started a hurried limp trying to get to cover but Max was on his tail and put another two bullets into his spine and head.

"Sit rep, Prince?" Flash asked.

"Yeah. One of them got a shot off. Any movement?"

"No, looks like they are all still just milling about."

"Roger. Must be enough noise in there to dampen the sound. Keep me posted. I am heading for the warehouse door. Four down in the yard."

"Copy, Prince."

Max dragged the two guards behind another shipping container out of sight. Shortly after, he arrived at a side door of the warehouse and turned the handle. He opened the door slowly not wanting it to creak. When the gap was large enough he slipped through and shut the door softly.

The space was enormous. Shipping containers, boxes and crates lined the interior. Rail tracks were carved out of the floor and a large crane moved busily hanging from the roof. Max watched as it lowered magnetic cables down and effortlessly lifted a container and sped off down the length of the warehouse. Orange lights flashed and an alarm sounded as it went. Autonomous forklifts moved cargo between sections of the warehouse. Each had its own orange warning light and alarm. No wonder no one heard the shot outside, inside it was noisy with all the machinery moving independently, their alarms sounding. It was all so different to the last time he was here. The warehouse now looked completely remote controlled and hi-tech.

Max was standing on a walkway that seemed to ring around the four walls of the space. It was painted white. He noticed yellow and red painted zones on the concrete floor, clearly warnings to visitors about safe zones. He heard two guards to his left, so he moved right. He followed the white zone along the wall, scanning the room, using the shadows to move undetected.

"Prince, it looks like you have five on the ground floor and three upstairs," Flash said over his comms unit. *"One of the heat signatures upstairs has not moved since we have been watching. Likely that's Sam. He is in a room at the far end in the centre of the structure."*

"Ack," Max said. "Two behind me. Where are the other three on the ground floor?"

"There are two on the far side and one in front of you. He is about forty metres at your ten o'clock."

"Ack."

Max crept forward quietly but fast, counting off the metres in his head as he moved. At thirty, he paused and listened. He could not hear the guard, but he could smell cigarette smoke.

Max climbed up onto one of the nearby shipping containers. He looked around the warehouse and watched as the machines whirled around moving the crates and containers with efficient speed. The last time he was here the warehouse was full of people. Their jobs now lost to technology.

He walked gently over the container towards the source of the smoke. As he got closer he lowered himself down onto his stomach and army crawled silently, painfully slowly, on the metal roof of the shipping container. The smell of the cigarette smoke grew stronger as he dragged himself over the last few feet. He laid flat on the dark green container only inches from the edge. Using his phone's camera, he looked over the end. The guard was leaning on the doors with his back to Max. He inched forward without making a sound until his right hand could hang over the edge of the metal container above the guard's head. Two shots spat from the silenced pistol in Max's right hand. The first hit the guard in the crown. The second hit the base of his skull at the top of the spine. Dead. The terrorist crumpled to the floor, the sound of the machinery and the various alarms masking the noise as he fell.

Max looked up and took in the scene. Ahead he could see a metal staircase, leading up to a row of raised offices. A series of metal gantries hung over the space. Maintenance walkways for the crane he guessed. He rolled right and lowered himself to the ground with a soft thump as he landed. Resuming his stance, he continued towards the staircase.

"Prince, stop!" Flash said. *"Cover."*

Max moved to the left, ducking behind the nearest crate.

"Guard coming down the stairs, twelve o'clock" Flash said. *"Twenty metres. Shit and the other two who were behind you are coming towards you at your three."*

"Count me in with the guy from the steps," Max said.

"Copy that, Prince, he is at eighteen metres. Now, fifteen metres. Ten metres. Five, four, three, two…"

Max watched as the guard walked past then he silently fell into step behind him. Max moved athletically and ghostly. Gaining on the guard, he holstered his pistol and took the knife in his right hand. When he was within reach, he grabbed a hand full of the guard's hair, pulled his head back and slashed his throat and in one move dragged him in between two crates.

"The other two are at the body of the guard you took down," Flash said.

Max sprung up and ran down the walkway towards the guards, drawing his pistol.

One of the guards had his back to Max. Three bullets hit the unsuspecting terrorist and he dropped to the ground next to his fallen smoker comrade. Max fired again but missed the second guy as he fled behind a shipping container. The bullet hit the steel container and rang out as the sound echoed through the space between the metal containers. Max took cover, leaning his back against the container in the same position as the guard he killed earlier. He stole a quick look around the corner, but whipped his head back as a bullet sailed past, impacting the neighbouring container.

"Put your head back out, Agent Shaw, I have a score to settle with you after leaving me to rot in gaol all those years and for burning my face with a soldering iron you fucking psychopath," Jackson yelled over the sound of the machinery.

Max paused for a moment considering his options. He could not go left because Jackson would be ready for it, so he jumped the two crumpled bodies and made his way down the rear of the container. Taking cover behind the corner of the container, he blindly shot twice in the direction of where Jackson had taken cover, then ducked his head around to find him. But he was not there.

Max heard a sound above and swung around as Jackson leapt from the top of the shipping container landing hard on Max. Both men dropped their weapons as they hit the ground, their guns scattered across the concrete floor. Max and Jackson wrestled and punched at each other, trying to get on top to pin the other to the floor. Max got behind Jackson and locked in a chokehold, but he was stronger than he looked and stood up with Max dangling on his back, hanging from his neck. Max wrapped his legs around him digging his knees into his sides and he held on firm with his chokehold. The inside of his elbow tightened around Jackson's throat. Jackson ran backwards slamming Max into the wall. Max felt his grip loosen as he was thumped hard against the wall for a second time. The impact forced Max to completely lose his grip and he let go falling to the ground. Jackson took the advantage and began kicking and stomping on him. Max curled up trying in vain to protect his head and vital organs from each kick. Then he saw his knife on the floor just beyond his reach. Each kick was a brutal blow but helped to inch Max closer to the knife. As Jackson wound up for another kick, Max pushed off a nearby shipping container and jumped for the knife. He grabbed it and sat up, lunging forward. He slashed Jackson across the thigh forcing him to stumble backwards, catching himself awkwardly on a nearby wooden box. Max held his ribs and winced as he struggled to his feet.

"How are those ribs, a bit tender I bet?" Jackson laughed. "I got pretty pumped in gaol. Nothing else to keep your mind occupied. Nothing but countless sit ups and push ups fuelled by a rage that can only be settled by killing the man who put you in there."

Max drew his second pistol and fired. The bullet went through Jackson's hand and into his already injured thigh causing him to fall to the ground. Jackson dragged himself backwards away from Max.

"You might have gotten fitter, but you didn't get any smarter," Max said.

Max stumbled holding his damaged ribs with his left arm, sighting Jackson over the pistol in his right hand. He watched as Jackson dragged himself into the orange zone and then the red zone, fleeing in panic from Max, trailing blood from hand and thigh.

"Please," Jackson said. "I'm sorry. I didn't know what I was getting into. I didn't know he would hurt civilians. I didn't know he would kidnap your boyfriend. I'm sorry."

"Where is Sam?" Max asked.

"Upstairs. In the crane maintenance room. He is chained up to a chair at the far end in the centre of the room."

"And Shadow?"

"He's up there too. In one of the offices."

"Which office?"

"I don't know. Please don't kill me."

"I don't make it a habit of killing unarmed men, but you did try to kill me. You are a traitor and a piece of shit like that arsehole upstairs. Although, like I said, you didn't get any smarter in prison. Turns out I don't have to kill you, you have killed yourself."

Max watched as Jackson's confusion turned to panic as he saw a shipping container racing towards him. He cried out and tried to crawl out of the way of the speeding metal wall coming at him but he could not get traction on the polished concrete and did not move fast enough. The container hit him with lethal force and dragged him away. Max watched the container disappear as the space before him opened up. Jackson was gone leaving behind a trail of blood on the polished concrete.

"Jesus, what was that?" Flash asked having watched one of the heat signatures race off at incredible speed towards the far end of the warehouse.

"Shipping container," Max said. "Jackson won't be selling anymore weapons to terrorists."

"Brutal."

"Better him than me. Have you got heat signatures on Sam and Shadow?"

"Yes. Top of the stairs. One still has not moved, got to be Sam. When you get to the top of the stairs, he is in the room on the left at the far end of the structure. It looks like it is hanging above the space. Shadow looks to be in the room opposite, down the end on the right."

"Got it. Thanks."

Max started briskly walking towards the stairs still clutching his ribs, gun raised in case there were any other guards the satellite was not picking up. At the base of the stairs, his radio crackled.

"Prince, the four guys from outside are running towards the building and Shadow is running towards the door of the office he's in!" Flash yelled.

Max sprinted up the stairs taking three at a time, wincing in pain with each step as his ribs shifted. As he reached the top step, bullets rang out from all around him. They pinged loudly as they hit the metal stairs and warehouse walls. He ran along the gangway outside the offices.

Scanning ahead, he saw the room where Sam was being held. It was suspended above the crane. The door to the right of the maintenance room opened and Max saw Shadow run across the gangway, heading for the maintenance room door. Max fired at the moving target while giving chase. Bullets hit the wall leaving a trail behind Shadow as he ran. One of the guards had made it up the stairs behind Max and started firing. Max dived through the door Shadow had left open across from the maintenance room for cover.

"I'm fucked Flash, I'm pinned down!" Max yelled.

"Hermes and I are already moving," Flash said breathing hard as he ran.

Max knelt on the floor taking cover behind the door frame. He fired blindly at the chasing guard who was forced to move to cover as bullets sailed past him.

"Prince, you have two on your side of the building close behind you. Both up the stairs. Thirty metres to your three o'clock. Four on the far side, moving up the stairs at your seven. Likely heading for the walkway at your nine o'clock to flank you."

"Ack," Max said ducking his head around to get a visual on the guards on the opposite side of the warehouse.

A bullet smashed the window above Max's head showering him with glass. Max laid on the floor and crawled forward to bend around the door frame. He fired towards the guard who had followed him up the stairs until the pistol clicked empty. He moved back to cover and swapped to the MP5. He took off the silencer and placed it in his vest then got into a crouch position and rolled himself around the door frame. Four bullets exploded from the barrel. Two went wide hitting the railing. The second two hit their mark impacting the chest and stomach of the guard who fell to the ground screaming in pain.

Shots blasted across the open space from the far wall. The second set of guards had arrived. Max returned fire, emptying the MP5 at the guards opposite. He watched as more bullets impacted either side of the terrorists. Blake had arrived at the top of the stairs opposite and was raining bullets down the walkway at the guards. Blake was in his full tactical gear, a much different look to his pristine black and white Navy uniform which Max had seen him wearing earlier in the day.

Max heard more gunfire to his left. Flash sprung up the last step, firing at the remaining guard on Max's side of the building. Max reloaded his guns and then sprinted for the maintenance room door while the remaining terrorists were occupied by Blake and Flash.

Max kicked the door open then jumped behind a large metal winch just as bullets ripped a line in the door and wall behind him.

"Got to hand it to you Prince, taking down half of my guys before I found out is pretty good," Lloyd said. "We have trained you well, but it is a pity you have gotten here too late. Oh and you brought friends which I told you not to do. Poor little Sam the surfer here is going to have to die."

Lloyd drew his pistol as Max sprung up from behind the winch and loosened off a volley of bullets towards Lloyd, wide and high enough to be clear of Sam. Max moved forward to a new cover position behind a wooden crate which splintered as Lloyd's return fire smashed into the box.

"Let him go, it's over, Shadow!" Max yelled. "You've lost. Take me instead. Give yourself one win for the day."

"You still do not get it, do you?" Lloyd said. "If I go down, I am going to go out knowing that I have broken the little Prince. You have been a pain in the arse since Hulk fucking hired you. I have been planning this day for years and you have gotten in my way so many times. You and your mentor, my dear old friend Hulk, could not see it. He is losing it in his old age. The two of you just kept chasing and fighting a Shadow. It is not just a call sign for me. I was right under your noses the whole time like I was when I was flying fast jets over Baghdad, in and out sight unseen."

"We have found you now though and everyone knows you are a traitor. There is no getting out of this. Let Sam go and throw down your guns."

"Maybe it is the fact that you do not seem to know when to quit. Maybe that is what Hulk sees in you? I must admit, since I lost my wife I have been hurting and there have been days I did not want to go on. I thought of quitting many times. But, it cannot be anything close to the pain of having to watch the person you love die in such a brutal fashion like you had to when Lachlan died in this very room."

Max's heart was racing, already fighting his emotions as he tried to choke down the pain of being back in the room.

"And, now to think I could make that happen again with little Samuel here. Is that what it is going to take, Max, will the death of another boyfriend finally break you? Remember it Max, the blood, the horror, the pain? Lachlan begged me not to kill him, you know? It was pathetic. 'Please, please don't kill me', he said. He was so weak. He cried so much. So much pain you inflicted on him. Should I take the tape off and see if Sam wants to beg too?"

Max was reeling. His heart was racing. He felt nauseous and lightheaded from the surge of adrenaline and realisation. Lloyd had killed Lachlan. He sat in silence. In shock.

"What's the matter Max? Didn't figure that out yet? I killed Lachlan. I took the love of your life away from you. Right here. With my favourite knife. History repeats itself Prince."

"Why?" Max asked choking through emotion.

"What's that I couldn't quite hear you?"

"Why did you kill him?!" Max yelled.

"Because you got involved in all of this!" Lloyd spat. "You kept getting closer to the truth. Closer to finding out about my involvement and closer to discovering my plans. I needed you to disappear. I wanted you out of the way. You clearly loved him, so I killed him to break you and force you to reconsider your work with AIS. But, you came back. You buried the pain deep inside. Hulk loved it, you know? You turned into him overnight. A ruthless arsehole, willing to do whatever it took. Torture. Assassination. You did it all for Queen and country. You should have left quietly but you did not. You turned your pain into a strength. I did not see it coming, but here we are again, and this time I will right my mistake."

"Yeah, here we are," Max said springing out from behind the crate and firing at Lloyd.

Lloyd dived left. A bullet tore into him, just above the hip. He scrambled pulling himself along the ground, leaving a trail of blood. Max kept firing as Lloyd made it to his knees and fell through a side door, closing it for cover as he went.

Max looked at Sam for the first time since entering the room. He was slumped over in the chair. His blond hair hanging over his face. Max could see he was duct taped to the chair. His mouth was taped shut. He was not moving. Max's heart raced as his mind slipped back in time to picture Lachlan taped to a steel chair.

Chapter Fifty-Two

It was just over three years ago. Lachlan and Max had a fight that tortured Max's thoughts each and every day since. It was when he told him he was a Federal Agent. Lachlan was upset that such a large part of Max's life had been hidden from him.

"That is why I am telling you babe," Max said. "It was killing me, keeping a secret from you. I don't want any secrets between us. I love you. I will do anything for you. If you want me to quit, I will. It doesn't matter to me at all. All that matters is you."

"That is not the point, Max," Lachlan said. "And, you know it. I am upset you could keep something this big from me. I love you too, but I am so hurt. It's a lot to process. Why didn't you tell me?"

"I couldn't. I was sworn to secrecy."

"So, why tell me now?"

"Because, we're going to spend the rest of our lives together. I don't want to keep any secrets from you. I don't want to lie to you. I want you to know exactly who I am and love me for everything that I am. And, you need to know and be comfortable with it. If you don't like it babe, I will quit the job. You mean more to me than any job ever could. I told you that when we first moved here."

"I remember," Lachlan smiled remembering that conversation. "Have you been a spy since then?"

"Yes."

Lachlan frowned.

"I'm sorry Lockie, but the deal was secrecy until I became a full agent and until I was sure you were the one. I have known you were the one since the day I met you, but I have only just been given clearance to tell you."

"Is it dangerous?"

Max shuffled and looked down.

"Max, I'm not sure I want you to do it if you will be in danger. I don't know what I would do if you got hurt Max or worse."

"I'm good at what I do and I have a great team working with me. They have got my back and I've got theirs'. We are very careful and well trained which lowers the risk."

"Like who? Have I met any of them?"

"I'm not supposed to tell you."

"For God's sake, Max. Another secret. I thought you didn't want any secrets."

"Okay, babe, but you cannot say anything about this alright?"

"Fine."

"Flash and Kate are on my team, and Blake works for my boss."

"Seriously? And, you have all kept this from me?"

"Yes."

"What about Jane, does she know?"

"Not yet. Flash is going to tell her soon too. It has been tearing us both up not being able to tell you."

"God, I need to think. I have to go to work, we will talk about this when I get home."

Max grabbed his hand and stopped him. Lachlan turned back to face Max. Max knew he was upset.

"I love you, Lockie. I'm sorry I hurt you. I didn't mean to."

"I love you too, Max. I know you didn't, but it's just a shock that's all. I really do have got to go."

Lachlan walked out of the room.

Max had gone to AIS that afternoon thinking about Lachlan. He was sitting in a conference room, staring at the ceiling. He was in pain knowing Lachlan was upset but there was something else. He had seen anger and confusion in Lachlan's eyes too, not just sadness. He hoped Lachlan would come around. Hoped he would forgive him. He did not want to lose him. Max meant what he said, he would walk away from it all if that was what Lachlan wanted. Their life together was all that mattered.

"Max," Blake said. "Hulk, is on his way? Can I get you anything?"

Max continued staring.

"Max?" Blake said.

"No, thanks mate," Max said. "Sorry, I was somewhere else there for a minute."

"Everything alright?"

"I told Lockie."

"I see. He didn't take it well?"

"No, he was pretty upset."

"Oh mate," Blake said taking the seat next to Max and put his hand on Max's back to comfort him. "He will come around. It is a pretty big deal, but he loves you. He will be fine."

"I'm thinking about quitting."

"Well, I can understand that, but why not give him a few days to think it all through? I'm sure he will be fine, once he has time to process it."

"Yeah, I guess you're right. Just feels shitty that I upset him. The look on his face was heartbreaking."

"It will be okay, Max," Blake said putting his arm around him.

Hulk walked into the room.

"Oh for fuck's sake, you two," Hulk said. "Why don't you just go in the other office and get it over with already?"

Blake's face flashed red from embarrassment and he pulled his arm back.

"What?" Max asked oblivious.

"Nothing," Blake said. "General, can I get you anything?"

"No, thanks Blake," Hulk said smiling sarcastically.

Blake shot Max an embarrassed smile and then left the room.

"Good work with the take down of our old friend Mr Smith," Hulk said. "He was selling State secrets to the Arabs. I hear you nearly got your dumb arse shot though."

"I thought I could talk him down."

"That was stupid, wasn't it?"

"Not, everything needs to be torture and death, Hulk."

"Wrong. A majority, if not all, of the time it is about shooting the fuckers before they shoot you. You have got to be willing to go all the way and even more importantly, they have to know you are willing to go all the way. If they sense any weakness, they will exploit it."

"Yeah, I guess. I've got it."

"Good, now I have another target for you," Hulk said sliding a file across the desk. "Middle-Eastern male. Five eleven. Average build. Trimmed beard. Links to businessmen operating out of Parramatta. We think they are funnelling money to terrorists operating here and abroad. Blake has done the initial leg work on this. He thinks the target is a messenger for local cells."

"Got it. Want him brought in or taken out?"

"Bring him in for a chat."

"A chat? Is that what you call it?"

"Max, there are times when some force is necessary to get things done. To get the information we need."

"Yeah, I get it, Hulk. Sorry I'm just a bit off today. I'll be fine. I'll bring him in."

"Good. Take Flash with you."

"Ack. Will do," Max said as Lloyd walked in the room.

"Off to save the world your Majesty?" Lloyd said.

"Something like that," Max replied.

"Who are you after today?"

Max flashed the file at Lloyd.

"Some terrorist messenger, Hulk wants a date with."

"Right. Mr Amir Shivani. Never heard of him. Do not let me keep you. Good luck and Godspeed."

"Thanks Shadow."

Max met Flash in the waiting Chevy sedan in the basement of the old AIS building. On the drive, he told Flash about the conversation with Lachlan. Like Blake, Flash said everything would be fine.

"Nothing will separate you two, you love each other too much for that," he had said.

Shivani was reportedly holed up in a townhouse not far from the CBD in Parramatta. Flash took the backdoor and Max the front. Max kicked the front door in and came face-to-face with Shivani who was running for the door with a backpack on.

"Get on the ground," Max said pointing the gun at Shivani.

"Please, no," Shivani said. "I am just the messenger, he will kill me."

"Who will?"

"The guy running our operations."

"Who is he?"

"They call him The Pilot."

"Where can I find him?" Max said as Flash arrived behind Shivani.

"I will not say anymore, not until I get protection."

"Fine, hands behind your head. Cuff him Flash."

Flash used flexicuffs to secure Shivani then picked up his backpack.

In the car, Max's phone rang. It was Lachlan.

"Answer it," Flash said.

"Hey babe," Max said.

"Babe? No, I am not your babe," a man's voice said. *"Disgusting. Unnatural acts will see you both burn for eternity."*

"Who the fuck is this? Where is Lockie?"

"Oh, he is here. He is fine, for now. As for me, you can call me The Pilot."

"What do you want?"

"I think you have something that belongs to me. I would like him returned. I propose a little trade. Your fiancé for my messenger."

"If you hurt him, I will fucking kill you!"

"Well, little Prince, I suggest you get here very quickly. And, come alone. If I see anyone else, I will kill Lachlan."

"Please, don't hurt him," Max said his voice full of emotion.

"I am at the docks. Warehouse three. Port Botany, Foreshore Road. Do we have a deal?"

"Yes," Max said his voice breaking.

The man ended the call.

"What's going on?" Flash asked.

"He's got Lockie," Max said tears in his eyes. "He wants to trade him for Shivani."

"Fuck, where is he?"

"Port Botany docks."

Flash pulled the handbrake and slid the car one-eighty, and gunned it towards the port.

"We will leave our friend here in the car and we will go in, and get Lockie back."

"He said to come alone. I can't risk it."

"You can't do it alone Max. We don't know how many people he has with him."

"No. I need to protect him. I got him into this, I need to get him out of it."

"I'll respect you call, Max, but you're wearing your comms unit and I will come in at the first sign of trouble. I've got your back."

"Thanks, Jacob."

They pulled up a block out. Max got his knife and pistol, and put a few mags in his pockets.

"Good luck," Flash said over the comms piece.

"Thanks."

Max made his way through the yard and into the warehouse. There were hundreds of workers in the space moving crates and shipping containers with manual trolleys and forklifts. He saw a line of offices and a maintenance room hanging above the open space. He swept left and right, then hit the stairs two at a time. The first room on the right was empty. A lunchroom. The second door led to an office. There were two people inside, a man behind a big desk and a woman at a desk near the door. Max moved on and cleared the remaining offices. He turned and headed for the maintenance room. He opened the door and was struck by the image of a man slumped over in a chair at the far end of the room. He had a black hood over his face, but Max knew it was Lachlan because he was in the clothes he had left home in.

His heart sank.

Bullets hit the doorframe beside him and he dived behind a big metal winch for cover.

"Where is Shivani?" the man said.

"In the car," Max said.

"How are we going to trade if he is outside and we are in here?"

"I am going to give you the keys. You can leave and I promise I won't follow. Please just leave us."

"Step out and throw down your weapons or I will kill him."

"Okay," Max agreed and he threw his pistol into the centre of the room and stepped out.

The man was standing behind Lachlan. His face covered by a balaclava. He was brandishing a knife and waving it in front of Lachlan. Max's heart was beating so hard. The adrenaline and fear was making him feel nauseous and lightheaded.

"I know you heard me say weapons before. You only threw down your gun."

Max pulled out his knife and threw it. It stuck in the floor next to his gun.

"There we go. Now, why don't you throw me your keys."

Max pulled out a set of keys and threw them to the Pilot.

"Chevy?"

"Yeah, how did you know?"

"Lucky guess. Now, tell me. Does your partner know to expect me?"

"What are you talking about?"

"Agent Jacob "Flash" Gordon. I presume he is sitting in the car babysitting Shivani?"

"No, I came alone."

"Maybe you did, maybe you didn't, but either way I cannot afford for you to come after me," the Pilot said before stabbing the knife down hard into Lachlan's stomach and tearing a huge wound.

"Lockie!" Max yelled, running towards Lachlan and the masked man.

He picked up his gun and knife as he went, and fired at the now fleeing man who was returning fire. He hit Max twice. Once in the upper left arm and once in the right leg, but he did not stop. Did not slow a beat. He just kept running. His pistol ran dry as he got to Lachlan. He dropped it and used his knife to cut away the tape that was securing Lachlan to the steel chair. He took the hood off and removed the tape covering his mouth.

"Max," Lachlan said tears streaming down his face.

"Lockie, oh God!" Max said. "I am so sorry. Flash get an ambulance! Hurry!"

Max dragged Lachlan from the chair and cradled him in his arms on the floor. Max was crying as he tried to apply pressure to Lachlan's wound. It was no use. The blood kept flowing from the large, deep cut.

"This is all my fault Lockie. God, I am so sorry. Please stay with me! Hang in there. Help is coming."

"It's alright, Max," Lachlan said with an unnerving calm to his voice. "This isn't your fault. He is a terrorist. I saw the hate in him. I get it now. What you do helps stop people like him. Promise me you will keep fighting to protect innocent people. I was being selfish this morning. I was worried about you getting hurt, but I know now that you do what you do to stop people like him. And to help people. You help those who can't help themselves. You are a caring and loving person, and now I know just how much. You risk yourself to protect others. I could not be prouder."

"I have been thinking about it all morning. I can't stand the idea of upsetting you or losing you, I'm going to quit and we can move to the beach. We can buy a big house overlooking the ocean and get married in our garden."

"I would love that, Max. You are everything I have ever dreamed of and I'm so glad I got to spend my life with you. I love you, Max."

"I love you too, Lockie, but please stay with me, I don't want to lose you."

Lachlan reached up and placed his hand on the side of Max's face. His thumb wiped away a stream of tears leaving in its place a trail of blood, as Flash ran into the room and stood behind Max. Pain filled Flash's eyes as he saw Lachlan's wound.

"Promise me you will find love and live your life. Promise me you will always protect innocent people and always fight for what is good in this world. Fight for a world without fear or terror. Fight for what is right and a world free of prejudice. Fight for love, Max. Fight so people can find love and happiness like ours."

"I promise," Max said his voice breaking. "I promise."

"Look after him, Jacob," Lachlan said looking past Max to Flash.

"Of course, I will Lockie," Flash said.

"I'm going to have to leave you now, Max," Lachlan said calmly, fully accepting his fate. "I have loved you since the first time we met and I have loved you more and more every day since. I am sorry we didn't go overseas to get married. I hope you know and our friends and family know that you are the love of my life and you are the only thing that matters to me in the whole world. I wish we had the chance to show the world how happy we were and how much we love each other.

I am sorry if I ever hurt you. Don't blame yourself for this. It was not you. Live your life. I love you, Max."

"Oh God, Lockie, you've never upset me, you have given my life so much happiness and joy, I love you so much," Max said unable to control his tears. "I can't live without you. You can't leave me. You are my world. 'You are my dream, you are my wish, you are my fantasy. You are my hope, you are my love, you are everything that I need'."

Lachlan smiled recognising the lyrics to *Truly, Madly, Deeply* the song they first danced to and the song playing when Max proposed. He weakly pulled Max closer and they kissed.

"I love you," Lachlan said and then his body went limp.

"Lockie," Max said softly shaking Lachlan's body before screaming out in pain and pulling Lachlan into his chest and sobbing uncontrollably. "Lachlan!"

Flash fell to his knees and wrapped his arms around Max, sharing the pain of his best friend.

Chapter Fifty-Three

Max ran to Sam and tore the tape from on his mouth.

"Sam. Sam!" he said shaking him. "Sam, are you okay? Wake up. Please, wake up."

He cut the tape on his wrists and dragged him from the chair. He cradled him on the floor in his arms. Overwhelmed by emotions and flashbacks of Lachlan he began to cry. Sam's face was bloodied and his eyes swollen from a beating he had received.

"Sam?" Max said as Flash and Blake kicked open the door.

They both froze. Flash froze because he had seen this scene before and Blake froze because Lachlan's case file was burnt into his mind so vividly he felt like he had been there before too.

"I'm here, Max," Sam said. "I heard everything. I am sorry about Lachlan. I cannot imagine your pain and how hard it is for you to be here again."

Sam opened his eyes and saw Max's pain, and reached up and hugged him tightly.

"I am fine, Max, go get that son of a bitch."

"I am glad you're alright, Sam," Max said and he kissed him softly. "Flash, Hermes, this is Sam. Look after him, will you? I've got something I need to do."

"Sure thing, Prince," Blake said, looking away shyly.

"We heard everything, Max, go kill that arsehole!" Flash said, watching Blake.

Max rested Sam against the chair.

"Be right back," he said drawing his other pistol and picking up his knife.

Max followed the trail of blood, scanning ahead with his pistol. It led down the stairs, across the warehouse and through a door on the far side. Max pushed the door open and he walked out into the yard. He looked left. Clear. Then he looked right and saw a trail of blood and some long swipe marks on the concrete. Lloyd must have fallen and had dragged himself along for a metre or so. Max scanned ahead and found Lloyd down near the water's edge.

Max walked towards Lloyd. Lloyd drew his pistol. Bullets sailed past Max, hitting shipping containers and the warehouse. Each one going wide as Lloyd's hand shook as he weakly held the pistol. Each would be a difficult shot from that distance with a pistol even if you weren't bleeding out. Max continued walking forward in a straight line. He heard the click of an empty magazine twenty metres from Lloyd and saw him move to reload the gun. Max fired two shots into the concrete next to him.

"Don't you fucking move!" Max yelled.

Lloyd moved. Max shot the pillar next to him. He stopped. Max was a few metres from Lloyd and stopped and stood looking down at him.

"You are responsible for the death of hundreds, if not thousands, of innocent people in the pursuit of money and chasing some payback for your supposed sacrifice. Your greed, selfishness and arrogance has made you a traitor to your country, to the uniform you used to wear and to everything you ever stood for. You are a terrorist!"

"Spare me," Lloyd said looking away.

Max walked forward and pressed his right boot into Lloyd's wounded hip. Lloyd grimaced in pain and gritted his teeth.

"You killed the love of my life and made me watch on as he died in my arms in agony," Max said. "You stole the only thing I cared about in this world and for what, to try to get me to stop working at AIS? I was going to quit, that day, to be with him. But then you took him from me!"

Tears ran down Max's face. His blood was pumping in anger.

"I am only here today and working for AIS because I made a promise to him that day to stop people like you," Max said. "You made me this way. You took my life away. There is an emptiness that I can never fill, a grief I will never get over and drive to see vengeance carried out in every terrorist I kill. And, it is all because of you."

Max threw his gun and knife back behind himself then bent down and dragged Lloyd to his feet. Max unhooked his vest and holsters and threw them to the ground. Lloyd laughed.

"Even with a bullet in my hip, I can beat you," Lloyd said. "I helped train you."

Lloyd moved quickly and threw a punch into Max's face sending him stumbling backwards.

"Told you," Lloyd said.

"I wanted you to get one shot in, hardly fair otherwise," Max said as he jumped up in the air off his left foot and brought his right fist down hard towards Lloyd's face.

Lloyd caught his fist and deflected the blow.

"I told you, I helped train you and you think I'm not ready for your go to left foot, right hook routine?" Lloyd said laughing. "So predictable."

Max unleashed a flurry of punches to Lloyd's mid-section as he tried in vain to block and cover. Max grabbed him by the shirt and threw his head violently into Lloyd's left eye. Within seconds it was swollen and starting to close. Max bounced around Lloyd, but Lloyd matched him which was surprising considering his wound. He lunged at Max, landing a left jab and right hook combination to Max's face. Max grabbed him around the head and dragged him in kneeing him in the ribs and into his wounded hip with his right knee. Lloyd groaned but struggled out of the hold and threw a Hail-Mary right hook which Max only just ducked.

"You should have kept your gun, Prince, such an arrogant rookie move," Lloyd said. "I am going to choke the life out of you and you can join your little fag boyfriend Lachlan burning in hell!"

Max's eyes went wild and he ran, and tackled Lloyd to the ground. He started punching Lloyd. Right after left. Lloyd raised his arms to block but the blows were too hard. Max unleashed all of his pain in every hit. Lloyd rolled flipping Max onto his back. They scrambled and wrestled on the concrete. Max broke free and sprung to his feet then bounced on the spot like a boxer. Lloyd struggled to his feet. His hip wound was bleeding heavily. He stumbled and Max took the opportunity to launch his left foot, right punch combination again. Lloyd read it but could not deflect the blow. He was weakening from blood loss.

As Max moved in again, Lloyd threw a right jab. Max grabbed his hand ducking around the incoming blow and threw a hard uppercut into Lloyd's elbow. There was a sickening crack before Lloyd's arm folded in the opposite direction. He cursed and yelled in pain, and started swinging wildly with his left hand. Max jumped back then planted his left foot on the concrete and side kicked Lloyd in the left knee snapping the knee cap. Lloyd fell to the ground and withered in pain.

"Well I will be fucked the little faggot had it in him all along," Lloyd spat.

Max ignored him and started walking away.

"Where are you going? It would be a mistake to keep me alive. I have friends in all sorts of places. I will get out and I will find you. I will kill every person you ever love."

Max stopped in his tracks.

"That's right. Lachlan was just the start. I will find Sam again and I will kill him. Then I will kill the next one and the next one."

Max took a knee, looking down at the concrete thinking about everything that had happened and what Lloyd had just said.

"That's right you fucking poofter, I will make sure you die alone, doomed to walk this earth stalked by a Shadow willing to kill everything you love, like I did when I plunged my knife into Lachlan."

In one smooth move, Max picked up his knife, stood, spun and threw it like a baseball. It sliced through the air end-over-end until it pierced Lloyd's stomach. Lloyd cradled the wound and the knife laughing. Max ran and leapt through the air at Lloyd. He landed on Lloyd and grabbed the handle of the knife, and pushed it deeper, tearing up into Lloyd's liver. He coughed up blood and moaned in pain, but he kept laughing through bloodied teeth. Max twisted the knife and cut deeper.

After a minute Lloyd's eyes widened and the laughing stopped as the pain took over.

"Feel it you arsehole, know what he felt," Max said twisting the knife. "You're the only one going to hell today."

Max sat there slicing the knife up through Lloyd's internal organs. His eyes never leaving Lloyd's.

"You are a traitor, a terrorist and, after today, a failure. Lockie would be happy knowing I have put an end to you. Your wife would ashamed of the man you have become."

Lloyd's eyes changed and filled with emotion thinking of his wife.

"Now, it's time for you to leave, not even a shadow of your former self," Max said. "See you down there."

Max ripped the knife free as he stood. Blood poured from Lloyd's stomach. He stepped back and watched as within seconds life drained from Lloyd. He slumped over and fell, his head hitting the concrete.

Max fell to his knees and cried. He fell forward onto his hands and screamed at the concrete as he sobbed uncontrollably.

He had his vengeance.

He had done what Lachlan had asked and stopped the reign of terror.

Flash, Blake and Sam walked out of the warehouse. Flash started to walk towards Max, but Sam grabbed his arm.

"Let me," Sam said.

Flash looked to Blake who nodded sheepishly.

Sam crossed the open concrete space and dropped down behind Max. Max lent back as Sam wrapped his arms around him.

They just sat there for a few minutes as Max let out his emotions.

"I am so sorry Max," Sam said. "I can't imagine what you are going through."

"Thanks, Sam," Max said. "Are you alright? I'm the sorry one. Sorry you got dragged into all of this. I never would have accepted that drink if I knew this would happen."

"I'm fine, Max, and I'm still glad you accepted the drink. And, knowing all this, I would do it all again in a heartbeat."

Max turned and looked at Sam. He had a cut above his right eye and it was black and purple. His cheek was puffy. Max smiled and gently placed his hand on his swollen cheek.

"You are very sweet, I am glad I met you too," Max said. "Come on, let's get out of this place."

The End.

Max Shaw will return in *Shaw Initiation*.

www.jwpublishing.com.au